Love Match

Book 2 (2010-2012)

by Kyell Gold

Dallas, TX

Love Match
Book 2 (2010-2012)

Production copyright FurPlanet Productions © 2018

Copyright © Kyell Gold 2018

Artwork © Rukis 2018
https://www.furaffinity.net/user/rukis/

Published by FurPlanet Productions
Dallas, Texas
www.FurPlanet.com

ISBN 978-1-61450-409-2

First Edition Trade Paperback 2018

Table of Contents

For my inspiring, talented, and patient writing group, not only colleagues but good friends: Ryan, David, and Watts.

Part Four: Deuce (2010)

Prologue (2015)

2015 States Open, Male Final: Rocky N'Guwe (12) v Braden Longacre (1)

($3 million prize to the winner, $1.5 million to runner up.)

"And that service break holds up for N'Guwe as he wins a very well-played second set 6-4. Alastair, it looks like N'Guwe found his footing there. His lefty serve didn't come up big in the first set, but in the second he served it out wide more often and took control of many of the points early on."

"Yes, indeed. You know, especially with a young player playing in his first major final, it can all be very overwhelming, and it looks like that's what N'Guwe was going through in that first set. The people are of course behind Longacre; no male player has won all four majors in almost fifty years, and everyone wants to witness history. And it looked like N'Guwe was overwhelmed by the moment."

"Heh heh. Were you ever in a position like that?"

"Of being young or of being able to break up a Grand Slam?"

"Either, I guess."

"No, I never faced anyone who was one major away from completing a Grand Slam. But my first major final, I was nineteen and it was at the Ozzie Open, which was nice."

"Home court."

"Indeed. I dropped the first set to the great Fernando Veles, the coati, you remember him."

"I certainly do. A great player."

"And I had the crowd behind me. Didn't do me any good, though. I won the second set just like N'Guwe here has, and Veles took the next two."

"We'll see if Longacre can regain his form. The crowd may be on his side, but they also want to see a good tennis match. They want Longacre to win, but they'd like it not to be easy. And we're going down to Bonnie Raymond, who is with Alicia Longacre."

"Thank you, Daren. Mrs. Longacre, your son is just two sets away from doing what no male player has done for forty years. When you started him on tennis lessons, did you ever think you'd see this?"

"Oh, I didn't really think about the future, you know. Braden always wanted to play tennis and he wasn't happy unless he was, so we let him play. I'm delighted that he's doing so well. We're very proud of him."

"I see you're up here with relatives, but since Miss Jacobs and your son split up, it's only family in your box. Does Braden have someone else in his life now?"

Silence. "Mrs. Longacre?"

"I do think Braden has had such a singular focus on tennis that it would be hard for him to think about anything else. That's why he and Cordelia split, you know. It was about tennis."

"Of course. Sorry to bring it up. Back to you, Daren."

"Thank you, Bonnie. Of course, our viewers know that Longacre's father also stopped coming to his matches early in this year, before the Gallic Open. Some people have linked that to his split with Miss Jacobs, but I can't imagine what the connection would be."

"You know, Daren, when I was playing, I absolutely hated it when the media would go on about my personal life. And it's ten times worse these days with all the computers and social media and everybody you-tubing every moment. There was one press session where I cursed at a reporter because he didn't know I'd lost the match and I was frustrated. Only a few people heard it, I apologized, it was over. These days it would get all over the Internet and we'd never hear the end of it."

"Point taken. Though it was Longacre himself who called a press conference with Miss Jacobs to introduce her to the media, while their breakup was all entirely behind the scenes. I don't necessarily favor prying into someone's private life, but when they make it public—and Longacre is very active on social media, you know—then I think it's fair game."

"Fair enough, although it's not Longacre himself on public media, but someone managing his accounts. All right, the fox is serving to open the third set. Let's see how this one goes."

* * *

I think about that first time we played a set at Palm Gables, there at night with only Marquize watching (poor Marquize), how that set changed me and Braden and our relationship. At the beginning of the set I was a Palm Gables student and Braden was the up and coming professional, playing me as a courtesy to his alma mater (and maybe to his former coach, too). At the end of the set, though, we were peers. Oh, not in the sense that we were on the same level. He would still have beaten me 99 out of 100 sets. Maybe 95. Or 90. But lots of them, anyway. No, the difference was that even though we weren't at the same skill level, he could tell I belonged on the professional circuit, and we knew that one day there'd be a match like this.

I don't mean *exactly* like this. We knew we were going to meet in the majors one day, and possibly in a final, but the chances of our meeting there regularly, building a rivalry like some of our heroes growing up, were slim because he was four years ahead of me in career path. At the time we played that set in Palm Gables, he was a precocious twenty-year-old fox starting to make a splash in the major circuit, the Champions, while I had yet to play a match as a professional, having only just registered for a Futures tournament. Realistically, at the age of 16, the majors were at least three years away for me. But there was enough overlap that I remember thinking, I could be facing him in a major final one day. I didn't imagine that it would be my first. And I didn't think that even as good as Braden was, he'd be going for a sweep of all the majors in tennis, a Grand Slam, at the age of 25.

The whole thing about tennis being composed of clubs? That's true at every level, but at the lowest level, the clubs are huge. Anyone who's studied at a tennis academy belongs to a club that excludes casual players (though not all pros went to a tennis academy, these days most of them did). Anyone who's won a match at a Futures tournament, anyone who's won a Futures tournament, anyone who's qualified for a Challlengers or Champions tournament, and so on. This is how your status is determined in tennis.

So that set in Palm Gables jumped me up in status, even though I hadn't technically won a Futures match yet. To Braden, I'd been a cub before that; afterwards he was more open when we emailed and he even helped me find a coach later on.

It's been four years since then. No, five, because I turned pro in 2010 just after that. Braden has been through a lot since then and so have I, and even though we have a lot of moments in our history to look back on, that one set stands out to me. He beat me pretty soundly, but I pushed him and got a chance to see what makes him great, the combination of raw athletic ability, intelligence, and adaptability that brought him here five years later.

After winning the second set to even the match, I'm ready for his serve. I'm still on, still dialed in to his game, and I crack his first serve right back at his feet for a winner. He's not rattled exactly (Braden doesn't get rattled), but I can see him wondering where the cracks are in my game for him to probe at. I grin at him; there are no cracks, not right now. I'm getting to everything. I just hope I can get through another set before the script flips and Braden's the one hitting every line, getting to every ball.

He screams an ace past me; nothing I can do about that. Next point, I jump on his second serve when he misses the first, and after a fierce rally, I drive a cross-court backhand out of his reach. He's in his head, muttering to himself, and when I break his serve, he doesn't look at me; he sets up and waits for me to start the next game.

* * *

"Great opening to the third set for N'Guwe. He's looking poised out there, not at all like a young player in his first major final. Alastair, we talked a little about Longacre and his family, but N'Guwe has had a really tough road to get here, and it's to his credit that he hasn't allowed that to diminish his focus."

"That's right, Daren. We ran that piece before the show about his home country. I've met N'Guwe several times, but he never talked about any of that as his personal challenge, to his credit. He prefers to raise awareness and aid for the people still living in Lunda."

"And of course the Lundan ambassador to the States is here—Bonnie talked to her before the match. She and her delegation are getting a good show. Longacre wins the point there."

"N'Guwe is up a break and he doesn't want to go into an 0-30 hole to Longacre."

"Second serve."

"Longacre jumped on that, sent it to the corner. N'Guwe got it back over the net in an impressive display, but Longacre was ready with the easy winner."

"Love-thirty, and Rocky's got to be careful here."

"N'Guwe with his fifth ace of the match, back to 15-30. He gets another good serve in, so it looks like he's not rattled by losing those points."

"30-all."

"He's still moving well, pushing Longacre around the court, setting up that backhand—there."

"Down the line for the winner, and he earned that point."

"Second serve coming. Longacre is on top of it again. He's really anticipating well this match."

"And that's what he's done all year, Daren. He got N'Guwe off balance, which is hard to do. Just a little, but the jackal didn't get as much behind that groundstroke as he wanted, and that makes a difference."

"Break point for Longacre coming up, a chance to get back on serve in the match."

"Longacre determined the pace of play on this point, and N'Guwe put it into the net. The jackal now to serve at 30-40."

"Longacre with the beautiful passing shot for the game and the fox breaks right back."

"N'Guwe had the shot he wanted, but it wasn't quite deep enough, and Longacre had plenty of time to get that where *he* wanted it. Back on serve in the third."

* * *

"After a spirited third set, Braden Longacre wins 7-6 in a tiebreak and is just one set away from the first Grand Slam in male tennis in almost fifty years."

"Daren, he's playing great tennis, just as he has been all year, and Rocky N'Guwe across the net from him is playing nearly as well, giving Braden more of a fight so far than his other finals opponents. We mentioned Rocky's family earlier, but I want to talk a little more about his education. We said that he and Longacre both went to Palm Gables, many years apart, of course, but they both overlapped the tenure of the infamous Coach Young while he was there."

"For those viewers who might not be familiar with what we're talking about, well, we don't want to go into too much detail. But Coach Young is a ferret who coached at Palm Gables while both N'Guwe and Longacre were there, and recently—well, not too recently—he was arrested, and Coach Murphy, who ran the school, lost his job."

"Well respected educator, and I still think to this day that he didn't know anything about what was going on."

"Maybe not, but it happened under his watch. You can't avoid responsibility for that."

"And he's remained in the tennis world as a consultant to some of the top players, although I heard that he offered his services to Longacre this year and was turned down."

"I can understand that. We should mention, too, that Palm Gables is much more than those two coaches. It's a fine school and the board conducted a thorough review of all the staff following that scandal. But because both of these players were there at the time…"

"Neither of them was implicated in the scandal, though."

"No, and I wasn't implying—"

"I want to make that clear. They both gave sealed testimony and the courts and the ITF both said that they were satisfied that neither one had anything to do with it."

"Right, absolutely. But you can't say that it didn't have an effect on them while they were there. They were called to testify—"

"Though that was much later."

"Yes, but it implies that they did know something about it."

"Let me tell you, Daren, when I was playing in the Gallic Open in 2001 and there was that doping scandal, of course they interviewed me because I was in the locker room with Fluvia and Masterson. But I didn't know anything about it, and it didn't affect me at all."

"I'll concede the point. They're coming back out onto the court to start the fourth."

Chapter One (2010)

I leaned across Marquize's lap as our airplane came in for a landing at Yerba. I'd never been west of Pensa, much less all the way to the West Coast, and though I'd crossed the Atlantic to come to the States, I had never seen the Pacific Ocean.

"It looks like the Atlantic," I told Ma, who was sitting in the aisle seat of the plane.

"But it's on the wrong side of the coast," Marquize said. "Look, that's south." He pointed toward the great bridge and the city crammed into the peninsula below it. "So the ocean should be on the right. It feels weird."

"Look how big the Bay is," I said as we circled around. "It's huge, nothing like the Intercoastal."

"The Intercoastal isn't a bay," Ma said.

"I know. Hey." I strained against the seatbelt. "Are we landing on the water?"

Marquize, who with the window seat could see farther than I could, pointed with one golden finger. "The airport's out in the bay. The runway's up there."

"Are you sure?"

"Yeah." He leaned back so I could look, but I still couldn't see.

Ma grabbed my arm. "Sit still, Rochi."

So I sat back and gripped my armrests. Someone around us was terrified, and the rank smell of their fear made my nose twitch. I managed to not be too afraid myself, though outside I could see the water getting closer and closer. But sure enough, Marquize was right and we landed on solid ground with a jolt.

When I wasn't focused on the water, I could appreciate how gorgeous this area was. The sun shone down, the water sparkled, and all the buildings up and down the shore of the Bay looked clean and well-maintained. Trees showed everywhere and the mountains framed the skyline with a natural-looking brown hue, unencumbered by the suburban sprawl they overlooked. Above us, a few puffy white clouds floated through a pristine blue sky.

Disembarking in the Union on our flight from Lunda two years ago had been like walking into the future. We'd stepped from the plane into an air-conditioned tunnel that had magically been extended to ensure our comfort between the plane and the terminal. The air smelled like Neutra-Scent and ammonia, and the airport wasn't crammed with people.

Now I took those comforts for granted as we hurried through the airport; the tournament started the next day about two hours away, so we had to rent a car and get to our hotel. By "we" I mean Ma, who had taken on all the responsibility for planning. Neither Marquize nor I knew how to drive, and we certainly weren't old enough to rent a car, so Ma had to do that anyway. In a couple years, when we were eighteen, we'd be able to get credit cards and drive, but even then apparently it would be a lot longer until we could rent a car. "By then," Marquize said from the back seat of our rental car as we drove over the bay we'd landed in, "we'll be making enough money that we'll hire cars to take us where we need to go."

"If you practice hard enough," Ma said.

"She's already in coach mode," I told Marquize.

He laughed. "Maybe we won't need to hire a coach."

"I haven't looked at your registrations because you said you managed those," Ma said. "But I did look around for practice courts because the arena where the tournament is doesn't have any available now. There's a school nearby that looks like it has tennis courts. We can practice there tonight."

We spent most of the rest of the drive talking about the scenery we were going past. After the flat Pensa suburbs, it was interesting to be going through green and brown hills, seeing farms full of cattle and even some wind turbines (I didn't know what they were and neither did Marquize, but we looked them up that night). We drove past fields of about six different kinds of crops and their smells filled the car.

The sun was setting as we arrived in Grey City, a town that mostly consisted of the University of Goldenwater's local campus. Marquize and I gawked at the campus buildings we passed and asked why there weren't any students around. "Their term ended last week," Ma told us, "which is why they're holding the tournament now."

"It looks like a nice place to go to school," Marquize said while I gawked at all the buildings. Palm Gables was an academic building and two athletic buildings as well as a lot of outdoor courts.

"How many people go to school here?" I asked.

Marquize rubbed his muzzle. "Dunno exactly, but a lot of colleges have fifty or sixty thousand people."

"That's more than lived in my hometown," I said.

"No, it's not," Ma told me. "It's more jackals than lived in Lundara, but there are several million people there."

"I knew that," I said, annoyed because we had in fact learned that in our cultures class. "I was thinking about our neighborhood, that's all."

"Here we are." Ma forestalled the argument, pointing up ahead to the tournament site.

Ma had to fill out some paperwork to register as our coach, but Marquize and I only had to show our state IDs; our names and species were already in the system. We got the badges that would let us into the player-only areas, and the mule deer behind the table said, "Welcome to the Grey City Futures Tournament," with a big smile as she slid them across. "The schedules are posted up here and in the players' lounge. Are you staying at the official hotel?"

"Um," I said, and Marquize shook his head.

"Okay." She pointed to a nearby wall with several pieces of paper taped to it. "Go ahead and find your names there and that'll tell you which court to be at and when. Good luck!"

"Thanks," we both said, and hurried off to see our names on the paper.

It was a strange feeling to look at a bracket of over a hundred names and to find mine there: "N'Guwe, R." I turned to Marquize. "I'm playing someone named Delvinic."

"I've got an Anderson," he said. "When's yours?"

"Ten a.m."

"Hey, that's when mine is too. When's our doubles match?"

We searched the schedule but didn't see our names there. So we went back to the registration desk where the mule deer told us that the doubles had filled up. "Once you've played a few tournaments and have a ranking, you'll get into more doubles draws," she said. "This one is popular because it's a fifteen K tournament. Are you playing the next series?"

Marquize and I looked at each other. "We hope to."

"That's a ten K, so you might be able to get in there."

We found Ma and told her that our matches were at ten. She nodded. "So we will arrive here tomorrow at eight. Time to find your court and your lockers and get in some practice."

"Can we practice tonight, too?"

"Of course we will. But first we will find our hotel and check in."

We weren't staying at a hotel; we were at the Gold Coast Motel. The rooms were not exactly luxurious. Ma had only booked one ("to save money," she said, "and when you have won enough to afford another room, you can have another"), which meant that she was going to sleep on a cot while Marquize and I took the two beds in the room. I argued with her, but she said that we were the ones playing and we needed our sleep. To be honest, I don't know that our beds were that much more comfortable than the cot, but we dumped our things on them, and after an hour of vigorous practice at the nearby courts (which were as nice as our Palm Gables courts, almost), comfort wasn't really an issue.

Chapter Two

We got to our first professional tennis tournament an hour and a half before our first match, at Ma's insistence. She packed our bags with our rackets (two each), towels, some overgrips (the tape you wind around the racket grip), and two bananas each. "For energy," she said. "They should have water bottles there for you to drink."

While she went to find the courts, we followed the signs to the players' locker rooms and looked for any indication of what lockers we should take. About a dozen players were getting dressed and chatting, everyone very familiar in this environment. Kind of like my first few days at Palm Gables, Marquize and I were surrounded by a group we were now technically—but not really—part of. At Palm Gables, I could've walked up to any one of the dozen people and started a conversation about school (maybe not so much in the last half year, but before that). Here I didn't know anyone's names, I didn't know what to talk to them about or even how to talk to them. And Marquize, always so confident, didn't either.

A red fox a couple inches shorter than me saw us looking around and walked over to us. He stuck out a paw. "First time?"

"Uh. Yeah." I scratched my ear while Marquize shook, and then took my turn.

"Is it obvious?" Marquize asked.

The fox grinned. "Welcome to the Futures. Grab a locker—any empty one is fine. I'm Nashan."

We introduced ourselves as well. "How long have you been pro?" I asked.

Nashan laughed. "About eight years. I made it to the Challenger circuit for a year, then dropped back here to beat up on you young cubs for a little while before I hang it up."

Eight years ago I'd been hitting balls on cracked courts against cement walls back in Lundara. I tried to imagine playing professionally for that long and never getting much beyond this level. "Hope I don't run into you in the tournament then."

The fox chuckled. "Don't be too worried. I broke a leg and missed a good chunk of last year, so my points are down. I have to win the qualifying tournament the same as you. So the chances of us both qualifying and then meeting in the main tournament aren't too good. You guys nervous?"

"No, but talk about it a bit more." Marquize's tone grew an edge.

"We're fine," I said. "We went to Palm Gables. We played lots of tournaments there."

"This is different," Nashan said. "You're not playing people you know, you're playing in front of bigger crowds."

"You don't need to psysch us out." Marquize gave Nashan a look as sharp as his voice.

"I'm not trying to. I'm telling you, this is going to happen, and the sooner you get over it, the better. If you go in thinking you're going to dominate the way you did at school, you're going to fall flat on your muzzle and that hurts. Better to go in realistically and be prepared to learn from what happens. Okay? Friends?"

"We'll see," Marquize said.

I smiled and held out a paw. "Thanks for the advice."

"Sure." Nashan shook. "I always like seeing the youngsters come up. Maybe one day I can say I knew them back when they didn't know what locker to go to."

I didn't really think it was going to be that different stepping onto the court for my first professional tournament. The arena wasn't that much larger than I'd played on at Palm Gables, and maybe the crowd was a little larger, but the court felt the same to me. The air was drier, the smells different, but I thought I could handle it.

Until that first serve. Delvinic was a lemming, a jumpy, quick guy half a foot shorter than me. He had a pretty good serve, but it wasn't anything I hadn't seen before. Still, for whatever reason I was a half-step late on it and my return landed just wide. And the line judge yelled, "Out."

I'd seen that on TV, and that simple thing, hearing a call of "Out," was enough to remind me that this was a professional tournament.

Then I got jittery because I'd missed the first point. I netted the next return, which should have been an easy point, and when I finally got a rally going, I sent a forehand long to lose the point. Thirty seconds and another wide return later, I'd lost the game.

On my serve, I double-faulted and missed my first serve two other times, but finally won my first point, down 0-40. I lost the break on the next point, but at least I'd won one.

I spent the third game talking to myself and trying to collect my thoughts. I stared at the crowd between points, finding Ma in it, wondering how Marquize was doing. Thinking about Ma and Marquize helped, and even though I lost the game, I finally remembered one of the centering exercises I'd learned at Palm Gables. As I collected balls from the ball boy (who might have been older than I was), I held one of them in my paw and stared down at it.

These balls: I knew them. I knew how they bounced, how they felt when I hit them right on the sweet spot of the racket. I turned the ball in my paw, looking at the white binding around the yellow felt. "The ball is the same no matter what," I told myself. I squeezed it and then looked up at the chair umpire to indicate that I was ready.

With a little of my focus back, I could see where I could attack Delvinic's game. He had a strong forehand (I would later learn that a lot of Siberian players start with that) but his backhand was weak. I had an advantage there: as a left-handed player, I could hit forehand shots to his backhand in some situations more powerfully than he was used to from other righties. The more points we played, the more I saw that he was afraid to go for the corners and lines with his shots, too; he kept them at least a foot inbounds. So I cheated a little on defense, figuring out where he was going to return my shots. He still had that forehand and he got a couple winners past me, and I lost the first set. But I broke his serve late in the second set to go up 5-3, and then held to pull even at one set apiece.

My first set win of my professional career had my tail twitching, wanting to wag as we rested between sets. If I could win one, I could win another one, right? I told myself that and believed it, and went out prepared to prove it.

As it turned out, it wasn't hard. Delvinic moved a step slower and that forehand didn't come as strongly. I broke his serve twice and won the match.

The moment took a little while to sink in. There wasn't any fanfare; a polite smattering of applause, and Delvinic walked up to the net to shake my paw. "Good match," he said in a Siberian-accented voice.

"You too." I followed him to the chair umpire, where we both shook, and then I went back to my bench. Delvinic packed up his stuff right away, so I did the same, taking the time to drink from a bottle of water. Someone nearby was still applauding; I looked up and saw Ma in the coaches' area, still standing, still clapping for me. When she met my eyes, she smiled and made her way to the exit, so I hurried to do the same.

"Very well done," she said, and hugged me. "Four more matches and you'll get paid."

"I was nervous the first set," I said. "But I figured it out."

"Yes. Figure it out faster next time. Save your energy."

I listened for the sound of tennis happening. "Is Marquize still playing?"

We found the cheetah in the locker room, already changed. "I lost in straight sets," he said, avoiding my eyes as I approached.

"Hey, it's okay. It's our first tournament. We'll get better."

"This guy just had me beat from the beginning."

I put a paw on his shoulder. "You'll figure it out. Me and Ma will help."

The cheetah looked up. "What about you? Did you win?"

"Yeah!" It burst out before I could restrain it, even though the word was followed by a rush of guilt over celebrating my victory when my friend—my boyfriend—was miserable from his loss. "I mean…the guy wasn't that good. Just lucky, I guess."

"No, no." Marquize met my eyes. "You're good, Rocky. Don't worry about it. Let's go get some lunch, and see when your match is tomorrow."

* * *

It was at the same time, first thing in the morning. So we followed the same routine, one which would become very familiar very quickly. We ate a healthy, filling breakfast a couple hours before the match, went to the arena, and changed. Marquize and I warmed up together, and Ma gave me some particulars on my opponent for that day.

She hadn't had time to research Delvinic, but when we found out I'd be playing Larntt, a red squirrel, she took the time to read up on him online. "He has a good forehand," she said. "And a two-handed backhand. Not much net game, likes baseline rallies."

"I'll try to play that way," Marquize said, and he did for the half hour we practiced.

It wasn't much help. Larntt was quicker than Marquize, and much better at hiding his intentions. When I served, we were pretty well matched. I could keep him on his heels, anticipate his ground-strokes, and if I were patient, I'd get a good approach to the net.

When he served, though, I got destroyed. I guessed wrong on his serves, barely got my returns in, and he played with much more confidence in those games. I lost all the games on his serve, and late in the first set he figured something out and broke my serve.

After dropping the first set, I fought back. I sat on the sidelines and ran through that game in my head while eating two bananas. Larntt had been pouncing on my backhand, which meant I was telegraphing something. Probably my footwork. I reached back to my lessons to remember what I was doing. Being too proper about my movements. Choose faster, move later, I told myself.

I hadn't had to worry about how my opponents were analyzing my game very often in the past. Now I had to do that while at the same time trying to find the cracks in his game. The problem was that while I knew he was vulnerable to net play, I wasn't sure how to get him off-balance enough in his baseline game to give myself openings at the net, at least not on his serve.

In the second set, I found my answer. We had a long rally from the baseline on his first service game during which I managed to disguise a few backhands successfully. He reminded me of some of the baseline pounders I'd played at school, but he had a much faster stroke, a really good snap of the wrist, and better placement than most of the guys at the Academy. He kept me off balance. But as I returned his shot, I saw where he'd go with the next one and had two seconds to plan my return. If I could pull him off to the side…

I caught the line and the ball hooked away from Larntt. He sprinted to the doubles alley and got his racket on it, and tried to hit it behind me as I went running for the net. I lunged and caught it, sending it into the open court as he ran to get back into position, but he was too far to even have a chance at it.

Two points later, I broke his serve for the first time. Then there were six tense games in which I had to hold my serve. I lost one, but broke him again, and I won the second set.

The third set came with me feeling very confident. What I hadn't reckoned on was being a little tired. Rather, I knew my legs were starting to drag, but that had never been a problem because my opponents were usually just as tired, and even when they weren't, like that match against Cleve, I could fight through it and still play my game. But Larntt was in great shape and still springing all over the court. He broke my serve early on, and I got discouraged enough that I stopped playing my game. He broke me again and that was that.

"What's next?" was the first thing Ma said to me when I trudged off the court.

"Next is stretching and cooling down," I said.

"There's another tournament next week," Marquize said.

Only we found that the deadline to register had already passed. "Well," Ma said. "You were so excited to register for your first tournament that you weren't thinking about the second."

"That's pretty obvious now," I said. "So?"

She cuffed me lightly on the back of the head. "So register for the third."

There was a series of three here in Golden, and we had time to register for the third one. Then, for good measure, we registered for the series of ten K tournaments in the Midwest. Again Marquize and I registered as a doubles team for all the tournaments, hoping we'd get a spot somewhere.

"In the meantime," I said, "I'm going to work out some more. I don't know why I was so tired today."

"The long flight," Marquize said. "I'll work out with you."

"And I will look for someone to coach you," Ma said.

* * *

The first of those things went better than the second. I remembered overhearing at the tournament that there were fitness rooms at the arena that were open for player use, so we worked out there among lots of other players. Some were our age, but most were older. Nashan wasn't there and neither were any of the ones we'd played, so we still didn't know how to make friends on the tour.

For the next week, we worked out in the gym and went to see some of the other matches. I made a point to watch the rest of Larntt's matches and was pleased to see him make it through the qualifiers into the main draw. I decided—whether it was true or not—that it had been bad luck that I'd been matched with him. If I worked and trained and got my stamina up and got a good coach, I'd be making it into main draws soon, I was sure.

Marquize and I made sure to go to the qualifying final, because Nashan had made it that far. I wanted to talk to him because he was the only person who'd been friendly to me on the tour so far, but when he lost the match, I wasn't sure he'd want some kid coming up and saying hi. Marquize didn't want to talk to him at all, and I almost agreed to leave the campus with him, but I couldn't bring myself to abandon the only connection I'd made so far.

Nashan, half-dressed, was gulping a bottle of PowerAde when I came into the locker room, Marquize trailing behind me. While the cheetah hung out near some of the other players, I went over to the red fox and said I was sorry about his match. "Thanks," he said. "Rocky, right?"

"Yeah." He remembered; that made my tail wag.

"You lost in the first round, I think?"

"Second."

"Oh!" His ears went up. "Won your first pro match? Nicely done. Where'd you go to school again?"

I told him, and he nodded. "Ah, that's a good place. No wonder. So are you going to be over in Calmo?"

"No, we missed the registration. We'll be in Euker, though."

The fox's ears flattened. "I think they have provisions to register if you played in the previous tournament in the series. No? Well, go over to registration and ask them about it, see if there's anything they can do."

"Registration here?"

"Yeah. Or get your coach to do it."

"Oh," I said. "We don't have a coach yet. I mean, my ma is coaching us, but we're looking for someone more…"

"Experienced in tennis?" Nashan finished when I trailed off.

"Yeah. That's a good way to say it."

"Hang on." He got his phone out and scrolled through something. "Here. You have something to write with?"

I got my own phone out, and he showed me his screen. "This guy, and I have one other. They're pretty good and they work with a lot of new pros."

He brought up the second name when I'd finished with the first one. I got them both down and thanked him. "Another friend of mine said he'd get me a couple names, but he hasn't gotten back to me yet." Then I thought he might be impressed if I knew Braden, and I wanted him to like me and be impressed with me, so I said, "Actually, he's not really a 'friend' friend, but he went to the same school and he said he'd help me go pro. Braden Longacre…don't know if you've heard of him."

Nashan obviously had. His ears swept back and his brow lowered. "Yeah, I know him. Don't hold your breath for that help."

Marquize had sort of been listening off to the side and now came over, stepping in while I searched for what to say. "Hi, uh, actually Braden came to the school and played a set with Rocky. I know he's an asshole; we've met him a bunch. But he seems to respect Rocky. And Rocky's really good."

The red fox shook his head. "I met him a couple years back when he was starting out just like you are. Except he was an arrogant prick."

"Still is," Marquize put in.

"He strutted in like he was already better than everyone else, even before he got his first hundred."

"Hundred?" I asked.

"Points. Ranking points. Your school explained that, right?"

"Oh, yeah." Coach Murphy had told me, but I already knew how players earned points with match wins that the ATP used to generate their ranking. The top players had thousands and thousands of points, and if I had somehow won four qualifying matches to get to the main draw, and then won six more matches to win the tournament, I would've earned 27 points. "So getting to your first hundred…"

Nashan waved a paw. "It means that at least you've gotten to a few quarters and semis. It's hard to get to a hundred just getting one or two points a tournament. Plus it usually gets your ranking into the top 500 and you can start getting automatically into main draws."

"How many did you get in this one?" Marquize asked before I could stop him.

"You don't get points unless you get into the main draw," Nashan told him. "You have to win at least one match in smaller tournaments, or two in larger ones. I think for this one if I'd gotten to the main draw and won in the round of sixteen, I'd have gotten," he held up one finger, "one point."

Marquize absorbed that. "You could play a hundred tournaments in a year."

"Sure," Nashan said. "There are some guys who do that. Family money so they can travel around, and they play well enough to be invited to some of the bigger tournaments, and they always lose. But if they're lucky, they get into an early round match with someone famous and then they can say they played him. You guys have family money?"

I looked at Marquize, but he shook his head. "No," I said.

"Good." Nashan's ears came back up and he smiled. "You're in it to win it. That's the way you've got to play." He shook each of our paws. "I'll see you guys in Euker for sure, right? Maybe Calmo, too. And you should start registering for the next set while you're at it."

"We already did, but yeah, let's head over there," I said. "Thanks"

The mule deer was at registration again, but there was a line. I wasn't sure who would be checking in this late and then as I listened to some of them, I realized that these were players in the main draw, who wouldn't be starting their matches until the next day.

When I got to the table, the mule deer recognized me. "N'Guwe, right? What can I do for you?"

So I asked her about the Calmo tournament, and she said she was sorry, but the registrations were closed. She did say I could still register for the Euker tournament, and I said I'd done that. She said she'd be working there and would hope to see me, so I felt good as I walked away, like I was becoming part of the tennis-playing community.

"They really should have an orientation," Marquize grumbled.

"They do, for seniors at Palm Gables, and I was sort of getting one before I left. People join the tour at all different times during the year."

"Still. Online or something."

(We found out later that there was an online page for joining the professional tour that nobody had pointed us to and we hadn't found, and also that there were sporadic attempts to have a seminar exactly like the one Marquize was imagining, but that the problem of people joining the tour at all different times meant that nobody really attended whenever they had one, and anyway people figured it out quickly enough or they gave up and went home.)

Chapter Three

Ma had looked up some coach's names, too, so it turned out to be a good thing that we hadn't registered for the Calmo tournament (optimistically assuming our time would've been taken up with winning matches there). Three of the coaches were already in the area coaching players, and we were able to get in touch with them and set up interviews; the fourth agreed to talk to us remotely over Skype.

The sticking point is that they wanted to see video of me and Marquize playing, but fortunately Palm Gables filmed their tournaments for this reason, so we actually had links to point them to. At that point one of the coaches sent back a polite note that he didn't think he'd be right for me.

That stung. Was I not good enough? Why didn't he say anything about Marquize? I didn't say anything to Ma because I didn't want to seem insecure, but I told myself I'd remember the coach's name and sometime later, I'd prove to him that he'd made a mistake.

(Within a year, I'd forgotten his name.)

In the week before we could head up to Calmo, Marquize and I practiced on the school courts, and when we weren't practicing, Ma made us read books. "You're going to keep learning some things, at least," she said, "and I'm going to keep teaching you."

Marquize grumbled privately to me as we were supposed to be studying, while Ma was in the bathroom. "Your mother had to be a teacher, didn't she?"

"What else would we do all day?"

He raised his eyebrows. "Find a place where we could be alone."

Ever since the night we'd been caught, we hadn't had any private time. Like, literally none, except when Ma was using the bathroom like now. Once we'd tried sneaking out of bed, but she sleeps very lightly and woke up immediately to ask where I was going, and I'd had to say I was using the bathroom (and then, because she was listening, I had to empty a water glass into the toilet). Whenever she went to the store or on an errand, she always took one of us with her. She was a strict chaperone, true to her word, and while we knew intellectually that that was probably best for us, it was also pretty damn frustrating.

"She won't let us."

Marquize tilted his head. "What if I rented another motel room and we stopped in there on our way back from practice?"

"And what, skip an hour of practice?"

"Half an hour, anyway."

"What if she comes back to the court to check on us?"

He shrugged. "Then we get in trouble. I'm willing to take the risk. I want to…"

The toilet flushed then, so we quieted down and bent back to our books. Ma didn't say anything when she came out, so I hoped she hadn't heard us.

* * *

At Calmo, we set up meetings with the two coaches who were there, a big, muscular lion and a skinny kit fox. Both of them wanted to meet with me and Marquize individually, and then with both of us and Ma together. The lion talked a lot about working out and building up my fundamentals, which sounded good to me. "Strength and conditioning are the most important part of tennis," he said.

The kit fox said that my mental game was very promising but could use some honing, and that I could use a lot of repetition on my fundamentals. "That's common to both of you," he said when Ma and Marquize joined me. "Most first-year players need some work on that."

Both of them had nutrition plans that seemed similar on the surface (they didn't give us a lot of details), and both had similar levels of experience. The kit fox was slightly more expensive than the lion, but that didn't make a difference with Ma.

"I don't like either of them," she said.

"What?" Marquize was as surprised as I was. "I thought they were both good. I could use work on my mental game and Rocky could use more strength training."

"I liked the fox more," I said, though in retrospect that was probably because he was a fox.

Ma shook her head. "They both talked about working on fundamentals. You're doing that already. Why do we need to pay someone to tell you that when I'm doing it now?"

"They understand the game," I said, because I could see Marquize thinking it. "They'll watch us and tell us how to improve."

"I can do that, too."

Ma had the money, so unless Marquize could convince his parents or she liked one of the coaches, we weren't going to get one. I hadn't seen anything wrong with either the lion or the kit fox, so maybe the third one, the one we were going to talk to over Skype, would be different.

He was a wolf, very curt and professional. "Saw your tape," he said. "Good potential. More in Rocky than Marquize, but you could both be top hundred if you work hard at it. You guys willing to work hard?"

"Yes, sir," I said, and Marquize echoed a moment later.

"Good." He went on to tell us his rates and then finished with a request that we get back to him in two days, as he was looking at another player as well.

I saw Ma's answer as soon as we broke the connection. "Oh, come on," I said. "What was wrong with him? He didn't even talk about fundamentals!"

"What did he talk about? 'Work hard.' You need to pay him to tell you that?" Ma shook her head. "When you are top hundred, you can hire a new coach with experience in important matches, one who knows things I don't. Until then, I'll watch your games and I'll coach you both. Besides," she said, cutting off our objections with a gleam in her eye, "it will keep me busy."

She was already keeping pretty busy what with the book-reading and the keeping us from having any alone time, but this didn't seem like the right time to bring that up.

I got to call my sister later that night. It'd been a while since I talked to her, though I'd called when I'd left Palm Gables and told her it would be a busy week or two.

"How was your first pro match?" she asked. "I looked on the Internet but I couldn't find you."

"Oh, we were there," I said. "I won a match and then lost. Until I start winning, I'm going to have to win four matches just to get a spot in a tournament."

"That sounds hard."

"Well," I said, "the guy I lost to today won a spot. And I could probably beat him if we play again. So I don't think it'll be that hard. But it's a lot of matches to play."

"You can do it. And I'm proud that you won your first match! How did Marquize do?"

"Lost. But he'll get better too." I told her briefly about our coaching search. "So I'm not sure we'll ever actually hire a coach. Ma wants to do it herself."

"If anyone can," Ori said, "I bet Ma can."

"I'm not so sure." I kept my voice down even though I was outside in the parking lot. "I mean, she knows a lot about tennis, but it's mostly really basic stuff we covered at Palm Gables. She's making us repeat a lot of workouts is all."

"It's got to be a big change for you now."

"Um…yeah. What does that have to do with it?"

"Take a few months and get used to the change. And take that time to talk Ma into getting you a coach."

"I guess that's all I can do. How are things with you and your village chief?"

She made an exasperated noise. "Kamina is pushing for him to come down here *sooner*. He was going to wait for a break in the weather, but it looks like it may continue raining for another week. Kamina doesn't want to wait."

"Another week?"

"Ugh. She says that as I've turned sixteen, 'the clock is ticking,' and she is still looking for other suitors for me so she wants to get me married before next year. Let's not talk about it. How's Marquize?"

"He's good. We don't get any time together because of Ma, and we've only been through one tournament and he lost, so he's grouchy, but I'm glad I have him here. Otherwise I'd be doing this alone."

"With Ma."

"So basically alone."

Ori laughed. "She's not that bad."

"She's making us read books."

"That's good. You should be reading books."

"Fine. Take her side."

"Ro, I'm reading books too. The difference is that I'm doing it when I can scrape together the time on my own because Kamina doesn't think it's important. She barely tolerates me doing it at all, in fact."

I sighed. "Just hold on for another year or two. When we have the money…"

"I know. I'll be fine, Ro. Go work on your tennis game, but don't neglect your books or your boy."

"I'll try." Talking about 'my boy' warmed my chest, but a moment later reminded me of Ori's boy Raji, still away, still missing in the midst of some war. I didn't want to mention him; if she'd gotten news of him, she would've told me, certainly.

Despite that sour note, it was good to hear her encouraging voice again. In the next tournament, I vowed, I'd do better.

* * *

Because the motel was cheap, we stayed there rather than going to the site of the next tournament. There was no point in going, Ma said, even though Marquize and I thought we could hang around and talk with more of the players, or at least watch the tournament. It seemed to be pretty easy to get in. Still, we couldn't argue that we didn't need the practice, so we stayed and worked out on the courts and read our books.

The downtime also allowed us to plan a moment alone. Or, as Marquize said, more than a moment. He snuck away to rent another room in the motel Tuesday morning while Ma and I were out getting groceries, and hid the key in our gear bags. We normally practiced in the morning, then studied in the early afternoon while the day was warm, and then went out again for an evening practice. Ma always watched us during the early practice, but sometimes left to start dinner before the late one was over, because we had to use the shared microwave in the motel office and sometimes there was a wait.

That's what we were counting on. I deliberately took longer with my reading than I normally would, so that our late practice would get a late start. And sure enough, an hour into it, Ma flicked her ears and lifted her nose to the scents of the families around us cooking their dinners. The light was starting to fade but wasn't gone yet, so we could play for another forty-five minutes.

"I'm going to go start dinner," she said. "Practice another half hour, then come home."

"Okay, Ma," I said. Marquize echoed the assent.

We hit the ball back and forth in soft rallies until she was gone around the corner. Then Marquize came to the net on his side, and I hurried up to meet him. "Think we can go now?" he whispered.

"Give her another five minutes," I said, tapping my own large, sensitive ears.

Marquize nodded and retreated to hit more rallies back and forth. He was clearly distracted, though, missing easy shots, not focusing on his footwork. I could guess what he was thinking about pretty easily, but weirdly, for me it was still about the tennis. I was trying to hit corners, practicing my groundstrokes, and Marquize was swatting the balls back without really paying much attention to where they were going.

I got frustrated with him, and then he let one of my lobs go (it dropped a foot inside the baseline) and said, "Can we go now?"

"Sure," I said, and walked to the bench to pick up the gear.

Marquize came over and put a paw on my shoulder. "Can't wait," he said. Then he must have noticed that my tail wasn't wagging, because he asked, "You okay?"

"I'm fine." I zipped up my racket and tossed the balls into the bag.

"Aren't you excited?"

"Yeah, of course."

He folded his arms. "We don't have to do this. I mean, I spent a bunch of money on the room, and we have the time, but if you're not interested…"

I sighed and turned around. "Of course I'm interested. I'm just in, like in tennis mode right now."

His expression didn't change. "Can you get out of tennis mode in five minutes?"

"Yeah," I said, though I wasn't sure.

He patted me again. "It's that intensity that's going to have you winning tournaments in no time."

His paw lingered on my shoulder, and that did get me thinking along more physical lines. He was trying hard to be nice, so I reminded myself that he was my boyfriend, after all, and that not being able to shake the memory of losing that qualifying match didn't mean I shouldn't enjoy time with him.

It took me a block or two to lose the annoyance at having to leave practice early. By the time we got to Marquize's motel room, I was more into the spirit of our illicit tryst. I sniffed the air for any trace of Ma, while Marquize looked around to make sure she wasn't spying on us from the door to our room before slipping his key into the lock and opening the door.

Then we were in a small clean room with two beds exactly like the ones we were sleeping in, except without our clothes and our scent, like a strange mirror world of the room we'd been calling home for nearly the last week. Marquize didn't waste any time, grabbing me and kissing me as soon as the door was closed. We dropped our gear bags and stumbled over to the bed, our paws sliding over clothes and under clothes, pulling them free.

"We only have about fifteen minutes," Marquize panted.

"I don't think that'll be a problem."

It was a little weird because light still came in through the curtains, but when I started to get up to close them, Marquize pulled me back to the bed. We had our paws in our pants within minutes and could feel how excited we both were, and within a minute or two the pants were down and our paws were around each other.

Marquize twisted around, his muzzle hanging open. "Ah," he panted. "On. On the sheets."

Better thinking than I was able to do in that moment. So I finished him, and then I turned over onto my paws and knees and he returned the favor.

The smell of what we'd done filled my nose. The excitement ebbed quickly, replaced by guilt and a little annoyance. I didn't want to be here with my pants around my ankles smelling this mess on the bed. Marquize's paw on me still felt good, and I still wanted to be with him, but it was in the middle of the day and we'd left tennis practice. "Should we clean that up?"

"The maids do it."

"Ugh." I said it before I could stop myself. My tail curled between my legs.

Marquize let me go and looked up at me. "What?"

"Someone else is going to…" I slid off the bed, went to the bathroom, and came back with a paw full of tissues.

"Rocky, you don't have to…" He watched as I cleaned up our messes. "Seriously. I paid for the room. Part of the room is the cleaning."

"It's okay." The tissues smelled. I took them to the bathroom, threw them in the toilet, and then washed my paws. "I just don't want someone else to have to touch that."

"Can you grab me a towel?" he called.

When I came out, I tossed the towel to him. He wiped himself and then dropped the towel on the bed. "It would've been dry by the time they come tomorrow."

I got myself a towel to clean up, too. "We probably don't have a lot of time left," I said.

He pulled his pants up and sat on the bed. "Did I do something wrong?"

"No." I said it automatically.

"So what's bothering you?"

I gestured at the room. "Sneaking around like this."

"We have to! Would you rather not have any time?"

"Leaving tennis practice…"

As soon as I said that, I saw that it was wrong somehow and searched for some way to back out. "I mean…"

The cheetah's expression closed and he looked away from me, at the window. "I get it. You'd rather do another half hour of tennis than have this time with me."

"No."

"That's what you said."

"It's not—" But it was close enough, so I changed tactics. "It's been really weird, being in school and then suddenly not. I'm glad I'm doing this with you. I'm just…remember when I was dating Shawna and you said she wasn't good for my tennis? I don't want this," I patted his paw, "to stop us from getting farther. And we have a long way to go."

He wasn't completely mollified. "I *know* that. I want to win, too. I just don't want to be one of those people who's eating, breathing, sleeping tennis. I want to have a life outside of it too, and I want you to be part of it. I don't think it hurts our tennis to steal a half hour here and there to have fun and remind ourselves that we're young and in love."

"It's just…" I sat on the bed and exhaled. "It's our first tournament. And there's so much to learn. I think I'm good, but I've only played two matches. If I'm going to get better, I have to be good enough to play a lot more."

Marquize scooted over to sit beside me and slid his arm around my waist. "Hey. You're good. You're going to win a lot of matches. You know, it's been less than a week since we left Pensa. You're not going to get to a major final in a week."

"I know." I leaned against him.

"So can we still sneak away? Once in a while?"

"I wish I was eighteen now. I wish I was making enough money to have my own room." Nearly two years seemed like a long time, far too long.

"Soon enough we both will."

Money would be months away, and there was Ori to think about, and all of it pushed my shoulders down and hunched my spine over. My tail curled in tightly against my leg and I wished in that moment that I'd never left Palm Gables. I wouldn't have to stay in a cheap motel and worry about who was going to clean the sheets, I wouldn't have to think about registering and worry about how we were going to get to some tournament or another or about where to find the right locker.

Then I remembered that Ma said she would take care of the registrations, and adrenaline punched me upright, out of Marquize's arms. "We gotta go. We gotta go!"

"Okay, okay!" He jumped up and reached for my arm, but I was already hurrying toward my gear bag, and then I doubled over and sniffed myself to see if any of our activity was still noticeable.

Marquize made it over to me as I ran for the bathroom, but this time he grabbed my wrist. "Where are you going?"

"I've got to clean up more!"

"Rocky. We'll take a shower when we get back to the room. You don't have time now. It's almost dark out."

I stared at the bathroom and then sagged back and let him lead me out of the room.

Ma didn't say anything, but I saw her nostrils flare when I walked by her, and after that day she didn't leave us alone at practice again for a while. It wasn't the sort of thing I would have noticed except that I was alert for it after that day. It didn't matter; Marquize didn't try to get private time with me again before we had to drive to Euker.

We'd worked out the schedule of tournaments and had figured out that by driving through the night in one or two cases, we could drive rather than fly, so Ma had spent some time looking around for used cars, and bought an inexpensive sedan that Marquize and I dubbed Big Blue because it was a deep, somewhat unsettling shade of royal blue. But it was comfortable, and she got it for the price of two plane trips for the three of us.

Euker was a larger town, with parks and tall office buildings and a motel called the King Yellow (the 'o' was burned out so the sign read "King Yell w," and Marquize and I dutifully yelled, "Double-U!" every time we drove up to it) a mile and a half from the tennis center. At the center, we encountered the mule deer again and got our credentials, and this time went to the locker room with more confidence.

I forget who it was I played that match, but I won and then won again. I got to the qualifying finals before being beaten this time, and Marquize again lost his first match. Ma watched all of our matches, and then made us watch the matches of the guy who beat me (I remember him: Yang, a Xaiqinese deer).

After the tournament she sat us down and ran through all the notes she'd taken. Even though Marquize had only played one match and I'd played four, she seemed to have a lot more notes for him. He picked up on that, but she reminded him that it was all meant to help him succeed, and he got over his pouting quickly.

Seeing Nashan again at this tournament was nice because even though we recognized a few of the other muzzles and names, he made us feel like we had another friend. He'd lost in the qualifying final again, but he wasn't angry about it. "These bigger tournaments," he said, "I don't make it to the main draw much anymore. Sometimes I get lucky, but most of my money I earn at the smaller ones, like these next three coming up."

We were sitting in the locker room after my last match. I'd already changed and was sitting on the bench, and he'd come in from losing his match at the same time, undressing as we talked. "I'm looking forward to those," I said.

"Hey, did either of those coaches work out?" he asked.

I shook my head. "We're sticking with my Ma for now. Until we find one we really like." He didn't say anything, but his ears went back. "Is there something wrong with that?"

"I don't want to tell you how to run your career, let alone your life," he said. "But I been doing this ten years now. I've seen a lot of guys come up and…" He traced trajectories with his paw. "Make it to Challenger, make it to Champions, make it to majors. I played against Tempest. Beat him once. That was three years before he won the Ocie, but still. Point is, guys who stick with their parents as coaches…they don't usually last long. Maybe that's not causality…"

There I had to ask him to explain that word. He rephrased it. "Maybe they're not failing out because their parents are coaches. Maybe they're the ones who never win enough to be able to afford to hire a coach. But the ones who make it to the next level with a parent

as a coach are so rare that it always stands out to me." He slid his underwear off as he said that and grabbed a towel. "Be right back."

I spent the ten minutes of his shower trying not to focus on the glimpse I'd seen of his privates, making sure I wasn't showing any signs of arousal in appearance or scent. I was pretty successful, and it's hard to smell anything in the locker room anyway, with all the Neutra-Scent and the smells of exertion and soap under that. If Nashan noticed anything when he came back, he didn't say. I did look away when he dropped the towel to start getting dressed, until things were covered up. Even though I was much more interested in what he had to say about tennis, I guess I was still interested in toned athletic male bodies, too.

"So what can I do?" I asked.

He shook his head. "You're going to have to work that out. Either you upset your mom or you risk your tennis career."

"I think Ma would understand if I explained to her that parents don't make good coaches."

"Good luck." Nashan pulled his arms through the sleeves of his shirt and grinned as he buttoned it up. "I haven't yet met a parent who didn't think they were the exception to that rule."

"Ma's pretty smart." But I remembered her attitude as we'd dismissed the other coaches. I'd liked some of them, too, and at least two of them had sounded like we could afford them.

"You know her, I don't." The red fox pulled on pants and tucked his shirt in. "All I know is what I've seen in the last decade."

"I won more matches this time."

"Oh sure. They can get you here." He held his paw around his chest height. "Maybe even here." Up to his shoulders. "But if you want to be here," as high as his arm could stretch, "my professional opinion is that you'll need a professional coach."

"Are, uh." I worked on the phrasing in my head. "Are you going to coach?"

"Maybe someday." He smiled. "Not right now. I've got a couple years, maybe four or five, to keep playing the tournaments. I'm gonna keep going until I can't anymore."

"Did you ever get to Champions?"

"Oh, for one month I was ranked in the top hundred." He laughed. "Ninety-two, that was my highest spot."

One month out of ten years? "That's great," I said.

"I know how it sounds." His tail flicked, and he sat down across from me. "But you know, I got there. For a little while, there were only ninety-one players in the world better than me. In the *world*. There are over a hundred players just in this tournament. Think about how that feels, how big the world is and how close you are to the top. Yeah, I could've maybe made it to the top 90 if a couple balls had dropped differently, but all in all, there's not that many people that can say they were top 100."

When he talked about the balls dropping differently, he slowed, and I could see him replaying the points in his head. But I didn't press him on it. "I sure can't, not yet."

"You've got a decade to change that." He leaned forward with a smile, back in the present moment. "You've got my number, right? Okay, any advice you need, just text me."

"Really?"

"Yeah. I take an interest in new kids, and I haven't seen much of you, but what I've seen is promising. Also, you're not an asshole, which is refreshing."

"How do I compare to Braden?" It burst out before I could stop it.

"Ha." He rocked back. "I already told you, you're not an asshole."

"I mean—"

"I know." He rubbed his whiskers. "I'd have to watch you more. Braden was...he was a force on the court. He's one of those players who imposes his will on the game, or tries to. When someone gets him out of his zone, he gets flustered. It's gotten harder and harder for other players to do that. You, though, you don't do that. Not that I've seen. But I don't know. I'll watch you out in Fort Ellsworth."

"Maybe I'll end up playing you."

He winked. "Then I'll for sure watch you closely."

I went back to Ma and Marquize that night but didn't say anything about my talk with Nashan. I couldn't say anything in front of Ma, and Marquize and I didn't have enough time alone to have a conversation. Ma was teaching me and Marquize to drive, and we were getting the hang of it without too much trouble (learning the rules of the road was harder, even with the manuals Ma download-ed). I filed Nashan's words away for a little later, when I might be able to do something about them.

But that night, I woke up with a very noticeable tension, and when I went to the bathroom to relieve it, I wasn't thinking about my boyfriend, but about the older, muscular physique of a red fox.

Chapter Four

All registered for the midwestern tournaments, we set out from Euker early one morning. Ma drove until we got out onto the freeway, and then a couple hours later, she pulled Big Blue over at a rest stop. "All right," she said, "which one of you would like to drive first?"

Marquize and I glanced at each other. I wanted to drive, but I knew he was down after our short tryst in the motel room and after two tournaments where I'd won four matches and he'd won none. So I said, "Go ahead," and he asked if I was sure, and I said, "Yeah, we've got plenty of driving. I'll get a chance."

So Marquize took the wheel. Ma drilled him on using his mirrors, keeping below (or at least around) the speed limit, being aware of other drivers, signaling, and a lot of other stuff that I zoned out for. I knew I'd get the same lecture when it was my turn.

Ma sat in front as Marquize eased Big Blue out onto the road. I sat up, excited for him, and I could tell he was nervous because he kept pulling the car from side to side. "Straighten it out," I said, trying to help, and Ma reached a paw back to shush me.

It took him a while to get up to seventy miles an hour. "Don't be scared," Ma kept telling him as cars honked and sped by us. "Go only as fast as you're comfortable with."

Marquize didn't say anything, hyper-focused on the road, but I could see him relax, the curl of his tail easing once he did get the car up to match the others on the highway. "Hey," he said a few minutes later, "this isn't so bad."

Ma wouldn't go faster than sixty on a road where the limit was seventy. Marquize had the car at seventy-three or so, and I could see Ma staring at the speedometer waiting to tell him to slow down.

"You're doing great," I said. "We're not getting honked at nearly as much."

That got Ma to shoot a look back at me. I smiled. "You told him to go whatever speed he was comfortable with."

"It's easier if I'm going the same speed as everyone else," Marquize said. "Getting up to that speed was hard."

I found that out when it was my turn, which I put off 'til the next day on the excuse that I was sleepy by the time Marquize was tired. Ma got us out on the highway again even though Marquize wanted to practice street driving, and at the first rest stop she pulled off and said, "Go ahead, Ro."

So I got behind the wheel. "Adjust the seat and the mirrors," Ma told me, and I did so, not really sure what I was doing, but I adjusted them until I could sort of see all around. Then I checked to make sure I could reach the pedals, and I eased the car down the ramp.

I'd thought that after watching Marquize, I would push the car up to seventy and lean back in the seat, all relaxed like in the movies. But when I pushed my foot down and the car leapt forward, I panicked and pulled my foot back, then eased it down again amid Ma's calm instructions. Fortunately, there weren't many cars on the road, so I got it up to what I thought was seventy, started breathing more easily as the tightness in my chest eased, and then looked at the speedometer and saw that I was barely over fifty.

"Go on, Rocky," Marquize said over my shoulder. "Open her up."

I didn't know that expression, but there was not much ambiguity around it. So I bit my lip and jammed my foot down harder on the accelerator.

At first it was scary, but I got used to it faster than I would've thought. Within about fifteen minutes I was comfortable at seventy, only tightening up every time we came up on a car that was going slower. But a few hours later, when we had to stop for gas and Ma asked if I wanted to change, I said, "I can keep going."

And we drove like that, switching between the three of us, across what felt like a dozen different states until we got to a hot, muggy town with flat cornfields and prairie all around. There were a few stories from that trip—the time Ma got mad at a diner for serving our food cold and got us a free meal, the time I was playing with Marquize's tail while he was driving and he almost drove off the road, and the southwestern cuisine restaurant staffed entirely by armadillos that served some chicken dish we all loved and have never seen anywhere else since. But mostly the trip was uneventful, except for Marquize becoming a much more confident driver by the end of it. I was okay, but he was a natural, better than Ma (in my opinion), even on city streets.

The town where the first of the three tournaments was being hosted had grown up around a large college campus, so there were a lot of people close to our age around. Still older, but at least Marquize and I felt more at home, as if we were back at Palm Gables.

In the first of the three tournaments, I entered the qualifying again and for the first time, I faced someone I'd faced before: Yang, the deer who'd beaten me back in Euker. This time we met in the semifinal of the qualifying round, and he used the same tactics he'd used on me the last time. I adjusted better this time, had a good serve going, and beat him in three sets.

My celebration didn't last long, as I lost in the third set of the qualifying final on a fluky bounce that landed clearly out—from my perspective. The officials didn't call it out, though. I raised a paw to the Chair Umpire, but they agreed with the call. I started to argue it, getting heated, but then remembered what our coaches had taught us about comportment and being gracious at all times. Bad calls would go both ways; that was part of the game.

So I lost that game, and then the set and the match, partly because I couldn't stop thinking about that bad call. All that stuff about it being part of the game didn't make it any easier when it happened to me. I walked up to shake the young tiger's paw at the net, forcing myself to smile past my clenched teeth. "I got lucky," he said with a smile.

I squeezed his paw back. "You played great," I said, because it was what I was supposed to say, and also because he had. "Good luck."

Marquize lost his first match here, again, but for the first time we played doubles. I thought we did well, winning one match but losing the next. Marquize didn't seem happy at having won his first professional match, even though Ma took us out for pie and ice cream that night to celebrate. We talked about the match and agreed that we had to work on our communication, but in general we'd done pretty well for as little as we'd played doubles. "If we win many matches," Marquize said, "it won't be because we're good, but because there aren't as many people competing in doubles."

"It'll also be because we're good," I pointed out. "We can't just stroll onto a tennis court and win doubles matches."

"I can't." He looked sideways at me. "You probably could grab your ma and win a match or two."

"Mar, stop that. You're a good player. Going pro is an adjustment, that's all."

"Didn't take you long."

We happened to be sitting outside the facility, so I pointed back at it. "Did you see how many people in our draw are over twenty? Over twenty-five? You have ten years or more to figure this out. Don't put it all on yourself in the first month."

"I know," he said, but I felt like he'd been about to say something else.

When I got time alone with Ma, cleaning up after dinner in the hotel room while Marquize took a walk, I asked her about it. "Is it hard for Marquize to adjust, with me doing well?"

"Don't you hold yourself back on his account." Ma whipped her head around to stare at me. "If I think for one second that that's happening, I'll get rid of him."

"Don't get rid of him," I said quickly, alarmed. "He's my, my friend."

"I know," she said, "but you will have many friends."

"Will I? We've been doing this for a couple months and I only really made one friend."

She switched tacks smoothly. "Friends aren't what's important. You have only one career, only one life. I won't see you waste it."

"I won't," I insisted. "I'm thinking about Ori, about making money for her. I'm not going to give up. In fact, I—"

Her eyes narrowed. "You what?"

I weighed whether to tell her. It might be good for her to know how I felt about tennis and Marquize, so I went ahead. "We had a fight because I wanted to keep practicing rather than relax with him." I thought that "relax" was the appropriate word to use there.

Ma seemed to understand what it meant. "Good," she said. "Keep that attitude."

* * *

The second tournament in the Midwest, about fifty miles away, started on a blazing hot day, and I think that played a part in what happened. The first match went quickly, the first time I won a match in straight sets. I thought that was a good omen, and in fact I won the next day as well. This time in the qualifying semis, I felt more confident and my opponent seemed tired in the third consecutive day of stifling heat, and I won again in three sets.

Marquize had played well and finally won a qualifying match, then won another when his opponent retired. But in the semis, he lost in straight sets. Meanwhile, though we played well, we lost our first doubles match. I wasn't entirely unhappy about that as it gave me the room to focus on singles.

And in the finals, I outlasted a panting coyote in three sets to win my first qualifying spot in a main draw.

At dinner that night, Ma bought me a glass of wine. "I'm sure this isn't your first alcohol," she said, "but your first entry into a main draw deserves celebration."

I worried about Marquize's attitude, but he seemed cheerful as well; maybe that's because he was also getting a glass of wine. Nobody at the restaurant asked for our IDs, which I filed away for future reference.

The wine was sharp, fruity, and full of complicated scents that kept popping up in my nose. "Is it supposed to smell like flowers?" I asked Ma, and then a moment later, "No, wait, it's…green peppers?"

"All of that," she said with a smile.

"I just get alcohol," Marquize said, sticking his nose into the glass and then wrinkling it. "And…wine flavor."

I tapped my nose. "It's not just good for sniffing who's around the corner."

We all laughed, and the warm glow of the wine relaxed me, and I felt like everything was going to work out. I thought I might even win the tournament.

That proved to be over-optimistic, though I did win my first match in the main draw. My opponent, a rabbit whose smooth and quick serve I tried to learn from even during the game, won the first set while I was trying to figure out how to get through his excellent court coverage. In the second set I used some drop shots to get him out of position and then took advantage, and that rattled him a little. He recovered in the third, but by then I was playing better and with more confidence and I broke his serve to win 6-4.

"Good match," he said at the net. "Imma keep my eye on you."

At the time, I was still figuring out how to respond to stuff like that, and so I said, "Thanks, I'll keep an eye on you too." As I was walking back to the bench, I remembered that the rabbit was 23 and had likely been trying to break into the Challenger circuit for a number of years already. How must he feel to have been beaten by a sixteen-year-old newcomer?

Well, I resolved as I put my equipment away, he and everyone else had better get used to it.

And with that confident swagger in my head, of course I went out and lost the next match.

It was another rabbit, a younger one, and I think in my head I was convinced I could play him the same way I'd played the previous rabbit. His style was different, though; he surprised me several times with drop shots and passing shots, mixing up his game well. I fell behind in the first set, vowed to do better in the second and actually beat him in a tiebreaker, but then he broke my serve in my first game of the third set and I never recovered.

"Good match," I said at the net. "Your drops are terrific."

"Thanks," he said, and squeezed my paw. "Keep at it, kiddo."

Ma and Marquize met me on my way back to the locker room and told me how well I'd played and that I was a couple points from getting to the quarterfinals. That was exciting, but not as exciting as, you know, making it to the quarterfinals.

Still, it was enough to collect a check from the tournament—
and get a single ranking point. I was told I could pick up my check
when the tournament was over, but I didn't get anything official for
my first ranking point. "You'll see it when the lists come out next
week," the squirrel at the table promised me.

I told Marquize and Ma about that at dinner. Ma gave me a long
smile and ruffled my ears. "First of many," she said.

Marquize's smile was shorter, and not only because of his muzzle.
"That's great," he said. "Hope we get some doubles ranking points
soon, too."

There wasn't much question what was bothering him, not when
he had to sit around and watch me play matches for three days.
Seeing me succeed in singles while he kept losing and we didn't fare
much better in doubles left him sure that he was the weak point, no
matter how much I told him that doubles was different from singles.

I wanted to buy dinner with my check, which was for $140,
but it was made out to Ma because I was still a minor. At least I got
to hold it and imagine a succession of checks with larger and larger
numbers, eventually accumulating enough to bring Ori over to the
States.

Marquize didn't talk much over dinner and Ma made it worse
by planning for the next tournament. When Marquize went to the
restroom, I said low to Ma, "Maybe we could wait until tomorrow to
plan the tournament? Marquize isn't in the mood."

"So?" She brushed it off. "If he can't be interested for you, he
should win some matches."

I sighed. "We could at least be considerate—"

"Ro. I'm not going to put your career on hold so your friend can
feel better." She put a sharp emphasis on 'friend,' "He's going to have
to learn to deal with this, or he should go home."

Truthfully, that's about what I was worried Marquize would do.

* * *

Before I worried about him, I had to call Ori back. She'd called during the match and again during the dinner. That she'd called a second

time was unusual; that made my fur prickle and my heart speed up. She'd heard about Raji, I guessed, and that's why I didn't pick up the phone during dinner. But my vision of a crying Ori devastated by the loss of her lion ate at me, so I excused myself after dinner, saying I'd meet Ma and Mar back at the motel. When they'd gone, I found a quiet bench in a small park and called.

She answered the phone on the first ring, and my vision of her sitting by the phone crying was so strong that I didn't notice that her voice was clear when she answered. "Are you okay?" I asked quickly.

"I'm fine. I wanted to tell you that I met this town chief today. And his wife."

"Town chief?" It had been a while since I'd talked to Ori and I'd been immersed in tennis. "Wait, the one who wants to marry you? He already has a wife?"

"He has two. I would be wife number three. Wife number two was the one who came with him."

"So what's he like? What's she like?" I leaned back against the bench.

She exhaled. "His wife is shorter than me, pretty markings over her eyes that I think she draws in. She's quiet and smells of casso and banana, but she's thin. She told me she likes to help cook in the town. The chief doesn't like that but he doesn't stop her."

"He doesn't like her cooking, or that she cooks?"

"That she cooks. He made a remark like, 'You don't have to tell them you cook, they can smell it,' and then laughed. He has a big laugh. He's bigger than Jean Chretien even. You remember him?"

The jackal who ran our neighborhood electronics store, a big fellow who'd still been taller than me at the time I left, with twice as many kilos on his broad frame. He'd smelled of solder and dust, and I'd always marveled that with his broad fingers he could fix such tiny gadgets. "Of course."

"Well, Bompaka—that's his name—is bigger than him. Fatter, anyway. He wears big robes and smells mostly like wormwood and those cigarettes that Pierre used to smoke."

"Menthol?"

"Yes. I suspect someone told him it smells good."

"Yuck." I fancied I could smell the strange combination.

"Oh, it's not *bad*. Just strange. Wife number two didn't seem to mind it."

"Does she have a name?"

"Probably? She talked very little."

"Charming family to join. How old is she?"

"My age."

A pair of lions walked past me, holding paws. I thought of Raji and sighed. "I'll make sure you don't have to stay there long."

"Thanks." She echoed my sigh. "How are you doing?"

"I won some matches." It seemed insignificant, so I didn't dwell on it. "I'm getting used to the competition. Don't worry, I'll be coming to get you before you know it."

"I'll be here, I promise. I'm not going anywhere."

"Except that village. What's it called?" I asked.

"Kitemini Troixième," she said. "A thousand people, perhaps not even that. More cows than people, Bompaka says. It's mostly jackals but there are some bat-eared foxes too."

"'Bompaka.' What's his last name?"

"That's all. No last name."

"Huh. How does he get his mail?"

She laughed, and I felt good for being able to make her laugh. She asked about Ma and about Marquize, and I told her they were doing fine. "It's a bit lonely," I said. "In Palm Gables I knew the students, but it's been months and I only know a few people."

"You're not taking classes together," Ori said. "How did you make friends at the tennis center here? You talked to people."

"It's harder. Everyone's got their own life to worry about. Not many people stand around after games and talk. If I knew a few people…" But Nashan hadn't introduced me to anyone else, not yet.

"Ro, give it time." I heard Kamina's sharp bark in the background. "I have to go," Ori said.

I'd wanted to go on and tell her about Ma, about my dilemma with finding a coach, but that would have to wait. "Travel safe. Be safe," I told her.

"I will. You get better. Win some tournaments. Make friends."

"I will."

And then she hung up and was gone.

* * *

I got time alone with Ma because Marquize, still quiet and with-drawn, curled up in bed to read social media on his phone. I asked if we could go outside, and she followed me out. She thought she knew what I wanted to talk about, because she put a paw on my shoulder. "Give him time," she said quietly. "He will understand that he also has to support you."

"I know." The change in subject stopped me momentarily. "No, that's not—did you know about Ori?" I knew that Ma talked to Kamina at different times.

"About her suitor? Yes. Kamina thinks highly of him. His town sits in a protected valley and he already has two wives, so the burden on Ori will not be as great. He hopes to purchase her to have cubs, and to help his other wives."

"Cubs? She can't have cubs." But of course jackals my age back home had cubs; if I thought about them very long, which I tried not to, I felt almost as though I'd stayed fourteen while they had grown into adulthood.

"She can, but I hope she will not."

"How are you going to stop her? Make Bompaka wear condoms?"

"Rochi!" she snapped.

I waved my paws. "If Ori has cubs—"

"If Ori has cubs," she cut me off, "she will bring them along as well when she comes over here. Everything has a price."

"Ma," I said desperately, "I barely made enough to pay for our motel this trip."

"Yes," she said. "You'll have to do better. Early practice tomorrow."

I practiced hard every day, and even the little times I got alone with Marquize were more tense those next few days. We'd gotten into the habit of stealing little kisses here and there, but with him pout-ing and me worried about Ori, even those little moments became less intimate. It wasn't that I was thinking about Nashan, because I wasn't, not that much. I felt guilty about those fantasies for a couple reasons. First, obviously, I should be thinking about Marquize's body, right? But also I was feeling bad because Nashan hadn't shown any indication that he was interested in me like that. What right did I have to picture him that way? And yet I couldn't quite help it.

On top of that I was worried about Ori. Technically she was still living with Kamina, but now her suitor had a name and a face; she'd met him and plans were in motion. When all of this was only possibility, it had felt like I had years to rescue her. Now I felt like I was standing in a train station watching her reach for me out of a window as her train gathered momentum and pulled away.

Entering the next tournament, my practices had been as good as ever as far as Ma was concerned, but I could feel myself slipping mentally. It was fine to practice serving over and over again, a routine mechanical physical motion; it was fine to practice against Marquize, whom I knew very well and who wasn't putting a lot of mental effort into his practice (and frankly, I felt bad about showing him up in practice now, so I wasn't practicing hard against him either). None of that was going to help me against a new opponent.

I told myself that I'd earned a ranking point. If I did that a few more times I would start getting placed directly into the main draw. The qualifiers were draining to get through, but I could do it in a few more tournaments. I kept repeating that to myself, trying to talk myself through the malaise I was in.

The upward trajectory I was forcing myself to visualize for my career got derailed in two days, as I won my first qualifying match and then lost the second. Marquize also won his first and lost his second, and I thought it might make him feel better to have me fail out at the same point he did. It didn't, though; if anything, he was more depressed. We hadn't even gotten into the doubles draw at that tournament, so we didn't have anything else to fall back on.

Neither of us talked much the next day, and Ma noticed that something was wrong. Going into the next series of tournaments she tried some new activities that she'd looked up on the Internet. After a practice, she found a trail and we went for a hike "to get outside of ourselves," she said, but I spent most of the hike flicking my ears to keep bugs away, and Marquize stepped on a sharp stick and hurt his foot—not badly, but enough that he exaggerated a limp all the way back to the car. So Ma tried jogging for conditioning, and it was while we were jogging along city streets that we passed a bunch of kids playing basketball, and I had another idea.

Those kids didn't want to play basketball with us, but Ma was willing to spend five dollars on a cheap basketball that Marquize and I could play around with, and after a bit more searching around, we found an empty court. There were a lot of basketball courts in this town, and only about half of them seemed to be in use at any time. We played one on one for a bit under Ma's supervision (she yelled at us from time to time not to get too physical, either because she didn't want us to get hurt or because she didn't want us to get distracted), and then we found quickly that any activity on a basketball court attracts a crowd. Before an hour was up, five other kids had shown up and asked if they could play with us: a couple coyotes, a deer, and two scruffy rats.

Marquize and I found it a lot harder to lose our focus when playing basketball. The game moves so quickly and you have to be attentive every second in case someone passes to you, or to find the spot where someone might pass to you. You wouldn't normally say that tennis is a slow-paced game, and in matches it's the same way: you have to be focused every moment on what's happening, what just happened, what's going to happen next. But it's hard to get that focus in practice.

We finished the game drained but happy, a little more engaged than we'd been in days. I hoped this would translate into more success when we went into the third tournament of the region, where we had gotten into the doubles draw. We both had our singles qualifying matches well before the doubles match, so we hoped we'd be able to focus better on singles and have good results to carry into our doubles.

And for the first time, Marquize won two matches. He finished short of the qualifying finals in his draw, but he still felt good about his performance—at least, he was more talkative after the match than he'd been in a couple weeks. I got to the qualifying finals in my draw but lost there, which was disappointing, but I took some lessons away from it that would serve me well next time, I hoped.

It was as I was changing after that match that I saw Nashan again. This time I was the one who'd just come back from the shower and was toweling my wet fur down when he came up in street clothes and sat beside me. He didn't seem to care that I was naked, but I sort of cared, so I hurried to get my shorts on. "Nice matches out there," the red fox said.

"Thanks. I saw you in the stands."

"You shouldn't be worrying about who's in the stands." He grinned. "I wanted to see how you were progressing since Golden. I know it's only been a few weeks."

"I got into the main draw in West Lefevre. Got my first ranking point."

"Very nice. Sorry I missed you there." He gestured to the locker room exit. "What happened here?"

"Ah…" I shrugged. "Goscoine is really good with his return."

"Not that good. It looked like you got caught off guard a few times."

I pulled on my shirt, trying not to feel ashamed. He was acting like I'd let him down. "I have a lot on my mind."

He nodded, his long tail swishing back and forth behind him. "Look, I'm gonna say again what I said before. I don't know how far you're going to get with your mother coaching you. She's the one who should be able to prepare you for Goscoine's return, for example, and it doesn't sound like she's doing that."

"I don't know how to change coaches, though," I said. "I can't afford to hire another one on my own."

"You talked to any teams?"

I shook my head. "I'm on a doubles team with Marquize, but…"

Nashan laughed, and he had a nice laugh. "A team. A group of young players. They travel together to save money on hotels and stuff, and often they share a coach. He usually works for a share of their winnings and sometimes helps them get sponsorships too. Sometimes they have a manager who does that, if they're starting to be successful."

"Oh." I thought about that. "That sounds like something that would be good for me and Marquize. If we could…I mean, if Ma would let…" I trailed off.

He nodded. "I can't help you figure out how to tell your Ma, but I do know one or two teams that might be interested in picking up new players."

"The school never told me about them. Although…well, I did sort of drop out before I was finished my classes."

"Yeah." He stood, straightening his shirt. "You're going to the next tournaments in a month, right? Lake Russo, Piedmont, Argent?"

"Yes. Already registered. We're hoping that we'll win a couple doubles matches here and get into the draw in all three."

"Mm. Good luck. I'll keep an eye on you."

He turned to leave, and I couldn't help myself. "Nashan."

"What's up?" He stopped, turned back.

"Why are you helping me?"

The fox's eyebrows rose and his ears perked. "I like to help the new players on the court. I told you that. A lot of the guys on the tour are pretty nice once you've shown you're in the club. When you get ranking points, people will start giving you advice and tips, and also people will start being hostile because now you're a threat."

"Okay." I wasn't sure he'd answered my question. "But if I join a team, they'll help me out, right?"

He grinned. "If you join a team, you're eventually going to have to leave the team and probably that coach, because you'll be able to afford a better one. So be prepared for that. Nothing's permanent in this life except for what you got right here." He tapped the center of his chest.

"What about family?"

"Sure, family. Your mother won't like being replaced as your coach and she might disappear from your life for a while, but she'll probably come back when you're good." He held up a paw to my protest. "Maybe yours is different. Parents I see are usually either cheerleaders from the sideline or they try to be coaches and then get offended and vanish when it doesn't work out. You'll have girl-friends, maybe get married, but that's all separate from the life too." He tapped his chest again. "You've got to learn to rely on yourself.

That's what's going to win games for you."

"On the court, sure. But what about off?"

"Off the court you've got to make the right choices to put you in the absolute best shape to step on that court. Right now that might be joining a team of your peers. In a few years you'll have to figure out which coach is right for you. Some players switch coaches every couple years. Some players stay with the same coach their whole careers. Only you," this time he tapped my chest, "know what's right for you."

"Thanks," I said. "Uh, hey, are you busy for dinner? Want to get something to eat?"

He relaxed with a broad smile. "Aw, thanks," he said, "but my wife's expecting me back. And she's paying a lot of the bills, so I should get back on time."

"Oh, okay. Maybe next time."

"Gonna be honest, I don't usually bring players home." He held his paws apart. "I try to keep that life separate from this one. But I'll catch up with you at Lake Russo, okay? I'll try to find a team to meet up with there."

"Sounds good. Thanks." And I watched his tail swish back and forth as he walked out of the locker room.

The Lake Russo tournament was a month away, late in August. Talking to the other players, I found that some were taking the time to practice and some were heading to Futures tournaments overseas. A few of the better ones had registered for the Challenger series but had to go through the qualifying process, the same as I was doing now. It tired me to think that after earning my place in the Futures series, I would have to go back to being a qualifier at the next level up, and probably the one after that as well.

But, I reminded myself, everyone had to do it, me and Bielovic and Braden Longacre equally. If they could do it, I could do it.

I wanted Marquize to be there with me, and I thought that after the last set of tournaments we'd turned a corner. For a week or two he practiced in better spirits. We couldn't practice doubles, but we had some good sessions back and forth, and it felt for a little while like we were back at Palm Gables, especially without the pressure of a tournament coming up.

A week and a half after the last tournament, though, he took me aside for another little bit of private time. We had what I thought was a good time together, and I didn't bring up tennis at all, but later in the evening he was moody. I felt like I'd done something wrong, but I didn't know what, and when I asked him, he said I shouldn't worry about it.

So of course I did, and our practices went downhill. I thought it might be the tennis again, so I was careful not to hit any shots that might show him up or remind him how much better I'd been doing than he was. The practices were also frustrating because I was doing the same things over and over, and Ma wasn't coming up with anything new for me to focus on. She told me I should get better at doing the fundamental things, and every so often she'd come up with a practice routine that I knew she'd gotten off the Internet because most of them we'd done my first year at Palm Gables.

There were a few good days in those weeks, but mostly I remember it being long and dreary. Marquize wasn't good company and I started to despair that I was going to be stuck in Futures for the rest of my life like Nashan, that in a decade I'd be giving out advice to a sixteen-year-old fox about what he was going to have to do to survive in the pros. I knew that was a long way away, but the prospect still frightened me.

Lake Rosso was a welcome relief. The tennis center was near enough the lake the town was named for that fresh lake scent filled the air, even inside. After months away from the water and humidity of Palm Gables, the smell invigorated me. I played well enough to win my first two qualifiers, getting back into the rhythm of actual matches. Marquize and I won our first doubles match, too, and he won his first two matches, so I was excited that this tournament might be the beginning of a better era for us. Then he lost his next qualifier, and I won, and in the doubles match he was lackadaisical and we lost in three sets.

He didn't talk much after that and I tried not to worry about him. I consulted Ma but she repeated the same old thing about letting him figure his own problems out. And Ma was having her own problems at this tournament.

During my second match, I wasn't looking at her, but the umpire had to stop the match. Apparently the opposing coach thought he'd caught Ma making hand signals at me. They called me over and the umpire asked me to answer truthfully if she was signaling me.

"Of course not," I said. "That's against the rules."

"I wouldn't cheat," Ma said.

The opposing coach, a ferret who thankfully did not remind me of Frio because he was taller, his fur was different shades, and his voice was deeper, didn't buy it. "You were signaling him. Course you're not going to admit it and neither will he. But I know what I saw."

"You're stopping the match because your player is losing," Ma snapped.

The ferret pointed at her. "I'm gonna keep my eye on you."

"Good," Ma said. "Then you won't have to watch your player lose."

I thought that was pretty snappy and I was proud of Ma. Afterwards in the locker room, though, I was making an effort to talk to a couple players and they were more reticent than usual. Finally, a cottontail rabbit told me that some of the players were saying that my coach was unprofessional. "It's not a big deal," he explained. "I mean, it's not you personally. They hate parent-coaches, especially when they're obnoxious."

"My Ma's not obnoxious." Though I guess she'd been a little rude, but the other coach had started it.

"Like I said, it's not personal. She's your mother, so that's why they don't like her." The rabbit paused. "But also she was yelling at Mazer during your match."

"The ferret?"

He nodded. "He's been around forever. Don't get on his bad side."

"I didn't try to." I saw another young player, a lemming, hovering nearby, and I made eye contact with him and nodded. He returned my nod. "Hey, are you part of a team?"

"Oh, uh, yeah." He squinted and glanced back to the lemming.

"We don't have rich families."

"Neither do I."

That stopped him. "Really?"

"Yeah." I leaned back against the locker. "Ma has to tutor students online to make money, and Marquize and I aren't making any money yet."

"So you are on a team?" When I looked confused, he said, "Marquize? He's another player?"

"Oh. I guess technically, but…" I shook my head. "It's just us and Ma. But if you don't mind me asking…how does it work? When you're on a team, I mean."

"Uh." The rabbit looked back at the lemming. "I mean, we travel together, we practice together, our team manager gets us endorsements. We give him a percentage of our winnings and he takes care of the travel arrangements."

"How did you get on the team?"

This time the lemming came forward. "We're out of the Schwender Academy. Our school hooked us up with a manager who was looking for a couple more players."

I guessed at the time that because I hadn't graduated from Palm Gables, I hadn't gotten that option. Later I would find out that that was part of it, but also that students at Palm Gables didn't join teams as often because they were usually better funded than students elsewhere—rich families.

I thanked them and took off, wondering where Nashan was and whether he'd come through with his offer of finding us a team. He'd given me his number, but I wasn't sure I wanted to text him and come off as needy, so I checked for his name in the scheduled games.

It turned out he was playing the same time as the match that turned out to be my last, and after we'd both lost, we met in the locker room. "Rocky," he said, greeting me with an outstretched paw before either of us had changed.

"Hi." I smiled. "Sorry about your match."

"Sorry about yours. What happened to you? You should've beaten him."

I straightened. "I lost focus, I guess. I've got a lot going on."

"Again? You need to learn to shut that out. You'll never have a career if you can only play to your full potential during good times." He pointed out toward where the courts were. "Out there, nothing else matters but this," he held up his racket, "and the ball."

"And the guy on the other side of the net."

"Yes, that." He smiled at me. "I got the info for that team if you want to contact them. Friend of mine manages it and I double-checked with him to make sure he's looking for two more players."

"Thanks. Definitely."

He gave me the info and then said, "Now…there might be a problem having your mother as the coach, but if you're really really set on it, you can probably work it out."

His eyes and tone told me what he thought of that option. I stared down at the number. "I'm not sure," I said. "She had some problems a couple days ago."

He put a paw on my shoulder. "It hasn't only been two days ago."

I got that creeping feeling that things had been going on behind my back, kind of like when Coach Murphy had called me into his office after my first night with Marquize. "What?"

"She's been arguing with coaches pretty much since the first tournaments you were in out in Golden. I thought you knew."

I shook my head. "What's she been saying?"

The red fox spread his paws. "I don't hear specifics. I know that when I mention you to people, they like your play but not your mother. She's pushy—on your behalf, of course."

"People talk about me?" The uneasy feeling grew stronger.

"Of course people talk about you. You're new, you're winning matches, you got a ranking point…trust me, people are talking about you."

"I never hear it." It was a dumb thing to say, but I still couldn't believe people were interested in a young jackal from overseas.

"You're hearing it now." He looked amused. All foxes look amused most of the time, I guess, but Nashan did look particularly so.

"Thanks. So…what should I do?"

"I told you what you should do. If you really want what's best for your career, you'll have to leave people behind sometimes."

Now I felt like not only were people plotting behind my back, they were planning my future for me. "I can't leave Ma."

"I said that wrong." Nashan put a paw on my shoulder. "You don't have to leave her behind. But she's not the best person to coach you. If she really cares about your future, she'll see that."

"She says…she says she can do anything the professional coaches can."

"She's wrong." He said it flatly. "Unless your mother's studied the game for twenty, thirty, forty years, unless she has experience teaching it to cubs—"

I jumped in. "She is a teacher. Er, an English teacher."

Nashan shook his head. I sighed. "I know," I said. "I know. All right. I'll call the manager."

The manager's name was Lochen, and he was a red fox like Nashan, but he had a bit of an accent, rolling his r's, so when he said my name I had to fight to keep from giggling. "Rocky," he said. "Nashan's told me about you. You're interested in joining a team?"

We were sitting in a little coffee shop near the tennis center. I'd told Ma that my friend Nashan had invited me out to talk tennis, which was not entirely a lie. I held a cup of coffee and felt very grown up. "What would that involve?"

He settled into a pitch. "I've got four other players, aged seventeen to nineteen, and we travel as a group. I have a deal with Marriott hotel chains so we get good rates on rooms there. You don't pay for the rooms; I'm explaining why we always stay in those properties. Besides me, there's a coach who takes charge of all the players. Nashan said you might be bringing your own coach?"

I took a breath. "No, I don't think so."

"Okay. That makes it easier. We travel together, we eat together, we practice together. You get time off in the evening and at least one day a week. You go to church?"

"No."

"All right, well, I'm not going to force you, but all the rest of us go." He paused. I didn't say anything. "You can find something else to do if you really don't want to go."

I didn't mention that Marquize was Muslim, because what if he refused us then? So I said, "Thanks, I'll think about it." And then, both to change the subject and because I was curious, I said, "What about sponsorships?"

"Ah, yeah. We get visits from companies who'll offer sponsorships if you get a few ranking points under your belt. Hang on, though, Nashan said you're from Africa somewhere?"

"Lunda, yes."

"Hm. That might be worth something too. If you come on board, I'll dig around. Lots of international players but not many from Africa. Are you good?"

I replied without thinking, "Yes, I am."

"Good. And you're a lefty too, so that's helpful. I'll come watch you the next couple tournaments and we'll see if we can't put something together for the fall."

He extended a paw across the table and I shook it. "Oh," I said as we got up, "could I meet some of the other players on the team? To see if I get along with them?"

"Of course. Though not all the guys on the team get along." He laughed. "You just have to be able to hold your own on the court."

Even though it sounded like everyone on the team was older than me, I was sure I could do that. "I'm looking forward to it," I said.

So over the next two tournaments, I played in front of Lochen and met his four-player team: Chris, a short, energetic squirrel; Les, a quiet rat; Paulie, a thin coyote; and Adam, a cheerful dingo with a thick Oceanic accent that made him hard to understand. I was taller than any of them, though Paulie was close. I got to see him and Les play, and decided I could probably beat either of them.

Paulie was also the most fun to talk to. The players mingled one evening at an informal gathering on the plaza outside the tennis center; we'd hung out around the edges of gatherings like this before, but nobody had talked to us then. Adam and Chris were the first to embrace me, proceeding to talk loudly about what a great team they were on, and Adam particularly got right up to my nose, uncomfortably so. Chris talked about tennis for five minutes and then said it was a blessing to be surrounded by such talented people and the Lord would provide for me if I wanted to join them.

It was later, when Paulie and Les had finished and the coyote came over to me that I got to talk to him. "Would be nice to have another canid around," he said. "Chris didn't scare you off with his God talk, did he?"

"No," I said, relieved. "Lochen mentioned that you all attend church."

"He's a Christian and he believes that 'religion will keep young people out of trouble.'" Paulie did a passable imitation of Lochen, then rolled his eyes. "It's not that bad, honestly. You get to kneel and if you learn the right times, you can doze off for a bit."

"I'll probably skip it," I said. "Ma and I pray at home."

"Hm. Not sure Lochen will go for that, but as long as you stay out of trouble, I guess it'll be fine." He winked at me. "That's why I go. Whatever trouble I get into, I just confess away my sins and," he steepled his paws together, "promise to do better. Something tells me you know what I mean. You've got the sniff of trouble around you. Not the obvious big kind of trouble like I get into, but…hm, a more subtle and devious trouble. I like it. You should come play with us."

"I don't know what you mean." But I was laughing as I said it and he winked at me.

"Anyway," he said, "it'd be nice to have someone who's a new challenge. I'ma warn you though, I beat these other guys all the time, so watch out."

"Maybe you'd better watch out," I said, and he laughed and shook my paw.

Marquize didn't get along with him quite as well, but he liked Adam. The two of them exchanged phone numbers before we'd even gotten any further with the negotiations over the team. "He's fun," Mar told me. "He likes to go out and have a good time. He knows that you can't live tennis twenty-four-seven. And he's doing well, too. Maybe that's what's holding me back, that I don't get to go out and have fun anymore."

"I'm not sure about that." I sighed. "So you want to join this team?"

"Hell, yes." He leaned in close with an eye to Ma, about thirty feet away. She had accepted the fact that we'd made some new young friends we wanted to talk with, and though she was keeping an eye on us, she was too far away to listen, even with her big jackal ears. "We'd get to live in a hotel room together," Marquize whispered.

"I'm pretty sure Ma will insist on coming along as a chaperone. Paulie told me there's another chaperone with the group."

"But she won't set our schedule. We'll have an easier time finding…time." His paw slid over to mine, between us where nobody could see.

"Yeah." His ears were perked and he was smiling so broadly that I didn't want to say that in the rush of potential friends and career movement, I hadn't even thought about that. "That'd be great."

His paw squeezed mine. "I know it's been rough," Marquize said. "I haven't been the best—" He looked around. Other people were in earshot. "The easiest to deal with. I keep wondering if this was a mistake for me. It clearly wasn't for you, but…I feel like I'm holding you back."

"You're not holding me back. It's so much better because I have someone else to do this with. I know you have more challenges but I'm sure you'll be able to start getting ranking points too. We're getting better at doubles for sure, and you're improving. You keep winning matches."

He nodded. "And this team might be the right environment to help me move forward."

Nashan came over then to ask how our talks had gone, so we quickly untangled our paws. I told him that we were seriously thinking about joining the team, but I'd have to tell Ma.

His lips pulled back into a long smile. "Good. I promise you, it's the right move." He looked around. "You guys done talking it over?" We nodded. "Then come on, you should meet some of the girls on the tour. That's what this mixer's all about."

We couldn't think of a reason not to, so we got up and walked over with him to a group of girls. I don't remember any of their names anymore, but we had a fun conversation.

When the mixer was breaking up, the girls left, and Marquize excused himself as well. He said it was to use the restroom, but really it was to leave me alone to have the beginning of the difficult conversation with Ma, who came over upon seeing that we were free. "Did you have fun with the other players?" she asked, and then, without waiting for an answer, "What would you like for dinner?"

I cleared my throat. "The guys we were talking to, Paulie and Adam and their friends, they're part of a team. They travel together, they have a manager, and they share costs and donate portions of their winnings to the manager to pay for it."

"That's good." She narrowed her eyes.

She knew, of course she knew. I blurted it out. "They have space for a couple guys on their team and Marquize and I want to join."

For a moment she didn't respond. Then she lifted a finger and tapped her whiskers. "I think that's a good idea. I had been looking for a way to share our costs, and this will also allow you to practice with other players."

At least she was okay with the easy part. Next came the hard part. "The thing is." I swallowed. "That team…they have a coach."

It was worse when she didn't say anything. "And, uh," I said, "they like for all their players to have the same coach."

"I'm sure they can make an exception if we ask." And when I didn't say anything, she folded her arms. "If you want to ask."

"I…I was thinking…" I hoped she would stop me, that she would say, "I see," and I wouldn't have to force the words through my throat one by one. But she stayed quiet, watching me, her ears up and her tail still. So I pulled the words out. "That it would be good for us to have a professional coach."

She nodded once but stayed quiet. Now I felt compelled to fill the silence. "He's part of the team. I mean, we don't have to pay him extra. And he's got lots of experience with younger players. Paulie says he's gotten way better since he joined the team. His style is sort of like mine. He's the coyote."

"Have you met this coach?"

I shook my head. Ma gave a decisive nod. "We will meet him, and I will decide whether he's right for you."

"No."

She inclined her head up at me. I stood straight and tried to feel as tall as I was. "I liked some of those other coaches we interviewed, the ones you said weren't right. And this is my career, and I think I need another coach. I need someone who's been around the game, who's studied the game, someone who knows how to get me past the obstacles I'm facing. It's not just about whether to work hard or whatever that wolf said."

"I know. That's what I want for you too."

"But." I pointed at my chest with a finger. "It should be my decision."

"You're not an adult yet."

"I know I can't make you let me decide," I said. "But Ma, my younger sister is getting married. My friends back home are parents. Don't you think I'm grown-up enough to decide?"

She sighed. "I worry that you'll make a mistake. There is so little chance to recover. What if you waste a year with this coach?"

"What if I waste a year not having a coach? What about Ori if I'm still making two-hundred dollar checks in a year?" She folded her ears back at that and I felt terrible, but I kept going. "I want to try this, Ma. If I make a mistake…then I make the mistake. I'll deal with it."

We stood looking at each other for two breaths, three breaths, four. And then she gave a quick nod. "Then you will make your mistakes."

"I still want you to be around," I said.

"Of course I will be around, Ro. Now if you'll excuse me, I should also use the restroom before we go." And with that, she walked off, leaving me alone on the large plaza outside the tennis center, with the breeze from the lake ruffling the fur on my head and tail.

Part Five: New Set
(2010-2011)

Interlude (2015)

With Longacre already up 1-0, he's looking at a break point and an opportunity to seize control of this fourth set and the match."

"A terrific rally on that last point. N'Guwe could not have played better defense, but Longacre painted the corner beautifully and the jackal just couldn't get to that last shot."

"But these two competitors are very evenly matched."

"We wouldn't have said that going in."

"No, but N'Guwe is playing the match of his life, and Longacre isn't quite at the level we've seen him at."

"Daren, I think it might be that they know each other very well. Longacre is playing quite well actually, only N'Guwe's defense against him has just been terrific."

"Longacre hasn't made many errors, but he's got fewer winners than his average this tournament."

"True."

"And Alastair, N'Guwe is a great returner but he's been unreal on Longacre's serve, holding down his points off first serve to 65%, the lowest in this tournament. In fact, that's the second lowest in any match Longacre's played this year."

"And still Longacre's up two sets to one, and part of the reason for that is that he's doing just as well against N'Guwe's serve and winning about half the points on second serve. Here we go, second serve for N'Guwe. He might be tightening up a little."

"That's long from N'Guwe! Longacre goes up a break in the fourth set and now all he has to do is hold his serve and the Grand Slam is his."

* * *

You can't be mad at yourself when you miss a forehand like that. It happens. You have to go for those shots and accept that maybe a third of the time you'll be too excited, or the wind will catch it, or your racket will be turned half an inch the wrong way. I had a great shot at the baseline for deuce—Braden ran for it but his racket was at least a foot away—and I pulled it long.

You can't be mad at yourself, but I am. Now I'm down a break and Braden isn't looking at me; he's rolling the balls in his paw and getting ready to serve. I've given away a precious game and now he only has to serve four more times to beat me.

He nets his first serve and I get ready for the second. It lands right where I thought it would, and in my peripheral vision I notice Braden jumping to defend the ad-side alley, so I step around the ball and scorch a forehand cross-court right in front of him.

The crowd cheers. They seem to be evenly split between him and me; the appeal of seeing a Grand Slam champion overwhelms Braden's unlikability, but also everyone loves an underdog.

Braden doesn't look at me, still. He crosses to the other court and prepares to serve. When he's focused like this, he doesn't want to look at anyone. His opponent becomes nothing more than an obstacle to be overcome. So I want to force him to acknowledge me, to understand that he isn't going to roll through this fourth set. If he wants the Grand Slam, he's going to have to take it.

* * *

"N'Guwe is not letting up at all. Third deuce of the game and he wants that break back."

"I don't think I've seen this kind of intensity from him before. He's not shrinking from the moment at all. So nice to see a young player poised for the stage when he finally gets there. Fourth set, down a break, and he is taking it to Longacre."

"Longacre's saved two break points this game and he does not want to face a third. There's the ace, right when he needed it."

"One more point to hold."

"And there it is. N'Guwe nets the forehand and Longacre is up three-love."

"N'Guwe starts this fourth game strong with a service winner. And there's another one. Longacre can't handle the lefty serve, and N'Guwe is up 30-0."

"This young jackal has really shown that he belongs here, Alastair. I expect we'll see him in many more major finals before his career is done."

* * *

On the changeover, I sit, take a drink, and stare ahead of me, trying not to look at the jackals up in my box next to my coach, trying not to look at the other foxes there, trying to keep my focus on the game. If I look up their way, I'll realize the weight of expectations and I'll risk distracting myself from what's important here: the racket in my paw, the ball in the air, and the lines on the court. Tennis is a simple game, my first professional coach taught me, only so many people let it get complicated because of the situation or the opponent or their own lives. Tennis doesn't care about any of that. Tennis is the racket, the ball, the lines.

It's early in the set, I tell myself when we get up. I had a couple break points; I'll have a couple more before the end of the set. Meanwhile, I have to keep him from getting any more, and I do that with a couple good serves to start. Then he gets into one of my serves and we start a baseline rally. I move him around until I can pin him to the ad-side corner, and then I send a forehand hard to deuce side and run to the net, but Braden knew I was going to do that and he flicks a lob over my head. I race back to the baseline, no time to plan, just reach out and smack it back and then skid to a stop, turn and see where it's coming back from, and it's coming back right at me, but this time I can plan for it so I poke a backhand past Braden, who's come to the net. Only it doesn't get past him; he slices a drop shot and I can see it coming down to the court in slow motion as my feet leap one step…two steps…and I slide my racket under the ball with a backhand tap and the ball just clears the top of the net, drops onto the line, and spins away from Braden's lunging racket. My point.

The crowd roars. This is the kind of tennis they paid to see.

Braden claps his paw to his racket, looking at me. Acknowledging me. I do the same back to him, then brace myself with my paws on my knees before trotting back to the service line.

After that, my ace to close out the game is almost anticlimactic. 3-1. Still only down a break, but time is running out.

Chapter Five (2010)

We joined the team in late September after another series of $15,000 tournaments in which Marquize's and my results did not drastically improve. I made one more main draw and got another ranking point, but it wasn't as exciting the second time around.

Ma still watched us closely, but she wasn't giving me as much encouragement. Our practices were quiet, tense affairs, and I was often left to concentrate on my own advancement. The only time I asked Ma for advice, she said, "I wouldn't want to interfere with what your new coach is going to teach you."

I got the hint pretty quickly and chose to keep things quiet. After all, in a month's time, I'd be in a new situation and then I wouldn't have to worry about any of this drama.

The last thing we had to work out was whether Ma would come with us as a chaperone. Lochen was not opposed to it in principle, but there were expenses to work out and logistics, and I would've thought it would be simple but apparently there were a bunch of other things to sign because Ma wasn't going to be competing and she wasn't officially a coach.

And Marquize was opposed to the whole idea. "Why are we going to more trouble to keep her around?" he asked irritably on what had been one of our nicer nights, a small interlude we'd stolen from practice time. We sat together in the bed but our words were pushing us apart. "Without her, we could have our time in hotel rooms. They're all churchy, they won't suspect anything. We'll be model players because we won't even be trying to sneak girls into our rooms!"

"She's my mother," I said for the hundredth time. "I can't abandon her. What would she do if she weren't involved in my career?"

"I don't know! Teach?"

"Don't yell at me." I kept my voice calm with some effort.

"I'm sorry. I…I'm having trouble understanding where you're coming from."

"Why? Because you don't love your parents?"

I regretted saying that as soon as the words had left my tongue, but Marquize didn't seem to mind. "Because you're sixteen. You should be finding out what your life will be like without your parents, not holding on to them."

"I'm allowed to love my mother, aren't I?"

"Ugh." He lay back on the bed. "Do you have to love her right up close? Can't you love her from afar? At least enough distance for to find out where this," he gestured between himself and me, "could go?"

"Where do you think it can go?" My voice rose despite myself. "It's going to the major tennis tournaments. You think we can go out in public together? You're talking about hiding from our teammates, so where is this going 'to go'?"

His face puckered and he looked away. "I'm not talking about publicity," he said. "I'm talking about…getting to know each other."

"All right." I checked the clock. "We have three minutes before we should start getting dressed. So tell me about yourself. Tell me about your family."

"Don't do this," he said.

"Why not? You know all about my family. You've lived with my Ma, you've heard me talk about Ori. So tell me about yours. I've only met your parents once. What was it like growing up Muslim?"

He folded his arms. "I prayed five times a day until I was twelve and then I stopped because my mom said I could. They believed in God, and I don't."

"At all?"

"Well…" He wavered. "I don't know. What's there to make me believe?"

"Nothing, but…" I thought about what Ma had told me, how we prayed together. "You just believe."

"Or you don't. Hey." He sat up and poked me in the chest. "You want parents and I don't. You want God and I don't. Deal with it."

"I'm trying to." I curled my tail. "What do you want, then?"

He looked steadily at me and then away. "I want to play tennis. I want to get better."

"Well, good. That's what I want." I reached out and held his wrist. "So what does it matter if Ma comes along with us? It's important to me."

"That's fine, Rocky," he said. "I'll tell you about my parents sometime and maybe you'll understand."

* * *

In the process of signing with the new team, Marquize and I met the new coach and had several workouts with him. Lochen liked us but had to get the coach's okay before anything was official, and watching us in tournaments wasn't good enough.

Marquize got in trouble right away. We'd been waiting at one of the practice courts when a field mouse came running up in athletic gear. "Finally," Marquize said. "So where's the coach?"

The mouse, a foot or so shorter than either of us, stopped and glared up. "I am the coach," he said. "Luka Šprem. I assume you are Marquize Alhazhari."

"Uh, yes." Marquize took a step back.

"And that would make you Rocky N'Guwe." I nodded. "All right, boys. Get on the court and show me what you've got."

His sharp, high-pitched words spurred us to action. We hurried onto the court and spent an hour following his instructions. "Serve wide. Now down the T—the middle. Again, but in the service box this time. Again. All right, N'Guwe, serve wide. Closer to the line. Again."

By the time he was done, I was panting and Marquize had slowed down. "You boys tired out?" Luka squeaked. "We can stop if you want."

"No," I said. "I'm good to keep going."

Marquize took a moment longer to say, "Yeah, I'm okay."

We passed—obviously—and even though our first encounter

with the coach had been rough, I liked him because from that first trial, he pushed me as hard as most of the coaches at Palm Gables had, and harder than some. When he challenged me to get more kick on my serve, I tried as hard as I could and felt a huge lift when I succeeded. I wanted challenges like that more often outside of games, ways to make myself better while keeping myself motivated.

When we signed with the team, I thought the workouts would stop, but Luka surprised me by scheduling another one. I asked if we'd be working out with the others on the team and he said no. "I do not divide my attention between more than two students. Paulie and Les practice together; Adam and Chris practice together. I will give you work to do when I cannot be with you personally. When I am with you, you will have my full attention."

I liked that. Marquize wasn't so sure. "So he's only with us a third of the time? At least your Ma was at every practice."

"You don't think Luka is going to make us better?"

"I don't know." We were sitting on one of the beds in our cheap motel while Ma read a book with her headphones in and pretended not to be listening to us. "He's expecting us to be at a level we can't make it to yet."

"At least he knows that level exists." I lowered my voice to a whisper, looking at Ma. "And he knows how to get us there. You heard how Paulie talked about him. Took his game to a whole new level. Paulie's getting into main draws in every tournament now. Soon he'll be skipping qualifying."

"I don't know." Marquize said. "What if I can't do what he wants and he cuts me from the team?"

"You can do it," I said. "I know you can."

But he still didn't believe it, and every time we went into session with Luka, Marquize refused to take any initiative or engage with the coach. So I wasn't too surprised when we got different practice plans our first week with the team. I was assigned Paulie as a partner and Marquize was assigned Les. "We've always practiced together," was as strongly as I dared protest to Luka.

"And see how far that has gotten you," he replied. "Paulie will be more of a challenge for your style and is close to your talent level.

Les…will challenge Marquize. I hope."

And he looked at Marquize, who was standing right there, but the cheetah looked down at the ground and didn't respond.

We had another argument that night and I ended up sleeping on the floor. There were two beds in the room, and usually Marquize and I switched off sleeping on the bed, but that night he curled up on the floor even though it was his turn to have the bed. Ma told me I should sleep on the bed but I grabbed a blanket and lay on the floor on the other side of the bed. I figured he'd feel bad in the morning or something.

It turned out I was the one who felt bad. I didn't get to sleep for an hour and a half, and when I woke up I had a pain in my shoulder. Marquize might or might not have felt guilty, but he wasn't talking much. So I didn't talk much either, and Ma wasn't talking because we were going off to our individual practices—though she was happy enough that we were practicing separately that I wondered if she'd managed to talk Luka into it somehow.

I didn't do well against Paulie, but he was energetic and he was good, and it was such a change playing against someone motivated and challenging that even though I was tired, I ended the practice in better spirits than I'd started it. And afterwards, when Paulie suggested going to a juice place for an energy drink, I said yes enthusiastically. Maybe I assumed Marquize and Les would join us, or maybe by this point I was tired of the cheetah and I didn't care.

Through October and November this pattern continued. Marquize and I had good days and bad days, and sometimes we would talk about our future, but it was always in far-off hypotheticals, never the near term. I still loved him, or so I thought at the time, and he loved me. Or so I thought at the time.

We continued to play doubles together because we were used to each other, and because the other teammates who played doubles (Les and Chris) were already paired up. Paulie told me he wanted to concentrate on singles because "doubles just adds to your workload. It feels like hedging your bets. I don't want to become a good doubles player. I want to become a great singles player."

I liked Paulie more and more, though I never felt the attraction for him that I had for Nashan, even when we were undressing together. I thought of him as an older brother and eventually told him about Ori and her situation back home.

It turned out he had three younger siblings, all girls, and even though he said they used to tease him constantly, he was looking forward to seeing them over the holidays. "I've been on the road for months. I get to call them every weekend when I talk to my folks, but I kinda miss just being around them." He laughed. "I'm sure by New Year's I'll be ready to come back on tour. Can't imagine being away from them for years, though. Must be hard."

"I get to talk to her every so often," I said, "though probably not when she goes off to that village."

"So look," Paulie said. "When you say 'village,' I'm imagining like straw huts and jackals in grass skirts. I know that's probably horribly wrong, so tell me what I'm looking at here."

I'd done that report on my country for class at Palm Gables, but nobody had asked me questions like this before. "Honestly," I said, "I spent my whole life in the city. We wore t-shirts—sometimes—and jeans, and we lived in an old brick building with a floor and indoor plumbing and everything. We didn't have our own bathroom, but we shared with four other jackal families on our floor, and there were cars—a lot of cars—in the street. I never went out to a village, but we sometimes saw jackals and lions and hyenas come into town wearing robes in bright colors. There were also some who came in wearing the clothes we get from relief organizations: loose cotton shirts and pants, and the women wear skirts and dresses. I think the houses in the villages can be anything: wood, brick, stone. They do have straw roofs a lot of the time but that's because they're more efficient. And cheaper."

"It doesn't sound so bad. Nice weather most of the time, simple life."

"I guess not if your family is there. They work, though; they keep cattle and plant crops and catch game. It's not all lying around in the sun."

"Oh, I didn't mean for me." Paulie looked out at the court. We'd taken a break from one of our practices and were drinking water from plastic bottles. "I feel bad for people who have to work to get to the next day and don't get anything else. You know? We work here and we get better and next tournament we do better. We get ranking points and we climb the ladder. But you're working to keep your cows alive or whatever, you keep them alive one day and then you go to sleep and start all over the next day. You never get so good at it that you get more cows."

"You do if you breed them," I said. "Did they not teach you where little cows come from in your lessons?"

He snorted and bumped my shoulder. "You know what I mean."

"Kind of. But I do think you get better at life if you try to learn from it, no matter what you do."

He gulped down some water and thought about that. "Maybe."

"But you have to try to learn."

"How can anyone not try to learn?" He gestured so expansively that he splashed water on my knee. "Sorry. But there's so much out there in the world. If I couldn't play tennis, I'd be studying history or writing music or something."

My ears perked. "You write music?"

He grinned and wiggled his paw. "Not really. But I bet I could learn how."

I almost said something about Marquize then, about shutting down and not learning anything from the world, but I resisted. "So," Paulie went on, "you're not going back to your country to see your sister over the holidays?"

"No. We'll get to talk to her. I hope."

"Will your aunt not let you talk?"

"Oh, she will. I just don't know if she'll be around. I don't know when she's going off to her village."

"Oh." He was quiet. "Sorry about that. I hope you get to talk to her. I'll send you pictures of Grace, Chaz, and Polleen if you want. They're coyotes, but it might make you feel better."

I smiled and stood. "Sure. I'd like to see them. Sorry, I don't think I can send a picture of Ori. I haven't gotten one in over a year."

He stood and held out his paw. "I hope you get a picture of her soon."

And then we practiced and I beat him pretty good.

* * *

Ma and I went back to Pensa for Christmas, back to our old apartment on the second floor away from traffic noise. She'd been subletting it to another teacher who had gone to her home for the holidays, so we could use it for a couple weeks. I stretched out on the couch the first night but couldn't get comfortable, and I could hear every time Ma shifted or her breathing changed in the bedroom. When I got up, I took three steps and I was in the bathroom. During breakfast, I couldn't move around Ma in the kitchen the way I'd used to. Ma didn't comment on anything but I took to sitting in a corner of the couch with my legs folded up to stay out of the way.

On Christmas Eve we sat down to a dinner of ham and potatoes, something fairly simple because Ma planned to make a nicer dinner the next day. We were quiet until she asked if I'd heard from Marquize.

"Oh. No, not yet. I mean, his family's Muslim, so they don't do Christmas. I'm not sure if they're doing anything special for it."

"Then he should be able to call you anytime. Maybe he is worried about intruding on your celebration."

"I'll call him after dinner," I promised.

The way we'd left things, though, I wasn't sure Marquize would want to talk to me. We'd had a fifteen-minute good-bye that involved more silence than words, and even though some of that silence was filled with groping and petting that was pretty nice, we still parted with an uneasy sense that our "I'll miss you" statements were tinged with relief. Partly I hadn't called him because it had been so hard dealing with him the past few months, and partly because I knew he hadn't been looking forward to visiting his parents, so I didn't want to bother him.

But I did call him after dinner and ask how things were going. "Not great," he said. "How about you?"

"What's happening?"

"I'll tell you later." He sighed. "Not over the phone. Tell me about your Christmas. Are you seeing any of the guys from class?"

So I told him we were keeping it simple, we weren't seeing anyone else, and we were going to get back to training right after New Year's. "And I'll see you then, right?"

There was a hesitation before he said, "Yeah," but he went on right after to say, "I hope you get to talk to Ori. Tell her Merry Christmas from me."

"I will."

"And I hope her lion turns up."

I sighed. "Me too. But it's been months. He would have by now, right?"

"Maybe not." He got more animated in tone. "Some of those operations keep guys out in the field for months. He might be in a conflict and unable to get back."

"I guess. I don't know how that works."

"Trust me. He'll be back eventually."

"All right. Thanks." I relaxed into the couch. "How's Port City?"

"There's slush all over and my ears freeze if I stay outside too long. But everything's lit up and people seem happier walking around. So there's that. And there's this new shopping development going up across from the store that's almost done. Cratch said they wanted to be done by Christmas but it got delayed so now they're aiming for a spring opening. They have tenants lined up to move in then."

"To move into a shopping development?"

"There's apartments over them."

"Cool. How are things going with your parents?"

"Uh." He didn't say anything for a bit. "You know. It's going. Hey, Rocky?"

"Yeah?"

"When I get back, I'm gonna try to be better. I know I've been shitty the past few months. I'm going to work on my attitude."

My chest warmed. "I could try to be more understanding too. It's just that tennis is so important."

"I know. Because of your sister and all."

"Not only that." I searched for words and remembered what Paulie had said. "It's a direction in life. Getting better gives me something to work towards. I know it'll be years, but the harder I work, the sooner I get there."

"That too."

He'd gotten distant again, but this time instead of walking away, I felt I should try to repair the damage. "That doesn't mean I can't work on us, too. It means I'll do both."

"I know." His tone warmed and I felt I'd done the right thing there.

"Good luck with your family. Hey, Ma says if you need somewhere to go you can always come here."

"Thanks." And his tone was warmer still. "That means a lot." He laughed. "You never know, I might need to take you up on that."

Ma glanced at me from the kitchen where she'd been cleaning up, ears perked back toward the living room. "You're welcome anytime," I said.

After we'd hung up, Ma dried her paws and came to sit next to me on the couch. "Rocky," she said. "I have made a decision I should tell you about."

I thought it was about Marquize because I'd been talking to him, so I said, "It sounded like things weren't going so well with Marquize and his parents. He might actually come down here."

"That's fine. He is welcome anytime. But I wanted to talk to you about my chaperoning."

"Oh. You're doing a good job. Lochen hasn't complained."

"No." She clasped her paws and put them in her lap. "But I am not doing very much for you. I think I will go back to teaching this semester if there is a vacancy, or in the fall if there is not."

I stared at her muzzle and her tranquil expression. "Are you sure?"

"Yes. I will trust," and she leaned on that word, "that you and Marquize will behave yourselves. You are of age and I only want to be sure you don't cause yourself trouble."

I leaned against the couch and listened to the sounds of traffic outside, a few individual cars hurrying to their Christmas Eves. "You really won't come on tour with us?"

Her tail twitched, but she remained otherwise composed. "To do what? Cheer for you? I will always do that. But here I can teach, I can help many cubs. You…you don't need me anymore."

"Ma." I reached out to her paw. "I still need you. Ori needs you. Who's going to help me when I have enough money to bring her over?"

"I will, of course." She held my paw. "But you don't need me with you every moment, not anymore. You are on the path to your future."

I pulled my knees in to my chest and thought about life on the tour without Ma. Behind her, our jackets hung on the apartment door. I thought about picking up my jacket and walking out without her. "Are you going to start teaching right away?"

"I've asked about openings. If there aren't any, I will come back with you in January."

I looked again at the door and hoped Ma would find a teaching post, but at the same time I was remembering Marquize's words about being on tour without her. Maybe if we didn't have to run around and hide from her, we'd be able to have a healthier relationship, and I could still call Ma in the evenings when I needed to talk to her. "I'll miss you," I said, which was truthful and didn't require me to sort out my conflicted feelings about it.

Christmas morning we called Ori. She had not participated in the Christmas pageant this year because she wasn't sure whether she would even be there. "Besides," she said dryly, "they said I'm too old to play anything but one of the wise men now."

"They didn't really." I laughed. "You'd be a wonderful Eve."

"But then Bompaka would have to come play Adam, or my honor would be called into question." She sighed. "It's fine, Ro. I'm just grateful he didn't call to have me brought to the village before the holiday."

"Do you know when he will call?"

"He calls to let Kamina know that he's still interested. That the time isn't quite right." She exhaled. "Kamina thinks he is waiting for the spring, after the rains. Nothing much happens in the winter and perhaps some of the important people are elsewhere. Or perhaps he is making us wait to make my price lower. We really don't know."

I leaned my ear against the phone. "I hope he makes you wait for years."

"How is your tennis going? I haven't read about you in any of the newspapers yet."

"No, and you won't for a while." I'd told her about our team, and now I spent a pleasant several minutes telling her about my practices, about Paulie and the team, and reported confidently that I would win a tournament in 2012.

"I believe in you," she said, and it was soon after that that I passed the phone back to Ma.

We hadn't talked about the call I knew she wanted to get and hadn't. Raji still wasn't back from wherever he'd gone, and Ori had no doubt felt it was a waste of her time to get close to anyone else, what with Bompaka's call dangling over her head. Things with Raji couldn't go anywhere anyway. But I knew she wanted to know, and I did, too.

Marquize did not come down that Christmas, though I found out later he had gone so far as to get onto a train, but got off again before it left the station. When I called, he didn't answer.

Ma and I went to a small gathering with two of her teacher friends, older people without other families who'd begun the tradition of spending Christmas with each other rather than alone. There I was able to forget Ori and Marquize and settle into the quiet delight that more than anything else defines Christmas for me.

I thought of Marquize later, when we were saying Grace around the modest Christmas dinner they'd prepared. He didn't follow the religion of his parents, didn't follow any religion, in fact. What void did that leave in his life? It wasn't as though I was one of those athletes who thanked my Lord and Savior after a win. But I believed that there was an order and a purpose to the world and that I was part of it and that there was a God (whom I nebulously saw as an old jackal about twice my size) who maybe didn't enforce the order but surely knew about it. Marquize—he was alone in the world. I felt a wave of sadness for him, enough that I almost got my phone out, but then the red wolf next to me started telling me about the Christmases he'd had growing up, and I couldn't call my friend without being very rude.

Later, I was full of food and playing Pictionary and just plain forgot. But he didn't call me, either.

Chapter Six

Because Ma wasn't sure about her situation, we bought a plane ticket for me to join the team in Kerina (in the state of Taysha, about a two-day drive from Pensa). As the holiday wound down and my plane flight approached, I got more nervous about flying alone. Finally, the day before my flight, Ma was talking on the phone to some people about a possible substitute teaching position while I paced back and forth in the living room, imagining being on tour without her. The team were all good guys, but what if Sunday churchgoing became an issue? What if something else happened?

She hung up, and I blurted out, "Please come back on tour with us."

Ma raised an eyebrow. Before she could talk, I said, "I know you said I don't need you, and maybe I don't. But." I took a breath. "I want you along. You help keep me in the right frame of mind to play and you take care of a lot of the things that I don't have to think about."

"Your manager will be taking care of those now," she said.

"But—"

"But if it will help your career, of course I will come along with you." She smiled. "I will drive Big Blue out and meet you there."

Once my wave of relief had passed, I watched Ma pack and wondered if that was what she'd been waiting for me to do all along.

Flying by myself was strange. Ma had taken care of most of our trips over the past year: she'd handled our tickets, checked us in, checked our bags, gotten us through airport security and to the right gate, out onto the tarmac and up the stairs to the plane.

I'd walked with her for all of that, but those memories didn't help me navigate the signs and counters. I was proud of myself for only getting lost twice in the airport and for reaching the correct gate half an hour before the plane started boarding (Ma had insisted I arrive at the airport two hours before the flight was to leave).

The flight itself went smoothly, and at three hours, felt shorter than I'd thought it would be. At the airport in Kerina, I had instructions from Lochen to take an airport shuttle to the Taysha University campus in Kerina, where the team was staying in a dorm that wasn't being used for the month of January while the school was on break.

Marquize and Chris hadn't gotten in yet, so the rest of us had dinner and talked about our holiday break. Everyone talked about Christmas Mass, and I felt self-conscious about not having gone to church at all. Ma and I had prayed and given thanks together, but that felt inadequate next to the pomp and grandeur of Paulie's church; Ma's telling of the story of the Baby Jesus paled next to Lochen's description of his pastor's ceremony. So I didn't say anything except that our Christmas was lovely as well, and I wondered what Marquize would have said if he'd been here with us.

He arrived the following morning while we were at practice, appearing at the fence around the court in a dark, sullen jacket with his fists stuffed in the pockets. I hadn't seen him arrive and he hadn't called out to me; I spotted him on a break and brought my water bottle over to the fence where he was standing as I drank.

"Getting right back into it," he said.

I gulped down the water. "Lochen doesn't want us to lose any time. Coach Luka's really good. I feel like I've picked up right where I left off and I'm getting even better. You gonna join us? Next tournament starts in two weeks."

"Two and a half." He sighed and brought his paws out of his pockets, gripping the fence with his fingers poking through to my side. "Sorry. I'll be ready tomorrow."

"We're going this afternoon as well."

"I have to unpack." He looked around. "So your ma stayed back in Pensa to teach?"

"Uh, no, she's on her way. She called this morning, said she hoped to be here tonight, but might not be." I flicked my ears back. "There weren't any teaching jobs so she decided to come out with us."

"Hmm." A crafty smile stole over his face, one that felt more suited to me or Paulie the coyote than a cheetah. "All right, I'll see you back at the room."

"Mar—"

"Don't." He pointed a finger at me. "We have a free night, or afternoon or something, and we're going to take advantage of it."

"That's fine." Paulie was calling me to come back to practice. "I was just going to tell you that Lochen and Coach have keys to our room, so don't lounge around naked or anything until I get back and we can put the lock on the door."

"Oh." His fingers reached for me through the fence. "All right."

I gripped his fingers quickly and then ran back to practice, relieved that he'd focused on our free afternoon and not on Ma coming back to join us.

* * *

Ma called around six to tell me she'd crossed the Taysha border and would be another two to three hours. We'd just sat down to dinner in the common area of the dorm—Lochen had gone grocery shopping while we were with Coach Luka, and had prepared a balanced meal in the dorm kitchen. "This is one of my favorite weeks of the year," he said, "because we can cook in most of the time. Tell me my lemon chicken isn't better than any takeout you've had."

It was delicious, but Marquize and I hurried through it and kicked our feet impatiently through the after-dinner "let's talk about our holiday again" session. Finally around 7:30 we excused ourselves, saying that Marquize needed to do some unpacking and that I was going to help.

And when he'd closed the door and locked it behind us, he threw his arms around me and pressed his muzzle to mine in a kiss. "I missed you," he said when we broke apart. "So much."

"Missed you too," I said, circling him in my arms. Our noses touched and I stared into his eyes, inhaling his scent up close. "Sorry you had a rough holiday."

"It's okay." He smiled and kissed my nose. "It was worth it."

"What? What happened?"

"Ah…" He licked at my lips and I parted them to let him kiss me again. When he pulled his head back he said, "Look, I don't want to talk about it right now. We've got an hour. Let's make good use of it."

And we did.

Chapter Seven

The beginning of the tennis year, all your points are frozen. As the year goes on, your ranking depends on how much better you do this year than you did the year before at each event. So for someone like me with two ranking points, unless I spend the year injured, I can't help but improve. Lochen had a meeting with all six of us where he laid out our tournament schedule for the year, and then had individual meetings where he told each of us his goals for us for 2011.

At least, that's what our meeting was about. I assume the meetings with the others were the same, but when I asked Marquize what Lochen talked to him about, he shrugged and said, "Wants me to get some ranking points."

To me, Lochen started with a long, slow breath and a recitation of my name, rolling the 'R' so it held my attention, the rest of my name almost an afterthought. "Rocky. I've only worked with you for a couple months, but I see a lot of potential. By July you'll be ranked high enough to get right into the main draws, and before the year's out you'll win a tournament. And in 2012, you'll probably leave the team and join the Challenger circuit, to be honest. Maybe late in the year, but if you work and live up to that potential, I can see it happening. So we're going to focus on singles with you." He saw my reaction and held up a paw. "You want to keep playing doubles, that's your call. It helps you out a good deal, and I know you want to make some money. That's fine, it's all good. This is your career. I told you that when you joined the team, and I'll remind you of it now and again."

He said 'career' with those wonderful rolling 'r's that momentarily distracted me from what he was saying. When I snapped back to attention, he seemed to be waiting for me to say something, so I said, "I understand, thank you."

His long thin muzzle nodded crisply once. He leaned back and laced his paws behind his head, his eyes still fixed on mine. "I've got you in more tournaments than the others. There are some small ones you could win and get a purse from, and to be honest it's cheaper for me to not pay for hotel rooms for five guys who aren't going to win back even one night's cost at that tournament for the one guy who might. Again, if you disagree, let me know."

"No," I said, ears perked and letting the 'r' in 'disagree' roll over them. "That sounds good."

"Good. Now don't agree with me just because I'm leading the team. You go back and think about this and let me know if you have any concerns."

"All right."

"But also." He waited until I leaned forward a little, attentive. "I am leading the team. I've done this before. Now, where you're going to make the money you want is through endorsements. I can help you line up several, and if you perform the way we've outlined here, you'll be making a few thousand dollars from them by the end of the year. When you go to the Challenger circuit, that'll jump up a level."

"To what?" I asked, unable to restrain myself.

He smiled, showing his fangs. "Depends on how well you do."

* * *

At the first tournament, I made it through the qualifiers in singles, and Marquize and I won a doubles match and almost another one. To be honest, I was carrying the both of us, though I didn't want to say it. I think he knew it too. He didn't even win one qualifying match.

I ended up playing Adam in the qualifying finals and won in straight sets. "Good job, mate," he said, keeping his cheerful demeanor even in a loss. "Gonna have to learn from ya."

"Anytime," I said, my mind already racing ahead to my next match, in the main draw.

An ermine named Melanovic took me to a third set, but in

that set I managed to exploit his tendency to come in to net with a lot of good passing shots, and I won the match, getting me into the round of 16 and earning me at least one ranking point.

In the next match I found myself facing Nashan. Before the match in the locker room, he came over to me and shook my paw. "Looks like the team is agreeing with you."

"Yes," I said cautiously, not quite sure what we were supposed to be agreeing about. "And you had a good vacation?"

"Pretty good. First time out of the qualifiers in a while." He swung his right arm in a circle. "Shoulder feels a lot better."

"Great." I grinned at him. "I want you to be at full strength when I beat you."

"Ha." He grinned back. "This'll be my best chance to take a match off you. I'm not going to waste it."

I stuck out my paw. "Good luck."

"You too." He grabbed and shook it. "Let's get out there."

So we walked out to the court, hit the ball around back and forth, and then practiced our serves. His looked crisp and fast, but I was also getting into good form after several matches.

I served first and got a good one in, keeping him pinned back to the baseline while I tried to remember what I knew from watching him play the previous year. We both played conservatively through the first set, each winning our service games until I was serving at 5-5, when Nashan changed his tactics. Where he'd been content to play a standard baseline game, now he changed it up with a drop shot and approach to net, earning him a break point. I got nervous, flubbed the first serve, and he smashed the second back into the corner to win the game.

He won his service game and the first set, and I spent the break mad at myself. And then I looked up at the stands and saw Luka there.

It had taken me most of my first match to get used to not seeing Ma in the coaches' area. Because Luka coached many of us, he hadn't attended all my matches, but of the team, I was the one still playing, so he was in attendance. Of course, he couldn't give me any signals, but just seeing him reminded me of how much his practices had helped me.

I looked across at Nashan, muzzle down in his towel. I knew he was near the end of his career and this was the farthest he'd gotten in a tournament in a long time. Might be the farthest he'd get for the rest of his life, his last chance to win one.

But this might also be my first chance to win a tournament.

Then the break was over and we were back on the court. I had to serve first and the ball was landing perfectly for me: I got four first serves in and won three, and I won the point where I had to drop a second serve in. And when I was on defense…well, things were about the same. Nashan kept mixing things up, keeping me off balance enough to win his service games, although I pressed him harder on his serve than he did on mine.

He was panting harder than I was by the time the set went to a tiebreak, and again I thought about him at the end of his career. I'd have more opportunities, wouldn't I? It would be nice to see him happy, winning a tournament, and it might give Marquize hope. He'd talked about following Nashan's career path, being stuck in the Futures forever.

But it wasn't easy to take the competitive edge off my game. My muscles followed a pattern I'd drilled into them over the past three, five, seven years. I could play defensively on his service points, remaining conservative and allowing him to dictate and eventually win the point. I did flub one of my service points early on, thinking that would be the difference, but then Nashan double-faulted and we were back even.

We got to me serving at 5-6, and here I really had to consider what I was doing. Effectively I was throwing the match. That was a big no-no; our coaches and teachers in Palm Gables had talked about tennis players who threw matches, but that had been for betting purposes, players promised big payoffs by gamblers. This was nothing like that. This was me doing a favor for a guy who'd been nice to me, a favor that didn't cost me anything.

But what if the difference in ranking points caught up to me at the end of the year? What if I came up one point short of the cutoff for entry into the Challenger circuit (if that was how it worked)? Would I look back on this game and regret it? So many people had told me over the years that tennis is the most selfish of sports, that there was no room for sentiment between those white lines.

I bounced the ball, pretending I was taking a while on my serve. In my head, the announcers calling the game (there weren't always announcers calling the game in my head, but sometimes on stressful points there were) were saying "N'Guwe knows this is a critical point. He's never advanced this far before."

It would be totally reasonable to be nervous at this point in my career. And yet I felt calm and collected. I could see the ball floating in the air after I tossed it, could see the perfect arc of my racket, watched the ball's flight right to the corner of the service box. I knew I could do it.

Pushing it just wide, though—could I do that on purpose? I was less sure about that. It wasn't just the ranking point; it was Ori, too. The difference here would be a hundred dollars, and would that make a difference of a week or a month in bringing her back?

And then I couldn't delay any longer without getting a warning from the umpire, so I lifted the ball over my head and served. The ball flew true just as I'd envisioned it, and landed an inch outside the line.

"Second serve," the umpire called, and Nashan moved a foot closer.

I took some pace off my second serve—"N'Guwe doesn't want to double-fault here," the announcers in my head said—and Nashan pounced on it. I sprinted after his cross-court return, but I didn't even have to fake miss it; it was a good hit and a foot beyond my racket. Set and match to Nashan.

I met the red fox at the net. We shook paws and embraced, and I felt pretty good, though he didn't say, "Good match," and I thought that was odd.

I found out why in the locker room after the game. "What the hell was that?" he said low to me, cornering me before I had a chance to change.

"What?" My fur prickled.

"That tiebreak." He waved out toward the court. "That second set. What happened? You taking money or something?"

"No!" I tried to recoil but my back was to a wall and I could only curl my tail up between my legs. "What are you—"

He shook his head. "I've seen you play enough to know that you were easing off on the second set. First set you just made a few mistakes. You should've at least won one set off me. So what was that, if not money?"

"You were better than me. You deserved to win."

I stared back into his eyes. He searched mine and then his brow lowered. "If it was a pity match, I don't need that either. If I can't beat you playing your best, I don't deserve to beat you."

"It wasn't," I said, but even to my own ears I could hear the unconvincing falter in my words.

He stabbed a finger at my chest. "Don't you ever do that again. It's hard enough to get what you can in this business without giving away matches. What if this ranking means the difference between getting invited to a Challenger tournament and staying home? That could be thousands of dollars and months of your career to make up."

I didn't know what to say. My ears lowered and I couldn't meet his eyes anymore. He waited a moment and then turned away. "You're a good kid, Rocky," he said. "Don't let that ruin your career."

In that moment, I wasn't as worried about my career as about whatever friendship I had with him. That black cloud followed me through my shower and dressing in street clothes, and then I had to contend with everyone trying to console me after the match. "You almost had him," Paulie said, and everyone else said variations on the same theme.

Of course, Nashan went on to lose his next match, so he didn't win the tournament, and in watching the player he lost to, I had the uncomfortable feeling that I could've won that match. I knew it was different watching than actually being there on the court, but I felt like my style would have matched up better. Nashan was right. What if I'd cost myself my first tournament win here? It gnawed at me that

I'd let Ori down, let myself down, and for what? Would Nashan have done the same for me?

At our first practice in the next city, Lochen and Coach Luka took me aside, their muzzles set and serious. My first thought was that they were going to yell at me like Nashan had, and I made a quick vow: I would never, ever lose a game on purpose again. But neither of them was angry. "You did real well last tournament," Lochen said.

"If you intend to continue with doubles," Luka went on, cutting through Lochen's small talk, "you should do it with a player who will teach you and help you grow. Marquize won't do that. We want you to pair with Chris."

"Chris?" I said.

"He's a better doubles than singles player, and playing with him will teach you more than practice sessions with me," the coach went on.

"I know it'll be difficult with Marquize," the fox said. "But it's about your growth as a player. If he can't respect that, he shouldn't be on this team with you."

"Shouldn't be difficult," Luka snorted. "Ivan Dulovik told me a month before Wimbledon that he was taking another doubles partner to the draw and it wasn't 'difficult.' I accepted it and found my own partner to play with."

"And did you win?" I asked.

"Of course not," the mouse snapped. "And neither did Dulovik. Because we didn't know our partners. But we grew to learn them. Just as you must grow to learn Chris's habits."

"Well…"

Lochen put a paw on my shoulder. "You always have a choice, Rocky. But you joined this team to benefit from our expertise. That's what our expertise tells you. Luka and I won't always agree, but when we do, we're pretty much right."

"All right." My tail drooped, but neither of them commented on it.

I did ask that they let me tell Marquize. That night, Ma wanted to talk about one of the books she'd brought us, a classic novel called

"The Grapes of Wrath" about a family that moves from their devastated homeland to a land that promises more opportunities. I had to take Marquize aside at a break and assure Ma that we were just going to talk. I think she got from the cheetah's surprise that we weren't going to fool around, so she left us for a few moments.

When I told Marquize that Lochen and Coach wanted me to play doubles with Chris, he snapped out, "That figures. I guess you said yes."

"What was I supposed to say?" I asked, trying not to get testy in return. "Why did we sign on with them if not to take their advice?"

"That's all it is, advice. You could've stuck up for me. Who are they pairing me with, Les?"

The rat was by mutual agreement the worst player on the team. "I don't know," I said honestly. "But if you don't want to play with Les—"

"What? Just tell them? What if they advise me to play with him? I guess I'd better listen then, huh?" He got up and paced to the window and back, tail lashing.

I didn't want to say what I was thinking, which was that Marquize hadn't been playing all that well, and that if he wanted us to keep playing together, maybe he should've tried a little harder. In the silence of my thoughts, Marquize kept going. "I know we weren't doing all that well, but I wish you'd stick your neck out a bit. Your career's going to be in singles; we both know that. You could afford to do something in doubles for your boyfriend."

I opened my muzzle, but he held up a paw, facing me again. "I know you want to raise money for your sister. I need money now too. It's not going to be that big a difference, winning a few more games."

But I was thinking of Nashan. Why had I been willing to risk my career for him, but not for Marquize? Part of it, obviously, had been that I'd been faced with my coach and my manager and that had been somewhat intimidating. In the game against Nashan, I'd made the decision myself. I was pretty sure Lochen would've told me not to throw away that match if he'd been allowed to talk to me during the match; as it was, Coach Luka had lectured me on keeping my focus and we'd worked exclusively on my serve in the next session.

"It's fine," Marquize said. "You don't have to justify yourself. I know your career comes first."

The anger was leaching out of his tone and I felt that maybe he really did mean that. And maybe also he was using the truth in it as a spear to wound me. So I turned it around on him. "Yeah," I said. "I'm glad you understand."

He frowned. "That's typical," he said, and then the door rattled and he shut up.

A moment later it opened and Ma came back in. She turned from him to me and said, "Are we ready to talk about the book?"

"Yeah." Marquize went to sit down on the other bed. "We're done. Thanks."

Chapter Eight

My first doubles practice with Chris went terribly. I was used to Marquize's passive play, but Chris jumped around the court—typical squirrel. Twice we collided; more times than I could count, we almost did until one of us jumped out of the way.

It didn't help that we were practicing against Les and Marquize, who had the opposite problem. "Get after that!" Coach Luka screamed at them time after time when they looked at each other as the ball landed between them. To us, mostly he yelled, "Call it!"

Marquize and I had never really had to call the ball. We knew each other well enough to know where the other would be and what they could take, and we'd always played well in sync. But I hadn't realized until I was playing with Chris just how much my responsibilities in our partnership had expanded over the years. Marquize should have been able to cover the same amount of court, or even more than me, and yet I routinely crossed over half the court to take a volley.

Chris did the same thing, maybe as a result of having played with Les. When we remembered to call out, "Got it!" things worked better, though many times we called that at the same time, which did not help our confusion. By the end of the practice, we were doing a lot better, and Coach said we were going to work out "fine, I suppose."

We all went to dinner together, but I sat next to Chris and talked to him more than I talked to Marquize. He talked tennis as readily as I did, dissecting our practice in a way Marquize and I hadn't done since Palm Gables, maybe ever. We talked movement, shot selection, and he remembered specific rallies from our practice as well as I did.

"If you'd stayed back," he said, and I would excitedly chime in with agreement. Or I would talk about a shot he'd made and suggest how he could've improved it or how we could've defended better against the return.

Across the table and down a little way, Marquize ate silently while Les and Paulie talked about the local church. When I cocked an ear to listen, I heard them debating whether they wanted to attend the bake sale the church was holding the following Saturday morning. Marquize had been quiet most of the dinner, but he must have noticed my ears, because he said, "Hey, can I go even if I didn't go to the church?"

Chris made another comment about our practice, so I cupped my ears forward and gave the squirrel all my attention.

* * *

For the rest of the week, Marquize didn't try to get any alone time with me, so we didn't have any. The whole week was spent practicing, and I told him I would still practice with him when we played singles, when Coach was working with the other players. "Fine," he said, and actually got a little spirit into his practice. And that's how we went every day when we weren't under Coach Luka's eye.

Meanwhile Chris and I had found a nice rhythm together and had gotten used to calling for our shots. The sensation of playing alongside him rather than Marquize still felt weird to me, but I was adjusting my game to his, figuring out for example that he had strong groundstrokes, especially off his forehand side. With Marquize, when I was at net I ran to try to get everything; with Chris, I could save my energy if a ball was headed for his forehand, knowing he'd get a good shot back.

Saturday morning, Marquize got ready to leave, and I asked where he was going. "The bake sale," he said. "Les and Paulie are heading over there at ten." He didn't ask if I was coming.

I threw clothes into suitcases and grumbled to myself for half an hour while Ma tried to talk to me, and then my bad mood was interrupted by a call from Ori.

"We are leaving in an hour," she said. "I don't know how long we'll be gone."

"Wait, leaving? For where? When?" Marquize and my packing and everything else vanished. I walked to the window, open to the breeze outside. "Sorry, you said that already. I mean, where are you going? Is it Bompaka?"

"Yes. He finally called. It's a week travel and Kamina is very anxious to leave."

"If he approves, will you stay there?" I felt as though I were hurtling down a cliff. This might be the last time I talked to Ori…until we could fly her over here, however long that would be.

"No. We will come back here and he must prepare the payment for the wedding. I don't know how long that will take."

I held my cell phone to my ear as the leaves in the trees outside rustled. "I don't have a lot of money. Lochen says I'll make money from endorsements once I start winning tournaments, but that probably won't be for a year or two."

"It's fine, Ro." She exhaled. "I'll be fine. But I wanted to tell you that I left your phone number with Raji's family. I met his sister Sarya and she's sweet. She knows—" Her voice caught and then steadied. "In case they hear from him, they will call you."

"Oh." I didn't know what to say. Ori was smart enough to know that if she hadn't heard by now, probably she should expect the worst, but maybe in this moment she needed that fiction to cling to. "All right, I'll make sure to pick up their call."

"I'm coming!" she said to Kamina, and then, to me, "Good-bye. Love you."

"Love you too." I took a breath. "Don't worry. I'll get you out."

But she'd already hung up. I turned off the phone and shoved it in my pocket, then set about finishing my packing.

I told Ma about Ori's call when she got back. Ma had always been calm and collected; I didn't expect her to sit down on the bed so fast that she didn't even sweep her tail out of the way.

"Ma?" I walked over to the bed. She wasn't reacting to anything, just staring straight ahead. I don't think she even saw me. "Ma?" I waved a paw in front of her muzzle.

She focused on me and smiled. "I'm fine. Thank you." When she saw that those words weren't very convincing, she flattened her ears. The smile remained, but it became more genuine, a smile of shared sadness and worry rather than the sunny "everything is fine" smile.

That moment sticks in my memory. Ma and I had done so much together, but even when I'd told her I would be joining a team, that she would no longer be my coach, she hadn't accorded me the respect of someone she could share problems with. It wasn't until this moment that she let me see the weight on her that came with raising two children across two continents.

"I had not expected this to happen so soon," she said. "Kamina was supposed to—" She shook her head. "It doesn't matter now. What matters is ensuring that Ori remains safe."

"Isn't she safe in that village? It's not near any of the wars or the fighting…"

Ma inclined her head upward at me. "It's best you continue to think that," she said. "Go finish your packing. In Greenwater, keep practicing. I will worry about Ori."

And she smiled again, that "everything is fine" smile. I hesitated, but she got up and began helping with my clothes, so I didn't say anything about it.

* * *

The next town might not have been Greenwater. They all blur together in my mind, these little college towns and suburbs with tennis clubs and college courts where I practiced and played those first few years. I can remember the stadiums, the way the bleachers stacked up and caught the sun when I played Nashan, the little flaw in the paint at the corner of the baseline the first time I played in a tournament final, the way the flags snapped in the wind when Chris and I… well, but I'm getting a little ahead of myself. The point is, maybe it was Greenwater or maybe it wasn't. Greenwater was one of the places we practiced and played a tournament, and of all the little towns and cheering crowds I played in front of, that might have been the next one.

Or it might not. But let's say it was.

So after the ride to Greenwater in the car (when the team took a bus, Ma drove, and this time I chose to ride with her), during which I thought a lot about Ori but neither me nor Ma spoke a word about it, I decided that if Ma said she was going to handle it, then the best thing I could do would be to let her handle it until she needed my help. As she often said, I had enough to concentrate on—in this case, navigating the personalities of the team.

Paulie was well-read in the world of tennis, even more so than I was, but where the others treated his knowledge like showing off, I wanted him to tell me more stories, and he was happy to oblige. So he told me about the epic 20-18 final set at the Ocie in 1979 between Tarq, a wolf, and Doppel, a rat; and their rematch at Wimbledon later that year when Tarq came back from 1-4 down in the final set to win 7-5 over a limping, exhausted Doppel. He talked about Tarq's power and precision and Jeffers' grace and Yelena's grit and Indiro's cool poise, about Doppel's creativity and Ancher's wild energy that annoyed and distracted his opponents and the way Widener could get to any shot, all with such joy and expressiveness that I felt as though I'd been there in the stands watching these epic matches from the late seventies through the nineties. "But there's only ever been one jackal champion," Paulie told me. "Mark Taba, won the States Open in '81. He was a great guy by all accounts."

"I never saw anything about him," I said, "but I heard the name." So in some of my spare time I researched Taba, a jackal who was born in the States. He'd played well before my time, but the reason I knew his name was that he'd stayed involved in the game, enough that announcers mentioned him often even after he retired.

The tennis stars I remembered watching Paulie knew as well, and we spent plenty of time discussing those. For those conversations, Les and Marquize joined in. Les, for all that he remained quiet in most conversations, had a deep knowledge of popular culture when you drew him out, and he could tell us things about the private lives of those tennis players—as well as movie stars, rock stars, politicians, and anyone else who at one point might have been on TV or profiled in one of the magazines he read.

Chris liked pop culture, but his level of knowledge was close to mine. His passion was sports, and in addition to tennis matches from the last two decades, he knew about football, basketball, baseball, hockey, and soccer. Our knowledge intersected at soccer and tennis, but I'd ask him for stories about the other sports and sometimes he'd get wrapped up for nearly half an hour remembering one game, his big bushy tail twitching and his paws punching the air in his excitement.

And Adam, like me, enjoyed feeding off of other people's passions and learning from them. I hadn't spent a lot of time with him until one evening when he and I happened to be the last ones out at practice hitting balls around idly. "Hey," he said. "Want to see if we can get to the roof of that building?"

I squinted at the tallest building nearby, a twelve-story office tower. "Why?"

He grinned. "Why not?"

We didn't get to the roof, but not for lack of trying. We almost got locked in a fire exit stair, and I would've been worried except that Adam never was. "Bugger," he said when the door shut behind us and we couldn't open it again. "Well, let's see if any of the upper floors open up."

The sixth floor door did, and allowed us to get to the elevator, which didn't take us to the roof or any of the other upper floors but did take us to the lobby, where we strolled out past a startled security guard. "Thanks, mate," Adam said with a wave. "G'night."

So when I wasn't with Marquize, that was how I passed my time. The others on the team wanted to know about the world outside the Union, which none of them had ever experienced, so I did my best to talk about home and the other places I'd studied in my World Cultures class. We all looked forward to getting to the Champions circuit when we could travel all around the world to play tournaments.

And of course, the conversations were the filler in between tennis. Practice in the morning, practice in the afternoon, sessions with Coach Luka, once-a-week conversations with Lochen to "keep us on track," nutrition lectures, and endurance exercises to keep us fit. Tournaments every so often, doubles and singles.

We grew used to the new doubles configurations quickly. Marquize stopped griping about not being my partner when he saw how successful Chris and I were together: we got to the quarterfinal in our first tournament together and in the second one, too, and two tournaments after that we got to the finals. We lost, but still celebrated.

And my singles play improved steadily as well. I met Nashan again in a qualifying final and beat him this time; shaking my paw afterwards, he fixed me with a stare and said, "Glad you learned that lesson."

I got knocked out in the round of 16 in that tournament, but every loss came with a new lesson from Coach Luka and a step forward in my training. By the time my birthday rolled around at the spring equinox, I'd made it to one semifinal and two quarters, and I felt great about my chances in the next quarter year.

The one thing that weighed on my mind was Ori. She'd said it would only be two weeks, but after three weeks Ma called Kamina to ask whether Ori was back. No, Kamina said, Bompaka had not been in touch. A week after that there was still no word, and when Ori had been gone for a month, Kamina said there was some trouble on the road from Kitemini Troixième and Bompaka felt it was not safe to risk the travel.

I tried to talk to Ma about it but she kept putting me off. "Let me worry about Ori," she said over and over again. "You worry about winning."

But I was worried, because she wasn't being nearly as vigilant around me and Marquize as she had been, and I knew it wasn't because she trusted Lochen to watch us. I would catch her on the phone sometimes talking very low, and when she saw me coming close, she would murmur something and hang up. I never asked her who she was talking to, but I knew it had something to do with Ori.

And I didn't press about it because it meant that Marquize and I got to celebrate my seventeenth birthday alone, after the team had celebrated it with the rare treat of a pizza dinner (pizza was high on the list of things that were nutritional no-nos while we were training). As we'd both eased into the rhythm of life on the road, our relationship had also settled into a routine where we shared quick kisses in private, and once or twice a week got time to be more intimate.

The first tournament after my birthday, I reached the final, playing against a veteran player I'd lost to the last time we met. This time I beat him in the second set after losing the first, but he took the third set to win the tournament. I didn't care—much—because I'd gotten enough ranking points from making the final that the following week, Lochen informed me that I wouldn't have to play through the qualifying rounds in the first May tournament, that I'd placed into the main draw. His prediction had come true two months early.

It was in the middle of celebrating that with Marquize, Chris, and Ma that I got a phone call from an international number I didn't recognize. *Ori*, I thought, and nearly toppled my chair getting up from the table to hurry out of the small restaurant so I could take the call.

Even though I didn't recognize the female voice that said my name, I said, "Ori?" hopefully.

"No. This is Sarya Muhammed."

I'm sure there was only a one-second pause between that and the next sentence, but it seemed to me to take forever. Who was Sarya? Was I supposed to know her? Did she have something to do with Ori? How had she gotten my number?

Then she said, "I'm—Raji's sister." And her voice broke there, and I knew everything.

Chapter Nine

I walked back into the restaurant in something of a daze. "Everything okay?" Marquize asked as I sat down again.

"Yeah." I stared at the remains of my meal, a half-eaten steak and a pile of vegetables. I thought about Ori, half a world away, maybe hoping that Raji would be waiting for her when she returned. I thought about Raji and wondered how long he'd been dead before they notified his family. Had he been dead when I talked to Ori over Christmas? Had he been dead within a week of saying good-bye to her?

Those thoughts didn't make me a very entertaining dinner companion, and since the dinner was supposed to be celebrating my accomplishment, it broke up quickly. Chris left first, saying he wanted to be fresh for practice tomorrow. Marquize waited a little longer, but Ma was the only one who talked to him, asking about his latest match. When that conversation lulled, Marquize turned to me. "Was that Ori on the phone?" he asked softly.

"No." I stared down at the pile of vegetables, all that was left. I couldn't make myself eat any more of them.

"Was it about Ori?"

"Not really." I didn't know how to have this conversation with Marquize. "It was about…a friend of hers. The lion I told you about."

The cheetah inclined his head. "Did they break up?"

"No. He went to fight…"

"That's right, you told me that." Marquize perked up with the memory, then his ears flattened as he realized what that meant. "Oh, no."

None of us said anything for several long, slow thuds of my heart. Ma kept her paws folded into her lap and her gaze on the table. Then Marquize turned from me to Ma and back. "I'll…you know, I should get some sleep too. Luka gets mad if I doze off on the court."

Neither of us laughed at his joke. He got up, shoved his chair awkwardly back at the table, and said, "See you back at the room."

When he was gone, Ma said, "Raji."

"That was his sister." I took a breath. "They heard yesterday."

"How long…?" Ma cut her question short at my quick shake of the head.

"I don't know. She didn't tell me if he was just…" I sucked breath between my teeth. "Or if they were only hearing about it now."

The waiter interrupted us then to ask if we wanted anything else. Over my no, Ma asked for more water. She rested her fingers on my arm when the waiter had gone. "Rochi," she said, "this is the world we live in. We can only protect a precious few, and those we give our all to. Others we must trust to themselves or to their precious ones, and sometimes the world is not kind."

"I'm not blaming myself. Or you." I wiped my eyes. "Or Ori," I added, though that should have been obvious.

"The war is terrible and senseless as well. You're doing all you can to bring Ori away from that…"

I stood up, and this time the chair did fall backwards, clattering to the floor. "Don't you understand?" My voice had gotten high and loud. In the background, pushed deep away where I didn't care about things, I heard the clink of silverware and the murmur of conversation die. "This isn't about why it happened. It just happened, it always happens, it's going to keep happening. We can't get Ori away from that. Even over here, that shit," I didn't care that I was swearing, "reaches out and finds us. You think we can escape where we come from? We can't. We'll always have friends there and relatives. Can we make enough to bring the whole country over here? Can we make enough to stop them from killing each other over and over again?"

I didn't expect an answer, but though Ma's ears stayed flat, there was nothing but sorrow in her eyes as she spoke. "We can only do our best," she said.

"And what if that's not enough?" The waiter, a tall zebra, had appeared with the two glasses of water, and that interruption snapped me back to being aware of my surroundings. "I'm sorry," I said to him and to Ma. "I didn't mean to yell."

Then it seemed best that I leave the restaurant, so I stumbled toward the exit, with murmurs growing in my wake. At the door, the hostess chirped, "Good night," but I ignored it and pushed the glass doors out of my way, gulping in the cool air of the evening.

I didn't even know Raji. When the tears came, they were for Ori, I thought. But I didn't understand why I was reacting so violently, not until Ma came out and put her arm around me. With her other paw, she handed me a paper towel that smelled of the restroom. "Let's walk," she said.

The towel got most of the tears out of my fur. I dropped it in the wastecan outside the restaurant and walked slowly back down the street with Ma. "Did you ever talk to him?" she asked.

"No." I sniffled. "But Ori talked about him a lot. How sweet he was, how kind. You could tell how much she loved him." I paused. "How did you find out about him?"

Ma drew in a breath. "I can tell when you cubs are happier because of someone in your life. I wish I'd had the chance to meet him. She could never have been with him, but kind souls are valuable and hard to find."

"Yeah." I exhaled. "She's going to be crushed." I knew that I was assuming we would get to talk to Ori again soon. I still believed that because the alternative was not acceptable.

"You've lost friends before."

"Kind of." I exhaled. "That was different. The boys from the tennis center, they just vanished. Like Dad. I know they're all prob-ably...dead." There I had to pause, that word unexpectedly difficult to say. "But I never got to know Dad. And the boys...I mean, I never heard for sure. I didn't know them all that well. We played together for a year or two, but..." But those memories faded. Even some of my early days at Palm Gables, nearly three years in my past now, were blurry to me. What was the name of that older kid Marquize and I had hung out with? Some kind of cat, I thought? "This is different. This is someone special to Ori."

"And Ori is away, too. You don't know what's happened to her." Ma reached up to stroke my ears. "If Raji can disappear and be killed, then why not Ori? That's what you're thinking."

"Is it?" It felt true, though, when she said it. Maybe that's why I was so shaken. "When will we hear from Ori again?"

"I would have been told if anything happened to her. We will hear from her soon, I promise you."

"Thanks, Ma." I leaned against her.

She hugged me as we walked, putting an arm around my ribs. "You are right, though."

I waited for her to go on. "About what?" I said finally.

"We can never leave it behind, not permanently. The war there will likely go on for the rest of my life, maybe the rest of yours as well, though I pray not. There are people of different tribes and religions and each one thinks the other has something that belongs to them, or has done them wrong in the past, or blames them for their troubles. Other countries have found their way out of war through prosperity, strong leadership, or because the wars have gained notoriety and the world stepped in to force peace. Our country is too big, the war too diffuse, to allow that." Her voice had grown distant, and then she stopped and I felt her breath and whiskers against my arm. "I am sorry that you had to learn this so young."

I shook my head. "I learned it a long time ago. I just forgot, that's all. You got me here, brought me to a better life. You gave us a chance to get Ori here too."

"You brought us here." She squeezed me. "Your talent, all the work you did to impress that scout. All the work you did at Palm Gables. You're working as hard as you can."

"I'm doing what they tell me. I feel like I could be doing more."

"You don't have to look far to see how much you outshine your peers."

"Outshine your peers" was one of those phrases I understood even if I didn't know exactly what it meant, so I ignored it and went on with my own thoughts. "Even if I start winning tournaments, even if I start getting endorsements, they only pay for my travel and boarding at first. That's what Paulie and Adam have. It's going to be another year before I can do anything about Ori. More, maybe. A year and a half."

"There are no shortcuts," Ma said, but at that point I worked through the phrase and ignored what she was saying.

"What do you mean, 'my peers'?" I said.

Her arm tensed around my ribs. "Look at the other people you went to school with," she said.

"That's not what you meant," I said. She sighed and released me. "You're talking about Marquize."

We'd stopped on a more or less deserted street two blocks from the motel where we were staying. Closed shops and quiet apartments with flickering TV light were the only witnesses to our argument. Once in a while a car drove by, headlights brightening out of the gloom and then passing us with a roar and rush of wind.

"Your coach and manager agree with me," Ma said.

"Oh, you've discussed it?" Of course this conspiracy had developed behind my back. Ma, knowing she would not be able to chaperone us once she left the team, would have told Luka and Lochen to separate us. No wonder she'd been so at peace with leaving. "You're the one who got them to change our doubles partners."

"No. I have not spoken to either of them. But even an idiot could see that you're better with Chris than with him."

I folded my arms. "That's not true."

"You've won more matches in three months than you did all last year!"

"I've gotten better." Of course she was right, but I didn't want to admit it. "Les has won more with Marquize than he did with Chris, too."

That might or might not have been true. Actually, I'm not sure it was. But Ma didn't know any better than I did, so she let it go. "Regardless," she said. "He is not as motivated as you are. He has had many chances to improve, but he hasn't taken many of them. He pulls you away from tennis practice, and—"

"He hasn't done that in forever." My ears burned. I had managed to fool myself into thinking Ma was oblivious to our fooling around. "And you said I'm getting better. I'm not taking off more time than

I can afford."

"But his attitude." She stared forward, as though she could see Marquize slacking off in the hotel room. "He's your closest friend and he is showing you by example that you need not spend your whole life thinking about tennis, when you do."

"You think I'm going to do whatever Marquize does? I've got Lochen and Luka and Paulie and Adam and Chris to remind me how important tennis is."

"None of them are your boyfriend," she said.

We both stopped, shocked at her bluntness. Her ears remained flat for a moment and then came up, matching the defiance in her stare. How odd that word sounded; how good to have it acknowledged and yet how violently it had been thrown at me. "No," I said. "If you were accusing me of cheating on Marquize, no."

She sighed and her frown deepened. "Love can take you down unusual paths. You may think you can resist him, but if the two of you are pulling in different directions, then one of you will be dragged along with the other. Maybe you will convince him to practice more and work harder. But maybe he will convince you that it doesn't matter to skip one practice, to go to bed early one night instead of studying, then perhaps to drink—"

"Neither of us drinks."

"Not now. But later. That is a thing that happens." She tried to take my paw and I pulled it away. "You need someone who will match your paws on the same path, and failing that, you should be alone."

"Maybe I don't want to be alone. Maybe I'd rather have someone to share my life with than a bunch of meaningless trophies."

"Ro." She saw that I didn't mean that, and I think she knew it wasn't worth arguing anymore, otherwise she would have reminded me that my family would always be there. "I am not saying you should break up. I'm saying that unless one of you changes, it will be very hard for you to keep together. Maybe more work than you can afford. You should be directing your energy toward winning and advancing."

"I am."

"And is he?"

"Yes!" I kicked at a rock in the street and sent it skittering away, into the concrete base of a storefront and back out into our path. "He's getting better. He's working on his doubles and his singles."

Ma didn't say anything. We walked up and when I reached the rock, I kicked it again. It spun out into the street and away. "You know that I want the best for you," she said. I didn't answer. "If I thought that you didn't want to win, we would find another way. But I watch you, I have watched you since you were old enough to stand. You outran boys twice your age. At tennis, remember when Prince the lion beat you and you came home and sulked for three days? You practiced, you worked, and you went back and beat him. I have seen this all your life."

I couldn't think of anything to say. Ma kept talking. "You also have a warm heart. You wouldn't let Ori beat you, but you are doing so much to help her. You have an impulse to put yourself at risk for others and I worry that this will lead you to do something you regret."

Did she know about Nashan? She'd watched the match. I swallowed the guilty secret down and said, "I'm going to keep winning."

"I know you will. Because you can be the best. And I'm going to watch you get there."

For a moment I wished I hadn't joined the team, that it was still just me and Ma (and Marquize, my mind added guiltily) touring the tennis world. I wished I'd believed in her a little bit more, had allowed her to find the rhythm of coaching. Maybe I would've improved anyway.

As soon as I thought that I knew the lie of it. The team was better for me and had made me a better player. More, it had positioned me to make friendships in the game, where previously Marquize and I had been isolated. I'd only befriended Nashan because he'd approached me, and my gratefulness for that friendship had led me to throw a match. Almost. If I really had. Now I had the guys on the team, and they knew other guys on the circuit and had introduced us. Not really like the Joads arriving in California in 'The Grapes of Wrath" because (Ma kept reminding me) for all our hardships, we had privileges and were never in any real danger. But I'd felt echoes of their homesickness, and in finding friendships with the other players, I felt a little like the workers the Joads joined with.

Of course, that was silly, because there was nobody keeping our wages down and nobody oppressing us except ourselves.

* * *

When I got back to the room, Marquize was lying on his bed staring at his phone. "You okay?" he asked when I came in.

"I'm fine."

"Sorry about your sister's friend."

"Thanks." I shrugged off my shirt and threw it in the corner, then flopped down on my bed.

After a moment, Marquize came over and sat next to me. He put a paw on my bare stomach and rested it there. After a moment I reached over and rested a paw on his hip. I was all cried out already, but the comfort of being close to him was nice. Ma didn't know what she was talking about. I needed this in my life.

And then the cheetah flicked his tail and said, "If you want to take off practice tomorrow, I'm sure coach would understand."

Damn it. I didn't want Ma to be right about him, but it was right there in front of me. I'd like to think that part of me understood that it wasn't malicious, that Marquize wasn't trying to drag me down from being the best. In the moment, though, I'm not sure that was the case. In the moment I was angry, angry that he didn't understand that tennis was the most important thing, angry that Ma had been right, angry that that meant she was probably right about us breaking up. "I'm not going to skip practice," I said.

He must have heard it in my tone. His paw lifted from my stomach and hesitated. "I didn't mean anything," he said, but when I didn't answer he got up and crossed back to his bed. "You know," he went on as I stayed silent, "you don't have to be shitty about things. You could talk to me."

"Oh yeah?" I shot back. "What happened over Christmas?"

His ears flattened and his eyes narrowed. He got into bed without a word and rolled away from me.

It wasn't malicious, his comment. He really did want the best for me. But he also didn't understand that tennis was the way to that best. Grief, anger, love, joy: all of them fueled my play and my drive to improve. For Marquize, tennis was important because he was good at it, but he believed he had to hold back, that he couldn't give all of himself to it. I didn't want Ma to be right, but in this case she was. I never before or since have wished so hard that she was not.

Well… that's not true.

Chapter Ten

Marquize and I didn't stay too mad at each other; that is to say, we made up the next morning in the way teenage boy-friends do when they wake up unchaperoned with physical needs more immediate than the previous night's remote fight. By breakfast we were talking about tennis again and looking forward to the day of practice. But as real as those needs and the emotions that accompanied the meeting of them were, they only papered over the death of Raji and the arguments between us.

For my part, I couldn't dwell on Raji because I couldn't risk my tennis. When I thought about the lion, I felt helpless and angry; if I turned my thoughts to rescuing my sister, I played with determination and drive. It was a tough day, but I got through it, and the next day, and the next. Ma and I talked a little, but she wasn't around for my practices, and a lot of the time we did have together she was pushing me and Marquize to do our high school equivalency work.

I never told Marquize why I was so upset. He knew that someone we knew had died and left it at that. Regardless, he picked up on my motivation. Maybe it was the argument (minor though it seemed) or maybe it was that in May, we played in the tournament where I'd been invited to the main draw.

The difference was incredible. Instead of having to fight my way through four matches with other qualifiers, I started with just one win to get into the round of 16, which I got. Playing those matches fresh rather than after three to four days of strenuous play made a huge difference. I got to the finals again and once again lost, now realizing that I was fighting against another subgroup of the Futures tour.

If you've won a Futures but haven't moved up yet, everyone

hates playing you. I wasn't quite there, so I got a lot of sympathetic remarks about my opponents, like "I can't believe that guy hasn't won enough," and "Isn't it time for him to move up already?" and "If you beat him, you'll keep him in Futures another few months and he'll hate that." That was mostly a couple players that the others didn't like; then there was the guy I lost to this time, Chafon Dzin, a red panda who talked to the others mostly through an interpreter. None of us asked how he could afford a full-time interpreter, but rumors were that the Xiaqinese government had paid for the sleek, well-mannered fox. Maybe everyone liked the interpreter better than the player, but it was impossible to tell; Dzin always looked very polite and semi-apologetic, or else broadly smiling and enthusiastic, and his interpreter said things like "Dzin wishes to express the high esteem in which he holds Mr. N'Guwe and his hope for a well-played, excellent contest."

We played three sets, and it was obvious to me that even though I won one, Dzin was a little out of my league. Not vastly, not even more than maybe three to four months of practice away from me, judging by how far I'd progressed in the last three months. But enough that over three sets, he made a couple more shots and caught me guessing one time too many. Beating him would not be a simple matter of learning his tendencies. It would involve learning his tendencies and then playing better than him. It would involve hitting that forehand a few thousand more times, that cross-court a few thousand more times, learning with my muscles how each shot would fall and how to hit it.

It would involve conditioning so I would always know my muscles would respond exactly as I wanted them to. It would involve listening to Lochen and Coach Luka and studying tennis and players. But I knew I could do it, that I could get to Dzin's level.

Marquize probably could too, though it would take a lot more work. He seemed willing to put the work in, though, as we rolled into the summer tournaments. He wasn't getting to my level, but he was definitely doing better than he had been—twice he made it to the main draw, and in general he had a more upbeat attitude.

In early May, we ended up back at the tournament the two of

us had visited the previous year, the Pensa one in Cowford a couple hours from Palm Gables. Ma asked if I wanted to visit the school; I thought about it, but I didn't really know who was there anymore. I wouldn't mind seeing Coach Murphy, but was it worth a day out of my practice schedule? I asked Lochen and he said we could accommodate it if I wanted, which didn't answer my question until I thought about it more closely and realized that if he'd thought it was worthwhile, he would've been more enthusiastic.

I sent Coach Murphy an email and got a response the next day congratulating me on how well I was doing and saying that he'd like to come down but that he was very busy planning the tournament and the evaluations. So it was surprising when I walked out for my first match (in the main draw, playing one of the higher seeds) and heard cheers behind me, my name being called out by a few voices. It was another second before I parsed those voices into familiar memories and matched them to the arctic fox and cougar in the stands.

"Hey guys!" I hurried over to Dom and Bret, both grinning widely. We shook paws and they clapped me on opposite shoulders. "How are you doing?"

"Still in school." Bret stuck out his tongue. "But look at you! Main draw already."

"Challenger next year?" Dom asked.

"That's what my manager says." I flattened my ears, self-conscious. "But I have to win one of these things first. It's just you two here?"

"Yeah." Dom grinned. "Coach told us you were playing, and we decided to take a little school-sponsored break and come watch." He saw me looking around and went on. "Let's see. Kim and Brittany are playing in Juniors tournaments. Yu is too. None of them are doing as well as you are, though. And Pom quit to go to prep school for pre-med, I think? He wants to be a sports doctor. Who else?"

Bret shook his whiskers. "Wait, you remember Verid? The groundhog?"

"Bret." Dom's tone was warning.

The cougar ignored him, leaning in close. "He got arrested for sexual assault."

"He hasn't been convicted," Dom said, arms folded.

"He and a couple friends were out drinking with some bear chick and got her super-drunk and did stuff to her while she was drunk. And one of the guys was taking video on his phone."

"Jeezum," I murmured.

Dom tilted his head, and I realized I'd picked up that expression from the team here. Before either of us could say anything about it, though, Bret went on. "Oh, and speaking of sexual assault—"

The arctic fox elbowed Bret, cutting him off. "Come on," Dom said. "That's even less proven than the Verid one."

"What? Come on, guys, I need to go warm up." My opponent was already hitting serves into my court, waiting for me.

"All right, all right." Bret lowered his voice to a whisper. Dom shook his head. "Coach Frio quit a couple months ago. Right in the middle of the semester, real suddenly. Nobody knows why. Coach Kotten took over his students and all he'd tell them was that Frio had to take some time off. But one of the new kids, this wolverine, he claims Frio would watch him in the shower. So we think maybe he did something with one of the students, and Coach Murphy found out."

"That's complete speculation," Dom said.

"You were alone with him that summer." The cougar leaned in close to me. "Did anything happen?"

"Bret, don't be an ass." Dom saved me from having to lie. "Leave Rocky alone. He's got a match to play, and Frio is not a sexual predator."

"Okay, smart fox, then why did he leave?" Bret put his paws on his hips. "What could have happened that they didn't want to tell us about?"

"I don't know," Dom shot back. "Maybe he has cancer and wants to keep it private. Maybe his mom has cancer. Maybe he was stealing from the club or maybe he insulted Coach Murphy or something. Or maybe he just quit and didn't tell anyone why."

"Davis says—"

"Oh, Davis." Dom scoffed. "I don't know how he could notice anyone watching him in the shower when he's so busy admiring himself. You ever seen how long he takes?"

"All right." I'd recovered from Bret's direct question. "Hey, you guys around tonight? Want to get dinner with me and Marquize?"

"Yeah, sure!" Bret brightened.

Dom slapped my arm. "Go get 'im," he said.

Despite the memories of Frio that the conversation had called up, I stayed focused and won my match, so I was in pretty good spirits when we all got together that night. Marquize was as delighted to see Bret and Dom as I'd been, and we spent a great couple hours telling them about life on the tour. They didn't have much more news of Palm Gables, but when they repeated the news about Frio, Marquize stayed pretty quiet. I wondered if he was thinking about the same thing I was: that summer night by the clay courts. Had Frio moved on to a new student, gotten caught, and been told to resign?

We talked a little about it after, but apart from reassuring each other that neither of us had called Coach Murphy about Frio's behavior that summer, we couldn't come to any conclusions. But remembering the ferret blaming me for his advances, I felt a little satisfaction when I went to bed that night, hoping that maybe justice had prevailed in some fashion. And yet still, the memory of his weight on the side of my bed would not go away easily.

Chapter Eleven

We were in another small town, a college campus this time, early in June. There was no breeze and it was a sweltering 30 degrees out—85 in Fahrenheit—and I'd made it to the semifinal of the tournament. Marquize had won his qualifiers and then lost his first match in the main draw, but we were celebrating anyway because he'd felt good about his match.

("Celebrating" in this case meant simply a nice dinner out with him, me, Ma, and Paulie. Nothing fancy, not like when I made it to my first final, but a little more social than we usually did meals.)

My phone rang, and when I pulled it out, I saw Kamina's phone number. It had been so many months that for a moment I wondered, Why is Aunt Kamina calling me? Then I remembered, and dread and hope exploded in me. I stabbed at the phone, hurrying away from the table as I had the last time Ori had called me, months ago. "Hello?" I said, and it took ages and ages for the voice to come back. Would it be Kamina telling me sad news? Would it be Ori?

It was my sister. "Hi, Ro," she said, sounding tired.

"Ori." I sagged against the wall. "How are you?"

"I'm back. Finally."

"To stay?"

She hesitated, then said, "For a while, anyway."

"Tell me about it." It was so good to hear her voice that I wanted her to keep talking for hours.

She took a breath. "Kitemini Troixième is in a pretty area. The huts are sturdy and warm and you get used to the smell of the people after a while. It's very strong, but after a couple weeks mine was part of it and I didn't mind it so much. There are hills around and herds of wild hartebeest that they hunt, and there are sometimes elephants but I didn't see any."

"Wild?"

"And people elephants too. I didn't see either. The village is all jackals except for one hyena family. I talked to the daughter but still don't know why they're living in a jackal village. It doesn't seem to matter; everyone gets along and works together. There are little arguments all over but nobody picks on them for being hyenas. Well, except the army, I guess."

"The army?" I stiffened, my ears going back. "They were there?"

"For a month or two they were fighting to the south of us, between the village and the capital. The fighting never got into the village but the soldiers would come in for water and food about once a week and we had to serve them. They kind of respected Bompaka but even he deferred to them. I think he was afraid he would get shot."

"You weren't supposed to be anywhere near the war!"

"The war is everywhere." She exhaled. "We weren't even out of it at home, were we? Dad and all those friends of ours who went away."

"So," I said quickly to put off the time I would have to tell her about Raji, "what did you do with your days?"

"Oh, I cleaned clothes and helped wife number one prepare food. And when they found out I could read, they had me teaching the cubs. I don't know how much good I did. They didn't have any teacher before that and they didn't want to take them twenty-two kilometers to the nearest schoolhouse."

"Twenty-two kilometers?"

"Through at least two places where the road washes out whenever it rains. That happened too, by the way. I'm so glad to be home and have even Kamina's gross scent powder again. It smells much better than mud and dirt."

I didn't know how to ask the next thing I wanted to know, so I stumbled around it. "Did Bompaka…did you have to…"

"No. Not until I'm officially his bride. I worried about that too, but the custom is very strict. Although first wife told me that there have definitely been times when that custom was broken."

"Is that still maybe happening? You being married, I mean."

"Maybe. I don't know. He talked to Kamina and then said there would be less fighting in the area in three months when the rains started and that he would come back then. It's going to be a while longer and I don't really know if he liked me. The thing with teaching the cubs—I thought it was good but whenever he went by he would put his ears back and stare down at me. But he never stopped me. Maybe he doesn't want them learning to read and write, or maybe he's worried about which one of them will take over the village. I don't know. He only talked to me a little when I arrived, to introduce me to everyone, and then right before we left to tell me to get ready."

"So…" I paced back and forth along the sidewalk. "He didn't talk to you at all?"

"Number one talked to me more than anyone else. She said he already knows that he wants me; he wants to make sure I can contribute to the welfare of the village and that everyone will get along with me and that I won't cause trouble if I'm living there."

"Oh." I understood that, but it felt weird that someone was evaluating a person they wanted to marry based more on how they fit in with their other wife and their town than with how well they got along together. I followed that thought out: Bompaka wasn't looking for a companion. He was looking for someone to support his village and bear cubs, and he didn't have to get along with her for her to be good at that.

"And I think," she said as I was reaching that conclusion, "that he always meant me to be there for six months. After two weeks I started asking about going back, and number one said, 'He'll take you back when it's time.'"

My fist clenched. "That…"

"It's how things are done. He lies, Kamina lies—"

"What did Kamina lie about?"

"My age, a little. My interests. She told him I like to sew. He found out quickly that that wasn't true. I know how, and I guess that was enough."

I exhaled. "I don't like any of this, Ori. I wish it wasn't going to be another year before I can get you over here."

"I'll be fine, Ro." She paused. "Have you heard from…"

I closed my eyes. I didn't want to have to tell her. Please, I prayed, let the phone's connection drop, let me not have to finish this conversation.

"Raji?" Ori went on. "Or his sister?"

"Uh." I could say no. I could lie, if only, if only it wasn't Ori. "His sister called."

There was a long, long silence, so long that I thought that my wish to have the connection broken had perversely been granted too late, and then Ori said a very small, "Oh."

"I'm so sorry," I said. "Ori, I can't imagine…I know you were hoping…"

Her breath hissed across the phone. "I wasn't. Not really. It had been so long, and he would have gotten in touch. If…" Her voice hitched there.

I wanted more than anything to be there with her, to wrap my arms around her. As I was thinking about it, I wondered how different she was now. I'd changed since the last time I'd seen her, and she'd surely changed as well. We'd stayed close by talking on the phone, but there were still parts of each other's lives that we were missing.

My determination to reunite us didn't need any more fuel. "I'm here with you," I said, wrapping my free arm around myself and pressing the phone to my ear. When she didn't answer, I repeated, "I'm so sorry," just to have something to say. It wasn't enough and would never be.

"I know," she said. "You know, in a way, it's maybe a good thing."

"What?"

"Now I won't have anything to miss when I have to go to Kitemini Troixième."

"What about me? And Ma?"

"Oh, Bompaka promised to get phones to the village soon, or at least one satellite phone we can use. I'll still be able to talk to you." Her voice had dulled.

"You bet you will," I said. "And in a couple years, I'll come get you."

"Yes." With that word, a small flicker of life came back to her voice, and then it was gone. "I can't wait to see you again. Tell me about yourself, Ro."

So I told her about tennis and about the tournaments, how I was getting better slowly or quickly, depending on who you asked, and Lochen's thoughts on my future. I told her about my teammates and how my doubles game was getting so much better with Chris.

"And how's Marquize?" she asked.

"He's fine," I said. I hesitated. "He's doing really well, too."

"Good," she said. "I can't wait to meet him."

With Ori back in Lundara, I called her every week. I'd missed her terribly and it was reassuring to be able to hear her voice, to tell her about the secret things I couldn't even tell Ma. I unburdened myself about my worries about Marquize and my hopes for him, and Ori reassured me that I should believe the best in him. "And if it turns out he's not right for you, you'll know it."

"How?"

"Oh, Ro, I don't know. That's what they say in the movies."

"Real life isn't like the movies." I sighed.

"You're doing better now, though, right?"

I was. I had enough points to be ranked in the 500s, which meant that technically I could enter some Challenger events whenever I wanted. But Lochen wanted me to wait until I'd won a few Futures tournaments, because a few wins would boost my ranking (he wanted me to be in the 400s at least), my confidence, and my endorsements.

My first endorsement came in that May, from an athletic gear company called Purrformance. They had a lot of cat spokespeople and wanted to get some canids as well, so they were targeting younger players in various sports, and Lochen brokered a deal for me. The way it worked was they provided me with free shirts to wear (mostly white, one red) with the Purrformance logo on them, and they paid me $50 per match I wore a shirt in. That doesn't sound like a lot, but it meant that over a three-tournament set, I could make $500 or so if I did well. Lochen told me that when I won a tournament, I could nudge that up to $70 a match, and when I moved up to Challenger it could go over $100.

Of course, when I "made" $500 over a month of tournaments,

Lochen got $100 of that and Ma took the rest, for expenses and (I hoped) saving up for Ori to come back. And Ma was busy on that score, too, talking to local media during the tournaments. I did an interview during the Pensa tournament because Palm Gables was close, but by the time July rolled around, it was standard for me to talk to one or two local news or TV stations. Depending on where we were, sometimes the interviews only showed up on sports blogs; once a cape fox with brightly dyed magenta fur interviewed me as part of a feature on African athletes in the States.

In July we landed in a small town called Benford in the north, where you wouldn't expect it to be as hot and humid as it was. Three lakes shimmered around the airport as we flew in, and we were told that there were a dozen more outside the town limits. Mosquitoes and other insects buzzed around our ears constantly, so that Chris and I complained by the end of the first day's practice that our ears were more tired from flicking them away than our legs were from running.

But we went out for the tournament with the same energy we always had. Coach Luka and Lochen kept us well hydrated and changed up our meals a bit so that we'd have good energy, and it showed. Chris and I won our first doubles match in straight sets, and I went out and won singles that afternoon. I was ranked fourth, tied for the highest I'd been ranked going into a tournament, so I was facing lower-ranked players (with higher seeding numbers) in the early rounds. So far, I hadn't lost to a lower-ranked player.

I won, and Chris won, and we won together. Then he lost to the second-seeded player, but our doubles kept on going. In the semifinal, we beat a team we'd lost to a month ago to make it to our first final.

In the meantime, I'd also gotten to the semifinals of the singles, where I faced the #1 seeded player, an elk in his early 30s who, like Nashan, was giving it one last go-round before retiring. He'd played in majors—never won—and in the locker room he captivated us younger players with stories of the fancy locker rooms, the attendants, and the personalities of the different players on the tour. Most, he told us, understood that we were all part of a community and kept a level of courtesy toward each other. Some remained stiff and aloof. A few took deliberately eccentric turns: swigging bottles of liquor in their locker before and after matches, or offering to fix up other players with female companionship, or singing loudly in their native language, or marching through the locker room nude offering to compare their penises to anyone who'd take them up on it (that, he said, was only one player, but he wouldn't name which one). Some of it might be genuine, some of it might be to psych out the opposition, but he told us that the only guaranteed result was that the other players didn't like the "weirdos," as he put it.

I wanted to ask him about gay players on the Champions tour, because it seemed like there it would be easier for them to be out, but I also couldn't think of a way to do that without giving myself away. So I settled for going out and playing my best, and I beat him in straight sets. At the net, he said, "What are you still doing in Futures?" and I mumbled something about my manager and wanting to establish myself. "You're established," he said. "Now get the fuck up to Challenger so I can maybe win a few more of these."

Of course, the final was the next day and I hadn't won anything yet, but my opponent in the final was a red squirrel who hadn't been ranked. He'd beaten the second seed, the guy who beat Chris, and then beat Paulie, who like me had been invited to the main draw. He was seventeen, my age, and in the writeup Ma showed me after the match, the reporter covering the tournament called us "the future of States tennis."

(I would run into the squirrel again in the Challenger series the following year, but he never won a tournament there.)

He played fast and smart, like red lightning zipping around the ball, and his shots burst off the court like mortar rounds. But he was too hyper, and though he was very good, he had a tendency to go for big shots. If I pinned him into his backhand corner, he'd get frustrated and eventually go for a risky shot. He hit a winner on some of those, but he'd miss three for every one he made.

On match point, at 5-4 in the second set, I served down the T when I thought he'd be looking for a serve out wide. I caught him guessing and his return floated long.

It didn't sink in right away that I'd won. The game, the set, sure. The match, a heartbeat later (the announcement of "Game, Set, and Match to Rocky N'Guwe" helped). And the cheers from the crowd, larger than any other match I'd won, let me know that I'd won the tournament. I mean, I knew it, of course. I knew that this was the final and that I'd won the match. But I was so focused on the game that the knowledge that there were no more matches, that I'd won the tournament, that I'd *won a tournament*, rolled over me in waves as I dropped my racket and raised my paws. And the next thing I remembered was that I had to go shake paws at the net. "You got a lot of good matches ahead of you," I told the squirrel.

"You too," he said.

I hadn't lost a set the entire tournament. The next day, Chris and I won the doubles and only lost one set along the way. "This is getting familiar," the tournament organizer joked with me as we stood up to receive our trophy and checks. "Great tournament."

"Thanks," I said. Though I'd never been in a trophy presentation in a real tournament before that weekend, I knew how to respond, how to be polite, and what to say if they offered me the microphone (they did not). Inside, though, I was buzzing. I grabbed Chris's paw and he grabbed mine back; it was his first win as well. We lifted our paws together in the air, then went and lifted the trophy.

Only a hundred or so people filled the bleachers, but they clapped like a thousand. Here was my affirmation, my confidence, my assurance that I could get to the next level. I could bring Ori home, and more importantly, I could be a champion.

I called Ori from the locker room to tell her the news, so giddy I flipped between Kikongo and English without realizing it. She laughed and told me I was the best, and that one day she'd be watching me win a real tournament. The phone call went so quickly that I only realized after I hung up that I hadn't asked her anything about her own life.

That night, Ma, Paulie, Marquize and I all went out, and Lochen joined us for a while. He said it was his tradition to buy a player a drink when he won his first tournament, but seeing as how all his players were underage when they won their first tournament, he generally made that drink a wheatgrass shot. It was one of the worst things I've ever tasted, but I gulped it and then everyone laughed at my disgusted face as I grabbed for the club soda to wash it down.

Lochen didn't stay long, but he toasted me before he left, saying, "To the future of States tennis!" with his accent that made me giggle. And when the red fox took off, the rest of us replayed the tournament, especially the final match. Chris and I made sure to give Paulie props as well—he'd made it pretty far—and not to leave out Marquize, because the cheetah was making it into the main draw consistently now. "See?" I said. "All we needed was a little time to settle in."

"It took me about six months to get my feet under me," Paulie said. "You guys are right on track. Except, you know, when Rocky got his feet under him…whoosh!" He sailed his paw up into the air.

"You're doing very well too," Ma said.

I thought she was talking to Paulie, but her muzzle was tilted and it was Marquize who answered. "I felt better the last few tournaments. It's starting to all come together now."

"Hard work pays off," Ma said. "Listening to your coaches."

"For sure." Paulie toasted her. "Rocky's lucky to have you around. Wish my mom could be on tour with us, but then who would my sisters complain to all day?"

There Marquize stayed silent, and so I figured I should say something to get the conversation off of parents. "I really feel like the team is a second family now. And Marquize is my oldest friend. All of you are important."

"I'll drink to that," Marquize said, and for the rest of the evening, everything was upbeat, smiles and wags.

Of the next four tournaments, I made it to three finals and won twice. I now had enough ranking points to join the Challenger circuit, but Lochen wanted me to stick around for another few months. "I'll be honest, I'd like to keep you through the end of the year. You or your Ma might believe that getting out there four months earlier will be best for you, and there's an argument to be made for that. But here's my argument: you're just starting to catch people's attention. If you stick with me for a few months, I can get you a good endorsement deal, and if you let me do that, I'll stay on as your agent."

"My agent?" I was panting hard, having just finished up a practice with Coach Luka (also because it was August and stiflingly warm).

"Sure." The rolling 'r' didn't distract me much anymore, except when he drew it out like he did here. "I'm the agent for half a dozen of my former players. I don't offer that to everyone, only the ones I think I can make a lot of money for."

"Well…"

"You think about it." He patted my shoulder. "You can think of these four months as a test run if you like. If I don't get you a major endorsement by the end of the year, go find a new agent and go on to Challenger with my blessing."

"All right. That sounds reasonable," I said. "I'll have to talk it over with Ma, though."

"Of course." And the fox let me go clean up.

Ma, because she was Ma, said she was going to investigate some other agents, but that Lochen had been pretty good for me and she didn't object to keeping him on as my agent. As for staying on the Futures tour, it wasn't as much money as the Challenger tour, but the tradeoff of getting more money from endorsements was an enticing risk.

In the meantime, I still had my Purrformance money, and Lochen brought me in on a call with them where we talked about upping my pay now that I was regularly appearing in finals. The rep was very nice but even though Lochen brought up the international angle, he didn't budge on the pay scale. "We just don't do a lot of business over in Africa," he said, "as impressive as it is that Mr. N'Guwe has risen to this level here."

"Never mind," Lochen said when he hung up. "They'll raise it when you move to Challenger. But that international angle is going to work sooner rather than later. I'm looking at some of the clothing companies that do sell in Africa. In the meantime it wouldn't hurt you to mention your home a little more in interviews. I notice that when reporters bring it up, you shy away from it."

Lochen didn't know a whole lot about what was going on in my home country; he and the other guys knew that my sister was still over there, but that was about it. They didn't know about marriages and wars and any of the other things I thought about every time I mentioned Lunda. "I'll try," I said.

"But not in a political way," he told me. "Talk about how important it is for you to remember where you came from, how much you love your home country and your adopted home. The whole 'adopted home' thing plays well. So over the next few weeks we'll practice some things you can say in tournaments, okay?"

"Okay." And practice we did. I had a little time with Lochen a couple times a week to get over my discomfort in talking about my homeland and for him to help me shape the comments I'd make. We had already gone over the generic things to say when interviewed after winning a tournament, so this was on top of that.

I took to it quickly, mostly thanks to Ma. She kept our high school lessons up, preparing me for the test to receive a diploma equivalent (the test was called the GED), which she planned for me to take once I turned eighteen. Marquize took the lessons too, mostly because it was something he could do with me. When Ma wasn't around, he said it was a waste of time. "We're athletes," he said. "What matters is what we do on the court. Even if we don't get the huge payday, we're going to be coaches or something. Don't need to be a high school graduate for that."

"But you have to get an education," I argued.

"No," he said, and poked me in the chest. "*You* have to get an education."

Still, he studied with me and took the tests and appeared to be working hard on it. And as I began to get more interviews at the end of tournaments, once or twice journalists told me that I was more articulate than most of the cubs they talked to. So I guess Ma's education was paying off in ways like that.

They were receptive when I talked about Lunda, too. Most of them didn't know much about it, but few of them asked me followup questions. I learned to have stock answers prepared: I grew up in Lundara, very happy childhood, lost my father to the wars, my mother took care of me, I hoped to bring my sister over to join me one day. This last one I insisted on including because Ma had said I would need to be famous to help Ori be admitted to the States, and I figured the sooner people knew about her, the better. Lochen wasn't convinced but also didn't see how it would hurt.

In October, Lochen set up a meeting with One Two Three, a firm with an international presence that made rackets and other tennis equipment. On a conference call with Lochen, me, and Ma, they asked about my off-court life, about how soon I would be on the Challenger circuit, and about my availability to do publicity work for them. It sounded like they could work around my schedule, and at the end of the call the rep said, "We'll be in touch."

Lochen said that meant that they would go back and make a decision and let him know. But he sounded hopeful, and he said he'd worked with the One Two Three people before and if they weren't interested they wouldn't have even taken the call.

"This could be it," I told Ma. "The money they were talking about, thousands of dollars…that would bring Ori over here, right?"

"It could happen next year." She smiled and put an arm around my shoulders. "Go ahead and call her."

"Yeah!" Ori hadn't been there the last time I'd called, and I was overjoyed to have really good news to tell her.

So I called, and Kamina answered again. "She's not here, Rochi," she said, a snappish edge to her voice.

"Well, tell her to call me, okay? It's been a week."

"Yes, yes," she said. "Is that all?"

"That's…all."

But I was suspicious, and I said as much to Ma. "I'm sure Ori is all right," she said.

Although I believed Ma, I still wanted to hear my sister's voice. Practices were all right; Coach Luka had helped me improve my concentration so that emotional issues didn't bother me quite so much, so my play wasn't suffering. I was proud of that, at least.

I tried to talk to Marquize at night, when we were lying together in my bed, but he didn't really understand what the problem was. "Your sister has a life, too. She's been away when you called before."

"Yeah, but Kamina sounded…weird. And she didn't ask me to

leave a message. She always asks that. Usually, I mean."

"Your sister's fine." He pressed up closer to me.

I wasn't yet good enough at boyfriend stuff to do that when I was worried about something. So Marquize got annoyed at me and went to sleep while I lay awake. Finally I figured it would be morning in Lundara, so I went out into the hallway and called again.

"She's not here, Rochi," Kamina said, and hung up without even saying anything else.

"Ma," I said the next morning over breakfast, "I called again and Kamina hung up on me."

She finished the bite of her scrambled eggs and wiped her mouth. "I'll look into it."

And those simple words made me feel a whole lot better.

The good feelings didn't last long. After a couple days I asked Ma if she'd heard anything and she said she'd tell me when she did. So I threw myself into tennis again, except for the time I spent with Marquize. And even that was tougher than it usually was. Marquize was working hard at tennis and so he didn't have a lot of energy left after practices. Besides that, my string of getting to finals was a sore point between us for a couple reasons.

First of all, there was the obvious point that Marquize was not getting to finals. At his current rate of improvement, he said gloomily one night, he would get to my level in about three years. I told him it wasn't like that, that at some point a switch would flip and he would start seeing the court better. But he didn't find that reassuring.

The other point was that I was going to be leaving for the Challenger circuit. Different tournaments, different cities, and we wouldn't be living or practicing together anymore. The prospect felt exciting and scary for me: it would be the first time I'd be entering a tennis world without Marquize. I tried to tell him how much it scared me several times, but every time he changed the subject. Fine, I thought, if he didn't want to talk about it, we wouldn't talk about it.

Chapter Twelve

We didn't dress up for Halloween, but here and there we saw bands of cubs dressed in superhero and monster costumes. We kept practicing even though there was only one tournament between Halloween and Thanksgiving. I put thoughts of Ori aside and brought all my skill to the court. By this point, there were only a few players who gave me any trouble, and we more or less knew each other. I won a three-set final against Dzin and got a cheerful smile and a firm shake of the paw after the match. In the locker room, his interpreter told me that he was going to the Challenger circuit next year, and I said I would see him there. The fox repeated my comment, listened for the answer, and inclined his head to me. "Dzin is very much looking forward to renewing your acquaintance and rivalry there."

"Me too," I said honestly, and as I shook his paw again I wondered what Yu was doing these days.

Marquize, Ma, and Paulie took me out for dinner as had become our custom. "Not too many of these tournaments left," Paulie said with a big coyote smile.

"One in December." I crossed my fingers. "If I play it. Lochen said if One Two Three comes back before Thanksgiving with an offer, I shouldn't."

"How long has it been with them?"

"Two weeks since the last phone call." I tried not to show my nervousness. "We had two other companies interview but they both came back with offers that Lochen didn't want to take."

"It's because he's a jackal," Ma said to Paulie.

"Ma."

"It is. If you were a fox, there would be no problem. Or a coyote."

She nodded to Paulie.

"They don't care about that," I said weakly, more because I didn't want to believe it than because I really didn't.

"Hmph," Ma said, and Marquize cleared his throat and said something about a movie he wanted to see.

* * *

Most of the team went home for Thanksgiving on the Monday of that week. Lochen booked an extended stay hotel room for me, Ma, and Marquize that had a little kitchen, a bedroom, and a comfortable sofa that Marquize and I took turns sleeping in. It also had a whole bunch of cable channels, which we didn't often get to enjoy, so we watched a lot of movies that week. Ma insisted on mixing in some "educational" movies with the fun ones—adaptations of books we'd read, like "The Grapes of Wrath," and other classics like "Les Miserables." Then we were allowed to watch our science fiction and action movies.

I'd sat down with Lochen and registered for the first Challenger tournaments of 2012. The process was the same as for the Futures tournaments, but the venues were different. I pictured the same small arenas I'd been playing in, but Lochen said some of them were much larger. "Not the size of the majors, of course, but pretty big still."

That skewed the picture in my mind. "Who will I stay with?"

"Your mother, probably. We'll work on getting you a coach, too, because Luka's going to stay with this team."

"Oh. Can't he come and see me one week a month or something?"

The fox turned to me. "Rocky," he said, "you're moving on. Don't worry, I'll help you find a new coach."

"I hope so. Last time Ma didn't like any of the coaches we interviewed."

"We'll be interviewing better coaches this time." He smiled. "Once One Two Three comes in, you'll have money to offer them. And I have another offer in the works, smaller than that one but they're already interested in you. They came to talk to me."

"Who is it?"

"Sport drink company, ah…" We were in his office, me leaning over his desk to see his laptop, and he pulled out a drawer and found a business card.

"Bolt?"

"No, no." He laughed. "When you win a couple majors, Bolt might come calling. No, this one is, well, the company is Gervitz Foods, but the drink they make and that they want you to endorse is Forge."

"I don't think I've ever had it."

"You will. It's sweet but okay. They're all the same anyway."

I took the business card and looked at it, then up at him. "I'm probably not supposed to say that."

He laughed. I thought it was a good sign that he was usually in a good mood when he was talking about my future and my endorsements. "No, you'll have to practice saying how great it is."

I left his office and even though practice was over for the day, I grabbed my racket and a bag of balls and went out to the court. Nobody else was around, so I served the whole bag out, aiming for various spots on the court, then walked around and collected them and did it again from the other side of the court. Slice out wide, flat down the T, slice into the body, kick down the T. I let all the worries about endorsements and new venues fade away into a repetitive rhythm of movement and practice.

By the end of that, I felt a lot better, and so when I started getting stressed over Thanksgiving weekend and Marquize wasn't helping, I went back out to the practice court and served over and over again.

Another of the problems Marquize and I were having was that he'd turned eighteen a month or so ago. We'd had a birthday party for him, and afterwards he and I had gotten some time alone, but we hadn't done anything. We weren't sure how things changed now that he was completely legal and I was still technically a minor; it might vary from one state to another, and although he trusted me and I trusted him, we were worried that if someone found out, he could be arrested. So we stayed clothed, we hugged and kissed, and counted down the days to my eighteenth birthday.

On December 13th, two days after the last tournament of the

year ended, we came back from practice and found Ma in our room packing her suitcase. "What's going on?" I asked.

She threw a few more clothes into the suitcase and closed it, then turned and came to stand next to me, reaching up to put her paws on my shoulders. "Rochi," she said, "Ori has been married to Bompaka. I have been talking to Kamina and there is very little I can do about it from here."

"From here?" I glanced at Marquize and then back at the suitcase. "I thought we were going to wait until I have enough money to bring her over."

"We were." She exhaled and lifted her nose to mine. "Ori told me something of the village and its location, and how many times she heard fighting while she was there. I fear it will be a year before you can bring her over, and I'm worried about her. The threat of war, the threat of having a cub in those conditions…"

"So…you're leaving?"

She kissed my nose. "There is no more I can do for you here. I am leaving you and Marquize the instructions to register for your GEDs." Here she looked at the cheetah. "I am charging each of you to make sure the other passes those tests in the next year."

"Yes, ma'am," Marquize said, shifting uncomfortably.

"And I will go back to Lunda and see what I may do about things from there." Ma touched the side of my muzzle. "I am very proud of you, Ro. Do not stop working, and you can accomplish anything."

My throat tightened. "Ma," I said, and then couldn't get out any more.

She saw what I meant, and smiled. "I'll always love you. Now, I've someone coming in two hours to buy the car."

"Big Blue?"

"And they will take me to the airport. I'm going to fly to DeLeon and try to get a standby ticket to Lunda as soon as possible. I will call you when I can."

"Today?" My voice got a little squeaky.

"I did not want you to be distracted during the tournament. Don't worry. I'll find Ori and keep her safe in Lunda until you can bring us both home. I promise. Don't worry about her or about me."

She smiled again, a tight smile, and even though I didn't know how I was going to be able to help worrying, I said, "Sure. Okay."

We sat and talked for the last two hours, with Marquize for some of it and without him after he left to give us some private time. There wasn't much Ma wanted to leave me with in the way of instruction for tennis or life. "You're growing into a wonderful jackal," she said. "Remember the things I've taught you."

"I will."

"And the things others have taught you."

"I'll remember everything," I told her. "And Marquize will too. I'll keep working on him."

"I think things will work out with him," she said, and though I wasn't quite convinced she was being sincere, I nodded and accepted the words as she wanted me to.

I asked her what had happened with Kamina, what was supposed to have happened, what had changed, but she only said that the war was closer than she'd thought. There was something else going on, though, something with Kamina, because Ma was usually very good at hiding her emotions, and when she talked about Kamina, her ears tensed like she wanted to flatten them but was restraining herself.

And finally we walked downstairs, where Marquize joined us as we met an old field mouse who gave Ma's car a look over and then nodded, satisfied. They exchanged a title paper for a stack of cash and then Ma put her suitcase into the back. She turned and gave Mar a hug, which surprised both me and him: his whiskers fluffed out and his tail lashed, and then he hugged her back.

Then it was my turn. I held her tight, and she held me, and she kissed my neck and said, "You can do whatever you set your mind to," in a low voice by my ear.

"I'll see you very soon," I said. "Love you."

"Love you too, Ro." And she kissed me, and then stepped back and waved. A moment later she was in the car, and Marquize and I waved as the mouse drove off toward the airport.

"Hey," Marquize said, putting an arm around my shoulder, "it'll be okay."

I leaned into him. "I know," I said. "I just wish it was okay *now*."

Chapter Thirteen

With Ma gone, it was even harder for Marquize and I to restrain ourselves around each other, and in the middle of December we did in fact, um, give in once. Panting afterwards, he nuzzled me and said, "We shouldn't do this again."

"No," I said, knowing we probably would.

But even though there were no more tournaments until January, there was plenty to do. Lochen helped me prepare for my Challenger tournaments, setting up accommodations with his hotel connections and sometimes with other players he knew. When I got invited to the main draw, he told me, most Challenger tournaments would pay for my accommodations, but I had a while to go until then. And he and Coach Luka coached me privately, trying to convey the kind of competition I'd face once I got to the new tournaments. They wanted to find me a few practice partners, but hadn't been able to secure anyone yet.

Late in December, the draw for my first tournament was published. I scanned the names, feeling like I was entering a foreign country; I'd become familiar with the core players in the Futures tournaments, but none of those were playing in this one. I was back in the qualifying draw with thirty or so anonymous players in the mid hundreds rankings, along with Dzin in another qualifying bracket. But wait—there, seeded number three in this tournament, was "B. Longacre."

It was worth a shot, I supposed. I went back to my computer and searched back through my e-mails for the last one from Braden. Had it really been a year or more since I'd e-mailed him?

Braden,
Hope all is well with you. Last year I joined a team and have won

a few Futures tournaments, so my manager is moving me to Challenger tournaments. I'm going to be playing at San Marcos in January and I saw you're going to be there too. Third seed, that's awesome. Anyway, because I'm new to the tour I don't have a practice partner.

I stopped there. "Would you be my partner?" sounded way too young-kid, in a way I was only starting to be aware of. I wanted to ask someone how to phrase it better, but Ma was gone, Marquize would not want to help me approach Braden, and I'd never told Lochen that I knew Braden. I felt weird bringing it up now, like he would think because I'd never told him about it that I was making it up or something. It doesn't make a lot of sense, looking back, but I was seventeen and already hiding a huge secret about my relationship, so my default was to keep secrets.

I guess I could've asked Coach Murphy, but I didn't really think of that at the time. I hadn't talked to him in over a year either. Later, he would get in touch with me again, and we would grow a good friendship, but at the time I wasn't in a position to do anything good for the school, and he was in the middle of a bunch of trouble that I didn't know anything about.

So I left that sentence hanging there and finished up the email.

Maybe I'll see you in the locker room. Merry Christmas!

Rocky

Braden has teased me about that e-mail more than once since then, especially when I'm going to a tournament for the first time. "Hey, you've never been to Salmandas before. Do you have a practice partner?" I cringe a bit when I think about the email, but I also laugh because given the way everything worked out, I'm really glad I sent it.

* * *

Christmas, in comparison to recent years, felt grey and dreary, and it wasn't just because we woke up Christmas morning in a garage next to Lochen's house on a day when the sky was the color of cigarette smoke and the air was cold and wet. Lochen had invited us to his house partly because we had nowhere else to go and partly because he told us he wouldn't pay for our hotel over the last two weeks of the year. His wife, a well-rounded vixen named Marta who sold real estate, remained polite as long as we were in the room, and made sure we got plenty to eat (she loved to bake, and there was never a shortage of fresh cookies, though Lochen reminded us to stay in shape). But when we were out of the room, my ears sometimes caught her complaints. "I get to see you a few times a year and I was hoping we'd have some time alone." Or, "I wanted to take an overnight to see the tree lighting at Plainsfield but I don't want to leave your guests in the house alone."

I never heard Lochen's replies. A couple times guilt drove us to say that we could afford a hotel over Christmas itself, that we didn't want to intrude, but Marta wouldn't hear of it. And Lochen reminded me that we had been promised an answer from One Two Three before Christmas.

That call came on the very last business day before Christmas, when the four of us happened to be sitting in Lochen's living room watching the year-end Masters tournament on TV. We had already gone through the obligatory-feeling "you two will be in there one day" from both Lochen and Marta, and then in the middle of one of the matches, Lochen's phone rang.

He picked it up and gestured me into the study right away. I hurried in and he closed the door behind us. "I'm here with Mr. N'Guwe," Lochen said. "I'll put you on speaker."

He set his cell phone down and tapped it, and the room filled with a crackly hiss. "Hello?" a high male voice said with a southern drawl.

"We're here." Lochen nodded his muzzle at me encouragingly.

"Hi." I cleared my throat. "I'm Rocky."

"Martin Gedekker," the voice said. "I'll cut to the chase, since I've got a dinner waiting for me at home and I still have to do some shopping, and sure y'all are in the same boat. Been crazy this year. I'm sorry to keep y'all waiting, but getting everyone in the same room has been like herding sparrows. We finally got sign off from the big guy this morning to do what we've been wanting to do for about a month now. We'd like to bring on Rocky N'Guwe as a client."

I'd guessed this was coming from the beginning of the phone

call, but I felt a warm flush like I'd won a tournament. "That's great to hear," Lochen said, his voice calmer than the huge smile he flashed me. "Rocky's very excited to work with One Two Three, aren't you?"

"Oh, uh, yeah," I said. "Very excited. Thanks very much." I tried to take my cue from Lochen, to be cooler in my words than I felt, and then I realized that I should've thanked the guy by name and that I'd already forgotten the name he'd given us. My eyes widened.

Lochen picked up quickly. "Mr. Gedekker," he said, and I stored the name in my head, repeating it to myself, "can you send over the contracts today or does it have to wait until 2012?"

"No, we can do it today. Well, I can email the particulars. We'll have to courier over the actual documents but you'll want to take a look at them first, I imagine."

"Sounds good. I'll wait for that e-mail. Go on and get home to your dinner."

"Thanks, Mr. Gedekker," I added. "Merry Christmas."

"Merry Christmas, you two."

When he'd hung up, Lochen's smile got bigger. "There you go," he said. "We'll look at the details, but I am guessing it's going to be about twice what you were getting from Purrformance, and that's going to go up as you get on the Challenger circuit too. Free rackets, I should imagine, and possibly strings, so that's more money saved. You'll be earning enough to bring your sister home next year."

I tried to imagine that, Ma and Ori getting off a plane and meeting me, and my chest got tight and warm and my throat closed up. "Thank you," I choked out, and had to wipe my eyes, and then it seemed better if I kept my paw there.

Lochen reached for a box of tissues and held it out to me. "Take as many as you need," he said, sounding amused and a little concerned.

"I'm fine," I sniffled, and grabbed a pawful of tissues to press to my eyes. "It's...it's the best Christmas present I've ever gotten."

"Ah, son," Lochen said. He splayed his ears and looked away. "Just doing my job. If, you know, you still want it to be my job."

"Yeah, of course." I laughed through the tears. He hadn't mentioned it to me, but Paulie had told me that he kept close track of how much he spent on each player and that if we left his agency, he'd politely present us with an invoice. At the time I had thought that sounded shady, but now I didn't care; he'd get paid back and then some. And Paulie had also told me, somewhat jealously, that Lochen hadn't remained the agent for most of the players on his team—two over the last five years. "Can you keep booking my hotels?"

"Sure. And some other stuff too. We can talk about it. I'll keep taking my fifteen percent and you're going to keep winning tournaments."

I wiped my nose and then my eyes again and sort of composed myself. "Sounds good."

"And if you want, I can start looking into the paperwork to get your sister back."

"Oh, would you really? I can pay you extra…"

He held up a paw and grinned, his tail swishing. "Let's see how much work it is. We can talk about it if it comes to that. But I'm pleased to do it. The less you have to worry about, the better you'll play, so it's worth it to me. And the other thing we're going to have to do is find you a coach. I have a few candidates in mind, so come January we'll interview them and see which ones you get along with best."

"Yeah." That made me think of Ma and the last time we'd interviewed coaches. I'd been so naïve then, I'd had no idea what to ask about or what to look for.

"But for now, all you have to do is send the One Two Three people your size and go enjoy Christmas."

"Thanks. I'm sorry I keep saying that, but I mean it."

He smiled and reached out to shake my paw. "I hope we're a good team for a while. Let's go see how that match turns out."

* * *

It wasn't until December twenty-third that I got a reply from Braden.

Rocky,

I know a couple people at your level. I'll pass your info along.

Welcome to Challengers. Merry Christmas.

Braden

It wasn't a lot, but it made my tail wag. Marquize, nearby, said,

"Good email?"

"Yeah," I said, and closed the laptop. He was just looking at stuff on his computer, so I hopped over to his bed and pounced him.

"Hey!" He laughed and pushed his computer aside. "Careful."

"Nobody's watching," I said. "I'm not going to be careful."

My tail wagged harder, and soon he smiled and kissed me. That it was Christmas again reminded me of Marquize's last Christmas, and I felt that whatever happened must have something to do with why he hadn't gone home for Christmas this year. But he didn't volunteer and I didn't ask. And at this moment, I was content that it would be just me and him.

Part Six: Main Draw (2012)

Interlude (2015)

That's a terrific passing shot from N'Guwe, and he's just one point from getting back on serve in the fourth."

"I have to admit, I thought this match was going to be over in four, but after a shaky start, N'Guwe has raised his level, and Longacre doesn't have an answer for him right now. As technically proficient as the fox is, the jackal is doing some creative things out there, just enough to keep him off balance."

"Alastair, you said before that you don't think N'Guwe is better than Longacre. Would you say after the last few games that he's nearly as good?"

"That's an interesting question. Over these few games, yes, for sure he's almost as good. But tennis isn't about how good you are at your peak. It's about how long you can sustain that. We saw in this very tournament, you remember Daric upsetting Yashimoto, how someone can have a great day and beat a better player having a not-so-good day. N'Guwe at his best probably is not as good as Longacre at his best, but these last few games, Rocky has been playing his best tennis, and Braden has not. Will it stay this way for the rest of the match?"

"Longacre to serve here."

"I guess we'll see."

"First serve is long."

"N'Guwe was fooled on that. He won't be fooled on this one, I'm pretty sure."

"Second serve."

"And Braden saves a break point with a great approach to net."

"N'Guwe was lining up the cross-court passing shot, but Longacre read it correctly and put it away."

"One break point saved. Longacre comes around to serve at 30-40, and he's taking his time."

"A little bit of mind games there from the fox. He's done that in previous matches, mostly when he's in tough spots like this one."

"And Longacre gets it to deuce! Excellent defense from N'Guwe, but he never recovered after that big serve."

"N'Guwe really did a valiant job there. Not much you can do with a first serve like that, but what there was to do, he did it."

"It's not over yet. He's got deuce and he can still get the break, but the momentum has swung back to Longacre."

* * *

There's a familiar feeling with Braden, when you think you've got him pinned down and then he manages to slip his way out of it. It's happened with our tennis matches often enough, though usually the matches are practice and I feel like he's letting me stay close and then he pulls away to win at the last second. Not this time. This time he was doing his best and I was matching him shot for shot, until that 15-40 point where he willed himself into another gear. Then a great serve, and a long rally where he pulled me all around the court. He can usually get himself out of trouble—when he gets into it.

I crouch down and wait for his serve. He stands looking at me, trying to guess what I'm thinking. And then, giving no clue what he himself is thinking, he tosses the ball into the air and serves.

It goes wide and I'm ready for it. I send a backhand down the line, and Braden steps around to strike it with his forehand. He sends it back to my backhand, which is up to the task. He returns steadily and I try to work myself around to the forehand without exposing too much of the court. He pins me to my backhand very well, so I start angling my shots farther along the court, trying to get him beyond the baseline so I can come up to net. And then one of my shots clips the net cord, pops straight up.

Braden's racing for it almost before the sound reaches our ears. But the ball hovers in the air, he's not going to get there in time, and it comes down and bounces on the court, once, twice, and then rolls back toward me. On my side.

The fox pulls up, meets my eye, and gives a tiny shrug. Them's the bounces.

It was a good shot, I think. It might've given me the advantage. But I can't focus on that. I've got to move on to the next point.

I guess I'm still a little bit rattled, because my return of Braden's first serve sails past him and lands a foot long. His game. He's up 5-2 and now if I want to stay in this match, I have to do something I've never done.

I have to win three straight games from Braden Longacre.

* * *

"I was thinking, Daren, about Longacre's first win. Remember, at the Ozzie in 2013."

"Of course. He's improved quite a bit since then."

"Yes, but what I was thinking was that his run there has quite a bit in common with N'Guwe's run to the final here. Longacre benefited from upsets in his bracket, beat one player ranked ahead of him, and went toe to toe with the world number one in the final."

"So you think N'Guwe has a chance here?"

"Not much of one now. He's down to one chance left to break Longacre, and the fox has got two chances to add to his lead. But I'll tell you, I've watched N'Guwe in several matches this year, and I've made the mistake of counting him out before, so I'm not going to do that again. This jackal has pulled himself out of some narrow spots."

"He's taking a lot of water on the changeover and looks very much at ease. If I didn't know, Alastair, I wouldn't say he was one game from losing the States Open Final."

"And that's what I mean. I spoke with him after the Deleon Open a few months ago, where he was runner-up to Dubois. But the match went three sets, and Dubois was up a set and a break in the second. Rocky came back and won that set and nearly won the third. And of course, here he defeated Dubois in the semifinal, so obviously he's learned something."

"And he's played Braden before."

"As I mentioned, they're very close friends. They practice together often, dine out together, so certainly they know each other. But they've only played in a tournament five times, and Braden's won all five, though some wins were easier than others."

"Do you think in cases like that that Longacre is hurting his chances in matches like this by allowing a challenger to get so close to him? To get to know his style that well?"

"It's hard to say, Daren. I'm sure he didn't expect to be playing Rocky in a final until next year, and perhaps he'd planned to put some distance between them by then. Or he might be so confident in his abilities that he doesn't see anyone as a threat."

"That would fit his personality."

"Indeed. Of course I think it's obvious that N'Guwe is putting up more of a fight than he'd anticipated. You have to remember, too, that as well as Rocky knows Braden, Braden knows Rocky too."

"They're taking the court again. Let's see if the jackal can give this crowd the fifth set they want."

"I think they'd be happy with a Longacre win, too."

"History in the making! No doubt about that. Here's N'Guwe to serve."

Chapter Fourteen (2012)

After the new year, Lochen sent Marquize back to the team, while he traveled with me to San Marcos. When Marquize and I said good-bye for the second time (the first time had been privately), we shook paws and wished each other luck on the upcoming tournaments. Watching him get into the car to the airport, I felt lonelier than I'd felt in a long time.

Lochen and I left for the airport an hour later. He'd shown me the online profiles of the three coaches he was looking to interview and we'd printed them out to review on the trip. "I don't want you to pass judgment early," he said, "so I'm going to let you read through them and then we'll make our own judgment in the interviews. I'll tell you my thoughts afterwards. But these are coaches I know who work with other players on the Challenger circuit and will be willing to give you some coaching for free when your schedules intersect or when you travel to them. If you start making really good endorsement money or get into the top hundred—I think that's 'when,' not 'if'—you can hire a coach who will travel with you. But then you have to pay for their travel, hotel, all that."

I must have looked bewildered, because he patted my shoulder and laughed. "A couple years out still. Let's worry about this for now."

Candidate one: a grey fox named Jay Cannion. He smiled and said "Great" a lot as I worked out for him, and overall I thought he was a pretty nice guy. In the half hour I was working out, though, he tried to correct my grip and my ball toss, and in both cases he touched my paw and stood too close to me. It was probably innocent, but it reminded me of Frio and I told Lochen afterwards that I didn't like him.

Candidate two: a brown bear. He grabbed my paw and said, "Rocky? I'm Coach Taw. Let's see if we can make a tennis player out of you."

I thought I was already a tennis player, given I'd been winning Futures tournaments and all. I started to go into my service motion and Taw said, "No, no. Start with footwork drills."

Lochen, beside him, nodded, and so I reached back to Luka's warmups and ran through a series of footwork drills. I'd only gotten through two, though, before he said, "No, no. Like this," and proceeded to show me a new exercise. I tried to do that one, and he frowned, then gave me another one. It wasn't until the last ten minutes of the workout that I actually got to serve and hit balls back to him.

"Don't you want to see me play more?" I asked. I'd shown off my forehand and backhand and lobs and drop shots for Coach Cannion.

"Don't need to," he said. "We're going to break you down to your fundamentals and everything else will flow from that. Don't worry, you won't need to take any time off from tournaments. Your existing style is obviously doing okay for you, but to get to the next level, you need to rebuild."

Rebuild? I wasn't sure what he meant, and he didn't elaborate, so I figured it was something I should know. How long would that take? But Lochen told me afterwards that that was a common thing for coaches to say when they were taking on new young players, and that all it meant was that he was going to go back to the beginning and teach me the fundamentals in the way he thought they should be taught. Usually, Lochen said, it improved a young player's game. "It's not that he thinks you've been taught wrong; it's that he wanted to add another dimension to the way you think of the game. Personally, I don't think you need it," he said. "But Taw's really bright. One of his two players has been in a nice run of finals."

Candidate three: Keely was a cottontail rabbit. Where the other coaches had shown up in polo shirts and casual pants, Keely came to meet me in a shirt and tie, even though we were in one of those indoor tennis facilities that always smells a little bit like the locker room even out in the public areas. But in contrast to his clothes, his manner was light and joking. "I hear you're looking for a coach," he said as he shook my paw. "Saw the sign in the window."

Lochen flicked his ears kind of back, which I knew meant he wasn't happy, but I liked the joke. "I am looking for a coach," I told him. "Did you bring one with you?"

He laughed. "Lok, I like this one. Where'd you find him? Your guys are usually stiffs." Before Lochen could answer, he said, "How do you get through church every Sunday?"

"Um." That seemed kind of personal for just having met someone.

"Rocky doesn't attend church with us," Lochen said. "Not that it should matter at all."

"Course not, course not. Means we can get an extra practice in Sunday morning if we need it." The rabbit winked at me. "All right, let's see what kind of tennis player you are."

I stood awkwardly. "So, uh...you want me to serve?"

He gestured at the court. "Whatever you want to show me. Lochen will hit with you if you need someone to hit with you."

That was weird. How would I show him my returns and game play if nobody was going to hit with me? But the way he'd said it implied that I didn't need someone to hit with me. I looked to Lochen for guidance and he grabbed one of my spare rackets and headed for the opposite court.

I served, volleyed with Lochen, returned his serves. Through all of it, Keely stayed attentive, watching our game, but he didn't take notes like the other coaches had done. And twenty minutes later, when I thought I'd run through everything I could, I picked up the tennis balls, pushed them into the loose pockets of my shorts, and said, "Is that enough?"

"Do you think that's enough?" the rabbit asked.

"Uh." I looked to Lochen, swishing his tail, but he wasn't any help. "Yes? Yes."

"All right." Keely motioned for me and Lochen to come over. "Your game, the basics are all very sound. Where you can really use coaching is up here." He tapped his head. "At Maple River in September, you had a call go against you and it went to your head and cost you a game and probably the match. At Curningham in November, you lost a set because it took you that long to figure out where your opponent—Dzin, the red panda—had a vulnerability, even though you'd played him before. Did Lochen have you watching film of him?"

"No," I said, and here I should stop and say a word or two about publicity. I realized, of course, that I was in a spotlight, but it wasn't as large or bright as the one shone on the players in the upper circuits. Journalists who covered the Futures recognized me now and remembered my previous matches. But I didn't get recognized even going out for dinner in the towns where I'd won, and few people seemed to follow me. That this coach had done research on me was impressive; I didn't even realize there was film from the Futures circuit.

"We don't usually watch film." Lochen's hackles were up a little and his accent came through more strongly.

"Not on Futures, no." Keely reached into his bag and brought out a small tablet computer. On it he showed us a bunch of video clips—of me playing tennis. "Doesn't mean other people aren't watching. So we're going to get into the habit. Tell me what you've been eating before matches."

The abrupt switch in subject caught me off guard, but Lochen was ready. "Bananas, complex carbs, pre-workout and post-workout protein, moderate fats and simple carbs."

"The Leshoe diet, right?"

"With some modifications." Lochen narrowed his eyes.

"It's not bad, but there's some research out this year that suggests—well, anyway, I'll print out the most up-to-date nutrition plan."

"We studied nutrition at Palm Gables," I said.

"Of course you did." The rabbit smiled.

Soon after that he left, and Lochen and I sat down to discuss the coaches. I didn't want Cannion, and he didn't ask why. I expected him to suggest Coach Taw because he clearly didn't like Keely, but he asked which of the two I liked more. "I liked Keely," I said, "but that doesn't necessarily mean anything, does it?"

"Means something," Lochen said.

"You didn't like him."

"I wouldn't have brought him in if I didn't think he'd be a good coach for you. I don't have to be his partner for the next many years. I just have to argue with him about your career sometimes."

When he put it like that... "Am I being lazy not wanting to rebuild with Coach Taw?"

The red fox shook his head. "Maybe. You would know best. Don't imagine Coach Keely won't be work, though."

"I'm not."

"I'll caution you that he is quite susceptible to fads, as you saw."

I nodded. "I'll be careful of that."

"Be judicious." Lochen pointed a narrow brown-furred finger at me. "When you hire a coach, you must commit to that coach, otherwise you're working at cross-purposes and wasting your money."

"I thought he was going to coach me for free."

The red fox laughed and slapped my shoulder. "This time, yes. In general, though. Give everything a chance and be honest with him if it isn't working."

"All right."

He smiled, showing his fangs. "You're going to make a lot of money, Rocky. Don't doubt that."

I said I wouldn't, and I was almost telling the truth.

Braden came through on his word the next week, connecting me with a grey squirrel named Danver who was close to my level. As Lochen worked out the terms of Coach Keely's contract with me, Danver and I met to hit the ball around.

It was weird not practicing with Marquize, but the differences were as obvious as when I'd switched to Diaz back at Palm Gables. (How was Diaz, I wondered? Still swearing?) Danver reminded me of that red squirrel I'd beaten in the final of one of the Futures tournaments, jumping around all hyper and full of energy. We would've had some good matches in tournaments, I thought, and he said the same.

In tennis, he kept his energy under control, but in conversations he let it have free rein. "You're Rocky," he said the first time we met as he grasped my paw. "Danver. Pleased to meet you. Braden said you're

from Lunda? That's far. I've only been out of the States a few times
when I went to overseas tournaments but I didn't really see anything
and I've never been to Africa. They don't have tournaments there,
do they? I think they should. Were there a lot of good players there?
I don't think I've met anyone who grew up there before. I've met
jackals but they were all born in the States. What do you think of
our food here? I'm on a strict diet but I admit it, I cheat sometimes.
Not often, and not before a tournament, but sometimes I just need
a hazelnut milkshake, you know what I mean? Probably not, you're
a carnivore. That's probably why Braden likes you. You carnivores
stick together, I've noticed. Hope you don't mind practicing with a
herbivore."

"I don't," I interjected there, having waited that whole time for
him to pause for breath.

(I would later find out, by the way, that Danver wasn't quite
right; there are tournaments in Africa, only mostly either in the very
northernmost countries or the very southernmost country. Nothing
within hundreds of kilometers of Lunda.)

And every conversation with him was like that. At first I found
it tiresome and wondered if perhaps Braden had recommended him
as a punishment for me daring to ask him for help, but as I got used
to him I found that he had a pretty good personality overall. And
the conversations grew to be relaxing for me because he didn't really
expect me to follow them, so I could let him talk and if there was
something I needed to answer, he didn't get angry if I asked him to
repeat it.

But that was a long ways off, and I was getting to know him in a
tennis way as well as a personal way that week leading up to my first
Challenger tournament.

There was a lot to learn. The tournament felt bigger and more
expensive from the get-go. My name badge was plastic and new and
it had some kind of chip in it that would scan for entry to all the
areas I was allowed into. "Keep this for all the tournaments," the
registration wolf told me. "If you lose it, it costs twenty bucks to
replace."

Danver already had one. "It's not the money that bothers me," he told me as we walked back to the locker room. "It's the hassle. You have to go log on to the website and order one, or if you get to the tournament and then can't find it you have to wait for hours for them to get their shit together and make one. I've lost three so far and that's the worst part. Sixty bucks, pssht, I'd pay double that if I didn't have to wait for it. Have you ever been to this facility? Grab an extra towel and stash it in your locker because by the middle of qualifying they run out. They restock for the main draw but you might end up reusing an old towel once or twice."

"We only got the one towel in the Futures tournaments," I said.

"Yeah, but this is the big leagues. Or closer to the big leagues. It's not really that big yet. But bigger than Futures. Check out the water bottles." We'd stopped at two lockers that were apparently going to be ours, and each one held a water bottle, a neatly folded towel, and a printed schedule of matches.

"Wow." I was most impressed by the schedule, honestly. I took it down and unfolded it. "In Futures we had to go look at where the match schedules were posted."

"Told you." Danver seemed pleased, as though he had arranged it all himself.

"Are you getting together with Braden during the tournament?" I asked as we dressed for practice.

"Ha ha! 'Getting together'? Sure, me and Braden, we're like this." He held up two fingers twined together. "We hang out and drink protein smoothies together all the time. Me and the top tennis prospect out of this country in the last ten years, we just chill all the time." He laughed again and doubled over. "Ah ha ha! That's awesome."

"So…" I frowned, annoyed. "How does he know you? Why did he recommend you to practice with me?"

"Oh, we played a few times. I mean, I've talked to him in the locker room. There's a board where we post if we're looking for practice partners, so I guess he got my name off it."

"Huh." Somehow I thought Braden had hooked me up with one of his friends. But all he'd done was go to a bulletin board and pick out a name he'd recognized. Still, it was cool of him to make the effort.

* * *

I had a good practice with Danver, and then I got a little time in with Coach Keely, who was there with some of his paying customers. He worked with me for half an hour and then gave me a little laminated card with food instructions and times before a match. "Follow this," he said, tapping it as I held it. "Different species process nutrients differently, and this one is tailored to jackals. Well, coyotes actually, because there aren't that many jackals. Sorry about that." His tall ears lay back for a moment; what was a flicking gesture for my triangular ears was a sweeping motion for him. "But that's close. And those are equivalences, so don't eat two eggs *and* a protein smoothie *and* a burger without bun here, for example. Just one. And they're listed in order of preference, so here the burger is last, because they have a bunch of fat there, too, but it's better than not getting protein at all."

"Okay," I said. When I looked at it like that, it looked pretty similar to what I'd been doing, maybe with different quantities and a more rigid timetable.

"And don't always eat the top choice. You need a little variety. Mix it up, y'know?"

"Yes, coach."

"Good." He clapped me on the back. "We're not going to do film this tournament. Might be a few months until we do. It's a subscription service, you know. I'll work *pro bono* for a while, but to get the film you need to sign up. Lochen will handle that when it happens. But when you do, I'll work with you on how to watch it."

"Thank you," I said. "Thanks so much."

He winked. "You'll repay me one day."

"Oh, sure, as soon as I start earning money—"

Keely held up a paw. "That'd be great, sure, if I'm free and if you still want to hire me, but I meant more by getting good. And when you do, tell people who coached you. That helps a lot more."

"Yes. Of course. Sure thing."

"Good boy." He pointed to the court. "Okay, get out there. Let's see your serve."

He had a different style from Coach Luka. Where the field mouse had barked orders, Coach Keely said things like, "Why don't you try standing with your feet an inch farther apart?" and "See how it feels if you keep your tail up. How's your balance?"

I didn't do great that tournament—won two qualifying matches and didn't have anyone to go celebrate with afterwards because Danver was still playing when I was done. But I hung out in the locker room and talked to the other States players and a few of the international ones. Having a team, I realized, had been great in that I had a big social group, but also it had removed any urge I felt to go talk to the other players. Here at this tournament, the most valuable experience I got—besides the experience of being in a larger Challenger tournament among five times more reporters and cameras, though few of them were interested in me—was applying the confidence I'd learned from Palm Gables and more recently my team to a setting where I knew nobody at all.

And around the end of the tournament, when Braden had won a semifinal and I finally got a chance to thank him in the locker room, he remembered me. "Rocky," he said. "How'd that squirrel work out for you?"

"Great," I said. "I wanted to thank you for setting us up."

His head tilted and then he nodded, all without smiling. "Yeah, sure," he said. "Glad it worked out."

"It did. Good luck in the final."

The cross fox flashed a thumbs up at me and then pointed outside. "Got reporters waiting. I'll catch you later."

Of course, then he lost in the finals, and though I was watching from the stands near the tunnel when he went in, he stomped past me and didn't say a word. But we'd reconnected, and I thought that was cool.

Marquize, on one of our calls, was not as convinced. "You're easy to remember because you're a jackal and he's met you a few times. He went and got you a name off a list you could've gotten yourself and he's trying to milk that for a bunch of credit."

I'd told him what Danver said, so he knew that whole deal. "I don't think so," I said.

"I know his type."

"Well, you weren't there."

There was a long silence then, as both of us thought about being on different tours. "Sorry," I said finally. "I wish you were here."

"Yeah." He let out a long breath. "Me too."

"Couple months," I said. "On my birthday. Still up for that?"

"Hell yes. Heh." I could see the warmth in his eyes and smile through his voice's energy. And that sparked him to talk about his own play. "Hey, I made it into the main draw again at our tournament here. Paulie beat me, the asshole."

And the tension slid back. "Tell me about it," I said, and settled in to listen.

I spent a lot of time on the phone with Marquize in those first couple months on the tour, leading up to March. There were lots of lonely nights in hotel rooms, me curled up on my bed with the headset clipped to my ear, talking about our days. I couldn't talk freely because after the first week, Danver asked if I wanted to share a hotel room with him and Lochen said that he could work out the finances with Danver's agent, so I did it. That meant I had to time my conversations with Marquize to when Danver was out—at least, some of the conversations.

The squirrel still pinged to the fact that I talked to Mar a lot, way more than is usual, and even my explanation that he was my best friend didn't prevent him from saying things like, "You two talk like a couple girls," which made me equal parts nervous and angry. I knew the expression and also knew that Ori and I talked about the same things, generally, as I did with Mar.

Kim would have responded sharply with some question like, oh, so what do girls talk like, then? But I kept my muzzle shut except to laugh and say, "We're funny that way." The second time, I'd come up with a better response, which was, "Don't you have anyone you talk to that much?" That set the squirrel off on an epic ten-minute monologue about his best friend from back home who was now in college for psychology and didn't have time for "late-night gabfests" anymore.

The phone calls grew shorter, but not because I was worried

about Danver. Once I'd told Mar about the novelty of the Challenger tour, all we had left was commiseration about losing our matches and his gossip about the team. And there I often knew about things before he did, because I also talked to Lochen at least twice a week. Now that I wasn't part of the team, the fox would let things slip now and then, maybe because he thought it would comfort me to hear news of my friends of the past year. "Paulie made it to a final," he told me once. "Without you to keep him down, he might win a few."

"I wasn't keeping him down," I protested, but he laughed that comment off.

"That's the way the game's played," he said. "If he wants to beat you, he's got to do it on the court. He's older than you, so he's not going to get past you by waiting."

Sometimes I asked Lochen how Mar was doing, but he never answered those questions directly. "He's making progress," he said once, and another time he said, "Coach is working with him."

To hear it from Mar himself, he was stagnating. "I lost in the qualifiers again," he complained bitterly in February. "I swear I had the match and then he hit this bullshit shot right in the corner on break point in the third. He was out in the doubles alley and I swear the shot curved like a foot out of bounds and then dropped in, pure luck. Anywhere else and I'd have won the point."

"I hate that," I said.

"I mean, what do you do after that?"

"You get ready to receive the next serve," I said, because that's what I would do.

Marquize was silent for a moment. "It was rhetorical," he said, and his voice was tinged with a sulky tone. I tried to salvage the conversation but still felt vaguely guilty by the time we hung up.

The other person I reached out to was Kamina. In January she was cordial to me; I called to tell her that Ma was on her way and she said, "It'll be lovely to see her, but I don't know what she hopes to accomplish."

"I think she wants to get Ori back."

Kamina sniffed at that. "She's welcome to try. Marriage contracts are legal and binding and this one is signed and set like clay in the sun."

Ma and I had had many conversations about exactly how binding marriage contracts were. In Ma's opinion, anything was negotiable, especially in cases like this where Bompaka was chief of the village. If he wanted to change something, then it would be changed. "Do you think it was the best thing for Ori?"

"Of course it was." Her voice rose. "What exactly are you saying?"

"I'm wondering how much this marriage benefited you," I said, and that was perhaps too blunt, because she hung up on me.

I talked to her again a month later, worried that she might hang up as soon as she heard it was me. But I had heard nothing from Ma since she'd called to tell me she'd landed in Lundara, and desperation drove me to try my aunt's number again.

She did not hang up when she heard it was me. "Rochi!" she cried. "Tell Diara to return to the States immediately!"

"I haven't heard from Ma in a month," I said. "What is she doing?"

"Tchah! What is she doing? She is causing trouble. She is talking to people she should not be talking to and asking things she should not ask. I should not have to answer these kind of questions." She sounded as agitated as the time she thought the government was going to take her house.

"What kind of questions?" Danver was in because we had matches the next day, lying on his back in bed playing a video game on a small device he had. He'd been ignoring me until this comment, when he looked my way, his bushy tail twitching.

"These people have no right to be in our country anyway. They say they come here to help, they bring a few clothes, and then they nose around, they claim they want to 'fix' our country. Nothing in Lunda is so broken that it needs their help. We managed for thousands of years before they arrived."

"The war—"

"You know why things are broken? It's because they came here. They came here and ruined everything and now they blame us for that ruin and they say they can fix it. They can fix it by leaving! And Diara is just the same now. She is meddling about in affairs that were settled and she should not, she should leave, Rochi, tell her to leave."

"Ma hasn't called me," I repeated. "But if she's trying to rescue Ori, I'm not going to tell her to stop."

"Oh, rescue. You think that's what she is doing?"

I met Danver's eyes over the portable game he held. He had no idea what this conversation was about, and at my questioning glance he shrugged. "That's what she said she was going to do."

"She is trying to make me lose standing!"

"Standing?"

"Tchah!" Her voice deepened to a growl. "You don't understand any better than she does."

"Don't hang up!" I said, feeling the conversation was heading for that same precipice. "Tell me what you mean. Uh, then if I hear from Ma I'll tell her."

"Your mother knows," Kamina said, "and you don't need to. Don't misunderstand me, Rochi. I am glad—we are all very glad for your good fortune. But we can't share it. You live your life, and forget about the ones you left behind."

"I can't do that," I protested.

"You wanted to bring Ori to join you," my aunt said. "What about me? What about your Uncle Goji and your cousins? Did you think of any of them?"

I hadn't. Ma hadn't, or if she had she'd never brought them up to me. "I—I can't save everybody," I stammered.

"No," she said. "You're Statian now. We're Lundan, and so is your sister."

I closed my eyes. "I'm not giving up on her."

"And Diara is also Statian, and she should return there and stop stirring up trouble. Tell her that. She might listen to you."

"Ma won't listen to anyone when she thinks she's right." I sat on the bed cross-legged and leaned back against the wall.

Kamina snorted. "You have the right of that. She was always that way."

It was one of the qualities I loved about Ma, but this didn't seem the right time to bring that up. It struck me that Kamina was not too far off that herself, but I didn't say that either. I couldn't actually think of anything else to say to her that wouldn't cause more problems, so that was the conversation ender.

"Tough family life," Danver said when I hung up. "You wanna talk about it at all?"

"Not really." He looked sad at that, so I said, "Not now. But sometime maybe."

That cheered him up. "Okay. You know, you need to get out more. One of these nights I'm gonna drag you out to the clubs. There's a few that are good for canids, you know, they don't allow smoking or heavy perfume and they Neutra-Scent the shit out of the air. Wait, do you like Neutra-Scent? I know some guys who don't, who say they'd rather have all the smells and it makes them feel weird when there's no smell. Anyway, a couple of them are all ages so you don't have to be old enough to drink or even old enough to vote."

"I don't care either way," I said. "But I'll go out with you after this tournament."

His ears perked up. "Really? You serious?"

I'd said it on the spur of the moment, but considering it as a serious option made me hesitate. I'd been warned so many times about living the party life that I could barely remember whether it had been Ma or Lochen or Coach Keely or even Nashan who'd said which specific words. But surely one night couldn't hurt. "Tell you what," I said. "If I get to the main draw in this tournament, I'll go out with you after."

He stayed bright. "I'll take those odds," he said, and then pointed at me. "And no tanking to get out of going out."

Chapter Fifteen

I didn't tank that tournament. I got to the main draw and won a match against this jaguar, S. Freta, before losing in the next round. Still, I was pretty pleased with how things had gone—my first win in a main draw on the Challenger tour. So I didn't resist when Danver insisted on dragging me out that night.

I'd talked to the jaguar in the locker room after our match. He seemed like a good guy, if a little quiet; after our match he'd said, "You're new, eh?"

"This year."

"Gonna go far," he said. "Who you practice with?"

"Danver. Uh, Peterson."

"Yeah, I know him." He eyed me. "Cool."

"Look," I said impulsively. "I don't know many guys on the tour yet. Can I get your number?"

I would learn that there are subtler ways to ask if a guy wants to exchange numbers. But Freta, maybe taken aback by my earnestness, took out his phone. "Sean," he said as he gave me his number. "With an 'e.'"

"Uh," I said. "So…'S'…"

He stared at me, trying to figure out if I was making fun of him. I blinked back. "E-A-N," he said, and watched me write the name down.

And that's how I happened to have Sean's number in my phone when Danver grabbed me to go out with him. "Hey, you know Sean the jaguar?" I asked the squirrel.

"Oh sure," Danver said. "I mean, not all that well. I played him a couple times, practiced with him, but our schedules didn't really mesh, I guess. He doesn't talk much, either. Not like you. You can hold a conversation, a guy doesn't feel like he's talking to a brick wall or something. With Sean, you know, you could be trying to talk to him about other guys on the tour, or about, I dunno, Shadow Knight shit or whatever, and the only thing you'll get out of him is like, 'Huh, cool.' At least you'll tell a guy what you're thinking, you know, like, *engage*."

I was learning how to break into Danver's monologues when I wanted to. "So you mind if I ask him to join us?"

"Hah!" Danver never minded when you interrupted him. He just went with the flow of the conversation. "Sure, he can come along. Wait, is he over 21? Could he buy beer? Never mind, I'm not gonna drink. Maybe just one beer. I had a rough tournament, don't have to practice tomorrow…I could have a beer."

So I called up Sean. "Me and—I mean, Danver and I are going out tonight. You want to come?"

There was silence, and then, "Where?"

"Where are we going?" I asked Danver.

"Little all-ages club. Wait, don't say 'all ages.' No, do. We're not sneaking into a bar with fake IDs or anything if that's what he's worried about. Unless he's 21. You don't have a fake ID, do you?"

"No."

"Oh."

"Do you?"

"No. I tried to get one once, but it was a lot of hassle and I wasn't sure I really wanted it…"

I let him talk and I went back to Sean. "A club," I said.

"Cool."

And Sean, much to Danver's surprise, met us in front of our hotel and walked the three blocks with us to the club. The jaguar and I had both dressed in a tennis shirt and jeans, unremarkable casual outfits, but Danver had pulled on a pair of near-white slacks that shimmered when they caught the light, and a collared shirt that was as busy and colorful as his pants were blank. He looked like he'd fallen into an artist's palette. And the shirt, made of something light like silk or rayon, fluttered in the breeze that ruffled his exposed chest fur. When we met Sean, Danver shook his paw, then set out and strode confidently along the sidewalk. Sean and I grinned at each other and then fell in behind on either side of him, that bushy squirrel tail waving between the two of us.

The place he led us to was a little brick building squeezed between an all-night deli and a restaurant that served something called "Pho," which we all pronounced "Foh." (Only years later would I learn it was pronounced "Fuh.") It smelled of beef and noodles and broth and spices as we walked by it. The club was called "The Red Raider," and above the door was a twisted neon sculpture of a fox in a pirate hat, all in red except for the great white feather in his broad-brimmed hat. Through the windows of the club came multicolored lights and subdued sound, tamer than the huge wild thumps we heard passing the clubs with lines to get in and velvet ropes and bears or tigers with folded arms guarding the entrances.

Nobody guarded this entrance; Danver opened the door and I held it for Sean to walk in. We stood, letting our eyes adjust to the stark contrast between the shadows of the interior and the stabbing colored lights strung haphazardly around the bar and in the corners. The music changed to a 90s song I knew, and my tail and hips swung in time to it. I caught myself, worried I was being too expressive, and then I saw Danver swinging his hips and clapping his hands in time, and I didn't feel as bad about my own little half-dance steps. Sean remained stolidly still.

"Over there," Danver pointed to a clear space of low cushioned chairs around a small circular table. We made for it and sat down, curling tails around our hips.

While we waited for a server to come find us, I looked around at the counter, which doubled as a bar, and at the people sitting around in the club, talking with each other, with bright smiles and tapping claws. A few were standing and half-dancing. "What do we do here?" I asked Danver.

Sean turned his ears to listen to the squirrel's answer. Danver, still tapping his feet to the music, leaned back with his elbows on the back of the couch. "Do? Enjoy the music, get a few drinks, get out of tennis for a bit. You've got to balance out your life, you can't be tennis 24-7." He waved around at the club. "Look at these people. You think they know about the tournament we just played? You think most of these people give a crap about it? Perspective."

Funny; from the way he was dressed, I'd expected him to say that his goal was to hook up, and I was preparing the argument that I was underage to exempt myself from that line of action. But he punctuated his insistence on "perspective" with a clenched paw, like he'd just won a difficult point in a match.

"Tennis is important," Sean said. "We got to believe that."

"Of course." Danver nodded. "Course we do. We wouldn't be doing this otherwise. But you have to relax. If you get too wound up in tennis, if you forget there's something else in the world outside, you go crazy. You burn out. You lose yourself. I," he tapped his chest, "am not gonna lose myself. I know how big the world is. Hi, yeah, can I get a virgin Planter's punch?"

The server who'd come over, a tall gazelle in a tight black dress, noted Danver's request with a nod of her head. "What about you two, darlins?"

I didn't know what a Planter's punch was. "Just a Coke," I said, because that's what I knew.

"Coke," Sean said.

"I'll be right back with those drinks." The gazelle flitted away again.

"Isn't this great?" Danver said into the silence. "I'm so glad you guys came out with me. I can't come to these places alone. I look like a tool, you know? But I really love being here in the music and having a drink, relaxing." His gaze drifted past me. "Hey, check it out. There's a couple squirrels over there." And before either Sean or I could react, he'd jumped out of his seat to make his way over to the bar where, indeed, two female squirrels were talking, one in a business suit and the other in a light yellow blouse and blue skirt.

Sean met my eye, a smile playing at the corners of his cheeks, and I returned it. "'Perspective'," I said, making air quotes of my fingers.

That got a laugh out of the jaguar. "Danver's okay," he said. "Exhausting. So what's your story?"

I gave him the abbreviated version: Lunda, Palm Gables, Lochen.

And then it was his turn. He'd never gone to a tennis academy; he'd played through high school and competitively in college, and had jumped right to the Challenger tour when he graduated. All of this was told in laconic sentences, like the way he described his goals, just as the gazelle returned with our drinks: "Win a few tournaments this year. Otherwise I'll hang it up. Got a management degree. Might as well use it." His slight Chevali drawl came out when he spoke more than a half-dozen words at a time.

My Coke had come in a thin, tall glass with an extended vertical lip for canids. I set it to my muzzle and tipped it back. Cold, fizzy, and a bit watery. I don't know why I expected Coke to be better in a place like this: the point of getting it was that it's the same everywhere. "Management? So you could manage other tennis players?"

Sean's Coke had come in the same kind of glass, but without the vertical lip. He brought it to his flatter muzzle and drank. "Business management. Guess I could manage players but it's not the same."

"So if you went to college, you must be…" I did figures in my head. "Twenty-three?"

"Four."

Seven years older than me, and at the same tennis level. When I was twenty-four, I wanted to be winning majors. But Sean also had a college degree, which I guess was a fair trade. "I'm only seventeen. Almost eighteen. What was college like?"

"Busy." He grinned and scanned the club before going on. "Classes all morning, tennis all afternoon, homework evenings, tennis weekends."

"The movies make it seem like there's a lot of parties."

He sipped his Coke. A new song came on, one that he tilted his head to, his expression puzzled and then clearing as the first verse started. "They don't make movies about good students."

Danver leapt back into our couch circle to grab his drink. "You guys doing okay? Those squirrels are hot, but I don't think anything's going to happen. But they wanted to hear more about tennis, so I'm gonna go. I'll be back though." He sipped his drink. "Woo! That's good."

He was gone before I could ask him for a taste of his Planter's punch. Virgin Planter's punch, I remembered, and that reminded me of my upcoming birthday. To distract myself from that, I asked Sean what a "virgin" drink was even though I was pretty sure it meant non-alcoholic. He confirmed that, and then my thoughts drifted back to my birthday and I stayed quiet.

We sat enjoying the music through two more songs before I felt awkward at being quiet so long. "Sorry," I said. "I'm not being very good company."

The jaguar arched an eyebrow. "Says who?"

"Uh…" I half-turned to see Danver, still chatting up the squirrels. "I'm not talking very much."

Sean smiled. "So?"

"All right." I relaxed back into the couch. "I guess I'll soak up the perspective, then."

He chuckled, a sharp, "Heh! Heh!" and then leaned forward. "We can talk if you want."

"I don't want to force you."

"Bah." He drank the last of his Coke. "Good for me, probably. All my business school profs told me I need to talk more. Make connections. Network." He grimaced. "Hate that word."

"Is that, uh. Is that what we're doing? Networking?"

"Maybe." He laughed again. "But hope not. Nah, if you're new to the tour, talk to people. Make friends. You need that to survive."

"I'm trying." Sean's tail was flicking like cats' tails do, and it made mine twitch too, even tucked against my hip. "But it's my first month. I had all these friends on the Futures tour…"

"Let's not talk tennis." The jaguar looked at his Coke glass and then signaled to the waitress.

"You want another one, hon?" She spotted my empty glass. "Both of you?"

I said yes, but Sean shook his head. "Just a water." And when she was gone, he said, "The Cokes here cost four dollars, in case you didn't know."

"What?" I stared at the little glass. It was less than I'd get in a one-dollar bottle from the machines at the tennis complex.

"Yup. Danver doesn't care. Price of entry to get laid. Cheaper than a prostitute."

We both turned to where Danver was still talking to the two squirrels at the bar, his paw on the hip of the one in the skirt. "He's gonna hook up with one of them?"

Sean shrugged. "Gonna try. You got a girl?"

I shook my head, telling myself it wasn't technically a lie. "You?"

"Nah. No time for it." Sean waved a paw. "Never got it. Play tennis, keep someone happy? Hard enough keeping myself happy."

I didn't want to talk about keeping a relationship going, "Four dollar Cokes help."

He eyed me and then laughed again. "But only one."

We chatted until Danver came back and told us that the squirrel ladies were busy. I thought he'd join us, but he took off when he saw a chinchilla by herself. And at that point Sean and I decided we'd had enough of the weird mineral-smelling water, and the two of us went back to our hotels. The walk back was much quieter, but it was still nice. Getting to know Danver had been great, but it was even better with the prospect of Sean to balance out the hyperactive squirrel. I had two friends, and they probably had friends, and before long I was going to have a lot of people to talk to and hang out with.

And when I was eighteen, Marquize and I could be proper boyfriends again.

Chapter Sixteen

I turned eighteen one week later, on March 23rd.

I'd already arranged for a day off, which was a lot easier than when I'd been on the team because I pretty much set my own hours and practice schedule these days. I did want to coordinate with Danver because he was my practice partner, so I told him that that Friday I wanted to go visit some friends. "Awesome," he said. "Friday night I'll hit some clubs. Come along later with your friends if they want. If they're local, I mean. And if they're cool."

"I'm taking a bus," I told him. We were staying with an older player Danver knew at his townhouse in Fort Allen, a Western town, and Marquize and his team were somewhere south closer to Kerina. So we'd arranged to meet at some hotel in Sequoyah City, a place called the Altamont Garden. I had to walk a mile and a half from the bus station to get to it, with my overnight bag slung over my shoulder. Fortunately the weather was nice and dry, and I even got to see a pretty sunset a little while before I got to the hotel.

Marquize had made all the arrangements, but he wouldn't arrive for another forty-five minutes or so—he'd texted me that he was driving a friend's car, which struck me as dangerous knowing what I did of Marquize's driving, but maybe he'd gotten better. Or maybe he was as desperately excited to see me as I was to see him.

I sat in the little hotel restaurant and got a chicken salad sandwich, a chef salad, and a $2.75 Coke. I didn't know if Marquize would have eaten on the drive; I'd texted him but I knew he wouldn't text me back while he was driving. The sandwich was dry and the salad dressing was too thick, but it wasn't bad and I wasn't hungry at the end of it, which was the main point. On the TV news, pictures kept coming up of a foreign country where a large oil tanker had foundered. It wasn't Lunda, wasn't even the same continent, but a lot of the people they showed seemed to live the same way we had. I watched the coverage and wished I could call Ma and find out how she was doing.

My phone chimed; I grabbed it and saw the text from Marquize: *Here.* I was halfway to the lobby before I realized I'd forgotten to pay the bill.

One paid bill later, we had hugged in the lobby and were in the elevator on our way up to the third floor, not touching even though there wasn't anyone else in the elevator. Palm Gables had made us wary of public and even semi-private spaces.

Once we were in the room, though, with the door closed, it was another matter. We were in private, away from the eyes of the world, and we were both eighteen. For the first time we could do whatever we liked without fear of discovery by anyone. Everything was the same and yet it was totally different.

We both dropped our suitcases in the front hallway and embraced in a tighter hug than we'd dared in the lobby. He pressed his lips to mine and his paws wandered down under my tail to hold my butt, and I let my fingers follow suit on his. We staggered across the room to one of the two beds and fell on it still twined together.

His heat soaked into me and still I tried to pull him closer. His paws pushed under my t-shirt to bare fur and then he pulled back from the kiss and pushed me down onto my back with a huge smile on his muzzle. I lay back as he unfastened my pants and pulled them down along with my underwear. I wriggled out of my shirt and lay naked beneath the cheetah straddling me as he tossed the pants off the side of the bed.

"I've missed you," he breathed, running his paws up my thighs, thumbs just tracing the outside of my sheath. He didn't trace the erection he'd already inspired, rubbing instead up to my stomach and chest and then leaning down to kiss me again.

My paws rested on his hips, holding him down and rubbing lightly there as we kissed. "Mmf," I said. "You going to keep your clothes on all night?"

"Not hardly." He grinned and pulled his shirt off, then worked his pants free as well, and soon he was as naked as I was—and clearly as excited for our night together. I wasn't as shy with my paws, cupping his sac and then reaching up to brush fingers along his erection, which gave me such a thrill that I closed my eyes to focus on the feeling.

Marquize stretched, arching his back under my touch, and I also liked—loved—that I could do that. This wasn't anything new, but it had been months since I'd done it, since Christmas, I remember thinking. His erection was slimmer and longer than mine, and a little rough toward the tip with bumps that he called "barbs." He was equally fascinated with my knot, which wasn't in evidence yet, but the pressure at my base meant it was on its way.

So I was rubbing his barbs with my thumb and he squirmed, his tail lashing across my legs. "Wh-whoa," he said, reaching down to grab my wrist. "I don't wanna come yet."

"We've got all night." I kept my paw where it was, smiling. "You'll be ready again in like an hour."

"Yeah, but…" He reached down and I thought he was going to grab my erection as well, but he reached instead down beneath my sac. "You're legal now and there's a thing we haven't done yet. I kinda wanted to tonight. If you're okay with it."

We'd talked about it a few times, but hadn't made any plans. It was hard to do that over the phone when you could only say, "I miss you," and not, "I like the way your length feels in my paw when you come," let alone, "I'd like to try taking you in my muzzle again." That was what I'd been hoping for and looking forward to tonight, although I'd be lying if I hadn't thought about going all the way—the "home run," I guess it would be in our high school code.

"I was thinking maybe I'd do it to you," I said.

"I thought about that." He slid his fingers around my erection. "But you're pretty thick and I'm not sure…plus then there's your knot…which I like a lot, but it's even thicker."

"But you've, uh…you told me you've tried it? With…with like, carrots or something?"

"Yeah." His eyes flicked away from me and then back. "You haven't?"

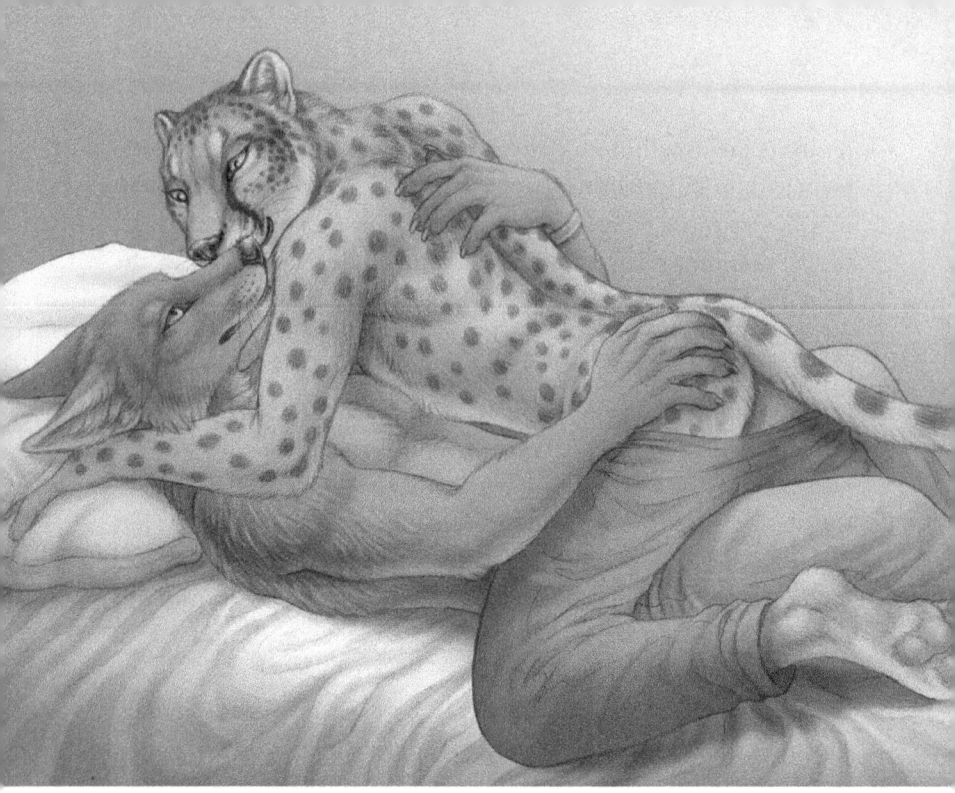

Honestly, I'd kept meaning to, but every time I pulled a carrot out of the fridge, I wondered what I'd do with it afterwards. I imagined throwing it out and having someone ask why I'd thrown it out. I imagined accidentally eating it. I imagined pushing it in too far and losing it. Not to mention it was almost always someone else's fridge, someone else's carrot. So I stuck to fingers. "I can get two fingers in," I said.

"That's probably enough. If you're willing."

He really wanted to, I could see that. And he wasn't thicker than two fingers. I did want to feel that too, and I wanted to feel it with him, and this was the time to do it. So I swallowed my apprehension. "Okay. Yeah."

"You want to?"

I nodded and squeezed his shaft. "I really do."

"All right." His expression lit up and he hopped off the bed. "I brought some stuff."

I rolled onto my side and watched his butt and the cute swing of his tail over it as he opened his bag and rummaged in it. He turned with a tube and a small cardboard box. "Condoms?" I asked, and he nodded. "I'm not gonna get pregnant."

I'd meant it jokingly, but his expression stayed serious. "There's disease and stuff."

"Oh," I said. "But I've never been with anyone else, and you…"

"You can pick up diseases from anywhere," he said. "I mean, even from, you know, you can't be too careful."

"All right." I smiled. "It's okay." The pressure that signaled my knot had decreased a little, and I wanted to get back into the mood. "I trust you. How do we do it?"

"Ah, well, this is for me." He held the box of condoms up in one paw, and with the other extended the tube out to me. "And this is for you."

I leaned over the bed and took it. It had a brand name and was marked, "Personal Lubricant." Marquize was still looking nervous, so I said, "Okay, I'll put this…back there?"

"Yeah." He worked his claws at the box and took out three condoms in a strip together.

That drew my attention from my own attempts to get whatever was in the tube out. "Are you going to use all three of those?"

"No!" He laughed and tore one off. "I mean…I guess, if you like it, we can do it again. They come in boxes of three, that's all."

"Oh, okay." I guess I was reading the wrong sites on the Internet that I didn't know all this stuff.

Don't get me wrong: I still looked at porn. But it seemed like there was always someone around, so I didn't have a lot of chances, and plus, Marquize had told me when we were at Lochen's place that if we were on someone else's wifi, they could maybe be tracking the sites we looked at. So for the few chances I got to look at porn online, I just looked at porn. I didn't look for "how to have sex" manuals.

I finally got the cap and the protective seal off the tube. I sniffed it; it smelled medicinal but not too bad. Worse, when I got it from my finger onto that spot under my tail, it was cold, but I didn't say anything because it warmed quickly and Marquize was having more trouble getting the condom rolled down over his shaft. We'd never used condoms, so I wasn't sure I'd be any better at it. Getting my slick finger up inside myself was a lot easier, that was for sure. I got the second one in beside it just as Marquize came over to the bed all wrapped up, paw out for the Personal Lubricant.

And when he had squeezed enough over his condom-covered shaft that it pooled and dripped off, he turned me onto my stomach and got up behind me. "Don't tense up," he said. "Try to relax."

Easy for him to say. I had no idea what to expect. And when his paw grabbed my tail and pulled it aside, a little harder than I thought was necessary, I couldn't help clenching the sheet in my paw. But I reminded myself that I trusted him, that Marquize knew more about this than I did, and that it was going to be good, better than the other stuff we'd done.

His finger pushed where mine had just been, around and then into me, and that was unexpected and good enough to make me gasp. And then he pulled it out and I felt his movement and something bigger, warmer, pushed at my entrance, a little off, and then pushing harder, sliding, finding the entrance and pop! He was inside me. We were having sex, real sex, for the first time.

That thought sent a thrill through me that erased most of the initial discomfort I felt. Marquize's shaft might be thin, but it still felt bigger than two of my fingers—though it slid back and forth more easily. It was a weird feeling, but the excitement over having sex after waiting so long—almost exactly two years, if you counted our relationship starting from the time of our kiss on my birthday— made it thrilling.

When his paw reached down to stroke me, he grasped me nice and hard the way I like it, and I stifled a moan because I was already so keyed up that it wasn't going to take long. He didn't notice or didn't care, just stroked me like normal while he pushed himself into me. And that got me shivering, shaking, and spilling myself onto the sheets just a couple minutes later.

Marquize kept stroking, so I had to reach back and stop him, panting, "I'm done, I'm done!"

"Mmf." He removed his paw and kept on thrusting.

It seemed to go on for a long time, long after the excitement of having sex had dulled, if not completely worn off. "Sorry," he gasped at one point. "It's…"

He never finished that sentence. He did eventually pull out, and I thought it was going to be over, but he grunted and stroked himself with his own paw for a while. Then, when he started to make more gasping noises, he shoved back into me and went back to thrusting. By this point I was getting sore, but I didn't want to say anything because it was our first time and I wanted him to finish too.

Finally, he let out a loud moan, pushed hard into me, and stopped thrusting. I thought that sounded like he'd finished, but I really had no way of knowing. "Did you…?"

"Yeah," he panted, and lay down on my back, one arm around my chest. "Yeah. Sorry."

"It's okay," I said. "But could you…?" I pulled my hips forward, trying to get him out of me.

"Oh yeah." He pulled back. "Let me get rid of this."

As he walked to the bathroom, he pulled the condom off. I looked long enough to see the telltale collected fluid in it, then lay down on my side. When he came back, he lay facing me. "I don't know why it took that long," he said. "I usually come quicker. Maybe it was the condom."

"We could try without," I said.

"No."

"Mar, if neither of us has been with anyone else—"

Again, he wouldn't look at me, and that time I finally figured out why. "You have. You've done this already."

Marquize didn't say anything. He looked away from me and picked at the bedsheets with his blunt claws. "Who was it?" I demanded. "One of the guys from the team?"

"No."

I hadn't thought so, but you never know with those good Christian boys, at least according to many stories I'd read. "Someone back in Port City?"

"Can we…" His eyes, wide and troubled, met mine. His paw reached out to my upper arm. "Can we not talk about this now? I promise I'll tell you sometime. I don't want to mess up tonight."

"Too late for that." I didn't stop him from touching me, but I didn't make any move to reciprocate either. "You might as well spill it all." When he sighed and didn't say anything, I said, "It's someone I know, isn't it? If it was a random hookup, you'd tell me."

His muzzle jerked down and up in a short nod. "It was…" He took another breath. "Jesus, this is hard." He had to look away, down at the sheets.

"Just say his name," I snapped.

"It was Frio." And then he stopped, as if the effort of pushing out those four syllables had closed his throat to further speech.

"Frio?" I pulled back from his paw, got up off the bed. "You slept with him?" He nodded. "After what he did to me—to us? He kicked you out of school!"

"It was before that." The cheetah's voice was dull. "I think he kicked me out because I stopped wanting to see him when you and I—when we started dating. But after you told me, I thought… I thought it wouldn't be bad if I approached him. You know, it wouldn't be a teacher pressuring a student, it'd be a student wanting to…"

"To hook up with a teacher."

"To take advantage—to get some experience."

I made some kind of noise in my throat and went to the bathroom, slamming the door behind me. Trembling, I stood at the counter and stared at my reflection in the mirror. My erection had retreated fully into my sheath, but I still felt slick under my tail, so I grabbed a hand towel and attacked that area until it felt dry and sore. And even then I could still smell the lubricant, so I turned the shower on and stood under the hot water, letting it soak into my fur.

The whole situation felt unreal to me. Marquize and Frio? The ferret who'd tried to fuck me in a hotel room and then turned it around to make out like it was me coming on to him? Was that what had happened to Marquize? Had Frio turned around their affair so Marquize thought it was all his fault? And—ugh, he'd touched Frio with the same paws he'd used to touch me, had maybe kissed him with the same mouth, had—had fucked him? Or been fucked? I grabbed the soap, squirted it into a paw, and lathered up under my tail. After a rinse, I washed it again, and if I could wash up inside myself I would've done that too.

Drying off, I felt calmer, but still no closer to understanding what had happened. First off, how could he? Second, how could he not tell me about it? We told each other everything…pretty much.

Tap tap tap.

I perked my ears to the door. "Rocky?" Marquize's voice came softly. "Hey, you don't have to talk or anything, but…I really gotta pee."

I wrapped the towel around my waist and yanked the door open. "Fine," I said, and stalked out into the room.

He didn't go in to pee. He followed me to the bed and when I went around to the side facing the wall and sat there, he leaned against the wall. I looked away but he spoke anyway. "One more thing."

"Oh, one *more* thing?" I looked up. "Did you sleep with Coach Murphy, too?"

"No." He inhaled. "Over Christmas, that time you rode with me to the airport? Frio paid for us to spend a couple days at the beach before I went home to Port City. That's where we…" His eyes flicked to the Personal Lubricant still on the bed. "That's where I did that for the first time."

"Were you on top?" My voice felt robotic.

He shook his head. "No, he wanted to."

"All right." I stared up at him. "Any more things?"

Slowly, he shook his head again. I pulled the blankets down on the bed I was sitting on. "All right. I'm going to sleep in this bed."

"Okay." His voice cracked. He went into the bathroom and shut the door.

I dropped the towel to the floor and slid under the blanket, lying on my side. I wasn't cold even though my fur was still damp, but I didn't want to be exposed.

A few moments later, the ear that wasn't pressed into the pillow heard the bathroom door open. Cheetahs can't retract their claws, so Marquize scratched his way across the carpet just like I did. He paused between the two beds. *Don't you dare*, I thought, and as if he'd heard me, he moved to the other bed and lay atop it.

Sleep, damn it, I ordered my brain, but it kept running through a barrage of thoughts that landed and then topspun away. Marquize in my position, Frio on top of him. I couldn't quite remember what Frio looked like anymore, but I could hear his voice and smell his scent, and I seemed to feel them on top of me. My tail curled tightly down between my legs, but that didn't stop my imagination from worming its way in there.

And then worse thoughts. *You're special*, Frio had told me, but then he went and slept with Marquize. How special did that make me? That had all been nothing but a seductive lie, an attempt to get me into his bed. He hadn't thought I was special at all, only an easy target, a cub confused about sex and sexuality who might let himself be fucked if Frio said the right thing. And he was good at saying the right thing. I'd been close, hadn't I? I'd lain in that hotel bed erect and wanting it, and only the barest effort of will had reminded me that I didn't want it from Frio.

Marquize's breathing hitched, like he was trying to hide that he was crying. Acting, or real? I didn't know, couldn't know. How could I trust him again? And yet, what if Frio had worked the same spell on him? I was the one who'd told Marquize about him, and I'd told Frio about Marquize. Granted, I'd hidden it, but with all the expert cunning of a sixteen-year-old jackal from Lunda who didn't know anything about relationships and not much about sexual predators, either. Jaded old eighteen-year-old Rocky looked back at that foolish cub now and squeezed his eyes shut, remembering the innocence with which he'd approached Frio.

What if Frio, expert charmer, had encouraged Marquize with words and movements? Holding our arms a little longer, Marquize had said once. What if he'd lured Marquize in so that the cheetah would be the one to ask and the clever ferret could always say that he had nothing to do with it, that it had been the student who'd seduced the teacher? Could that make him less culpable? And Marquize, for all that he'd hidden his affair from me, had been barely more cunning than I'd been. I'd just been too innocent to think to ask about him taking a regional airline to Port City, or about not texting me at all the day we went to OzWorld.

Frio had threatened me; probably he'd threatened Marquize as well. Maybe he didn't really want to keep the secret and now I'd forced it out of him. On the flip side, though, we'd been out of Palm Gables for almost two years at this point. How much longer did he need to keep the secret?

On the other bed, my boyfriend's breathing evened out. Guess he had less trouble getting to sleep than I did. Good for him.

I wished I had someone to call, to vent to about this. Ma was gone (and good thing for Marquize, because if I told her what he'd done and she was within striking distance, he might find himself without the means to fuck anyone ever again). Ori was gone. I didn't know Paulie well enough to call him up and talk, let alone Danver or Sean. Maybe Lochen, and at some point I probably would have to have the conversation about my sexuality with him, but I didn't want to lead into it with this. No, I had nobody but myself to talk to, to volley thoughts back and forth with, to try to balance comforting myself at Marquize's betrayal with feeling empathy for him, seduced (maybe) by Frio, forced to carry around that secret with him for years and then having it pried out of him at the worst possible moment.

Back and forth I went, feeling sorry for myself and angry at myself and angry at Marquize and sorry for Marquize, and without realizing it, I slipped into a dream where I was yelling at Ma about the crate of tennis balls we were supposed to have gotten and how without them I wouldn't be able to play in the final. She was telling me that they hadn't arrived fast enough and that I should have known before I ordered them from that place I'd ordered them from. And then I was blinking the sun out of my crusted eyes and rubbing my head into a damp pillow in a hotel room in Sequoyah City, and I had to pee.

Chapter Seventeen

When I came back from the bathroom, Marquize was sitting up in his bed staring at his phone. I crouched down beside my bed and dressed quickly, pulling clothes on over my matted and disheveled fur. We'd planned to have breakfast before going off to my bus back to Fort Allen, which left at eleven, but my previous attitude of anger and worry had simmered into a vaguely noxious unease that hung around my stomach and in other places I preferred not to think about.

I stood up, fully dressed, and threw everything into my bag. "Rocky," Marquize said.

"Yeah?"

"Can I call you?"

I paused. It seemed like a simple question and yet it held a lot for me to think about. But the answer was easy. "Of course," I said. "Our phones still work."

"Yeah, I mean…" He set his phone aside. "There's a lot of stuff I want to tell you."

The clock read 7:43. I leaned against the wall. "All right. Go ahead."

He turned toward me. "Right now?" I shrugged, and he fidgeted with the covers. "I figured you might want some time to cool off."

"I'm cool."

"Do, uh." He stared down at his paws, the tawny yellow with black patches against the white of the hotel sheets. "Do you still want to be boyfriends?"

"I don't know if I want to be," I said, "but we still are."

"Are we?" His greenish hazel eyes glimmered in the light even though he was turned away from the window.

"We haven't said we're not, so we still are. Right?"

"But not if you don't want to be."

I exhaled, frustrated. "I guess that's something we should talk about. Or do you want me to dump you and walk out?"

"No," he said quickly.

"All right then." I didn't want to look at him. In the back of my mind I thought that that probably wasn't a good sign. "We'll talk about it. But not now."

"I knew you weren't cool," he said.

"You know me pretty well." I folded my arms. "What else did you want to tell me? Go on. We have time." He still didn't say anything. "I don't want to make any decisions about our relationship," I said. "I don't want to have a big movie scene and all that. But that doesn't mean I can't listen to whatever else you want to tell me. Unless it's about someone else you fucked." The profanity sat ugly and sharp on my tongue and I relished it. I was eighteen, I could call things what they were.

"Fair enough." He laid his paws out flat on the sheets. The tip of his tail poked out, remaining very still. "I decided last night and this morning that I should tell you everything. What we did, what we said, and so on. Then you'll know and you can decide what you want to do."

I'd just told him that *we* would decide what to do about us, but I let that pass. Honestly, I didn't really want to hear the litany of sex acts I was sure would follow, or really anything about him and Frio, but I guessed I owed him the chance to talk it out.

(Looking back, I probably—definitely—did not.)

"After you told me what he did, I kept thinking about him. I know we didn't want to do…what we did last night…because we were underage. But I figured that if he was willing to come on to you, he probably didn't care about age. And with him, if we got caught, I mean, he'd get in way worse trouble than I would. So I'd have the advantage.

"I didn't go talk to him right away. I found excuses to stand close to him and talk to him outside of lessons and I think—I thought—he really liked me. Like the way he liked you, you know?"

I didn't say anything. He looked at me but I kept my eyes fixed on the window. "So anyway, one day after practice I told you I forgot something in the locker room and I went back when it was just him there. And I told him I heard that…" He closed his eyes. "I said I heard he liked to walk around naked in front of the students and why didn't he do that here?"

"Seriously?" The word came out before I could stop it.

"It sounds dumb, I know."

"You told him that I told you about him?" My paw slammed the wall behind me. "What were you trying to do?"

His eyes widened. "I—he never said anything about you. I figured if he did it with you, he must have done it with other students."

"Oh, and he wouldn't put it together that you probably heard it from your *best friend*?"

"Yeah, I mean, I'm not dumb, but—"

"You're not convincing me of that."

He started to say something, then took a breath. "I figured he might think it was likely but he wouldn't know for certain. And anyway I told him I wasn't going to tell anyone and that nobody else knew I was asking him."

"You could've gotten me expelled."

"Oh yeah." Now he regained a little spark. "Golden boy, best student since Braden Longacre? Even when we got caught, Coach wouldn't throw you out."

"If Frio wanted me expelled, he'd have found a way."

The spark died again. "All right. I'm sorry about that. I didn't think it would hurt you. And it didn't. But sorry. One more thing I'm sorry for."

I shook my head but kept my ears up and let him go on. "So anyway. He said if I wanted to see him naked, I should go to a hotel room. Or something about he only does that in hotel rooms. The point is…the point is, we went to a motel that weekend. One of the nights you were working. And he, uh. He took his clothes off and I took mine off." His eyes flicked to me. "But we didn't do it, not that night. We touched each other, got off with paws. Like, uh."

He'd been about to say, "Like you and I did," I was sure. At least he had enough sense to stop himself. "Anyway, it was good. It was frightening and dangerous and it felt pretty good. You and I weren't having sex at all. And the next time he, uh, he sucked me off, and he let me try on him, and he taught me some things."

Marquize's blow jobs had always been good, and he'd occasionally taught me things that he'd told me he'd learned from the Internet. I kept my jaw shut. "Two weekends later we did it again, and I told him I wanted to do more stuff. So he said that we could go to a place over Christmas break for a couple days, a really nice beach where nobody knew us, and he could teach me a lot about it. We could take our time and ease into it. That was exciting, it was a chance to go out and get away from everyone and have real sex with this guy who liked me, who was paying for all of it, who said my tennis was really coming along."

And I'd ridden in the cab with him to the airport and he'd given me a friendship bracelet that I still wore on my left wrist, a cloth band in the colors of Lunda's flag. "So I went. And we had sex like… four times in two days. He said I was really good, and talked about maybe coming on tour with me when I went pro.

"But when you turned sixteen, when we started dating…I was so excited. Rocky…it was nothing like with him. I cared about you and being with you was ten times better than with him. So as soon as we started, I stopped with him."

Now I met his eyes. "You didn't do anything with him after I turned sixteen? After that first date?"

His muzzle lowered. "We didn't have sex right away," he said. "You and me, I mean."

"So you kept seeing him. Until that first night?"

"I told him I didn't want to anymore. I felt like I was cheating on you."

"Because you were."

His ears flattened. "We only had sex twice while I was dating you. I promise. And then I said it was over."

"Was either of those times after that first night we did it?"

"No. He was mad at me, remember? That's why he told Coach Murphy. That's why he was watching the cameras. He knew I was probably doing something with you and he wanted to catch me. I mean, I think. He didn't tell me any of that, but he told me I should've been more careful and I should've realized who was really looking out for me. So I think…I mean, that's what I think happened."

"Sounds about right." I glanced down at my bag, then at the clock. 7:58. It seemed impossible that it wasn't even eight o'clock yet.

"Look," Marquize said after a minute. "You want to get some breakfast? Your bus isn't for three hours. You don't have to spend all that time with me, but…I'm hungry."

His contrite demeanor worked on me. I was still mad at him, but after all, he'd gotten expelled from Palm Gables, thrust onto tour before he was ready, and he was still struggling with that. I'd advanced to the next level while he was stagnating, and who could say whether another year in school would have prepared him better? By contrast, I'd left at the right time (seemingly) and was on my way up. That's what everyone said. Would I have left at the right time if it hadn't been for him?

And as bad as it was that he'd done anything with Frio, he'd broken it off when we started sleeping together. He'd cheated on me a couple times before that, but people forgave each other for cheating all the time in the movies. Sometimes their relationships ended up stronger afterwards. There were no more secrets between us now.

(But what about that last Christmas with his family, I wondered? Well—it wasn't likely he'd slept with any of them.)

"I guess I need something to eat," I said grudgingly.

He smiled, and I hated and loved how much that smile made me happy, that I could do that for him. "I'll get dressed," he said, and hurried to the bathroom.

The mix of emotions went back and forth in me. Unable to figure out how I should handle it, I reached out for help from Ma. She would have been calm, she would have looked at it logically. She would have told me that Marquize had been by my side for a year and a half—no, almost two years now; it had been May we'd had sex for the first time—since breaking up with Frio and that obviously he cared about me. Ma wouldn't let him off the hook for the cheating, nor for the really bad decision to attempt to seduce a coach, not to mention the emotional impact on me because he was sleeping with the guy who'd tried to seduce *me*.

And that, of course, was why he'd kept it secret. God. He just shouldn't have done it to begin with.

But I'd done things when I was younger, too, things I wished people would forget. I'd never intentionally betrayed a friend, much less Marquize…unless…no, moving to the Challenger tour wasn't a betrayal, was it? That was for my career. We'd always said that we would respect each other's careers and he'd understood that I was ready to move on. Besides, his affair with Frio had happened years ago. And there hadn't been any harm done…

My eyes lit on the discarded condom wrapper as Marquize left the bathroom and hurried to put his clothes on. His tail curled up again and he was smiling. "There's a Waffle House down the street. I thought we could get the pecan waffles again. Remember, like in—"

"Peachtree, yeah," I said. "Hey, you used condoms with…him, right?"

"Of course," Marquize said, losing his cheer. "He insisted." He pulled on his shirt quickly. "Ready?" he said, as though I might change my mind.

I kept staring at the condom wrapper. "For everything?"

"Uh." He stopped and stared down at the bed. "I mean, for like, what we just did, yeah."

"That's the first time we've used condoms. Did you do…muzzle stuff with him too?"

He stepped back, still staring down at the floor. "I mean, yeah, a couple times…"

I folded my arms. "Did he come in your mouth?"

He saw where I was going right away. "He's a ferret, so there's no species-specific diseases I could catch from him. And the big one, you can't really catch that through the mouth."

"Really? That's not what they told us in that health seminar our first year. Or our second year. 'All contact,' they said."

"Where there's an open wound," Marquize said. "When we do it…like that…there's a chance of small tears, there's lots of places for, uh, but not so much in the mouth. If you get rid of it quick, the chance is almost zero."

"Almost." I kept my voice calm, though it was a struggle now. "Not zero."

"No, but…" He trailed off.

"And what about the skin diseases? You can transmit those through contact, can't you?"

"He didn't have any."

"That you noticed."

"He said he didn't have anything."

"Oh, he's super trustworthy, I'm sure. A coach who'd sleep with his students. Lots of them too, not just you."

That stung him enough to look up at me. "What, did he sleep with you too and you never told me?"

"He would have," I said. "And you don't get to be angry with me."

He dropped his eyes again. "Sorry. I don't know how many times I can say I'm sorry."

"I don't know." Anger dominated the roil of emotions in me again. "What else did you do? Cheated on me, maybe gave me some disease from cheating on me…anything else?"

"You'd have noticed," he said with a hitch in his voice. "If you'd caught anything. It'd have shown up."

"Is that so? I seem to remember a lesson about some diseases not showing symptoms. Do you remember that?"

He didn't say anything. I reached over to the dresser and grabbed my bag. "I'll get my own breakfast. See you around."

"Rocky." He called after me before I'd gone more than a step.

I stopped but didn't turn around. My ears cupped back. After a moment, Marquize went on. "There's free clinics. You can go and be tested anonymously. It's better than going to the doctor. If you use your doctor and your real name, people might talk."

"Free clinics?"

"Yeah, I'll…I'll send you a list of the ones in Fort Allen. That's where you're staying this week, right?"

I paused. "Yeah."

"All right."

I moved toward the door. As I opened it, he said, again, "I'm sorry."

I didn't pause and didn't respond. The door swung shut behind me with a loud thunk.

Chapter Eighteen

Sequoyah City on a Saturday morning at quarter after eight is not a very busy town. A few cars rumbled desultorily down the main street, and not many more people walked by me on the sidewalks, tails mostly down. I strode as quickly as I could toward the bus station, intending to camp out there for two and a half hours until my bus left. As I got closer, though, I passed a fast food place I didn't know, and it looked like they were local and had barbecue-flavored breakfasts. My stomach rumbled, so I wandered in.

The barbecue sauce set my taste buds tingling, but I couldn't enjoy it all that much. I kept thinking about what disease I might have courtesy of Frio and Marquize. And I couldn't decide whether or not that bothered me more or less than Marquize's betrayal. At the core of it, I thought as I chewed mechanically on a breakfast barbecue burrito wrap, the worst part was that I'd thought we were sharing this first experience together. And for him it hadn't been a first, it had been something he'd done before and now was doing with me. It wasn't special for him at all, and now I'd never be able to share my first time with anyone else again.

I finished the burrito and sat there licking the barbecue sauce out of my finger pads, staring at the little bits of egg and pepper and bacon scattered over my paper plate. Still more than two hours to the bus, and nothing to do but turn over the events of last night in my head. It had all gone from what was supposed to be the best night of my life so far to approaching the worst. I took out my phone and tried to call Ma, which I knew I wasn't supposed to do and wouldn't do any good anyway because I'd make a bigger mess than I had of the burrito if I tried to tell her about everything. But I was dialing the number anyway and listening to a series of clicks and then a harsh strident tone and a message telling me the line had been disconnected.

Of course it had. Ma couldn't use it over in Lunda and she wouldn't have kept up the payments. I don't know why I'd even tried to call.

Kamina's number came up next. I dialed it. It rang and rang and rang and nobody answered.

I put the phone back in my pocket and played with the cloth band around my wrist as I sat there in the restaurant, alone.

Chapter Nineteen

Marquize texted me twice on the bus ride home. I deleted both messages without looking at them. I know that's not the way a boyfriend should act, but I had spent a lot of the morning thinking about going to a free clinic and getting more and more scared and angry about it. What if someone recognized me? What if it turned out Marquize had gotten something from Frio and passed it on to me? What would I have to do next? I couldn't stop from thinking over and over about the worst-case scenarios and so I knew I wasn't in any mood to talk to Marquize or even read what he had to say. I told myself I would text him later, when I felt more able to deal with things.

Then there was Frio, too. Had he seduced Marquize because he knew it would get back to me? He knew we were friends, and I couldn't help but think that his paying so much attention to Marquize had in some way been a message aimed at me. Arrogant, self-centered maybe, but my last meeting with the ferret had convinced me that he held a grudge for my rejection. Escaping Palm Gables should have gotten me away from him, and yet here he was reaching out again to ruin what should have been a beautiful moment for me.

The bus ride took forever, just as it had on the way to Sequoyah City, but for a very different reason. I slept for a few of the six hours on and off, each time hoping that I'd woken up at Fort Allen and scared I'd slept past it. When we finally pulled into Fort Allen, I grabbed my bag and stalked off the bus, and rather than get into one of the taxis, I decided to walk the ten miles back to the condo I was staying in, figuring that maybe the exercise would help me cool down, and also realizing that I didn't want to talk to Danver either.

I stopped for dinner on the way back and got to the condo

around 8:30, worn out. I knew I was going to have to practice on Sunday, but I didn't really feel like it. I didn't feel like doing anything, and my hope that Danver was already out was dashed when the squirrel came running down the stairs as soon as I got in the door. "Rocky! Hey, how was your night out? Was it good to see your friend again? Did you guys get lucky at all? Where'd you go? You just get back now? You gotta come out to this place I found last night. It's great. They don't card, so you can totally come, not that I got any alcohol at all, I know that's bad, I gotta stay in shape. But woo, you should see the action there. Plus they got live music Friday and Saturday night and I wanna go back tonight, this cacomistle said the Saturday night band is great. If you're up for it, I mean. It's over in Silver, that's half an hour away, and they start at ten so you've got, uh, an hour or so to freshen up if you want."

"Let me get settled," I said, but unfortunately he and I were sharing a room with twin beds in it, so he followed me back to our room, chattering the whole time. Finally I said I'd go in the hope that it would shut him up, and it sort of worked, because he ran to the bathroom to get ready.

I almost told him I wasn't going, but he was still in the bathroom when I thought that, and by the time he was out I'd scolded myself into going along. What else was I going to do tonight? Sit on my bed and get angry or sad? At least going out would be a distraction.

And it was, but it turned out it didn't help. Even through Danver's incessant chatter about how lucky he'd gotten the night before and his tips about how I should behave, I turned over the confessions of the previous night and that morning in my head. The question I kept coming back to was whether I should dump Marquize or not. He'd betrayed me, but he'd also supported me for a long time after that and had sworn not to hurt me again. And where was I going to find someone else who was gay and could support my tennis career? No tennis player would admit to being gay; if I dumped Marquize I'd have to find someone gay who could at least adapt to my life.

Or else I could become that guy in the movies who had a series of hookups and didn't have a steady person in their life. I didn't like that as much. Times like now when I really needed someone to talk to, the loneliness felt like a prison I was beating my head against. But I'd have Ma, and I'd have Ori. If I got through this time, then maybe I could satisfy my urge for sex with visits to clubs like Danver did (or said he did; I'd never seen him actually hook up).

We got out of the cab on a loud, neon-bright street. "College town," Danver said of Silver. "Lots of places we can go here, lots of college gals looking for mature guys. That's us." He plucked the lapel of his jacket.

Mature? Eighteen was both older and younger than I'd thought it would be, confusing as hell and about as far from mature as I could imagine. But Danver's chatter as we walked up the street looking for a club did provide me with a new question: could I pick up someone and sleep with her? I'd dated Shawna for a while so I was pretty sure I could fake my way through sex with a female. That would be cheating on Marquize, of course, unless I called him and broke up right now.

Tempting. But hasty. I still wasn't sure I wanted to be his boyfriend, but I also wasn't sure I didn't, so it was best to leave it there. My brain went on to tell me that if I cheated on Marquize it would make us even, but that wasn't the kind of even I wanted to be with him. *Two wrongs don't make a right*, Ma said. I wanted to be even with Marquize by forgiving him for what he'd done, and I definitely was not there yet.

And as I was trailing Danver wondering whether I could actually convince anyone to even try to have sex with me, I glanced down an alley and saw a neon rainbow flag in the window of a club two blocks away. So maybe there was an opportunity to meet a male interested in sex—or at least see what that kind of club was like.

But no, I couldn't stroll into a gay club. What if I was recognized? What were the chances, furthermore, that it was all-ages? What if Danver caught me coming out of it?

"Come on," Danver said. "The band's already started."

Like I couldn't tell. My ears flattened, but the upside to the blaring, strident music was that if I didn't focus my ears on the squirrel, I couldn't hear him, and my oblivious small-eared friend went on chattering as we walked in and found standing room near the bar.

There I had to listen to him again, and worse, I had to find responses to his questions. He'd reached one of those moments where he would say, "Wow, I talk too much!" and pepper me with questions as a way to make up for it. Where had me and my friend gone? How was it? We were slated to hit the Sequoyah City tournament in six months, should we go back to this club?

"It wasn't a club," I muttered in an ill-advised moment of honesty, which led to more questions, and finally I remembered that there'd been a bowling alley next to the hotel and said, "We went bowling and hung out."

That did the trick. Danver said, "You can mess up your elbow bowling, you should be careful." But he didn't want to hear any more about it. And soon enough he was dragging me to the bar to be his "sidekick" in his attempt to pick up a pair of chinchillas.

I couldn't handle that for long, so after fifteen excruciating minutes during which I and the chinchilla Danver wasn't interested in exchanged a total of about five words, I mumbled and pointed at the bathroom, which fortunately happened to be in the same part of the club as a bright red EXIT sign glowing like a beacon through the dim haze.

Out back, the cold air invigorated my lungs almost as much as the silence relaxed my mind. I walked a block or two before remembering the bar with the rainbow flag. Probably they were over-21 only, but it was a college town, Danver'd said; it was worth a shot.

A few minutes later, I found it, a small building with the name "Politics" over the door. Though a faded "WE CARD" sticker adorned the window, nobody was actually checking IDs. It smelled warm and masculine inside, with a lot of beer that made my nose wrinkle, but conversation drowned out the music, and I liked that. And nobody I knew was visible through the dark windows, nor when I cautiously slipped in the door. So I made my way to the back and waited until I caught the attention of the wolf behind the bar in a white tank top with a blue checked collared shirt open over it.

"Hey," he said, and pulled a paper wristband out from behind the bar. "Let's see some ID."

"I just want a Coke."

He squinted at me. "Just Coke?"

"Yeah."

He had a lot of grey on his muzzle and ears, and I caught the scent of wood dust and beer on him as he looked me up and down. Finally he tucked the wristband back under the counter. "All right," he said, "but drink it at the bar here."

"Uh…" I slid onto the nearest stool. "Sure."

"If I see you adding anything to it, you're out of here," he warned.

"I won't, I promise."

He grabbed a glass from below the counter and aimed a nozzle on a hose into it until it foamed with Coke, then slid it over the bar. "Three dollars."

Remembering Danver's tipping, I fished out a five and said, "Keep it."

"Thanks." He pocketed the bill and walked away.

Left alone with a cold Coke and time to think, my mood slowly improved. This whole bar was full of gay guys, presumably; even the bartender sported six small earrings in the pride colors down the edge of his right ear. There were more gay guys here than I'd met (knowingly) in my life. They laughed, talked, and rested paws on each others' arms and hips and tails while I watched from the end of the bar. The scene interested me but didn't attract me; someday I was sure I'd want to be part of that crowd, but at that moment the memory of the night with Marquize was too fresh. It occurred to me that someone here might be able to listen to my problem, but even that was more than I wanted to do.

Even though I felt separate, being in the bar calmed me and reassured me. There were a lot of guys here, a big crowd of boys who liked boys. If things didn't work out with Marquize, it wasn't the end of the world. I had options, and a lot of them were my age and kinda cute.

I made a game out of picking the cute ones. At first I was doing it because it was something I'd heard guys talking about (mostly about girls); as it went on, I started enjoying imagining myself with them. They would be dependable and trustworthy and wouldn't go behind my back fucking my child molester coach. There was a rat in a cute blue sweater who looked like he had good muscles, and the light caught his smile when he turned his head. A wild cat—it took me a few minutes to come up with "genet"—wore his shirt open and the fur and lines of his chest caught my eye, as did the movement of his tail and his rear when he turned around. A marmot shuffled back and forth to the music playing in the background, clapping his paws, and I liked the energy and rhythm he had.

And then a fox caught my eye. He reminded me of Nashan a little, over six feet tall, and I only knew he was a fox because I saw his dark bushy tail with the white tip gleaming in the light. He wore a hoodie over his ears and most of his muzzle, but his pants showed off his muscular thighs and rear. Not bad. And this was different from being in the locker room with Nashan. This guy was in a gay club. His butt was fair game.

So, I guessed, was mine. I snuck looks to see if anyone was checking me out, but it was hard to tell. I wagged my tail at the thought of it though, and adjusted the way I was sitting to show my butt off a little more (I thought—I couldn't tell, to be honest). It'd be nice to be approached, to have someone be interested in me even if I couldn't do anything about it tonight.

The cloth bracelet on my wrist intruded on my awareness more tonight than it had been since the week I'd started wearing it. I'd gotten used to it so that I barely noticed it, but all through the bus ride I'd played with it, and all through the evening my paws kept returning to it, picking at it, as though maybe if I loosened enough threads it would fall off of its own accord.

The bartender came back and, without asking, pointed his soda nozzle at my glass and refilled it. "Thanks," I said, and he nodded.

My phone buzzed. I hesitated, thinking it might be Marquize, but it was Danver: *Hey wered ya go*

He wouldn't come looking for me in Politics, I was sure, but I didn't want him to try. *Needed some air*, I wrote back. *Sorry.*

I promised him I'd be back at that club soon. I wasn't ready to go back yet, though. I liked being in this place where guys could kiss other guys (that genet was kissing a tall, slender pine marten) and where you could imagine that one of these guys might want to go to a hotel room with you. And likely they would.

But not me, not tonight. I pulled at the cloth bracelet and looked down at my Coke. Once I'd finished I should go back and rejoin Danver. This was a nice escape, but I had a lot to think about before I could come back to a place like this and worry about whether I had the courage to go up to the marmot, or the genet, or even that fox, who'd moved to a table a little ways away from me and was deep in conversation with a rabbit.

"Hey." The rat I'd been looking at slid in next to me at the bar. He had a nice scent, something store-bought but not bad, floral and probably light to his nose.

"Hi." I took a drink of Coke because I didn't know what to say next.

"Saw you looking at me." He leaned his elbows on the bar. "Haven't seen you in here before. Freshman?"

I almost said that I hadn't been in a while, but then I remembered someone telling me that the labels reset when you got to college, so an eighteen-year-old would be a freshman again in his first year. "Kind of," I said.

"I'm Allen."

"Uh, Rocky."

"Rocky?" He chuckled. "Is that a nickname or something?"

"Well, my name's Rochi," I said, "but when I came to the States I changed it so it'd be easier to say."

"Also cooler. I like it. Where'd you come to the States from?"

"Africa," I said, so as not to be too specific.

"Nice. What's your major?"

It was too hard to think of a lie or a way to evade questions for me at this point. "I'm not really a freshman," I said. "I'm eighteen but I'm actually a tennis player."

His ears flicked. "A tennis player? Like that's your job?"

"Uh-huh. There's a guy I'm staying with in, uh," I realized at the last minute I shouldn't tell him where I was staying, "a condo around here. There's a tournament here, and, uh." Too late I realized I didn't know him at all and I was giving him information to track me down.

He reacted with only mild interest. "Oh. So if I find it on TV I could see you play?"

"Maybe. But I think you'd need to have a local TV station. I'm not at the tournaments that get onto national TV. Yet."

He grinned and then leaned in close. "So you wanna get out of here?"

I did, but I shook my head. "I can't. I just came in for a drink." He looked hurt, and then I realized that I could explain the situation honestly and that he would understand. "I have a boyfriend. We just had a huge fight."

"Ohhh." He nodded and the hurt vanished. "Look, if you want to blow off some steam…"

Was that a euphemism for a sex act? "No, I'm fine."

He accepted that. "What was the fight about?"

"Oh, I found out he slept with someone else like a year or so ago and he never told me."

"Ah." Allen patted my arm. "What an asshole. But you're still together?"

"Until we break up, I guess. I didn't dump him."

"Good for you. Are you going to?"

I eyed him, and he laughed, holding a paw up. "I'm not hittin' on you. Promise. Just listening now."

So I told him I didn't know what I was going to do, and explained a little about how difficult it was and how close the two of us had been, how we'd been the only ones there for each other for so long. At the end of it, Allen made a "hmm" noise and said, "I think maybe he was taking advantage of you guys being so isolated. There's lots of guys out there, Rocky."

"But I really do love him. Or, I used to."

"If you do," the rat said, "work that out. But don't stick with him because you think you don't have another choice." His paw swept the air in front of us, indicating the room. "Look, you got lots of choices."

"I was thinking that." I finished my Coke. "I've never been in a gay bar before."

"Come back to this one sometime. It's pretty chill."

"Yeah, but for right now I gotta go meet my friend." His eyebrow rose, so I clarified. "My straight friend. Who doesn't know where I am. Or why I'd be, uh, here."

Then Allen laughed as I stood. "Cool," he said. "But hey, do you want my number? Like if you want to talk to someone sometime?"

Damn, it was tempting. Looking back, I wish I'd said yes. But I was scared of making attachments and I still felt like he wanted to sleep with me. Giving him my phone number would establish a connection that I wasn't ready for. So I shook my head. "I appreciate the talk, but sorry, I'd rather not."

"All right." I couldn't tell whether or not he was offended. His ears stayed up as he got up with me, said good-bye, and headed toward a table near the large wall painting of a naked rabbit kept modest by purple rose blossoms.

Outside, I breathed in the chilly air and rubbed my nose. Danver was probably still at that other bar.

I'd taken one step in that direction when a paw landed on my shoulder. Before I could fully turn to see the fox in the hoodie, he growled almost right in my ear. "Don't tell people you're a professional tennis player."

"What?" There was something about his voice, but I couldn't really see his muzzle. Only his eyes shone out from under the hood.

"You think it's hard for people to look up a jackal? You think it won't be news maybe when you're more famous?"

"Why—I mean, who—"

"Just say you work in construction. Nobody asks questions about that. All right?"

The flicking of his white tail tip drew my eyes, and then I saw that what I'd assumed to be a russet tail in the dim light of the bar was actually a darker brown, like a mix of fall leaves. And then it clicked: the voice, the tail, the warning. "Braden?"

"My name is Joe. I work in construction," he said, and put a finger to the end of his muzzle. Then he turned and walked away.

Chapter Twenty

E ven Danver's chatter couldn't penetrate my thoughts for the rest of that night. Braden Longacre, in a college gay bar? Of course he was in Fort Allen for the same reason I was; of course he would've thought that Silver was far enough that he didn't have to risk running into anyone who knew him. Or maybe it was just that Politics was a really good gay bar. It was the only one I'd ever been in, so I had no way of judging.

But Braden had been in a gay bar. So he was gay, too? He'd been hitting on a guy, or chatting with a guy…it was possible that he was just there with a friend, right? But no, he'd left me with that line about being in construction, which was what he'd told me to say. So he was gay, and experienced in going out to bars and hooking up for a night.

Could I talk to him about it? He certainly hadn't seemed all that interested in having a conversation, though that might have been the circumstances: out on a public street where anyone could hear. But oh, I wanted to talk to him about Marquize and about Frio—

Frio. Braden and Frio had gone off and had that conversation the time he'd come to play me at Palm Gables, a meeting which now took on a different cast knowing that both of them were gay. When Braden had been a student, had Frio come on to him? Did the ferret have a string of gay students, one a year or more, stretching back to whenever he'd started?

That possibility put Marquize's betrayal into perspective. He was as much a victim as perpetrator; even if he'd truly initiated the contact with Frio, he'd only done so after Frio had come on to me and I'd told him. Frio had done this before and he was the one I should be mad at.

The funny thing was that even though I could work through all of that logically, it didn't change how I was feeling. I still didn't want to talk to Marquize. I'd rather talk to Braden, but I wasn't sure he would want to talk to me.

By the time we got back to the condo, I'd allowed Danver to tell me about his night, which included the usual parade of lovely ladies he would totally have gone off with if he didn't have to come back to the condo tonight, or if he'd had the money to buy them one more drink, or if their friends hadn't shown up at just the wrong time. He did claim that one pretty drunk chinchilla had given him a good groping, and even though I wasn't sure how much credence to give any of his stories, that one was so tame that I believed it.

* * *

Marquize sent me the address of a clinic in Fort Allen, but they didn't have any appointment openings until the last week of the tournament. Fortunately—or not—I lost my second match, so by that last Tuesday, I wasn't playing anymore. After practice, I told Danver I was going out to meet a friend and I hopped in a cab.

The cab was twenty each way, which was a lot, but not so much that I couldn't afford it. Marquize had told me to send him whatever it cost me to get there and back, and anything else, but I didn't want to take him up on it. Partly I think I was punishing him: paying for my cab would make him feel better, and I didn't want him to feel better. I still blamed Frio for most of it, but as the cab pulled up in front of a smelly, run-down block, I hated the fact that I had to come here, hated that I was scared about what might happen here, and I was angry at Marquize for putting me in this situation.

I looked for the street number and found a squat taupe building, cleaner than the ones around it, with blue letters across the top that read, "Community Health Clinic." A squirrel and a zebra leaned against one of the front windows passing a cigarette back and forth. I took a breath and pushed the door open.

I'd worn my rattiest non-tennis clothes, jeans I'd outgrown over a year ago and a t-shirt I'd ripped longer ago than that. And when I pushed open the door of the clinic and walked in, I felt self-conscious about my pants ending above my ankles. The waiting room was crowded with people and all of them turned to look at me. Braden had me paranoid: did any of them follow tennis? Recognize me maybe? But nobody made any sign that they did.

I walked up to the window that said, "REGISTER HERE," behind a fennec fox in a leather vest whose piercings clinked when he moved and a skinny Bengal tiger whose tail flicked over the waistband of jeans slung so low I could see half his butt. It seemed to take forever for them to get processed, leaving me apprehensive about how complicated the registration could be because I was trying not to listen to their conversations.

It was hard with the fennec, though. He kept trying to give specifics about what sex acts he'd done to the receptionist and asking, "Can you catch it from that?" The tall red wolf patiently asked him to write down the information on the form, which finally he did.

When it was my turn, I wanted to talk as little as possible, and I think she appreciated that. I gave her my appointment number and got back a form and a little card with four stickers on it. One went on each copy of the triplicate form, and the last I was supposed to give to the person who drew my blood. The stickers had a barcode and a number and the red wolf stressed that I was never to use my name, only that number. On the form, all I had to fill out was the date, my gender and age range, and there was an optional section if I wanted to test for only certain diseases. I hesitated and left it blank. Might as well get tested for all of them.

She examined the form when I'd given it back to her and nodded, pulling the triplicate sheets apart. She gave me back the bottom paper. "After you get tested, it'll be three days. Make sure you bring this form in when you come to pick it up."

"Ah…three days?" I stared down at the paper, then up at the wolf. "I'll be somewhere else by then."

"We'll hold the results for six months." She was already looking behind me.

"Can't I…call in?" I looked for a phone number on my paper. "Or something?"

She gave me a tired look. "If you can show us that barcode over the phone, you can call in."

I sighed and took the paper to a vacant chair, figuring out when in the next many months I would be able to get back to Fort Allen to pick up my test results. I still hadn't figured it out twenty minutes later when they called my number.

The nurse, a male I thought was an armadillo until I got closer and saw the overlapping scales, sat me down in a chair and brought out a rubber band he wrapped around my arm just above the elbow. "Small shave," he said, though his accent was thick enough that I didn't quite get it until he brought out a scalpel. The thought ran through my head that he was going to stab my arm with it, but there was also a syringe on the tray next to me with a needle attached to it and that seemed much more likely to be the bloodletting tool, so I just breathed deeply.

"First time?" he asked as he applied the scalpel to a small area of fur on the inside of my elbow, efficiently shaving it down to the skin.

That I understood. "Yes."

He had a long smile with even rows of low, flat teeth. "Don't to worry. Small poke, very easy. Don't to look if don't want to."

"Okay. Thank you." I stared at the scales. "If you don't mind me asking…what are you?"

"Pangolin. From Myanmar." He smiled again and swabbed the bare skin with some cool liquid. "And what are you? Not coyote, not fox."

"Jackal." It relaxed me to think that he didn't know me any more than I knew him.

"Okay, jackal," he said. "Relax here, small poke."

I looked away. There was a jab at the inside of my elbow that tightened up all my muscles, and then the pangolin said, "Easy, easy. Relax. Little more. Little more. Okay." And then his paws moved deftly and the little pain in my elbow was gone, replaced with pressure as he held a bandage over the wound. "Hold here please?"

I pressed my thumb down over the pad. He fiddled with the syringe, full of a dark red liquid, and then took the sticker from my card. "This your sticker, yes? You watch." And I watched as he peeled off the sticker and put it on my syringe. "Your blood, no mistake."

"Thanks." I stared at my blood in the syringe. What was in there? What would they find? It was strange and slightly nauseating to think that there might be germs in there that had made their way from Frio to me through Marquize, and from who knows whom before that. It wasn't out of the question that if Frio and Braden had had sex, I might share more with Braden than a preference for the male body. How far did those commonalities spread, I wondered?

"You feel okay?" He peered at me closely as he removed the needle and set the vial in a tray with several others.

"Fine," I lied, already planning to go to a pharmacy on the way back and buy the biggest box of condoms I could find and use them for everything.

"Good." He gave me a thick rubber band to wrap around my elbow to hold the bandage in place. "Keep this on one hour. After that, small Band-Aid, is fine."

"Thanks," I said again, and got up. He watched me as though worried I might topple over, but I walked out of the clinic without a problem. Without a physical problem, anyway.

All the way back to the condo, I agonized, and finally decided I had to call Lochen to see if I could get a later flight out of Fort Allen. When he asked why, I had a lie ready. "I messed up my racket and the place is going to take three days to restring it."

Unfortunately, Lochen had an answer. "That's ridiculous. What place is it? Go get it today and bring it to Coverset. I know a place there that'll do it in a day."

"They might've already started," I said.

"Doesn't matter. Didn't I tell you if you need a restring to go to a place that caters to pros? They're a little more pricey, but you can't sit around waiting three days for a racket. Three days!"

"I, uh, I don't know if I can get it back," I said.

He was quiet for a moment. "Are you in some sort of trouble?" When I didn't answer, he said, "If you owe someone money, we can take care of that. Don't worry about it. I mean, worry, because we're going to have a conversation about your money management or gambling habit or something, but right now I want to help make the problem go away."

"No," I said. "Nothing like that." I took a breath.

"Rocky, what is it?"

"I had to get a blood test," I said. "They won't have the results for three days."

I waited for him to ask more questions. *Blood test? Why, did you have gay sex? Are you gay?* But he just laughed. "Ah, kid, so you picked up some girl and forgot to wrap up your dick? That's no problem. You shoulda just told me. Went to a free clinic or something?"

"Yeah." My throat was dry. I'd forgotten that you could get diseases from straight sex, too.

"Well, happy eighteenth birthday. Welcome to the adult world. You need me to get you some condoms?"

"No, I got 'em now."

"Okay. Let's see, three days, so…let me get the schedule here. Hm. That gets you in the night before qualifiers start. I'll call the tournament and get you a medical to come in late. You just have to fill out a couple things and we'll be all set. Look for the forms in your inbox in a few hours. Okay?"

"Yeah. Thanks." I still could barely talk.

"No problem, Rock. I'm here to take care of you. Hey, speaking of which, I meant to call you. I got another client, I think you'd do well with him in doubles. He's an arctic fox, Aliq Loize." He pronounced it "Loy-zha" and then spelled it for me. "Real workaholic, good guy. He'll be in Coverset and if you guys hit it off I'll enter you in the next set of tournaments down in Pensa."

"Sure," I said. I probably would've agreed to anything he said at that point.

"Great. See you in Coverset. And good luck. If the test comes back positive, let me know. You should probably get another one in three months just to be sure. I'll set it up as part of a routine physical, don't worry about it. Oh. If anyone asks why you had a blood test, tell 'em it was an anti-doping thing."

"Doping?"

"Performance-enhancing drugs. They do random testing here and there, not very much in tennis, but enough. I mean, if you don't want to talk about your sex life, which it seems like maybe you don't."

213

"Not really. Thank you."

"No problem, Rocky. It's what I'm here for."

The conversation didn't make me feel any better about the potential results of the blood test, but it did at least reassure me that if I got into trouble in the future, I could count on my manager to help me out with it as discreetly as possible. That was the first time I really thought about whether I could tell him I was gay. But there was no longer a need to, and wouldn't be as long as the test came back negative.

* * *

The ride back to the clinic was worse than the first trip. I knew I was going to get news one way or another and I couldn't stay calm. It's probably nothing, I thought. Probably nothing. But what if it's something? What will I do?

Being able to fall back on Lochen was comforting, a little bit, but even he wouldn't be able to erase whatever was already in my bloodstream. I'd done some research on the various ailments I might've gotten, and they ranged from annoying and embarrassing sores or warts to a disease that would require expensive medications and might ultimately still kill me in ten or twenty years.

There was a different window at the clinic for results. No line at this one, because the transaction was simple: I walked up, handed my form to the coyote behind the counter, and she scanned the barcode, then turned to the file cabinets behind her and pulled a sealed envelope out of it. We compared the sticker on the form stapled to the envelope with my sticker and form, and then she gave me the envelope.

I walked outside, heart pounding, envelope clutched in my paw. If I didn't open it, a nonsensical voice said in my head, it would never be confirmed one way or another. If I left it sealed, I would always maybe have a disease but never definitely.

And then I seemed to hear Ma telling me, "Ro, that's nonsense. You have what you have, and right now the only thing you definitely don't have is knowledge. Would you choose to go into a tennis match not knowing if your opponent would be Marquize or Braden

Longacre? Know your opponent."

I don't know if Ma would actually have used Braden as an example; probably she would have picked then-number one player Tempest. But that's how my mind painted her words, and like a plunge into an ice bath, they shocked me alert. I slipped a claw under the flap of the envelope and tore.

NEGATIVE.

I read that word first, in big bold letters, and then all the other words around it. "For all tests." "Blood sample submitted March 29, 2012." And below, the list of diseases tested for, with a smaller "negative" next to every one of them. Every single one. I scanned the list twice and then shoved the paper back into the envelope.

"Thanks, Ma," I whispered, and called a cab to take me back to the condo.

* * *

I made two phone calls before leaving Fort Allen. One was to Kamina, telling her to have Ma call me. She was frostily cordial, but I believed she would do as I asked.

The other was to Marquize. "I got my test results back," I said.

"Yeah?"

"I don't have anything."

He exhaled across the phone. "Good."

"They said test three months after last exposure and it's been three months since I last…more or less, I mean. So anyway. Looks like I'm clean. Thought you'd want to know."

"I did." When I didn't say anything, he said, "Rocky?"

"Yeah?"

"How are you?"

How was I? I'd gone through this nerve-wracking ordeal of being tested, juggling my schedule, not to mention I kept thinking about Frio now when I'd think about any kind of relationship. I didn't have anyone I trusted anymore, not as fully as I had Marquize. About the only positives that came out of this had been that I trusted Lochen more, and I felt like I was starting my sexual history over again with a clean slate. "Fine," I said.

"You're in Coverset?"

"Going today. I had to get my test results."

"Oh." He digested that. "I was thinking, your Pensa tournament is just a week off mine. We'll both be there around the same time."

"Uh huh."

"So I'll give you a call? Maybe we can…get a drink or something?"

"Maybe. I'll see how I feel then."

A longer pause. I wanted to make him hang up, and eventually he did. "Okay, I'll call you. See ya, Rocky."

I felt bad as soon as we hung up. Why was it that when I was talking to him I was mad at him, but when I acted angry at him, I felt bad about it afterwards? My relationship with Shawna hadn't been anywhere near this complicated. I'd liked her, and then I'd liked tennis more than her, and then I'd been mad at her. Now I was mad at Marquize and hurt, but I still loved him and felt bad when I saw him feeling bad, doubly so when it was because of me.

The remedy, as it had been with Shawna, was tennis. I got my gear together and read through the info Coach Keely had sent me on my upcoming opponents. His reports were short, but I was learning to read them so I could envision myself on the court, imagining what the opponent would play like, mentally going through my responses. Coach Keely had taught me that technique, and while it was difficult to pick up, it had helped me out in one or two matches and I could see where it would work. So that's what got me through that night and on to Coverset.

Chapter Twenty-One

Aliq Loize was an arctic fox shorter than me by a few inches, but with a more muscular frame that showed under his close-shaved fur. Where Dom had let his grow out and molt, Aliq kept his neatly groomed all the time, and as a consequence I could see the rounded curves of his biceps and chest, and even a small ridge of fur tracing the outline of his abdominal muscles.

I'd caught him in the middle of practice, so I watched him volley with his partner. He wore only a pair of mid-thigh blue shorts that did little to conceal that his butt was as tight as the rest of him. Last week I'd have felt guilty for admiring his body; this week I let myself do it, entertaining a brief fantasy in which he confessed to me that he, too, was gay. Even though I knew that wouldn't happen, I still enjoyed watching him.

He knew who I was right away, and came over to shake my paw when his practice was over, holding a bottle of some weird branded drink from which he took frequent gulps. "Hey, Rocky, right?"

"Yeah. Aliq?"

"Uh huh." Gulp of drink. "When are you practicing?"

"Already did one session. I have another one in a few hours."

"Good. Good to space 'em out." He looked me up and down appraisingly. "What gym do you use?"

"Whatever's at the facility or the hotel."

"Oh, boy." He shook his head. "You gotta get a gym membership. You can't do all the focused work you need to in a hotel gym. I do an hour and a half every morning before I even pick up a tennis racket."

"Doesn't that, ah, wear you out?"

"Nah. I don't do it on match days, y'see, so those days I got all

this extra energy to spare." Gulp. "I can hook you up with a program if you want."

"I'll take a look, sure. How much doubles have you played?"

He drained the bottle and tossed it in a nearby trash can. I walked with him to the bench where his gear was. "A year or so. Only been on the Challenger circuit a few months."

"Me too. Was in Futures for a year and a half before that."

"Ah." He waved a paw. "I played for my high school team. Won the state finals with them and took fourth in Nationals. Lochen contacted me and said I should go right to Challenger. He said there'd be a few tough years but better to start at that level." He peered at me. "So you didn't graduate high school?"

I thought about Ma and her equivalency studies, which I'd been neglecting since she'd left. "I went to a tennis academy—"

"Which one?"

"Palm Gables."

"Nice."

"For two years on a scholarship and then I decided to leave and turn pro."

"Not bad." He grinned. "So when do you want to start practicing? Can't wait to get out on the court with ya."

We set a time for the next day and shook paws. He had a firm grip, a little firmer than it needed to be, so I squeezed back and matched his grin with mine. This partnership might not include all the things mine and Marquize had, but I had a feeling it was going to be fun.

* * *

I still had those equivalency degree textbooks. That night, I got them out again and went back to where I'd left off. I found the last math problem I'd done—that Marquize and I had done. We'd joked about some of the trigonometry terms: which one of us would be the sine and which the cosine. I couldn't remember now, only a few months later, which was which, or if we'd settled the argument with a kiss before it reached any resolution.

I shook that off to focus on the math problem again. Even

without Marquize, I could do this. I didn't know whether he was going to keep pursuing his equivalency, but I wasn't going to let mine lapse.

I'd gotten through three of the math problems when my phone rang. My first split-second thought was that it was Lochen calling, but a moment later, even before I'd spotted the international number, I discarded that thought. "Hello?"

"Rocky?" Ma's voice, scratchy, far away.

"Ma, oh my God, how are you? Where are you?"

"In Lunda still. This is a very complicated matter. But Kamina passed your message to me and I realized I must call you."

"Why haven't you called?"

"I am sorry. I didn't want to call until I had definite news, and it was always just one more week, one more week, until it was months. Kamina is mad at me and at you, and the friends I am staying with must pay for international calls. But I should have called you before now."

"So still no news?"

"No news. I am in negotiations, but there is always another person to include, someone else to pay. I am calling in favors from all my friends, but it may still take weeks. Perhaps months."

"Months?"

"I hoped it would not even take this long. Always they assure me, 'this person can make the deal, this person has Bompaka's ear.' I have only met the chief himself once and I have not yet seen Ori, though I have been assured that she is in good health."

"That's good."

"It's good to talk to you, Ro. Tell me what you've been doing."

So I told her about the tennis, about how difficult Challenger level was but that I was slowly improving, and about Aliq. "And how is Marquize?" she asked when I was done with that.

"He's…fine. Doing the same in Futures."

"'The same' meaning he is getting better too, or he is doing the same as he was?"

"The same as he was."

"Hm. And how are you two?"

Pressure built behind my eyes. "Not…ah. Not great."

I told her all of it, having sex on my eighteenth birthday and Marquize and Frio, the clinic and the test and the results, the stories pouring out of me leaving me sagging in my chair when I was done. She stayed quiet, and if not for the static on the line, I would've thought she'd hung up or been disconnected. "Ma?"

"I think you have done a good job of taking care of yourself," she said with a flat tone. "But it is lucky for that cheetah that I am an ocean away."

The pressure diverted, turned into semi-hysterical laughter. "Very lucky," I agreed. "I think he's suffering enough. Ma, I don't know what to do. I keep wanting to punish him, but there were also good times, real…" I hesitated. "Loving times."

"When Shawna was making your tennis worse," Ma said.

"She was never making it *worse*."

"When she was making it worse, you did what you had to do. This life apart from Marquize, the worry about his actions, is that helping you?"

"I don't think about it all that much." But my laughter had already faded as the pressure of tears eased up, and now it felt as though all those unshed tears were collecting in a cold, heavy mass in my chest and throat.

"You are making new friends now?"

"Yes."

"Might any of them fill that same role?"

"I don't know. It's hard. You can't be public about it. There's maybe…" But Braden's secret wasn't mine to tell. "I don't know, I'm just not sure."

"And if it came down to choosing between being the best in the world at tennis or pursuing a relationship?"

She only asked that question because she knew there was no doubt about the answer.

* * *

Aliq and I had a pretty good doubles practice the next day. I found it easier to learn to play with him than it had been to learn to play with

Chris. Either he and I were more compatible or more experienced; whatever it was, we communicated well from the very start. Buoyed by that and by Ma's phone call, I did better in Coverset than I'd done on the Challenger circuit yet, winning a spot in the main draw before losing in the round of 16. At the next tournament, we kept up our practices and Aliq introduced me to a rabbit named Caboll, who reminded me of Dom in that he was glued to his phone when he wasn't on the court. Unlike Dom, he didn't spend the time talking to friends so much as reading news not just from the States but from four other continents and (he told me proudly) from all sides of the political spectrum.

On the court he played in very much a rabbity style, covering the court in bounds and playing great defense. He had trouble with both strategy and tactics (again, his words) in that he found it hard to plan for an opponent and hard to stick to a plan once he'd made it. But being able to get to most every shot will get you a long way in the qualifying rounds of a tournament, and he had the most success of any of us early on.

I introduced those guys to Sean and Danver and was pleased to find that we all got along pretty well. Danver's chatter worked much better spread out over four of us, and often Sean and Caboll would sit in the back of our group while Danver chattered on and Aliq and I exchanged amused smiles and interjected now and then. We played conversations like we played doubles, learning who could head off an epic Danver monologue best and who could tackle a particular topic with enough ease to send it into a direction we could all enjoy.

None of them were gay, at least as far as I could tell. Caboll had a girlfriend, a rabbit who was higher up in the female rankings than he was in the male. Aliq was happy enough to go off with Danver and the two of them actually hooked up with a pair of nutria down in Pensa. And Sean didn't seem interested in any sort of relationship, so he and I sometimes went out with a few other players on nights when the others were going to "hookup joints," as Danver called them. If Caboll wasn't meeting up with his girlfriend, he'd come along, but often those nights coincided.

It was easy to fall into a pattern: travel to a city, set up practices, go out with my friends, play in the tournament, watch a few more matches, pack up, reset, repeat. As April slid into May, though, I made sure to add studying to my pattern. I didn't know when I'd hear from Ma again, but I wanted to be well on the way to taking my equivalency test when I did.

When Aliq and I started playing doubles, it shook my routine up a little, but not a lot, and the extra practice was worth it. We got better quickly; at the last tournament in May, we won a qualifying spot and made it all the way up to the quarterfinals before losing a tough match. Afterwards, we celebrated, and Aliq said, "You could be really good at doubles if you give up singles."

"Maybe someday," I said. "I'm not ready to do that yet."

"Hey," Danver said, reaching across the small table we were all sitting around, "Rocky's gonna be a great singles player too."

"We're gonna be the next big five." I raised my Coke to the table even though Sean wasn't with us at the moment.

"Nah." Danver wiggled his paw. "I'm gonna get into the top 50 for a while, make some money, maybe win a few mid-tier tournaments, and then drop back down to this circuit and coast here for a few years. I know what my ceiling is and it'd be nice to be a top five player but I really don't think it's in my DNA."

(Looking back on that, it's scary how close he was.)

"Just need to work out more." Aliq flexed his fist and forearm. "If you had better conditioning you'd have won at least three more matches this year."

"I'm in okay shape," Danver said. "Can't be in bad shape and play tennis."

"You could be in better shape." The arctic fox looked at the pretzels in front of the squirrel and shook his head at me. "You could cut back on the carbs, too."

"They're just pretzels. I can't eat meat all the time like you guys, it upsets my stomach, and anyway it's not good for you." Danver popped a pawful of pretzels into his mouth as a that'll-show-you gesture, but the side effect of it was that his speech devolved into a shower of crumbs down his shirt and onto the table, giving the others a chance to respond.

"I don't eat meat either," Caboll said, stretching out, "but I try to balance out beans for protein and veggies and carbs."

"And there are veggie protein supplements," Aliq said. "I eat them sometimes too."

I leaned back, smiling and enjoying the back and forth. Coach Keely had me on a restrictive diet on game days, but I was allowed Coke and some other indulgences. He said that if you get treats every so often, you won't want them so badly that you'll just "binge out" on them (I had to ask Danver what that one meant because I'd only heard "binge" in the context of drinking).

Marquize never liked our restrictive diet, and that was back in the day when it hadn't been as restrictive. I wondered how he'd get along with these guys. Probably well, although he still didn't play tennis well enough to be in our group. There was an unspoken barrier to entry into the group and it hinged around our ranking numbers. We were all in the 200-300 range, with Sean at 210 the highest and Danver at 295 the lowest (those were this current week). I had climbed to 278, and Aliq and I were ranked a sparkling 204 in doubles. But Marquize was still down in the 500s.

"Rocky knows." Aliq tapped my shoulder. "I got him coming to the gym with me and taking protein supplements along with his diet. Look, you can see how much bigger his arms are."

There followed an uncomfortable moment of scrutiny after which Danver said, "He's always been big in the arms. He's a tennis player."

He took a breath to go on, and I cut in. "I can take my shirt off if it'd make it easier for you guys."

Caboll laughed, and a moment later Danver joined in. Aliq flashed me a quick smile that said he understood I'd been trying to get Danver unsettled and he appreciated the tactic.

As much as I appreciated my new group of friends, I went home that evening thinking more about Marquize than I had in a long time. So I wrote him a quick email telling him how I was doing and asking how he was doing. I didn't talk too much about the new crowd in case Marquize thought I was replacing him, but I did say that I had a new doubles partner.

He replied within an hour, telling me that he was struggling, annoyed at himself for not getting better, and mad at himself for what he'd done to me. He asked if we could have a phone call. And I thought about it and decided that it wouldn't hurt to talk to him.

* * *

Our schedule synced up a couple days later, when both our tournaments had ended. I felt unusually nervous; it had been over a month since I'd talked to him. That had been on his mind, too: the first thing he said was, "It's been a while."

"I know. Life is busy. Play, practice, travel."

"I know. I'm doing the same thing."

I still felt jumpy, so I avoided the subject of our relationship. "How's the team?"

"Everyone's good. They ask about you sometimes. Not so much lately."

I lay on my back in bed in the hotel room I shared with Danver; the squirrel was out with Sean. I'd noticed that if I didn't come along, Aliq and Caboll went and did their own thing ("Danver's a lot less fun when you're not around," the arctic fox confided in me). That made me feel good, to be the glue of our little group. "Glad everyone's doing well. Are you playing doubles?"

"No. Chris went back with Les. Lochen says he's looking to find me a partner but nothing yet."

I stared at the ceiling and pressed the phone to my ear to block out the sounds of traffic outside. "Did you see that doubles match in the Kingstown final?"

"Sharper and Liu? Yeah. Great stuff."

"I watched it three times trying to figure out how Liu moves so well."

"He's a genius."

"Aliq says I could move like him with a little more practice. But I don't have his backhand."

"Who does?"

Marquize's short reply sounded wounded, which I interpreted as being hurt that I was still playing doubles and he wasn't. "I talked to Ma," I said.

That did perk him up. "Oh yeah?"

So I told him about her call, how Ori's situation was still not resolved, and how I was going to study for my equivalency test. "Are you still studying?"

"Uh…yeah." He paused and then said, "Not really. I crack a book open every week or so, but…"

"Without you around I stopped. But I'm picking it up again."

Marquize didn't say anything for a second and then spoke hesitantly. "Maybe we could…check in on each other? Not start studying again, but just…you know, keep each other…"

"Honest?" The word came out a little sharper than I'd intended.

"Motivated."

"Oh." I closed my eyes. "Sure. I think that's a good idea. None of the guys here are still studying."

"Okay." His breathing sounded loud, like the phone was up real close to his mouth. "Have you thought about Pensa next month?"

"Not really."

"Oh."

I sighed. Talking about our GEDs reminded me of Ma. "I just don't know, Mar. I don't want this to screw up my tennis. I have to go down there and be focused and if I have a fight with you then—"

"Whoa, whoa. Who said we're going to fight?" He listened, and when I didn't answer: "Are you still mad?"

"Should I not be?"

"Rocky, you—I made a mistake. I'm sorry. You're not sick, I'm not sick, so can't we put it behind us?"

"I don't know." I had to press my free paw to my eyes at the hurt in his voice.

He went quiet, still breathing right into the mic. "So do I have a boyfriend still?"

"I don't know, Mar."

"If I need to know right now, what do you say? Yes or no, no in between."

I exhaled. "Fine. I'll meet you in Pensa."

"You didn't answer the question."

"Yes, all right? We're still boyfriends, I'll meet you in Pensa."

"Okay." He sounded relieved. "I'll look forward to it. When do you want to meet up?"

"I gotta go," I said. "We can work it out later."

I didn't feel good about that conversation, which was fast becoming a familiar aftereffect of talking to Marquize. It twisted my stomach up to think about what might happen when we met in Pensa. Would I feel similarly angry to his face? Would he expect that we'd have sex or at least some kind of physical contact? Right now, sex was off the table as far as I was concerned. Though it had been a while, and my own paw wasn't as satisfying as having someone next to me. Would I be able to resist if he pressed for it?

I'd have to. Somehow.

Chapter Twenty-Two

I agonized over the meeting with Marquize for weeks. We talked on the phone two more times and nothing he said gave me any indication of what he was going to expect from the meeting. Partly that was because I was afraid to bring it up, but I think he was worried about it too.

The good part of those weeks was that Aliq and Danver did a great job keeping me focused. I practiced singles with Danver and doubles with Aliq, and Aliq's workout regimen, though I didn't follow all of it, had gotten me in better shape so that I wasn't panting at the end of our practice sessions. And I was able to leave the trouble with Marquize behind me when I stepped onto the court. Once I was standing on the warm asphalt, white lines all around me, that was all there was.

It helped that Aliq and Danver were genuinely good guys. I enjoyed Danver's chatter and came to look forward to our nights out because they allowed me to relax, and Aliq introduced me to punk music, which I hadn't liked when I'd heard it back in Lunda, but it turned out I hadn't heard the bands he liked. Danver called it "anarchist noise" and didn't want to be around it, but I loved the energy and freedom of it. Danver did appreciate the punk-pop that had evolved from it into a more mainstream sound, and Aliq tolerated it, so when the three of us were together, we'd listen to stuff like Green Day, Social Distortion, and Blink-182.

Aliq tried to get me to go to a show, but it was so hard to fit that into our practice schedules. I know it sounds like we had all this time to go out, or to sit around listening to music, but really those nights out were once a week, if that, and listening to music happened mostly when we were working out in the gym or stretching after a match. My days were structured down to the minute on match days and pretty rigidly at other times, with Coach Keely asking for reports when he couldn't be around in person. I hoped for the day I could hire a dedicated coach and trainer, but none of the other guys had them yet either.

In early June, with the Pensa tournament a week away, I got a call from Ma.

It came in the middle of a practice session, so I didn't see it until we were done and I checked my phone. When I saw the number, I dropped my water bottle and pulled up the voicemail right away. She didn't say much, only that she had news and that she'd be at this number for another hour, and at the same time for the next three days until I called her back.

I started dialing, but the numbers flew out of my head, so I had to listen to the message again to write them down. "What's going on?" Aliq asked, looking over my shoulder.

"My Ma called." We had a Sharpie to mark dead tennis balls with, and I wrote the number on one of those dead balls. When I'd gotten it all down, I turned. "I haven't heard from her in weeks. She's trying to get my sister out of Lunda."

"Oh, shit." Aliq crouched down next to me. "Why's your sister in Lunda?"

"She never came over with us. She got married to some village chief." I raised a paw. "I'll tell you in a minute."

"Yeah, sure, dude." The arctic fox stood and stepped back. "I got your gear." He picked up both bags and retreated to the far end of the court, giving me space.

I nodded acknowledgment, dialing, and stood up as the phone rang with that hollow, distant sound it makes when you're connecting overseas. One ring, two rings, and my heart beat faster with every one. Had I missed her already?

Click. "Hello?"

"Ma?"

"Rochi." Her warmth came through the phone. "How are you?"

Her accent was stronger than it had been, or else my ear had grown unaccustomed to hearing it. "I'm fine, I'm practicing doubles,

I'm—how are *you*? What's going on?"

She remained as calm as always. "I believe I have reached an agreement, but I need an extra five thousand dollars. There is a jackal here who will give you instructions on where to wire it; you may trust him."

"Five thousand—Ma, I don't have that much."

"Can you get it?"

I thought about my connections. Lochen had advanced me money in the past, but always a hundred here, a hundred there. I didn't know how he'd feel about five thousand dollars. None of my friends were any better off than I was, and Sean particularly kept talking about how long he had before he would have to give up the tour, how he was living month to month. Between the five of us we couldn't come up with five grand. But I knew there'd have to be a way. "I can get it."

"Thank you, Rochi. I'm sorry. I wouldn't ask this if there were any other way."

"It's fine, I can do it, I can help. How are you? How is Ori?"

"I'm well. Ori is well. We are both looking forward to seeing you again. How are your matches going?"

Aliq bounced tennis balls at the far end of the court. I watched the motion, the quick, sure snap of his paws. "They're good. I think I'll do better at doubles than singles, at least for now. How soon do you need the money?"

"Whenever you can get it. Ori is not going anywhere. She says her next season is in August, so before then would be preferable."

From that I gathered that she wasn't yet pregnant. My resolve stiffened. "I'll get it before then. I promise."

"Thank you. Now tell me about your new doubles partner."

Aliq swished his tail and looked my way as though knowing we were talking about him. "He's a great guy, really workout-focused. He's getting me in better shape. We listen to music together and sometimes we rent movies. Coach Keely is helping us both with our techniques. I'm number 260 in singles but we just broke into the top 200 in doubles last week. We should start getting invited to main draws over the next couple months."

"Congratulations. How is the prize money?"

"Ah, well, it's more, but not that much, not until we start winning. The endorsements are helping but not a lot. Honestly I probably still owe Lochen a bunch of money." I rubbed my ears. "He's been really great. Coach Keely is still helping me for free."

"I'm glad to hear that. Ro, if you can't get the money—"

"I can get it. I will. I'll talk to Lochen. Or…" I'd had another idea, but I didn't want to talk to Ma about it. So I said, "Don't worry. When can I call you again?"

"You can call this number for the next week. The jackal I'm passing you to will be able to get messages to me if I'm not here. And I will call you when I have a chance. I promise."

"Thanks, Ma." I stood and braced myself against the chain link fence. "I miss you."

"I miss you too, Ro. Be good. I hope I'll see you soon."

"Me too."

Only after I'd hung up did I remember that I was going to tell her I was still studying for my equivalency test. Maybe I'd make it a surprise. I'd pass it before she got back and then I could show her my diploma, or certificate, or whatever it was.

"Everything okay?" Aliq asked.

"Yeah," I said. "I've got to do some studying tonight."

* * *

Studying helped distract me from the meeting with Marquize while I was off the court, although as we boarded our plane for Pensa I was tense for a different reason. I knew Marquize's parents were well off, and I thought that of all the people I knew, he was most likely to be able to get me five thousand dollars in short order. It probably wasn't the most diplomatic thing for me to ask at our first meeting since my birthday, but I didn't have a lot of other options.

And of course, my mind played out a whole lot of scenarios. Would he ask me to have sex again in exchange for the money? (Not directly, but…maybe.) Would I do it? (Probably.) Would that make me a prostitute? (I wasn't keeping the money for myself, so…no?) I played out variations of all the conversations in my head over and over again, and none of them felt realistic or probable, and yet I couldn't stop doing it.

He called the day after we landed. "I'm in qualifying here," he said. "All this week and then if I win, the weekend is when the main draw starts. So I'll probably be free by Saturday. What about you?"

"I'm starting qualifying next week, singles, and then doubles two days later. So I'm free over the weekend. But you might make it to the main draw."

"Ha." There wasn't any humor in his laugh. "I'll see you Saturday. We can text around noon or so?"

"Sounds good. I'll take a bus up to Cowford."

"You sure? I can come down to Hellentown."

"It's fine. I wouldn't mind seeing the old place again. Last year Dom and Bret showed up."

"They're both still at Palm Gables. You want me to send them a note? We could all get together."

I considered that. It would certainly remove the danger that Marquize would want to have sex, but it would also make it harder for me to ask him for money. Seeing Bret and Dom again would be cool, though. I was honestly curious what they'd be up to at this point. Were they going to join the tour? "Sure," I said finally. "If they're around."

"Done. All right, Rocky. See you Saturday."

So Saturday morning I got onto a bus for Cowford and leaned back with my music and earphones and closed my eyes, trying not to think about what was going to happen when I got there. Unfortunately I didn't do so well with that, and even though I didn't want to have sex, my body was very aware that it hadn't had any in a while. So my mind kept wandering into those scenarios that my body wanted, and my sheath kept responding. I wasn't worried that my seatmate, a bobcat, would smell the arousal, because the bus was pretty rank as it was. I was more worried that I'd get aroused around Marquize and do something I shouldn't and didn't want to do.

As he'd promised, he texted around noon when I was still a half hour out. Bret and Dom had come up to meet him, and they were all sitting at a Friday Night bar and grill waiting for me. It was a short walk from the bus station, but I admit I dawdled a little; it was almost one by the time I showed up.

They all stood up to greet me, hugged me and shook my paw. For the first hour, we talked about little stuff. The guys wanted to hear about the Challenger tour, so I told them stories about the amenities in the locker rooms and the increased press. Then I wanted to hear about Palm Gables and they told me about the new coaches, the new ninth and tenth graders, and it all sounded very familiar and fun.

"So what are you guys going to do when you graduate?" I asked.

Dom and Bret looked at each other. "I'm gonna go to college," Dom said. "I can get a lot more out of college."

"I'm going on tour." Bret grinned at me. "So I might see you at some events. It's gonna be hard at first, though. My parents are gonna pay for my first year, but then I have to start earning money or…" He mimed pulling a plug out of a socket. "Yoink."

"Tough," Marquize said. "But you can do it."

"You're the one we're looking up to." Bret turned to me. "I don't know if you can give me pointers or anything…"

"Sure," I said immediately. "Look me up when you get out on tour. I'll hook you up."

"Cool," he said. "Thanks, Rocky. You're a good guy."

I didn't meet Marquize's eyes.

The conversation was fun, but I couldn't ask Marquize for money with Bret and Dom around. They were going to have to leave around four to get back to Palm Gables; my last non-overnight bus was at five, and I didn't want to spend the night sleeping on a bus. It wouldn't be good for my prospects in the tournament and if Aliq found out, he'd have a fit.

So when Bret and Dom got up and said they had to get back, I shook their paws, told them to keep in touch, and stood beside Marquize as they left.

"I'm glad we'll get a little time to talk alone," he said.

I avoided his hopeful eyes. "Not a lot. I need to be at the bus station in like forty-five minutes."

"That's fine," he said. "I didn't think this was going to be a, y'know, super-long visit."

Which at least settled the question of whether he thought we were going to have sex this time. My mind was relieved, my body disappointed. "Yeah, sorry," I said. "But I need to ask you something, and it's really important."

"Yeah?" We walked through the park adjacent to the tennis center where Marquize's tournament was, a small patch of green grass and park benches with a fountain near the middle around which a huge flock of seagulls clustered. The cheetah pointed across the street. "We can go back to my hotel if you want."

"No, that's fine." We were surrounded by people, but none of them were paying attention to us. "I would like to grab something to eat before I get on a four-hour bus ride back, though."

He rubbed his whiskers. "There's, ah, there's a Bamboo Garden around the corner there."

That was the place we'd often gotten food from at the food court near Palm Gables. I nodded. "That's fine."

So we went into the little store with its familiar smells of soy and wok oil, and I got the same black bean chicken with noodles dish that I'd always gotten, and Marquize got the same orange chicken dish that he'd always gotten, and we sat down across from each other at a red plastic table near the window where the afternoon sun streamed in over our heads. "I haven't had this in forever," I said.

"Me neither." Marquize laughed. "Sports diet."

"Yeah." I slurped up noodles. "So...I heard from Ma."

His eyebrows rose. "Really?"

I nodded. "She's making some progress with getting Ori back."

"That's great!" He was genuinely excited, which relaxed me.

"Yeah," I said. "I can't wait to see Ori again. It's been years. I haven't even talked to her this year at all."

"How soon does your ma think she'll be back?"

I spun a noodle around with my plastic fork. "That's the problem. She needs like five thousand dollars."

"Oh, shit." His whiskers drooped. "Do you have that? Can you get it from Lochen?"

"No," I breathed in. "I was thinking...I was hoping..." I could see the answer in his expression before I finished, but I had to plow ahead. "I mean, could I borrow it from your parents?"

He froze. I'd heard that before as an expression, but Mar really did stop moving completely. Only his eyes flicked to the side, away from mine. I waited a moment, then another, and just as I was about to say something, he swallowed. "I don't think that'd work," he said.

I knew him well enough to know that something was really wrong there. And I'd already known this was a long shot. All that time we were on the Futures tour together, even when we went to the Northeast to play, Marquize never once mentioned his parents coming to see him play. Never once mentioned having talked to them on the phone. I knew they didn't get along, but I was hoping that in a crisis like this they might be able to help. "You wouldn't have to talk to them," I said. "I met them when they brought you down to school that one time, remember? I could just call them myself."

He pushed his plate away. "I said, I don't think that'll work."

"I've got to try. If there's any chance—"

"I told them about us."

It was my turn to freeze, though I didn't do it as literally as he had. I laid my ears back and rested my muzzle on my paws. "When?"

"Christmas. That Christmas I came back early from home? I had a big fight with my dad."

I remembered him being in a tense mood. "It's been a year and a half since then."

He nodded. "And they haven't called." He took a breath. "Being gay—acting on it—it's forbidden for Muslims. So me telling him that I was sleeping with you was basically me defying his whole faith."

"But you've never really been practicing. Neither of us is."

"Right, but…" He shook his head. "Dad always thought I'd come back. To the faith, I mean. Which was dumb to begin with because I was never really in the faith. I got out as soon as I could. I don't say any of the daily prayers, I drink alcohol…I just don't believe in that crap. So I told him that. He said I didn't mean it, and I said I was on tour with my boyfriend and that we were having sex, and that proved that I didn't believe in it." He shrugged with a carelessness belied by his low, raw voice. "He told me to get out and not come back. And he hasn't called or tried to get in touch with me since then. Mom either."

"You should reach out to them," I said.

"Look, Rocky, I'd love to get your money, but I don't want to go back begging."

"No, not about the money. Sorry." I reached out and put a paw on his. "Just about reconnecting with your parents."

"I don't need to reconnect," he said. "I'm done. They're done with me and I'm done with them and that's all there is to it."

"But—"

He gazed steadily at me. "I'd rather spend some time figuring out how else we can get your five grand."

There wasn't going to be any more discussion about his parents, not right now. So I nodded. "Thanks. Anything you can think of that might help, I'd appreciate."

His fork traced soy sauce trails around his plastic plate. "Thought about asking Bret? His parents are pretty well off. Or Kim. Are you still in touch with her?"

"Occasional emails. She's hoping to move up to Challenger next year and she's doing really well in Futures, so I think she'll be able to. But she's separated from her parents, remember? I'm not sure they had that much money anyway."

"Oh, right." He dropped his fork and rubbed a paw across his whiskers. "It doesn't seem fair. You're eighteen. You shouldn't have to raise five thousand dollars to save your sister."

"Who else is going to? Ma's over there making all the arrangements, and my father's dead. My aunt is useless; she thinks Ori should stay married. There's literally nobody else to do this."

"I know." He shook his head. "It's just a lot. I mean a lot on your plate."

I ran through the list of my classmates from Palm Gables. "Pom? What were his parents like?"

Marquize shook his head. "I mean, maybe, but he went to college this year, early entry or something. Got in at seventeen because he's crazy smart. I don't think anyone's heard from him since."

"And how would it look for me to show up after two years and be like, 'hey, haven't talked in a while, but do you have five thousand dollars?'?"

"Yeah."

We sat together in silence, the meal over. I checked my phone. "I should go in about ten minutes," I said.

"I'll walk you to the bus."

I wasn't sure I wanted him to, but objecting would have caused more problems, so I nodded.

"Hey," he said, "you heard about that big court decision?"

Of course I had. The highest court in the country had decided that gay people could get married and all the states were going to have to comply with that. The implications were huge, but I hadn't read very much about it. Not many of the guys on the tour talked about it; Danver had laughed and said something about how did they decide which one of them had to wear the dress. None of the rest of the guys were amused by his joke, which I appreciated, but neither did they seem particularly excited about the ruling. It was a thing that had happened for some other people in another world, and it affected our tennis life not one bit. "Pretty cool," I said. "You're not going to propose, are you?"

"No." He took a breath and went on, fingers tapping nervously on the table. "But I still want to be your boyfriend, Rocky."

I knew this was coming, and I hadn't been sure what I'd say to it. Now my answer surprised me. "Why?"

I surprised him, too. He sat up and tilted his head, the sun hitting the tops of his black ears. His fingers stopped tapping the table. "What?"

"Why do you still want to be my boyfriend?" I followed the train of thought. "I mean, we've barely talked in weeks. We live separately now."

"That doesn't have to be a barrier."

"I know. But I'm asking: why?"

He leaned forward. "Do you still want to?"

"I'm not saying I don't. I'm asking you why you do."

He frowned, creases in his golden fur, and then leaned back in his chair. "All right. I guess…I mean, we're close, we care about each other. I still want to get to the majors with you."

I swallowed back the question, *Do you really think that can happen?* Instead I said, "How's your game coming along?"

"Oh, you know." He looked away. "It's hard. I'm practicing all the time."

I made a mental note to write Paulie and ask him for his view of Marquize's work ethic. "Yeah?"

Now he squinted at me. "Are you saying that you don't want to date me if I'm not as good at tennis as you?"

"No," I said, but I wondered.

We walked through the warm afternoon air to the bus stop. Like Palm Gables, Cowford is a lot of low stucco buildings framed by palm trees, but unlike Palm Gables, there's a city center that looks like every other city center: a mix of blue glass and concrete towers with one or two distinctive structures tossed in among the cookie-cutter ones in an attempt to give the city some kind of identity. Two years ago I'd seen one small States city; now I was looking at city centers with a weary eye and ranking them in my head.

"Oh," Marquize said as we rounded a corner and the bus stop came into view. "There's one more idea. I mean, it's not a great one, but…"

"An idea about what?" I was distracted by trying to decide whether Cowford was more or less picturesque than the Midwestern Johnsonville, and whether the originality of the names counted toward that.

He wouldn't look at me directly. "The money. The five grand. There's—well, I mean, I wouldn't normally—but it's your sister, right, and that's gotta be more important than—than whatever."

"Just tell me already." I shoved his arm.

"Okay, well." He rubbed his ears, which were flat. "He told me if I ever needed money to call him, and…I mean, I'm sure he'd do the same for you."

"He who?"

"Uh." We took four more steps before Marquize said the name. "Frio."

Then he did look at me, and his wide eyes showed that he was scared of my reaction. Which was about right because I wanted to stalk back to the bus station without saying goodbye to him. That name still sent my gut into turmoil, twisting into knots; I was legitimately afraid I might puke up all that Xiaqinese food. But I kept it together. "I don't want to talk to him—"

"I know," Marquize said quickly, and put a paw on my arm as though he sensed I wanted to run off. "But if it meant getting your sister back…I mean, you could pay him back. I can help, I can send like fifty—a hundred a month, maybe."

"Ugh," I said, but I let his paw stay on my arm. Would that make up for it? Would it be worth whatever I'd have to do with Frio for five thousand dollars to get Ori back? I'd already decided I'd sleep with Marquize; wouldn't it be easier to sleep with Frio because there wouldn't be any emotion involved? And what could he ask me to do that would be worse than that?

"At least maybe talk to him."

"What if I talk to Coach Murphy?" I asked.

Marquize nodded. "Sure, you can try that. But you know, they fired Frio, and we might've been involved in that…" He sensed that he was on shaky ground and retreated. "Anyway, I guess it's worth trying him first, yeah."

He didn't say anything more about it. We did our public hug at the bus station and I got on the bus, where I had hours to think about what he'd proposed. I'd much rather talk to Coach Murphy, but I wasn't sure how he'd view a student coming back and asking for money. Frio had gotten me a job when I'd needed money back in school, so he seemed more likely to have connections that could help out. The problem was that even thinking about talking to him put a bad taste on my tongue and kept that knot twisting around in my gut.

I got back in time for a late night practice with Aliq, and as usual, tennis helped me escape my problems. But Ori wasn't going anywhere, not until I came up with the money for her, and so the next morning, I called up Palm Gables and asked for Coach Murphy.

They didn't know where he was, because it was Sunday. I should've known that. I left him a message and my number and told them I was at the Challenger event in Hellentown.

Hellentown, by the way, is a more interesting city than Cowford, if only because of OzWorld nearby it. But more than that, it feels younger and more alive than Cowford. I have no idea if it's really a younger city, but it's brighter and more active, especially at night. Lots of places for Danver to go and attempt to drag us, but I begged off this night. I know it would probably have done me good to take my mind off my problems, but I couldn't just shunt them to the side like that.

It wasn't half an hour before I was aching for a distraction. So I went online to look at the scheduling for the match to see when my singles and doubles matches would be. I knew, but I wanted to see the times again to fix them in my mind. And then I perused the other players to see who I might be playing against in later rounds, and my eye lit on one bracket, the player who'd be playing the winner of my qualifying bracket. My claw traced the name "B. Longacre."

Chapter Twenty-Three

Coach Murphy hadn't gotten back to me by Monday, which was when my first match was. Braden, having been invited to the main draw (as the second seed), wouldn't start play until Friday. I kept an eye out for him on the practice courts, but if he was practicing, it was somewhere private. So I played my first singles match, won it, and then got on the phone to call Coach Murphy again as soon as I was out of the locker room.

This time his secretary put me through to his office. "Rocky," he said cautiously. "What can I do for you?"

Glad that he remembered me, I took a breath, walking down the Hellentown street. "I'm in a little trouble—or rather, my sister is."

"I'm sorry to hear that," he said, still guarded. "What do you think I can do about it?"

"I need money to release her from her marriage in Lunda," I said, having spent the day trying and failing to come up with a better way to say it.

He exhaled. "How much?" he asked, with a touch of relief in his voice. I wondered what he'd thought I was going to ask him for.

"Five thousand dollars."

"Oh, Jesus, Rocky."

"It's a lot, I know. I don't know anyone else who could get it for me. I'm sorry, I know I haven't talked to you for a while."

He was quiet for a moment. "I just want to get clear what you're asking for here."

It had been a long time since someone hadn't understood what I meant. "I'm—uh, I need five thousand dollars. I'll pay it back, I promise."

"Or?"

The conversation was feeling more and more surreal to me. "Or—or my sister won't be able to come to the States."

"Right. You said that." The relief came through more strongly. "All right, so…look, I can't just take five grand out of the school, and I don't have that kind of money. Maybe in a few months…I could hit up the alumni, make it a cause people could get behind."

"I need it by August," I said.

"Oh. That'll be more tricky. Um. Tell you what…this is your phone, this number?"

"Yeah."

"Okay. I'll make a couple calls, see what I can do, and if anything turns up, I'll call you."

I tried to keep the disappointment out of my voice. "Okay. Thanks, Coach."

I didn't hold out much hope that he'd help. Once, maybe, I'd have taken his lukewarm promises at face value, but no longer.

The problem of Ori gnawed at me as I dressed and practiced, but on the court I left it all behind. Inside the white lines I knew what problems would be coming at me and how I could send them back. I was getting better and better at it, and I won this match in straight sets.

Over the next few days, as I continued to hear nothing from Coach, I set that frustration aside and tore my way through the qualifying tournament. Braden still hadn't made an appearance, but that was fine. He'd show up for the main draw, and if I made it there too, he wouldn't be able to avoid me.

In the qualifying finals, I met Georgi, a wolf with a killer forehand and sharp reflexes who made things difficult for me. But my reflexes were pretty good too, and though I struggled through a four-game stretch in the second set where I couldn't seem to get anything to drop inbounds, I recovered and won that set 7-5, and with it the match.

"A date with Braden Longacre," Aliq said that evening after

our practice. We had doubles coming up the next day, which was also when my next match was. "Lucky you. Maybe he'll go easy and let you win a game or two."

"I've played him before," I said. "I won a game off him."

"Get out. When?"

"Oh, uh, he came by Palm Gables while I was there. We played a bit."

"Huh." Aliq put his racket back in his bag and gulped down another half-bottle of BoltAde. "Wouldn't have figured Longacre for the charitable appearance type."

"School loyalty," I said. "What do you know about this pair tomorrow?"

And we talked about our opponents in doubles while I thought about Braden and the prospect of playing him in a real match, in a real tournament, for the first time. I was fairly sure I would lose; my more urgent question was the one I wanted to ask him off the court.

Fortunately, we won our doubles match that morning, leaving me somewhat tired but in good spirits to face Braden. I got some rest over lunch, loaded up on carbs and a protein drink, and felt pretty good as I stepped out onto the court to warm up. I knew Braden was better than me—he was already ranked in the top 60 and was seeded second at this tournament—but I'd gotten better over the previous years and I thought I could at least hold serve against him for a little while. I'd never beaten a top-100 opponent, but I knew I'd have to sometime.

Within two games, I knew it wasn't going to be that day. Braden's forehands came in laser-precise, kicking up on the hard court so that I had to adjust my returns quickly, and he varied the spins so I had to be really good at reading them, which I was not. He served well both wide and down the T, and held his first service game without allowing me a point ("at love"). When I served, he pounced on the balls, and though I won two points, he broke my serve distressingly easily.

So I lost the first set 6-0, and that depressed me going into the next set. I mean, I'd been doing pretty well up to then, but running into Braden was like rounding a corner and slamming into a brick wall. I didn't score a point on his first service game of the second set either. Then it was my turn to serve, and Braden wasn't saying anything, but his body language was relaxed, like he knew this wasn't going to be a problem.

He'd said hi when we met in the locker room. I'd said congrats on his success on the tour, and he'd said it was good to see me in the main draw. We didn't talk about Palm Gables or the gay club at all. Now I felt like he wasn't going to have any respect for me if I didn't start playing better, so I kicked myself mentally. Get into gear, jackal, I ordered my brain. He's got a crack in that game. Find it.

So I tried some new things on serve. I continued mixing up the placement of my serves, but leaned more on the wide serves because that was where Coach Keely told me my lefty serve would be the most trouble for righties. I shifted toward the deuce side after serving so I wouldn't get pinned in the backhand corner by his returns. When we got to a rally, I watched his patterns and followed a feeling I had about where to hit the ball back. He adjusted, returned it, and the return felt familiar. I had a brainstorm in that moment. Braden was following something like a formula about where to hit the ball. It wasn't highly rigid, within a foot or anything, but it was in certain areas of the court. He was great with spin and kick on the ball, but what that meant was that I could often tell where the ball was going on the court about a half second before he hit it. And that was an advantage.

Not a huge one, not like it was going to turn the match around, but it was enough that I could prepare myself better for some of the points. And that helped. I won that service game, and then I contested Braden's next one. The crowd, mostly there to see Braden, stirred. The fox's ears perked up and when I came around to serve, he put a little extra on some of his strokes. But that meant he had fractionally less time to place them, and I got good racket on them most of the time. I won my next service game as well, and actually got him to deuce in his service game after that.

But then he closed the door. He hit a gear where it didn't matter if I knew where the balls were; they were placed perfectly and either flat or with spin, and though I won another service game, that was it.

I lost the set 6-3, which is at least a respectable losing score.

And afterwards, I waited for Braden to talk to the media people and come back to the locker room. There were a few other players there, so I thought I'd wait, but he came up to me at my locker. "Good game," he said, and extended a paw.

I shook it. "Thanks. You too. Obviously."

We were both still panting, but not a lot. I had my shirt off, but Braden was still dressed as he'd been when he walked off the court, white shirt with green trim on the collar and cuffs, shorts with a matching green line down the sides and a "3K" logo on them. He had a good body too, more muscular than mine, I noted. I should spend more time in the gym with Aliq. "You're better than you were a couple years ago."

"So are you."

"Keep working." He gave me a tight smile and made to leave.

"Hey," I said. "Can I ask you something?"

His ears went back and he gestured at his locker. "I got a thing."

"It's not about…uh, construction. It's about Palm Gables."

Those ears came back up. "Short question?" I nodded. "Okay, shoot."

"Well…I need five thousand dollars to get my sister out of Lunda," I said. "And my friend told me that, ah, Coach Young told him if he ever needed money—"

"No," he said, with a raw edge to his voice.

I stopped, disconcerted. His fur had bristled and he looked as though I'd suggested I could murder someone for money. "I just—"

He smoothed his hackles and went on, back to his polished manner. "You don't want to be in debt, is what I mean. There are other ways."

"I don't have a lot of them," I said. It was clear that he meant, *You don't want to be in debt to* him.

"There's got to be one better than that." Braden's eyes bored into mine.

I nodded. "I get that, but…my sister needs to get over here. She's married in some village, and she's got to get out before she starts a family. That was the deal: I come here and play tennis and I send for her."

He folded his arms. "Would she want you to fuck up your life to save hers?"

Hesitantly, I shook my head. "But a debt…I can get out of it."

"Not that kind of debt." He shook his head, then turned to glare at a pine marten walking by who'd slowed. The marten ducked his head and hurried on his way. "Find someone else."

"All right," I said. "Honestly that's the way I was leaning but I'm so desperate."

Braden looked me up and down. "How old are you?"

"Eighteen."

He nodded. "You're four years younger than me and honestly, you're better than I was at eighteen. You just played me a more competitive second set than three quarters of the players on tour could. In a year or so you'll be winning these tournaments and then you can pick up five thousand in a month. If your sister can wait, I'd advise you to keep your head down and work hard."

"I've been doing that," I said. "I hoped I'd have more time, but it's taking so long."

"It takes a long time." He ran a paw over his ears, smoothing them back and down, and they sprang up again as he lowered his paw. "There's no shortcuts."

I eyed the logo on his shorts. "What about endorsements?"

"Still gotta win to get the endorsements." He looked down at my shorts as well, the "I-II-III" design on the hem. "Can't you go to one of these companies?"

"And what? Ask them for more money to do the same thing?"

He huffed through his nose. "Your manager should be able to help."

"Yeah, I could…I need to ask him. But I already owe him a bunch of money."

Braden's ears perked up. "What? How do you owe him money? Doesn't he only make money when you make money?"

A wolf near us snorted. I hadn't realized he was listening. Braden ignored him, so I did too. "Yeah, but he also pays for my hotel and transportation and all that. I think I'm breaking even with him now but I still owe him for a year of putting me up."

"Oh." Braden's eyes, a soft hazel, stared into mine as though he'd only just realized the possibility that I might be poor. "Like I said. Another year should do it."

"Thanks," I said. "Good luck tomorrow."

"Thanks." He stuck out his paw again. "Good match."

I grasped it and it felt like he held the clasp for a little longer this time. Then he let go and walked over to his locker.

The wolf who'd been listening came over to me as I was finishing up getting dressed. "Don't worry about him," he said. "Born with a silver spoon and can't understand why other people can't buy anything they want."

"I think he understands," I said. "I just don't think he thinks about it much."

"You sure changed that," the wolf said. He stuck out a paw. "Lowry."

"Rocky." I shook his paw. "And I know who you are. I saw you win back in Chesterton, the doubles final."

"Oh yeah." He grinned and perked up. "And you're the one who plays with that arctic fox. You guys are getting good."

"Hope so," I said. "Maybe we'll play you guys this tournament."

"Hope not." He patted me on the shoulder. "And hey, good luck with your sister. I really hope something works out."

"Thanks." I hefted my equipment bag and closed my locker. "Me too."

After my loss to Braden, Aliq and I did pretty well, getting to the quarterfinals before losing a tough match to Lowry, whose partner was a short maned wolf I'd beaten in singles at a previous tournament. As well as Aliq and I were playing together, those two had been a team for two years and had clearly developed strategies several moves ahead, so I'd find myself preparing to hit the ball and Lowry or the other one would already be in position to return it. We made it competitive but lost in straight sets anyway.

Talking in the locker room afterwards, it turned out that the maned wolf knew Danver a bit, so all of us ended up grabbing dinner together and talking tennis for what was a pretty enjoyable evening.

The socialization helped me forget my money worries, or at least put them aside for a night. The next day, with no tennis to distract me, they came back in force. So when I was on the phone with Lochen talking about future tournaments and my upcoming travel plans to Gardalina for the next tournament, I blurted out, "My sister's in a dangerous marriage in Lunda and I need five thousand dollars to get her out."

There was silence for a moment, and then Lochen said, "What do you mean, 'dangerous'?"

"As in she's married to a village chief in a war zone without adequate medical facilities and she goes into season in August and if she has a cub she might die."

There was a longer silence. "Rocky, I been managing tennis players for almost twenty years now. I thought I'd lost the ability to be surprised."

"Sorry," I said.

"Don't be. Aye, well, I don't know that we can get all that together by August, but certainly by the end of the year it should be manageable. Hopefully she can hold out that long, eh?"

"Do you really think we can get the money by then?"

"Probably. If you and Aliq keep winning, that is. I've got calls in to a couple more endorsers, and winning always shortens the time it takes for them to call you back." He laughed. "Business. You know how it is."

I did, but only hazily; that was the point of having him manage it for me. But I forced a laugh and said, "Yeah."

"All right, you guys keep doing what you're doing. I'll keep doing what I'm doing. And don't worry about your sister. We'll get her out of there."

I thanked him and hung up, and went to find Aliq because we were going to watch the doubles semis together.

The team that ended up winning the tournament beat Lowry and his partner in the final. Aliq and I watched the match and spent a long time talking about the communication and strategy we saw in both teams, and how to improve ours. It wasn't easy because a lot of it was very short verbal cues and much of it seemed to be an unspoken understanding of how they each played. We decided we needed to play together more and practice together more, but both of us felt that we had a shot at being that good. "It's not the tennis," as Aliq was fond of saying.

"Except your serve." I elbowed him.

He snorted. "You need to get better at hitting their returns since you know they're gonna come back."

I grinned. "I'm trying. It would help if you could at least serve to the same part of the box every time."

"Fuck you," he said, and lifted his muzzle haughtily. "My unpredictability is my greatest weapon."

"It's really not." I tossed a tennis ball up and caught it on my racket, bouncing it up and down. "Even a little spin or kick would help."

He watched. "Show off. All right, I'll work on my serve."

* * *

Aliq and I were now getting invited to every main draw, and I got my first singles invitation to a main draw in July for a tournament in September. Lochen hadn't turned up any endorsement opportunities and Coach Murphy hadn't gotten back to me. August was around the corner, and I still didn't have any ideas about how to get five thousand dollars to Ma.

We were playing a smallish tournament in Cuyahoga, but even a small tournament would get me about ten thousand in prize money if I won. I'd made it through the qualifiers again and had won my first main draw match, so this next one was to get into the singles quarterfinals. My singles ranking was 210, and I was going up against Grigor Markov, a pine marten who was ranked #75 in the world.

Coach Keely actually called me before the match to look over Grigor's game. "Guarantee he's not looking at your tape. Take that advantage while you can get it." We watched his games and looked at weaknesses in his serve (not many) and his forehand and backhand.

"You can beat his serve," Keely said. "I'm pretty sure you can. And you match up pretty well with him. Don't be afraid to come to the net; his passing shot isn't great. Remember he tends to go deep to the deuce side in rallies, so lean to your backhand side. He might catch you with the occasional cross-court angle to your forehand, but don't overplay that shot—he doesn't hit it that often."

"Thanks," I said. I'd never beaten a top 100 player, but Coach's confidence in me helped my nerves when I walked onto the court. Grigor jumped around with a ton of energy on his end and his serve sizzled in the practice before the match. Mine wasn't hopping quite as much but I still felt good about it.

There wasn't a lot I could do against his serve in the first set. When I got a racket on it, he was jumping to where I'd hit it and controlling the point. And in the fourth game he broke my serve, really drilling his returns back, and that was the set.

But in the second set, I'd seen enough of his game that I could start implementing Coach Keely's advice. I anticipated his serve much better and got a few good returns in in the early games, then more in the later games. At the same time my serve was getting better as I started figuring out his tendencies. He couldn't break me in the second set and I broke him in the middle and then again to win the set.

Then the third set wasn't much of a contest. He was flustered because I think he hadn't been prepared to lose to a 200-ranked player, and he took a lot more chances. I stayed disciplined like Coach taught me and I broke his serve twice again and won the match, 4-6, 6-3, 6-2. At the net he shook my paw and said, "You return serve like Bielovic," naming the number three player in the world, so I took that as a pretty nice compliment.

I called Marquize that night from the hotel room to tell him about it, but he wasn't in a great mood. He'd just lost in the qualifiers of a Futures tournament, a fluky loss, but it upset him. "That's great," he said flatly when I told him about my match.

"And he was really nice about it. Like I have to remember to be that nice when some snotty cub beats me in a few years," I said, trying to be funny. He didn't answer. "What?"

"You trying to get me to say what I said to the cub that beat me?"

"I didn't even know it was a cub."

"He was sixteen, I think."

I frowned and my ears flattened. "So, what, two years younger than you?"

"I walked off the court and didn't say anything. Does that make me a bad person?"

"Mar—" I didn't know what to say. The loss was bothering him, of course it was, and I felt guilty that maybe my calling to share my accomplishment had felt like bragging to him. "Look, I'll call you back."

"No," he sighed. "I'm sorry. I'm just not in a great mood. I'm going nowhere."

"You're not. You just had a bad day."

"I have a lot of bad days."

I exhaled. "You need to keep working." I should have known better than to say that, I guess, but I was used to saying it over and over again to him and it just came out.

"I know I don't work as hard as you. You don't have to keep rubbing it in."

"Jeez, Mar. I didn't mean that. I know you work hard."

His voice got louder, raspier. "Then why do you have to keep telling me to work? Huh?" When I didn't answer, he said, "There's only two cases. Either I'm not as talented as you or I don't work as hard. Right?"

"I know you're talented," I said, and that was another mistake.

"So it's that I don't work."

"I didn't—"

He talked over me. "I already know you're better than me. You're playing in Challenger tournaments, you're beating good players, you and that fox are winning doubles matches. I get it. You don't have to call all the time."

I should've hung up the phone then, but I was torn between guilt at making Marquize feel bad and anger that I'd only called to share good news and he'd turned it into an argument. "I was calling because I was happy. You don't have to be a dick about it. And I don't tell you that you need to work all the time."

"Whenever you bother to call, you do."

"Oh, sorry," I said. "I didn't realize you'd gotten one of those phones that only takes incoming calls."

He softened his voice. "I never know when you're busy, and you didn't want to talk to me for a while."

"Because you fucking cheated on me!"

"I thought we'd be past that by now."

Now I was the one getting agitated. "Oh, you did, did you? Because, what, nothing happened from it so it was all okay?"

"I apologized! Like a hundred times! It's been months!"

"Since I found out."

He paused. "Uh, yeah. I mean…I would've apologized sooner but then—" I think he realized there was no good way to end that sentence, because he broke it off. "Anyway, the point is, I clearly left it up to you to call me and you hardly ever do."

"Yeah, well," I said. "I'm calling you now. And you're yelling at me about, what, telling you to work hard?"

"I don't want to fight when we talk."

"Then don't start a fight!" I rubbed my paw between my eyes. "Jesus Dog. Ma said…"

"What?" When I kept quiet, he got louder. "What did your mom tell you? That I was holding you back?"

Probably 99 times out of 100 I would have made some kind of evasive remark. But I was tired of his bullshit and I was mad because I'd called with good news and now we were fighting. So fuck him. "Yeah. Kind of."

"Okay, well, she's gone. So do you have to listen to her or can you make your own decisions?"

Someone knocked at my door, and Sean called in. "Hey Rocky, you busy?"

"I can make my own decisions," I said. "And I'm deciding to end this conversation." I put my paw over the mic and said to Sean, "Yeah, just a sec."

"Don't hang up," Marquize said. "We're talking."

"We're not talking. We're yelling at each other."

"We have to get through the yelling before we can talk."

"Maybe we can do without the yelling next time," I said. "Bye." And I hung up the phone and went to meet Sean at the door.

Chapter Twenty-Four

Going out with the guys improved my mood, and even though I lost my next singles match (capping my singles earnings at five thousand minus three for expenses), Aliq and I were on a tear. We upset the top-seeded team in the quarterfinals and then won two tough matches in a row to win our first tournament. He leapt into my arms when our opponents' final shot went long and I hugged him back, laughing in short incredulous bursts. "Holy shit, Rocky, holy shit," he kept saying as we went to the net to shake our opponents' paws and then to thank the chair umpire. We hadn't gotten all our gear together before one of the tournament officials, a red squirrel, came over to tell us where the trophy presentation was going to be.

The crowds were cheering and Sean and Danver were a few rows back on the other side of the court going nuts. So Aliq and I went over and they jumped up and hugged us. "You guys are awesome!" Danver said. "That one point where Rocky clipped the net and Molian recovered and tapped it back and Aliq got to it and then somehow Goren whipped it right at Rocky and somehow, dude, I dunno how you got back over and right down the middle."

I knew the point he was talking about. "You just react," I said. "We gotta stick around."

"For the trophy presentation!" Aliq burst out. "You guys we're gonna get a trophy!"

Sean had a big wide grin on his jaguar muzzle. "Good job," he said.

It wasn't just the trophy I was thinking about. We also got to split the nearly $25,000 check between the two of us.

The most we'd made prior to that was for our quarterfinal

appearance, about $5,000 for both of us. Between travel, hotel, and meals, the tour cost us about three thousand a month depending on where we were, and if I made it out of the qualifying round in singles I could pretty much cover that. So getting over twelve thousand in a month—plus the five thousand I'd won for my singles match—was amazing to me. And more, it meant I could send five thousand dollars to Ma.

I wanted to call Lochen right away, but I only had time to tell him that we'd won doubles before Aliq dragged me back to the locker room to change. Lochen said he already knew and was excited and then he let me go.

I sat on the bench and collected myself. It wasn't just winning the tournament, it was the knowledge of the paycheck and that I would have the spare money to send to Ma to bring Ori home. Home. I pressed a paw to my chest, trying to contain the sunburst exploding there.

Aliq kept walking back and forth in the locker room rubbing his paws together. "We won. We won! Wow, I can't believe it. We're gonna go back out there and get a trophy. With our names on it!"

And the check, the big check that Lochen could cash and send money to Ma.

The arctic fox came over to put a paw on my shoulder. "You doing okay?"

"Yeah." I cleared my throat. "I—I think I can get my sister home now."

Saying the words made it real. We were going to get the money and Ori was going to be free, get on a plane, and for the first time in three years we were going to clasp paws, talk face to face instead of over a telephone line. She and Ma and I would be together again.

"Hey," Aliq said. "Hey, hey, you okay?"

I shuddered and pressed my face into my paws. "For so long," I said, "I've been trying to rescue her, and, and, I never thought we'd be able to do it." I wiped tears away. "I mean, I always believed, but it's been so long, it stopped being real. It's like winning a tournament. We'll do it one day but..."

"We'll do it soon." He put a paw lightly on my shoulder and

then withdrew it again. "But I know what you mean. You, ah, you need a tissue or something?"

I grabbed a workout towel and rubbed my eyes with it. "I'm fine," I said. "Everything's fine."

The fox had taken a step back from me, his ears set to the side, tail curled around one leg. "I didn't know," he said. "I mean, didn't know that was all on the line out there."

"We would've made it sooner or later." I breathed into the comforting laundry smell of the towel. "But having it before August is good because—you know, never mind. I hadn't expected…" I looked up at him. "Thanks. I mean, it's because of you that we won."

"Ha." His ears came forward. "It's more because of you."

"We're a team," I reminded him.

His tail uncurled to swing free. "All right, sure. We're a team. Glad I could help."

I cleared my throat again, wiped my muzzle, and stood up. "They're probably waiting for us."

"Let 'em wait." He waved a paw. "Take all the time you need."

"Nah." I dropped the towel. "I'm good."

The ceremony is a blur in my memory. It turned out we didn't get a real trophy, like a gold cup or something. We each got a block of lucite that had "2012 Doubles Champions" on it that our names would get engraved on in a month or so, the official promised us. I know we each said a few things, and I know what I said because Danver recorded a video of it, but it feels like I'm watching someone else's highlight when I watch it. There's a moment in the video, though, where they go to bring out the big novelty check and I duck behind Aliq and bring my paw to my eyes, and I remember that moment, and I know what I'm thinking.

* * *

"It's too bad you're not legal to drink," Danver told me and Aliq after the ceremony. "We'll have to have a private party in the room after."

"It's fine," Aliq said before I could get to. "I don't need to drink to celebrate."

"You won your first fucking tournament," Danver said. "You're going to have a drink. It can just be beer or something, whatever."

The fox and I glanced at each other and shared a "we'll work it out when we get there" look. "Fine," I said.

The whole evening, I answered questions when I was asked, but when I wasn't, the conversation flowed around me and I let it go, imagining what Ori might look like and what her scent might be like. We'd both grown, we'd both had triumphs and losses. And I'd bring her over here and we could share our lives going forward. Or else she could go to school maybe, and I'd see her between tournaments. Or maybe, or maybe, or maybe…there were so many possibilities.

Danver brought our evening to a close, having drunk so much at the restaurant that when he got back to our room, he sat down on the bed "for a minute" and ended up snoring on his side. Aliq grinned at me and grabbed my paw. "Sleep well," he said.

"You too." I grinned back. "And then we start getting ready for the next one."

"Yeah." He paused. "What do you think we'll be? 150?"

"Close to that. Maybe 160," I said. "We beat a few good teams."

"It was great." He shook his head. "Don't know if we can do that every time."

"I'd settle for every other time." I wagged my tail. "Thanks for being my partner."

"Hey, back atcha." He pointed a finger at me. "I was going nowhere before you. So, gym tomorrow?"

The question was playful, but I gave it a serious nod. "Yeah."

He blinked. "Wait, really?"

"Yeah. I need to get stronger. I'm going to work out with you more."

He pumped his fist. "Finally."

"I meant to do it after that last tournament, the one with Braden, but kinda lost track of things. But I want to keep our momentum going."

"And your singles momentum too. You're gonna be top 200 by the end of the year."

I held up two crossed fingers. "Here's hoping."

He turned to leave and then stopped with his paw on the door. "Hey," he said. "I'm looking forward to meeting your sister."

I swallowed the lump in my throat. "Can't wait for her to meet you. And all you guys."

I wasn't tired, and Lochen had said to call him anytime, so I called. "So," I said, "I'm right about this being enough to spare five thousand?"

"That's right. You go ahead and let me know what to do with it and I'll take care of the transfer, if you're sure."

"Of course I'm sure. Why wouldn't I be?"

The excitement drained from his voice somewhat. "Rocky, I read up a little bit on Lunda, and…I know you lived there, but there's a lot of stories about money going astray or not getting to the right paws. I just want to make sure this is all you need, that it isn't going to be five thousand now and then five thousand next year and then ten thousand the year after that. You can end up sending a lot of money down a sinkhole if you're not careful."

"Ma's there," I said. "She's managing it. She said five thousand and I trust her."

"This jackal your Ma referred you to. Does he speak English?" When I told him yes, he said, "Then give me his number and I'll handle it. You worry about tennis."

I hesitated, because I knew Lunda better than Lochen did, but at my hesitation he said, "If I run into any trouble, I promise you I'll call you. I won't go ahead if I'm at all unsure about anything. Besides, it's more official if I do it, aye? You go to practice. I'll call tomorrow morning and I'll call you as soon as it's done."

"Thank you," I said. "Thanks so much."

Danver was dead to the world, so if I'd wanted to, I could have called Marquize. But I was feeling pretty good, and I didn't want to ruin that, so I didn't.

As it turned out, we were at 168 the week following our win. It wasn't as high as we'd hoped, but it was still pretty good. We figured that if we kept going, we could talk about maybe going to majors and some international tournaments the following year as a doubles team, and that was pretty exciting. When he called back to confirm the transfer, Lochen told me to put him on speaker with Aliq and told us both that he was very impressed with our work. Not only could we go to the majors next year, he thought, but we might be close to affording a full-time coach.

That was exciting too. I asked if it could be Coach Keely, because I really liked working with him, and Lochen said that it would depend on his availability. Aliq liked his coach, too, a gazelle named Bowan, but he too was getting help on a part-time basis. Secretly I thought that Coach Keely would like to be my full-time coach; he'd hinted as much once or twice and he coached our doubles play, which Aliq's coach did not.

All through August I waited impatiently to hear from Ori. Lochen gave me regular updates, and right at the beginning of August he told me that One Two Three had contacted him and wanted me for an international campaign. "And get this," he said. "They're paying you five thousand dollars for it."

I blinked, sitting in bed. Danver was in the bathroom. "That's a lot."

"That's right. It's a big campaign. They said they had a couple established stars and then five or six 'up and comers,' and that's you."

My tail thumped the bed. "That's great!"

"You've earned it. I told you, keep on going and you'll earn more and more."

I tried. Aliq and I got to the semifinals of the Gardalina tournament in September, and that was the first one I was entered into the main draw without having to go through qualifiers. I did pretty well, losing one round short of the quarterfinals to the eventual runner-up of the tournament. That was where I filmed the short spot for One Two Three, an hour of filming for what I think ended up being five seconds of commercial time. It seemed excessive, but for five thousand they could have me for a bunch of hours, plus I did get a new pack of tennis shorts out of it.

And Marquize called me back after my singles loss. I was guarded, but he seemed apologetic. "You have time to talk?"

Remembering him complaining about me always being busy, I

said, "Yes," even though I'd been about to head out to dinner with Danver and Sean. I waved at them to go on without me; I knew where they were going. They nodded understanding and left me alone in the hotel room.

"Sorry for being snappy earlier," Marquize said. "It's just stressful here."

"I know. Here too." That didn't seem helpful, especially with as well as the tournament was going, so I said, "Thanks for calling back."

"Yeah, well." He still sounded down. "I talked to Lochen and he mentioned you'd won a tournament. Thought I should say congratulations."

"Oh, thanks. It was pretty cool. I did a bunch of interviews and got my picture taken."

"Nice. How much did you win?"

"Um, like twelve thousand or so."

"Wow." His voice stayed flat but then picked up. "That's great. So I guess Ori's taken care of?"

"Oh yeah. Yeah, I can't wait to see her again. I can't believe it's happening."

He absorbed that and then said, "Well, good. I'm glad. So, uh, what's up with you guys in the doubles?"

I told him a little about our upcoming opponents in the semi-final match the next day. "I don't know that we have much of a chance. Wan is a great returner and he's gonna eat up Aliq's serve. Probably mine too, to be honest. We do best when we can get the ball in play and some rallies going. Our communication's getting a lot better, and Coach Keely's helping with our strategy."

"Ah, cool," he said. "You know, a bunch of people think you might win that match."

"What people?" I asked, laughing. "Seriously?"

"Oh, I just read a little bit on some tennis website. Anyway, good luck. Hope you can win another tournament."

"Thanks," I said.

We made a little more conversation, and then, hoping I wasn't coming off busy or brushing him off, I said, "I'm getting hungry, so I should probably eat something or I'll definitely lose the match tomorrow."

"Yeah, yeah, go," he said. "Thanks for talking."

"Sure," I said. "Thanks for calling."

Aliq and I did lose that match, and it went pretty much the way I'd expected. The other team went off to practice for their final and we went to work out our frustrations at the gym. Marquize didn't call back, but at least I didn't feel angry when I thought of him, the way I had before he'd called.

Chapter Twenty-Five

In the heat of early September, we had a week off before the next tournament started, and I spent a lot of it at the gym. Aliq invited me and Danver back to his home outside of Freestone to train, and it was cheaper than staying in a hotel, so we went. His parents had a spare room that Danver and I took over, and they lived around the corner from a gym. Tennis courts were harder to find, but there was a set around six blocks away that we could take over if we went early in the morning. Harder was finding a way to practice our doubles with only three people, but Danver would position himself opposite me and Aliq like a doubles player with an imaginary partner. The points didn't last very long, but they were still useful to us in terms of working on placement and strategy.

It was Wednesday, September 12 at about 3 am—technically Wednesday morning, but it felt like Tuesday night—that my phone jolted me out of sleep. I fumbled for it, blinked at the international number, and felt sleep vanish in a wash of excitement and adrenaline. "Hello," I said, and pressed my ear to the receiver.

And for the first time in a year, I heard Ori's voice. "Ro?"

"It's me," I said. "Oh my god, Ori, where are you? I'm so happy to hear you."

"Oh, Ro." And then she was crying into the phone.

"Shh, Ori, shh."

Danver stirred in his bed. I didn't want to wake him, but I also didn't want to try to sneak through an unfamiliar house. I settled for going to the bathroom and closing the door. One of the things that had surprised me (in a good way) about Aliq's house was that his family, being foxes, had taken pains to soundproof all their bathrooms. Between growing up in Lunda and going to school in a dorm

and living in hotel rooms (whose bathrooms were definitely not soundproof), I was used to hearing everyone's bathroom business. Even at Lochen's, the bathrooms hadn't been this quiet.

When I closed the door behind me, the little rustles and creaks of the house and the sighs and movements of the sleeping foxes and squirrel vanished from my hearing, and all that was left was Ori's panting into the phone. By the time I sat on the closed toilet, she had calmed down a little. I curled my tail around my hips. "Are you at Kamina's?"

"No. I'm at Raji's sister's place. Oh, Ro. Ma—"

She broke down crying again and now my fur prickled. "What happened? Where's Ma?"

Sniffles, and then her voice came through in broken phrases. "We were coming…Bompaka's village…he didn't like letting me go…but we paid him…we were driving back…there was fighting, gunfire…we drove very fast, but Ma…she pushed me down on the seat…they hit Ma…"

The silence of the house seeped into my bones, into my chest, clenched around my throat. I made a noise but couldn't shape it into words. I tried again. "Where—is she okay?"

She sniffled again. "We tried…we got her to the hospital. But she was…" She gulped and sniffed. "We were too late."

I didn't say anything, hunched over with the phone pressed to my ear. It was so remote that I couldn't process what the words meant. Ma had been gone for eight months, but I'd always thought she'd come back eventually. Ori's words on the phone told my brain that that was no longer a possibility, but the news hadn't reached deep inside of me yet. Ma had always been there; she couldn't be gone. She'd come to get me at the school when I was five that time there was a storm; she'd rescued me from Lundara; she'd grabbed a cake knife at my birthday party to defend me. There was no reconciling the vivid, lively memories with the words that Ori was saying.

"Ro?"

"I'm here."

"I'm sorry."

Her emotion cracked the walls of my certainty. Ma wasn't here now in this room with me. "It wasn't your fault." Emptiness seeped into my skin. Force yourself to breathe. In. Out. "If I'd gotten the money sooner."

"No. Ma said you did everything you could have. She was so happy. I owe you both…"

"You stayed while I left." I closed my eyes and pressed my free paw to my head. "If we'd brought you over to start with…"

"You couldn't."

"I'm sorry, Ori."

"For what?"

"You had to go through all that." I took a breath and tried to focus on my living sister. "Are you safe?"

"Yes," she answered immediately. "Sarya and her husband are very kind."

"Is this number the one I should call to reach you?"

"Yes. They said you can call anytime."

"All right," I said. What was next? Ma was taking care of that. No; Ma couldn't take care of it. I had to be the head of the family now. I was all Ori had left. "All right. So when can you fly over here?"

Now she hesitated. "There's paperwork. I don't know…"

Raji's sister and her family must not know about emigration procedure. I would have suggested Ori overcome her prejudices and ask Kamina, but for two things. One, when I thought of Kamina and the way she'd talked about Ma, anger flared against the grief; and two, I was sure Kamina wouldn't know any more than Sarya did. "Is there an American consulate there?"

"I can look."

"Oh." I had an idea. "We called a jackal to send the money along. Maybe I can call him and see if he can help."

"That's a good idea."

We sat quietly for another few seconds. My eyes felt warm and my throat tight whenever my thoughts circled back to Ma, so I tried to focus on Ori and the fact that she was safe, that we would be bringing her over here to the States soon.

"I should get some sleep," she said.

"How big is their house there?" I asked, not because I cared, but because I didn't want to let go of this connection. "Do you have your own room?"

"No, I'm in a room with Sarya's daughter. She's five."

"Oh, okay."

We were quiet again, until Ori said, "Where are you staying?"

So I told her about Aliq and his parents, and that held us together for another few minutes.

"This phone call is probably expensive for Sarya," Ori said finally.

"Sorry." Guilt wasn't enough to make me let her go.

"What time is it there?"

"Don't worry about it."

"Love you, Ro."

"Love you, Ori." And then, because I couldn't postpone the good-bye any longer, "I'll talk to you soon."

I hung up the phone and sat there, clutching it in my paw. It wasn't true, what Ori had said. It couldn't be. It was some macabre joke. I would get up now and go back to bed, and when I got up in the morning I would call that number and Ma would answer and tell me about getting Ori back.

Except my legs wouldn't support me when I tried to stand, my body leaden. I could barely sit up straight. All right, then. I would stay hunched over here until I felt better.

I didn't realize I was crying until the first tears dripped onto my paws.

Chapter Twenty-Six

A knock on the bathroom door came a while later. "Hey," Aliq's voice came through the door. "Uh, Rocky? You feeling okay?"

I checked my phone. It was 5:15 am. I knew I'd been drifting in and out of sleep and crying most of the time. Had I been making noise? I rubbed my eyes. "Uh, I'm. I'm…"

I didn't think that "okay" worked, but I couldn't think of another word. Aliq grew more concerned. "Are you sick? Do you need help?"

The fur around my eyes wasn't getting any drier. I stood, wobbly, and grabbed a hand towel, rubbing at my face. "You can come in," I said.

The doorknob turned slowly, and Aliq, in a t-shirt and boxers, stepped into the bathroom. He padded up to the sink beside me. "You feeling okay? Did you puke?" He opened the medicine cabinet. "We got Pepto, um, some anti-nausea my mom keeps around, I don't see it, though…"

"I didn't puke." Every time I tried to take a breath, I felt like I might, though. I steadied myself with both paws on the long counter and inhaled deeply, my body shaking. I didn't want to say it aloud but I was going to have to tell him. And he was patient, waiting, watching. Aliq was a good guy, a good doubles partner. "I. I got a phone call. From my sister."

His ears perked up, but the smile didn't get far before he reconciled the news with my state. "Oh, shit. Something…went wrong?"

"My mom," I said, and I couldn't force out the words, but shaking my head and rubbing tears from my eyes got the message across.

"Ah, crap," he said. "I'm sorry, Rocky."

He dithered, not sure whether to hug me or not, I think. I wasn't really processing stuff. "I'm sorry," I said. "I'll go back to bed."

He flicked his tail out of my way as I stepped to the door. "I gotta pee," he said. "Um, you want to go to the gym? In a bit?"

"No," I said dully, and walked back to the room I was sharing with Danver.

I sat on my bed and turned my phone over and over in my paws, tail curled around my hips. My thoughts kept going back to Ma and then skittering away, replaying what Ori had said and trying to remember the last time I'd talked to Ma. She'd never know I'd won a tournament. She'd never know what was happening with me and Marquize, or even how I'd gotten the money for Ori. I hadn't told her on the phone and now I never could. She'd never see Ori and me reunited in the States, or see me and Aliq going to a major tournament, or an international one. She'd never see me get my high school equivalency—which I was determined more than ever to get now.

A light knock came at the door, and it creaked open. A white muzzle poked through. "Hi," Aliq's mother said softly. "Aliq told me you had some bad news."

"Yeah."

She came in, box of tissues in one paw which she held out to me. "You doing okay?"

I pulled a tissue and put it to my face. It came away wet. "Thanks. Um. Yeah. I'm—no, I'm not."

"Come on," she said, and led me out of the room.

We sat in their living room on the couch and she tried to coax me to talk. I didn't feel like talking much, though, so she ended up telling me about her mother, who'd recently died after a year and a half struggle with breast cancer. It sounded like a terrible ordeal for the family, and Aliq's grandmother sounded like a nice person, but to be honest I couldn't concentrate on the story. His mother had her paw on my wrist, though, which was nice and helped me feel a little better.

Partway through, I realized that I really wanted someone to hold me, and the only person who was going to do that was Marquize. And he'd known Ma too. I should call and tell him.

So I excused myself, telling Aliq's mom that I had some people to call, and she said she would make me some fish soup. An old family recipe, she said, which made me wonder if she had a recipe to make when someone died. I shook those morbid thoughts away and went to my room.

Danver was getting dressed, so I had to tell him what had happened too, and he got a weird twisted up expression on his muzzle. "Aw, geez," he said. "That sucks. I'm sorry."

"Yeah," I said. "Look, I gotta call…some people."

"Sure," he said, and yanked the shirt on over his head. "I'll get outta your fur." But in the thirty seconds it took him to grab his stuff, he managed to keep talking. "You know, if you want to drink or something, I can get some booze for you. I know it's not your thing, but my dad said it helped take the edge off when he was worried about his job so I don't know. For me it just relaxes me, maybe you need that more than staying sober? Just let me know."

I didn't respond, and he left the room, closing the door behind him.

I know he wanted to give me privacy, but that made me feel even more alone and isolated, and then I got my phone out and called Marquize, and he didn't answer. So I left a voicemail. "Hey, Mar, I, uh, I got some bad news. I need to talk to you. Call me back."

My voice was all weird and I didn't know if he would pick up on that or not. But as it turned out, I only had to wait for two minutes, because he called me back right away. "Rocky? It's four in the morning here. What's going on?"

"Uh." I stalled, still hating the shape of the words in my mouth. But I had to push them out or else this conversation would be even more anguished. "Ma died."

"What? *Your* Ma? That's—how?"

So I told him what I knew, in halting broken sentences, and he didn't say anything until I was done, when he breathed, "Fuck. I'm so sorry."

Everyone was sorry. Already I was getting tired of hearing that phrase, or else I was numb to it. "I was wondering if I could come out there and see you."

"What—now?"

"Well, whenever I can book a flight."

"You know I'm like an hour outside Pelagia, right?"

"Yeah, so?"

"I mean, I start a tournament tomorrow. Qualifying and everything. Don't you have a tournament next week?"

I growled so I wouldn't start crying again. "I'm not going to play in a tournament next week. I mean, for one thing, I need to take care of stuff. Ori and…and just stuff, and I'm not going to have time…" The growling wasn't working. "I'm just not, that's all."

"Did you cancel already?"

"Don't try to talk me into playing. Losing a match and letting Aliq down isn't going to make me feel better."

"No, no, I didn't mean that," he said hurriedly. "I think time off is good."

"I'm going to call Lochen right after I call you. He'll take care of it."

Marquize took a breath. "Maybe don't call him right now. I mean, look, if you want, I can call him for you. I'll have him email you for confirmation."

The prospect of not having to talk to one more person was a huge relief. "Yeah, if you would. That'd be a help. Thanks, Mar. And I'll look for a flight."

"Oh, uh. You know, I'd love to, but…I mean, if you come out, we'll figure out something, but it's…I mean, sure, come if you want to."

"All right," I said. "I'll let you know. And thanks for taking care of things with Lochen."

"Sure, Rocky. Whatever I can do."

When we'd hung up, I lay back on the bed and stared at the ceiling. Even here, with Danver's clothes all over the floor and arctic fox scent on everything around me, the voice of my still-maybe-boyfriend in my recent memory, I felt alone.

Chapter Twenty-Seven

The house was quiet when I woke, which meant that Danver and Aliq had gone out to practice. My stomach was empty but I didn't register it as hunger. Aliq's mom had put a bowl of their fish soup on a little table outside my door, covered, and I picked at it. It was lukewarm but still tasted good; I just didn't have any appetite.

If I were going to visit Marquize, I should book the flight to Pelagia. I opened the computer, searched on "buy plane ticket," and found myself on a website that was going to let me do that. But as I was looking at all the options, I couldn't figure out which would be best to get me there, and I didn't know when I was going to want to come back. Everything felt so overwhelming that I closed the computer and lay back on the bed again.

By the time the sun was coloring the sky red, I really did need something to eat besides the now-cold fish soup. I wandered down through the house, but everyone was out. Someone had left a note under the bedroom door that said I could help myself to whatever I wanted in the fridge, but I felt weird taking their food. So I went out in my t-shirt and jeans, walking around to see what I could find.

Three blocks away I found a little strip mall with a cluster of fast food restaurants. They had different names from the ones in Pensa but the menus were pretty much the same. I got two burgers, pulled the buns off them, and ate the meat. Then I ordered another one and did the same. By that time I was feeling a little better, but I still didn't want to go back to Aliq's.

Then I remembered that place, Politics, out in Silver. I brought up my phone to see if there were any gay clubs in this area, and lo and behold, one popped up about a half mile from where I was.

Well, I thought, the walk will do me good.

That turned out not to be true. I had headphones and music but it still left me too much time and space to think, to circle around the impossibility of Ma being dead and the reality of her death. Twice I almost called Ori, but I was afraid that talking to her would make it more real even though I knew she probably wanted to reach out to me. After the club, I told myself.

I missed it at first, walking past the door lost in thought, and only turned around because I saw two male porcupines holding paws walking the other direction. I turned and followed them, and then saw the rainbow flag sticker in the window of the old building.

And it was a bar, not a club, a dark, musky place where people sat and drank and flirted. I was prepared to make the same deal with the bartender that I had at Politics, but nobody challenged me for my ID when I went in, nor did the waiter who came to my table. He was a squirrel, which reminded me that Danver had recommended booze, and that stopped me from ordering the Coke I was going to. What kinds of things did Danver say to waiters in the clubs we'd been to? I came up with, "What's local?"

The waiter rubbed a paw on his apron. "You mean beer?"

"Yeah."

He rattled off a few names and I picked one at random. He took a note of it and went away.

So maybe it was that easy to get alcohol in some places. I sat alone and stared at my paws until the squirrel came back, setting a thick glass mug down on the wood table with a thunk. "Anything else right now?"

I shook my head. "I'm good, thanks."

And off he went again, leaving me alone. I picked up the beer and sipped it, and the flavor was a little bit of a surprise, yeasty and malty with a strong citrus undertone. It wasn't bad, though, and the sip turned into a drink.

By the time the glass was empty, the tight knot in my chest was looser. I felt floaty, more relaxed, and when the squirrel came by, I ordered another beer. I had enough cash for probably, I calculated, three of them, and a credit card if I needed it, but I didn't want to use the credit card because that might require getting out my id, and then they'd know I wasn't old enough to drink. That was fine; I could be careful.

Halfway through my second beer, I was liking the taste more and more, but I kept thinking about whether Ma would have liked it and what she would've thought about my drinking. She probably wouldn't have cared as long as I was responsible, because Ma was great that way. Had been great. I had to rub my eyes more and more, and I wasn't honestly sure if the beer was helping or hurting. I did feel like my grief was more real than it had been, and while that hurt, I thought it was also healthy.

And then a cacomistle in a yellow polo shirt stopped by my table. "Mind if I join you?" he said.

"Sure." I waved him to one of the other chairs and he pulled it out with a scrape across the floor.

He swept his long ringed tail to one side and sat down. "I'm Manny."

I reached for his extended paw and shook it. "Rocky," I said.

He held the grasp for a little while. "Looks like you're having a rough time."

"Uh…kind of." I pulled my paw back and gulped some more beer.

He leaned in. "Can I guess? Someone left you."

"Yeah," I said, a little surprised.

"That really sucks." He rested a paw on mine. "You think these things are going to be forever."

"I thought so." Manny was right. I'd thought Ma would always be with me. He smelled nice, too, a pleasant scent of masculinity over the beer scent clogging my muzzle. "I mean, you never think… and I still can't believe it…"

His paw tightened around mine. "You want to talk about it?"

I sniffed. "Maybe." It was really nice that someone was so concerned about me. "I think part of the problem is that I heard it over the phone."

"Over the phone?" He shook his head. "You poor kid."

"My sister wouldn't lie," I went on. "I know. And I don't want to be there in person, but at the same time I don't know if I can really believe it otherwise."

His grip didn't waver, but his tone did. "Your…sister?"

"She was there. She saw it happen. Oh, poor Ori. I should call her."

"Hold up." He tapped my paw to get my attention. "I think I'm missing something. What did your sister see?"

"My Ma," I said. His frown didn't lighten, so I said, "My Ma was killed."

The pressure around my paw lifted as his fingers spread, and for a moment his paw rose, but then it settled down again. "Killed?"

I nodded. "Over in Lunda."

"Ah." He seemed to think about something for a moment and then took my paw again. "You poor thing. What was she doing in Lunda?"

So I told him about her going over to get my sister out of a marriage, and was careful to tell him that I work in construction; true to Braden's advice, he didn't ask any more questions, just ran a paw up my arm and said that it showed. That was around the time he offered to buy me my fourth beer, and the combination of the contact and the drink finally got through to my brain.

"Oh, uh," I said. "I have a boyfriend."

I should've said it more tactfully, but I'd downed three beers in an hour and a half after maybe drinking three my entire previous life, and tact wasn't happening anymore. But Manny didn't blink. He had a really nice, warm smile that curved all the way around his short muzzle, and his expressive ears flicked around. "Where is he?"

"Huh?"

"Your boyfriend?" He looked around the bar. "He meeting you here later?"

I shook my head, part of me marveling that we were talking so casually about boyfriends, something I could do with hardly anyone else in my life. "He's in Pelagia. I was going to fly out there. But." I wasn't sure I should tell this guy about Marquize, but heck, I'd told him about Ma, hadn't I? "It didn't really sound like he wanted me out there. I mean, I'm sure he does, but it's a long way and he's playing, uh, he's really busy these days."

"He's playing busy?" Manny raised his eyebrows. "You think he's pretending to be busy so he don't have to see you? You know, I was dating a guy like that once. He never said anything straight out, but when he got tired of me it was all 'gotta work late tonight' and 'gotta visit my parents,' and after a month of that he dumped me."

"Oh," I said. "No. I mean, he's not, he's not going to…" But then I started thinking, where *was* Marquize? I really needed him now, and he hadn't said for me to fly out. He hadn't said not to, but…it was hard to remember exactly what he had said, to be honest. It definitely wasn't "yes, come out here right away," or I would've come out there. I wouldn't be here alone in this bar—no, not alone, leaning against this really nice cacomistle.

After the fourth beer, I got out my cash because I was feeling pretty drunk at that point. Since then I've been more drunk, but that was definitely a first. It doesn't excuse what happened, mind you, but at least it explains it. A little.

Manny had told me a little about himself, too. He worked as a mid-level manager at a technology company ("we design stuff that other people use to make home appliances," he said, and I didn't press because I wouldn't have understood him even sober). He'd broken up with his steady boyfriend the year before and hadn't found anyone else since, though he'd dated a lot. He lived somewhere called "Planton," where he had a "split-level duplex," a phrase I nodded at but was secretly sure he'd made up. And he liked the same superhero movies I did, and said the thing that I'd only dared say to Marquize, which was that Red Lightning was hotter than WonderWolf.

My phone buzzed a couple times, texts from Danver and Aliq, and I hadn't responded at first because I didn't want to let them know where I was. But Manny, noticing, said I should at least tell them I was ok, because I might be taking Ma's death hard and they might be worried about my safety. That was pretty nice of him, I thought, so I texted them back and said I was fine.

It had been an hour and I felt comfortable with the cacomistle, enough to tell him that I shouldn't drink anymore. "No," he said, "I agree. You want me to give you a ride home? Did you drive here?"

I shook my head. "Don't have a car," I said.

"I hate to think of you going home to that bed all alone," he said. "You want company? I've got some coffee at my place. You could sober up there before you go home."

"Yeah, that sounds good." I had a huge feeling of relief. Already I'd been picturing myself walking back into Aliq's parents' house drunk and smelling of beer. A chance to clean up a bit beforehand was perfect.

Manny had a little red car that was hard for my tall frame to fit into. "Sorry about the space," he said as I folded my knees up. "Hope the leather seats make up for it. They got heaters for when it gets cold, y'know?"

"Nice," I said, though I tried to imagine hot air blowing through the leather and couldn't.

He lived not too far away. We parked in a multi-level garage next to a complex of apartments and Manny led me through a small courtyard that smelled of flowers to an elevator, and then down a hallway where I leaned against a wall while he unlocked the door. The car ride had been bouncy and unsettled my stomach, even though I hadn't eaten much that night, and the elevator's bouncing hadn't helped matters at all.

"Doing okay?" Manny asked.

I nodded and burped. That helped matters long enough for me to get into his apartment.

If I hadn't just come from Aliq's parents' place, I would have been impressed with his living room. It looked like a hotel room, but friendlier. There was a poofy couch, blue and soft-looking, a wooden coffee table with a few magazines spread out under a cluster of remotes, and a matching wood entertainment unit that held a plasma TV, a game console, and a rack of electronic appliances behind a glass door. On top of the unit, a green parakeet chirped away, hopping back and forth in an ornate birdcage.

"Hang on," Manny said, hurrying to the cage. "Let me feed him."

I still felt uneasy, so I checked for a bathroom and found it opposite the kitchen. Knowing where it was made me comfortable

275

enough to plop down on the couch, and that was nice. It was as soft against my fingerpads as it looked. I brushed it up and down as the cacomistle tipped birdseed into the cage's feeder. "You ever let him out?" I asked.

"Sometimes," he said, putting the canister back on the shelf below the cage. "But not tonight. He sometimes makes messes and I don't want to have to clean them up right now."

I didn't see any bird messes around the apartment, though there was a distinct smell of bird. But I closed my eyes and didn't worry about it. Manny moved back to the kitchen, where he ran some water and then turned on a coffee machine. "It'll be about ten minutes," he said.

"Great," I murmured. "Thanks."

I wasn't sure he could hear me over there, so when he came to sit beside me on the sofa, I said, "Thanks," again.

"Hey, it's no trouble." He slid an arm around my shoulders, and it was comfortable, so I leaned into it. Then something fluffy landed in my lap and I had a paw on it before I realized it was his tail.

"Oh, sorry." I lifted my paw.

He laughed. "Go ahead. I keep it conditioned and clean."

So I let my paws stroke the fur on his tail. He was right: it was soft and it smelled like flowers. Some people let their tails drag along the ground and get grimy and gross. I kept mine pretty clean, but I'd have wanted to wash it if I thought some guy was going to run his paws through it. Manny clearly had prepared for that eventuality. And it was nice and soothing stroking his tail, just like his paw rubbing my shoulder was nice and the smell of him was nice and the embrace was nice. I hadn't forgotten Ma—I couldn't—but at least this made me feel like I wasn't alone.

He shifted toward me and his other paw landed on my stomach. The touch was what I'd been craving, so I exhaled and leaned into it further.

A couple minutes in, I noticed that I was getting kind of hard. I hoped Manny couldn't tell; he was being so friendly and here I was getting worked up. It was only because I was next to a cute guy, I thought, with my hormones working the way they did. I certainly didn't think he was going to be interested in sex with a drunk jackal, and with Ma's death, I wasn't really in the mood even if I didn't have a (far away) boyfriend.

Fortunately, his tail was covering my lap, and that's when the second thing registered with me, which was that his tail was actually pressing down on my groin as I rubbed it. Was that my fault or his? I tried to shift his tail, but after a moment it curled back to rub my erection. I moved it again, and Manny definitely noticed this time, because he took that as permission for his paw to wander down from my stomach. "Seems like you're feeling a little better," he said.

His paw rubbing my cock felt good—when doesn't it—and I squirmed, leaving it there. "Uh," I said. "I'm…"

"I know." His breath tickled my ear. "You have a boyfriend. But he's not here to make you feel better, and I am."

Marquize wasn't here. And that almost worked. But even drunk, or partly drunk, my thoughts were about Ma and what she would say. She didn't care that I was gay, but she would've been mad if I'd cheated on my boyfriend. Especially after he cheated on me. What would that say about me? That we were right for each other after all, that we belonged together, and maybe that I belonged down on the Futures circuit and not rising through the Challenger circuit aspiring after majors. Was that what I wanted for myself?

My thoughts whirled around those subjects and then asked, Had I already cheated? By going to this guy's house and letting him rub my cock through my pants? No, that wasn't—I hadn't intended—

And then Manny started undoing my pants and his fingers slipped past the waistband.

"No! Sorry!" I got up, wobbled, tried to brace myself on the arm of the sofa and missed but caught myself before I fell all the way to the floor. From my knees I studied his muzzle, saw disappointment smoothed over with charm. "It's just, my Ma, I don't feel, I mean, maybe some other time, but…"

From the kitchen, the coffee machine whined. "It's all right," Manny said, rising as gracefully as I'd been clumsy. "I'll pour you a coffee and you can call a cab."

"I don't have money for a cab," I blurted out, refastening my pants.

"Then you can call a friend." He got out two mugs and poured coffee into each of them.

There followed the most uncomfortable cup of coffee I've ever had in my life, and not because the cup didn't have an extended lip for canid muzzles. I sipped it in silence, trying to ignore the bitter taste while also trying to figure out how to ask Manny for a ride back to Aliq's parents' place, or at least the bar. Worse, my erection wasn't going away, and was probably responsible for the little voice whispering in the back of my head that I could have sex *right now* if I'd only loosen up a little. Manny was clean and was probably pretty good, and I'd never had sex with anyone else.

In the end, I couldn't ask Manny either for sex or a ride. But I had thought of something to tell Aliq and Danver, so I texted them that I'd gone out walking and got lost, named the street I was on, and asked if one of them could come pick me up. Aliq got back to me right away and said he'd be here in fifteen minutes.

I got through about two thirds of the cup of coffee and then said, "My friend'll be here soon. I should go."

"All right," Manny said. "You ever dump that boyfriend or the prissy attitude, come on by."

If there was any part of me that still wanted to see him again, it gave up at that remark. "Yeah," I said, relieved that I felt a lot more sober and steady both inside and out. "Sure thing."

Outside, I only had to wait a few minutes before Aliq pulled up. "You okay?" he asked when I got in.

I nodded. "I had to clear my head."

Aliq swung the car into a U-turn right in the middle of the street. My stomach lurched again and then settled, thankfully. I leaned back against the seat rest and remembered that I should call Ori when I got back. If only Marquize was here, or I was with him; until Manny had gotten too insistent, having someone to hold me had been really nice. At least my erection had gone away.

"Did you have coffee?" The arctic fox sniffed the air. "And beer?"

"Uh, yeah. There's a bar around, I had a few beers and then I got a little woozy so I drank some coffee."

"The bar served you, huh?" Aliq shook his head. "Which one was it?"

I froze. "I, uh, don't remember the name."

"Hey, I'm not going to report them or anything. Just curious."

"I really don't remember," I insisted. For a moment he reminded me of Dom, and I thought about his baseball code. Would I say that Manny got to second base? Or almost got to third? That he was thrown out trying to stretch a double into a triple? My confusing tangle of emotions threatened to bubble up into a giggle, which was almost sure to turn into sobs, so I bit the inside of my cheek until the feeling went away.

"All right, all right. Ah, crap, I need to make this turn." He gunned the engine and swerved around a slower car to the tune of several honking horns. I resolved to keep my eyes closed for the rest of the drive back, and also to never let Aliq drive me anywhere again.

Chapter Twenty-Eight

I was sober enough to call Ori when I got back. We asked how each other were doing, and she said she was fine, that Raji's family was a big help. They had already had to deal with the grief of losing a son and brother, so they understood her pain. For the first time in years, I envied Ori her community in Lunda, where losing people was common enough that you could always find support, people who understood what it meant to have someone vanish from your life. The next moment, I felt guilty about that—did I want my friends here to have lost relatives just so they'd be better at comforting me? Did I wish more suffering on the people in Lunda? But as unfair as it was, I couldn't help feeling it.

And Ori was a big help. We didn't talk really about Ma, but loss permeated all of our words. I told her I was going to contact some people to help her come here to the States; unspoken was that Ma should have been setting up those meetings. Even the simple fact of Ori staying with Sarya rather than Kamina underscored that Ma wasn't there to smooth things over. The fact that it was me and Ori planning our future rather than me, Ori, and Ma stayed with me long after the phone call.

In the morning, I had messages from Danver, Aliq, and Lochen. The first two were in the house, checking up to make sure I was okay. They coaxed me into coming out for breakfast, and my appetite had returned enough that Aliq's insistence that I stay nourished made sense.

During breakfast, I listened to Lochen's message. "Hey," he said. "Just talked to Marquize and he said your mom passed away. So sorry, Rocky. Can you send me a quick text confirming your withdrawal from the tournament and I'll make sure to get that processed."

I thought it was a little weird that Lochen hadn't called until late, when Marquize had said he'd call him yesterday morning, but maybe he had a lot on his plate. So I sent him the text and got back another condolences text, and that one I didn't feel I had to respond to.

"Hey," Aliq said after breakfast, "we gotta get going to the airport this afternoon. But I talked to my mom and she said you can stay here as long as you want. Which means a couple weeks." He grinned, kind of lopsided, and patted my arm. "But you'll be back on the circuit by then."

"Yeah." The ache inside me came and went, but seemed to subside when I thought about playing tennis. "You going to find someone else for doubles?"

The arctic fox shook his head. "Too late for that, and anyway, we're doing good. I'm not going to try to figure out how to play with someone else. I'll focus on singles this tournament and then you'll be back for the next one."

"What if I'm not?"

"Hey," he said with a smile. "You will be."

I accepted his confidence, but it didn't seem like two weeks was going to be enough to heal the break inside me.

* * *

I talked to Ori a lot over the next week, and then I finally called Lochen a few days later because I didn't want to put off starting the process of getting my sister over here. Of course, the first thing the red fox wanted to know was whether I was going to play in the next tournament after the one I was skipping.

"I suppose I'd better," I said.

"If you're feeling okay. You've been through something bad." He paused. "You're still going through it."

"I'm doing better. Talking to my sister helps a lot."

"Right. And you want to get her over here." The rustling of paper sounded. "I don't really know anyone in the government, but I've made a couple phone calls to a guy I know who knows a guy who knows a guy." He laughed. "Anyway, expecting a call back. They don't just hand out visas, you know, but for someone famous we can pull strings."

I swallowed. "Am I famous enough?"

"Ehhh. To be honest, not yet. Winning Challenger-level doubles tournaments doesn't really ping on most people's radar. Win some singles tournaments, make a showing in some majors, and we'll have a better argument. Of course, there's always the legit path, but I suspect that from a place like Lunda we're talking two years or more. So we should probably get that started. And for that, uh…I mean, she's probably going to have to talk to someone in government about everything she's gone through. The guy I'm waiting to hear back from, he specializes in refugees and asylum. You know what that means?"

"Means it isn't safe for her there so she can come here?"

"More or less. I'll let you know when I find out more."

"Thanks."

"And you focus on the tournaments, all right?"

"I will."

And I did. Not that day, but the next, I picked up the tennis racket again and walked down to the tennis court. I stepped into the white lines of the court and again, most of the rest of the world melted away. But not everything this time. An ache in my chest persisted no matter how many balls I hit. At least it was a little better, a little more bearable. And remembering how to hit, letting those physical memories take over, that helped.

I practiced again the next day, and the next. And then I went to the gym and worked out and practiced again. If I had an opponent to figure out, I hoped the mental exercises would help me ignore the ache still more.

Aliq's parents were lovely to me during this time, feeding me and letting me have my privacy if I wanted it. Sometimes I wanted to talk about Ma or about loss, and once I asked his mother how long it took to get over her mother's death. "Oh, bubelah," she said with a smile on her snow-white muzzle (she had taken to calling me that), "I never got over it. I miss her still. Only it's not every day anymore. It's more like once a week, maybe once every two weeks. There'll be a memory, or something she would have liked. I wish she could've seen her grandson playing tennis, winning tournaments." She laid a paw over mine. "And thank you for helping me at least see that."

"He's fun to play with," I said. Even though we were talking about loss, her enthusiasm for her son warmed me.

By the second week, I was impatient and ready to get back onto the court. As Aliq's mom said, I wasn't over Ma's death, but my calls with Ori helped. Both of us talked about the future; she was going to go back to work at that Muslim charity, and I was going back to tournaments. I told her what Lochen had told me, and she found out where the States Consulate was so that she could go once Lochen's friend (friend's friend's friend?) was ready to start the process. It still hurt too much to talk about Ma, and in the nights when I lay in bed alone, I thought about her often and cried a lot. But getting back on the tennis court felt good, and I knew it was what she would have wanted.

So I flew to Deleon, so warm and humid and sticky that Aliq's mother pressed a bottle of conditioner on me as I was leaving. "Otherwise your fur gets all," she waved her paws. "Mishegas." (I had to ask her what that meant: "crazy," she said.)

I wasn't any stranger to the humid summers of Pensa, but Deleon was warmer than I was used to. I was panting within ten minutes of getting off the plane even at nine at night, and that continued all the way to the hotel room. I'd expected Danver to be out, but he and Sean and Aliq and Caboll were all waiting for me, and when I came in, they got up and greeted me with solemn grasps of the paw and warm smiles, as though they wanted to hug me either in delight at my return or in sympathy for my loss, but weren't quite sure it would be okay. And that was fine; the firm grips on my paw were nice.

For the first few minutes, they were cautious, but as I talked about tennis and getting ready for the tournament, everyone loosened up. Aliq told me the gym nearby was barely adequate but he was still going over in the morning, and I agreed to go with him.

Eventually he and Sean and Caboll retired to their rooms, leaving me and Danver alone. Danver was unusually quiet after they left, but when we turned out the lights, he started talking, all in a rush, like he did. "Hey, Rocky, I don't wanna be inappropriate or anything but are you doing okay? I was thinking, I mean, Aliq and I were talking, and I realized, like, I've never lost anyone. So I dunno what it's like. I dunno what I'm supposed to do. Should I just leave you alone? You can tell me and I won't be offended. Or if you want to talk about it, I promise I can shut up and listen. And hey, if you don't want to talk about it, we can talk about tennis or whatever you want, or I can take you out…" He trailed off. "So, uh, anything you want to tell me?"

I'd started out uncomfortable, but Danver's earnestness won me over by the end of his speech. "I appreciate it," I said into the darkness. "I think right now just acting normal is the best thing, but I'll let you know if anything changes."

"Okay." He exhaled and rustled around in his bed. "Thanks. Sorry, I usually know what to do but like I said, I haven't really lost anyone that I remember. I guess my great-grandfather died when I was two, but I don't really remember him at all."

"It's fine," I said. "Thanks."

And I thought about Marquize, who had called me a couple times and also didn't seem to quite know what to say. He'd talked tennis, more optimistic about my future than about his even though I'd told him to keep working. He didn't say whether he was disappointed that I hadn't flown out to visit him; he'd only asked me if I still wanted to, and I said I'd be okay in Freestone, and we dropped it. I kind of wanted to tell him about Manny, but not over the phone.

But that night, lying in bed, I missed Marquize lying beside me. It had been over five months at this point, and as I was thinking about him and about Ma, some words Ma had said when we first left Lunda came back to me. I'd been worried about losing touch with Ori, and Ma said, "We're all floating on an ocean, and sometimes we'll drift apart from people. But family, we're tied together." She'd made a little motion with her paw, like fastening a rope between herself and me. "And we'll all drift together."

It was clear from the phone calls with Ori that she and I were still close even though we hadn't talked in months. But I wondered whether Marquize and I were drifting apart.

Chapter Twenty-Nine

So I settled back into the routine of tennis, familiar thoughts and muscle movements like choreography designed to keep my mind and body on a certain track. Concerns like Ma, Ori, and Marquize were outside that track.

It was only in the evenings when my body was pleasantly exhausted and my mind supposed to be anticipating the following day's exercise that it wandered. My friends were very good about taking me out, talking to me, keeping me occupied. Nevertheless, there were holes they couldn't fill or even patch. Ori filled part of it, the reassurance that my family was still around me. And Marquize should have been around to fill the other. I missed him, but not quite him. I missed who he used to be, the relationship we used to have. The Marquize on the phone was an echo of that, and maybe I was an echo of the Rocky he used to date, and we were holding onto nothing but memories. Or maybe this was something we had to go through, something all couples went through. I didn't know, and I didn't have anyone to ask about it.

Plus I couldn't talk to the guys about Ma any more than I already had. I'm sure they would've listened, but they couldn't tell me anything they hadn't already, and I couldn't ask more of them. To try to explain what was missing from my life when I could barely get my mind around it myself would have distracted us all from tennis. So I lived with the nighttime grief and hoped that, as Aliq's mother had said, it would one day lessen.

A couple days in, I told the guys that I was going to go out on my own. They all said that was fine, none of them asking me to check in or anything like that, which was freeing and at the same time heightened my loneliness. But that was why I was going to a gay bar

I'd found a half mile from the tournament site.

This one was giving out wristbands at the door with your ID, and so it didn't matter that I wasn't 21; I just didn't get one of the wristbands that would've told the servers it was okay for me to have alcohol. I sat down and ordered a Coke.

Not everyone in these places could be as sex-driven as Manny had been. Truthfully, I was in a better place now, and if not for Marquize, I wouldn't mind a hookup. But I couldn't cheat on him, not after I'd gotten so mad at him for cheating on me. If I really wanted to break up with him, I was going to have to do it myself. I kept thinking about it, which made me think I probably should, but at the same time he was pledging to try hard, to work to be a better boyfriend, and I didn't want to turn my back on him without giving him a chance. But if I waited much longer, the currents of life would pull us more and more apart.

For whatever reason—maybe because I was clearly not wrist-banded, maybe because I was dressed down in t-shirt and jeans while the rest of the patrons sported flashy shirts, glittering jewelry, even bright beads in their fur—only a couple people came over to talk to me. One fox had a series of studs running up the length of each ear in the six Pride colors, and I reflected that it would be nice to be able to be that open about my orientation. Some players wore crosses around their necks, but otherwise there wasn't a lot of jewelry on the tour. It tends to fly about when you're playing.

So as the evening wore on, my loneliness got worse. I thought about calling Marquize, but then I'd have to tell him I was in a gay bar and that might lead to more awkward questions. I kept looking around and picking out guys I'd like to put my arm around, but that led to me thinking about doing more with them. I felt a bit guilty and then decided that it didn't matter as long as they stayed thoughts.

And then I spotted a fox in a hoodie. I hadn't seen him come in, but he'd moved across my field of vision and sat right in my line of sight. My ears perked up and I watched him for the next five minutes, trying to see if he had a cross fox's markings. He was tall enough for sure.

Yes. It was him. His head turned underneath one of the overhead lights and I recognized Braden. I didn't know whether he'd seen me yet or not; he hadn't come over and he wasn't looking anywhere near me.

On any other night I would've let him be. But tonight I saw a chance to talk to someone about Marquize, maybe the only person in the world whom I could turn to now. So I got up and walked over to where he was sitting, alone, looking around the same as I'd been. I leaned against the brass rail at the bar, putting myself in his line of sight so he couldn't help but notice me.

Still, it took him a good minute before his eyes lit on mine and recognition spread in them, followed by a frown. He dropped his head back to his drink, something clear and bubbly, and sipped it through the straw. I waited. After a moment, he lifted his head and looked at me again, then shook his head and muttered something to himself and got up. I braced myself for him to come over to me, but he walked right to the door and out.

What the hell? I watched the door close behind him. The bartender said something behind me but I didn't really process what it was. My mind buzzed with the mood I was in, and I strode across the bar, yanked the door open, and stomped out past the surprised bouncer and a pair of antelopes getting wristbands.

The hoodied fox was only a block away and not walking fast, his six-foot height easy to spot and catch on the moderately busy street. He heard me coming and turned as I got close to him, putting his paws up. "Hey," he said. "What the fuck?"

"What the fuck is with you?" I hissed, conscious that there were people all around us and that Braden's big ears could hear me perfectly well at a very low volume.

He gestured back to the bar. "You come up on me in a public place like this, what the fuck do you want?" His paw moved from the bar to point up at my muzzle. "And if you say 'what do you think?' so help me I'll…" The threat was clear even if he didn't want to verbalize it.

"I just want…" What I wanted felt clear in my head, sharp as a bell, but I had trouble saying the words. "I want to talk to someone."

"You have friends," he said, and then raised an eyebrow, making it a question.

I shook my head and looked back to the bar. "Not who know."

"Jesus Fox." He flattened his ears and looked around, but nobody was paying much attention to us. "If you want someone to hold your paw and tell you it's okay to be gay, go find a therapist."

It looked like he was going to walk away. The loneliness threatened to overwhelm me, and I thought that if I started crying in front of him, he should know why, so I said in a low voice, "My mother just died and my best friend is the problem."

That stopped him, though it didn't get rid of the frown. He rolled his eyes, his head bumping the wall behind him as he tilted his muzzle back. "For fuck's sake," he muttered.

I moved against the wall beside him so I'd be out of the way of the people on the sidewalk. "I know you don't owe me anything," I said hurriedly, almost in a whisper. "In fact, I owe you a lot. And I promise, I intend to repay it someday. But right now I'm lost and I'm messed up and I just want to talk to someone."

He shook his head and didn't look at me. "You know the Calcott Hotel?"

"No."

"Can you find it?" I nodded. "Okay. Room 822, in," he pulled out his phone and looked at it. "Half an hour. Ten-fifteen. Okay?"

I gulped. "Calcott Hotel. 822. Thank you."

He looked around again. "And be discreet about it." He moved away from the wall and then turned back. "One more thing. This is a one-time only deal, one hour only. No all-night crying relationship advice shit. I've got practice in the morning."

"I do too," I said, annoyance creeping into the gratitude. "I'm not going to be up past midnight. I'm in the life too."

"All right," he said, and his expression seemed to me to be a little more relaxed. "See you in half an hour." And he walked away, the warning not to follow him very clear. I let him get out of sight and then looked up the hotel on my phone.

The Calcott was a nicer hotel than any I'd ever stayed in on tour, and at the time I thought the coral-pink exterior and seashell windows were really neat, especially when lit with orange spotlights under weather that wasn't quite mist and wasn't quite drizzle but was somewhere in between. The whole place had a feel like something out of one of the fantasy movies I liked, except for the harsh salt smell of the ocean combined with the odor of the trash littering the beach, not to mention the car exhaust.

Inside, all those objectionable smells vanished as if by magic. Fancy places spread Neutra-Scent around their public areas to diminish the fug of crowds and then also mist scents in with their air circulation. The scent in the Calcott wasn't one I would have picked, kind of a cotton-candy sweetness, but it was better than ocean garbage. And everyone in the lobby wore at least a polo shirt, most of them wearing nice button-downs with jackets or dresses. I rubbed the fur of my arms below the t-shirt sleeves and hurried across the lobby, following the sign that read "ROOMS."

I knocked once at 822, and Braden opened the door. He'd changed out of his hoodie and wore only a t-shirt and loose sweatpants. As I stepped in, he walked over to the king bed and gestured to the chair in front of the desk. "Have a seat."

I swung my tail through the back of the chair and sat down, feeling less self-conscious about my clothes. The room was pretty nice and smelled more like Braden than the hotel's cotton-candy scent. Curtains covered the large window, and two bags of tennis gear lay on the floor; on the desk behind me were two Royal brand rackets and a can of balls. The scent of Braden, I realized, came mostly from the bathroom and was probably some combination of his own scent and whatever fur products he used.

Braden sat on the bed cross-legged and swept his tail around his hips. "Well?"

My attention snapped back to him. His ears were up, his expression bored. "I have practice tomorrow. You wanted to talk, so talk."

"Right, sorry." I felt self-conscious again, but not because of my clothes. Why was I going to bore this guy with my problems? He didn't give a crap about me or about them. "You know, maybe I should—I mean, you don't want to hear a lot of crap about boyfriends and—"

I started to get up, and he said, "Hey," which stopped me. "Don't bail. You leave now, you're going to be bugging me again later, right? You got something you need to get off your chest. So talk."

I sat back down and took a breath, watching his muzzle. Despite his bored expression, his eyes stayed focused on mine like he was actually interested in what I had to say. So I gave him a short history of me and Marquize, from my birthday party to my moving on to the Challenger tour, to Ma leaving and my eighteenth birthday, and there I hesitated, because I wanted to talk about Marquize cheating, but I wasn't sure I should reveal Frio's name. "He'd had sex with a… an older guy," I said. "While we were at Palm Gables."

And there Braden sat up straighter. "This was the cheetah with you when we played that match at the school."

I'd already told him that, but I nodded. "And it was—I felt like he'd betrayed me, but you know, we couldn't have sex—"

"Because you weren't eighteen." Braden shook his head. "Right. Whatever. This guy, did he tell you who it was?"

"Uh." I looked down at the floor.

He scooted forward, his legs dropping off the edge of the bed. "He did. And you don't want to tell me. If I guess, will you tell me if I'm right?"

I swallowed and nodded, knowing what name he was going to say before he even said, "That damn ferret."

"Frio."

"Yeah." He scowled. "That guy's a piece of fuckin' work."

"How, uh." I started asking the question and then realized I might not want to know the answer.

Braden raised his eyebrows. "How did I know?" I nodded. He leaned back and studied me. "He bragged about it to me that night."

"Wha—" My mouth gaped. "He told you?"

"Oh yeah. If you didn't already know he's a piece of shit pedophile, he's also a grade-A asshole. And—well, yeah. Be glad you're clear of him."

"That's why you told me not to go back to him for money? You thought he'd ask for sex for money?" I thought about how close I'd been to agreeing to that.

"Ah, something like that." His eyes flicked away a moment; a painful memory, I thought, and that was when I realized that Braden had probably also been molested by Frio while a student there.

"Shit," I said. "I'm sorry."

"Assholes are all over," he said. "You've got to keep clear of them. Be glad he didn't try anything on you."

"He did." I didn't have time to wonder whether I should say anything. "We were in a hotel by these clay courts up north."

"Ah, the Pelotas Rojas trip." Braden shook his head. "You'd think he'd update his playbook."

"So you know. The shower, the open door…coming out all naked…"

"Subtlety is not his strong suit." The cross fox eyed me. "But you said no."

"Yeah. And…" I remembered now. "That was thanks to you."

"Me?"

I leaned forward, elbows on my knees. My tail swished back and forth. "You sent me that email telling me I didn't owe him anything, that I didn't have to listen to him. I guess…you knew?" He gave a quick nod. "Anyway, I thought about that and about Ma and…it was confusing. I wanted him to like me, but it didn't feel right."

"Good for you. Glad that helped." He rubbed a paw along the side of his muzzle. "So where'd you leave things with the cheetah? You guys still together?"

"Sort of? I don't know." I flicked my ears back. "We've seen each other in person once and we talked for an hour and nothing got resolved. I miss being with him but I can't get past being angry at him for lying to me. I want to work things out but also it's so hard not being able to tell anyone, and I can't tell if we're both holding on to something that's already gone."

We were both quiet for a little while. I didn't even know what I was thinking about, much less what was on Braden's mind. But after a moment he said, "I'm probably the worst person in the world to talk to about relationships. I've barely even tried to have one. But I need to ask you one really important question before I tell you what I think."

He had a gleam in his eye. I nodded. "Go ahead."

"Have you really not had sex since March?"

I sat up straighter. "Uh. I mean, not with someone else. I've…I mean, I take care of myself. When my roommate's out."

The corner of his mouth twitched. "All right. For the love of god, go get laid. I get the whole boyfriend-long-distance thing, but don't be celibate for months. There were a bunch of guys in that bar tonight who would've happily taken you home and fucked you silly. It releases tension, gives you endorphins, it's good for you."

"I, uh…"

He held up a paw. "You don't have a lot of experience picking up guys in a bar. It's fine. Just smile at people and make conversation when they come over. Say yes when they ask if you want to go somewhere more private. And use a condom, use two if they look skeevy. It's not more complicated than that, not when you're young and have an athlete's body. And for god's sake, remember you're in construction."

"I know." I still didn't feel right about betraying Marquize the way he'd betrayed me, even with Braden's compelling argument. But maybe we could agree to see other people while we were apart, as long as we were careful. I tested that thought in my head and it didn't completely upset me. Maybe worth thinking about.

"But here's the real thing." He pointed to the desk behind me. "That's the only true boyfriend you're ever going to have."

I half-turned to see the two rackets there, then turned back. "The handles look a little…big…"

"Not like that." Then he laughed shortly. "I mean, if you want to and can fit them, sure, why not. But I mean, tennis is the only relationship worth pursuing. He won't always put out, but if you put a lot of work into it, he'll reward you. And any time you spend with someone outside tennis is like cheating. You give your life to tennis and you'll go to the places you want to go. You want to go there, right? To the majors, to titles and trophies and standing alone on the court when everyone else has tried to beat you and failed?"

"Yeah," I said.

"That's the path. Work hard at it. Sacrifice anyone else you need to."

He spoke softly but with a firm resolve, and the words wrapped themselves around my chest and settled there like a chilled wet blanket. I wrapped my arms around myself. "That sounds bleak."

His long muzzle nodded once, a short, sharp affirmative like one of his forehands. "If it was easy, everyone would do it."

"That's from a movie."

He nodded again, but a slower nod with a smile; a lob rather than a sizzling groundstroke. "Yeah." And then his ears flattened back, and the smile vanished. "I'm sorry about your mom. I didn't mean—"

Again we were silent, until this time I broke the silence. "It's okay. I didn't think you meant that." And then, when he didn't say anything, "She, ah, she went to Lunda at the beginning of the year to rescue my sister. She hasn't been coaching me since then."

"Better for you not to have your parents coaching. They never know as much as a professional coach and they can be…weird about it." He scratched his ear. "Who's your coach?"

"Keely."

"Oh, I sort of know him. Not bad."

This time, the silence began to feel awkward. I stood, and Braden didn't stop me. "So look, you've got practice. I should go."

He stood too, and extended a paw. "Sorry about your mom."

"Thanks. And thanks for…for taking the time, for talking to me. I owe you more now." I tried to summon a smile. "I meant what I said about paying you back."

Braden snorted. "Don't come up to me in gay bars anymore and we're square."

"Yeah, sorry." My ears flattened. "I wasn't having a good night."

"All right. See you on the court."

And I walked out of that hotel room into the cotton candy air, and then out into the humid, salty night. It still hadn't been a great evening, but I felt more resolved, and I knew I would have to call Marquize soon.

Chapter Thirty

Aliq and I won our early matches and I won my first singles match too, though it was tougher than I thought it should be. My serve was fine: that was a time when I could bring all my focus to the game. The lapses came not in the sense of me forgetting how to play or anything like that, but more in the sense of not thinking far enough ahead, letting my reflexes dictate where the ball was hit rather than planning based on my opponent. In the best case it made no difference or extended the point a shot or two; in the worst cases it set my opponent up with an easy return.

I'd thought I should wait to call Marquize until after the tournament, but three matches in, I started to worry that the distraction might cost me a match. That was fine for singles, but I didn't want to let Aliq down. And as we started to play better competition, I was going to let him down if I wasn't on top of my game.

So that night I called up Marquize's entry on my cell. I hit Call before I could change my mind.

"Aren't you in the middle of a tournament?" he asked.

"Beginning of one," I said. "Listen, I needed to talk to you."

"Now you need to talk to me." He sounded tired.

"Yeah, I…"

"It's been six months, but now you need to talk to me."

"What's your problem?" I asked.

"My problem? I dunno, Rocky. Does it matter? You wanted to talk, go ahead and talk."

"Mar—"

"No. You called me. Talk."

I exhaled. "Look. We're apart, and we haven't…I mean, I've been faithful to you. I haven't done anything with anyone else." He was quiet. "I'm assuming you haven't either." He stayed quiet. "I hadn't realized it'd be hard this way."

He laughed, then. "Hard. Really. It's hard for you?"

"My mother is dead," I said flatly. "Yeah, it's hard for me."

The laughter cut off as though I'd lost the signal. "I'm sorry about that."

"So sorry you didn't want me to come out there."

"I didn't say that." The edge crept back into his voice. "I told you we could work something out."

"That's not the point. Or maybe it is. The point is…I needed someone. I didn't go get anyone, but…look, maybe until we work things out, we should figure out some arrangement…"

I thought he'd be understanding, at least. But he made a "whoof" kind of noise. "'Until we work things out.' And when will that be, Rocky? It's been six months."

"We're both busy."

"Right. We had an hour or so together, we talked, it was nice. I thought we'd get closer after that. I waited. And waited. And waited."

This was unexpected. "I, uh."

"And you finally called me when you needed something. Not because you were worried about me. Because you needed someone to hold on to. Did it matter that it was me?"

He was uncomfortably close to the truth I didn't want to admit. "But I called you."

"You don't have any idea what I've been doing for you. You just call when you need something."

"I called—" I didn't know what to say. What had he been doing? I tried to summon the anger I'd had before. "You don't get to be mad at me."

"Why not? I made one mistake. Does that give you a 'Get Out of Jail Free' card for anything else you do, for any indignity you subject me to?" I tried to get a word in, but he kept going. "Yeah, I made a mistake. A bad mistake. You could've dumped me, and I'd have been sad about it, but yeah, it would've made sense. You're a good guy and I screwed up. But you gave me a second chance, and I was grateful. I took it. And then…nothing."

"We're in different cities all the time."

"Of course we are. But the phones still work. We could've talked this out. But you left me hanging and hanging, and then you call when you need a shoulder to cry on, and now you call because you're horny and you want my permission to fuck some other guy."

"That's not—"

"You know what? You've got it. You want to go fuck someone else, go do it. And don't worry about cheating on your boyfriend. You don't have one anymore."

"What?"

"You heard me. We're through. I'm tired of sitting here waiting for you to forgive me for something I did two years ago." He sounded angrier than I was. "And of being afraid to call you when I need to talk. And of you making me feel bad for how I'm doing in tennis, for how I'm not on the Challenger circuit yet, not even winning Futures tournaments. Look, maybe I'm not as good as you. No, strike that. I'm not as good as you. I'm not afraid to say it."

"You don't have to—"

"No, Rocky, I don't have to. But you know what saying that does? It lets me feel better about myself. Maybe it's not something I'm doing *wrong*, maybe it's just the way I am. There are a lot of guys who spend years in the Futures tournaments, and you think all of them could be winning majors if they only practiced more? Maybe I'm one of those guys. I'm not at your level, Rocky. No amount of practice is gonna change that. And if you'd see that—if you'd seen that, if you'd been happy having a partner who could just be your boyfriend and didn't have to be your practice partner too, your doubles partner, your tennis lifemate, then maybe you'd have felt like you wanted to pick up the phone and talk to me."

All of this washed over me like cold water, like I'd walked into a prank in a cartoon where a bucket was propped over a door. "I'm—I'm sorry—"

"I'm sure you are now that I'm laying it all out for you. It's fine, Rocky. You want to feel better about yourself, call it even. I fucked up, you fucked up, we're over and done and sadder and wiser or whatever you want to call it."

I knew I should be sad about the relationship ending, or angry at Marquize, or guilty about myself. But I didn't feel any of that. I was trying to envision myself as single again when for the last almost three years I'd been a guy with a secret boyfriend. Now I was a guy with a secret ex-boyfriend. And weirdly, all I could think of in that moment was Braden telling me to sacrifice anyone I needed to. And maybe this would be better for my career.

So I said, "All right. If that's what you want."

"Oh, don't give me that," Marquize snapped. "It's what you want, too, only you haven't had the balls to say it. You don't love me anymore."

"That's not true."

"Well." His voice softened a little. "Not in the same way."

"Okay. You don't love me either, though."

"Don't I?" He answered his own question. "Maybe not the same way. But I have to have loved you at least a little to—to wait around for six months."

That reminded me why he'd been waiting for six months, which gave me a foothold back into my anger. "And I have to have loved you at least a little to stay with you after you fucked our coach."

There was silence, and then he said, "I know what I did. I feel like I've paid for it."

"Maybe you feel that way," I said, "but maybe you don't understand what that meant to me."

"I tried, but—"

"Maybe you didn't realize that you're the only person I could trust, with Ori and Ma gone. That I'd just moved to a new tour where I didn't know anyone, and you weren't only my boyfriend, you were my best friend. And maybe you didn't remember that Frio tried to fuck me, too, and that he spied on us and got you kicked out of school. I hated him for that. So maybe you didn't realize that betraying me with him was more than taking away the only person I could trust in the world. It was like you preferred this horrible person to me."

"Rocky—" He was weaker now. "I didn't—"

"And, and how much did I want my boyfriend and best friend

back, how much did I want it all to work out? Every time I talked to you I couldn't stop thinking about what you did, and every time I hung up I wanted to hold you. It was confusing! It still is. So maybe this is best. Maybe you making the decision for us is the best thing. Now I don't have to wonder if I'll ever get you back. I know."

He didn't say anything. The earpiece pinched my ear, so I fiddled with it as I said, "Thank you."

Marquize said, tiredly, "Yeah. I guess I'll talk to you…" He stopped.

"Sometime."

"Yeah. I'd, uh. I'd like to know what happens with your sister."

"I'll let you know. And…I'd like to know about your tennis."

"Rocky—"

"No expectations. Just…whatever you decide to do."

"All right." He sighed. "Good night."

"Good bye," I said, and hung up the phone.

I sat there and then lifted my wrist, the one with the tattered cloth bracelet still on it. In a quick motion, I gripped the bracelet in my teeth, bit down, and yanked. It came apart more easily than I would have thought. I held it for a moment and then dropped it into the trash.

Chapter Thirty-One

I went out the day after that phone call and absolutely crushed my singles opponent, a kangaroo as tall as I was. He served great, with placement and kick, but I was seeing everything sharp as glass and hitting every angle, and he only won one game. He looked dazed when we shook at the net, and afterwards Sean, who'd watched the match, told me I looked like a top ten player.

It didn't last; I got to the quarterfinals in singles and lost a tough three-set match. Aliq and I got to the finals again, though, and despite losing we felt pretty good about the tournament. My income was steadier than it had been in…well, ever, and our little group of friends stayed tight. We practiced together, rose in the rankings together, and went out or stayed in together most nights. After my talk with Braden and the call with Marquize, I felt strangely more at peace with losing Ma. I mean, I was still sad, but I asked the guys if they'd mind hearing about her from time to time. I wished—I wish—they could have met her, and her them. But my stories were a way for that to happen, and they enjoyed them more than I would've thought required by friendship. So that made me feel like they appreciated how special she was.

And I texted Marquize after the tournament. "Got to qtrs in singles & lost fin in dbls. Hope you did ok."

He texted back an hour later: "Lost in Qs. Congrats."

It wasn't much, but it made me feel a little better that we were talking. As angry as I was with him some of the time, I realized it was as hard for him as it was for me to be apart, and harder because he hadn't been in control since my birthday. With a little distance from him—emotional rather than physical—I could see that.

Of course, none of my friends were terribly helpful, not only

because they didn't know I was gay, but because none of them were in relationships, apart from Caboll, and he didn't talk much about his girlfriend. I did ask him how they made the long-distance thing work, and he frowned like I'd asked him how he breathed. "We talk on the phone and we get together when we can," he said, and I couldn't think of how to ask the followup question of how to make phone calls meaningful.

That wasn't a problem with Ori. My phone calls with her were full of emotion. I told her about Marquize and she said loyally that he was a jerk. Then, in a way that reminded me of Ma, she said, "But Ro, you might have made a decision sooner."

Ma wouldn't have allowed me to string Marquize along for months, I realized now. I hadn't seen that earlier. But Ori saw it right away, and told me about it in a way that didn't hurt.

I also spent a lot of time on the phone with Lochen, not all at once but in a number of short calls. We talked about my endorsements and about Ori's situation, both of which he said were improving. "Keep doing what you're doing," he said, and I told him I'd do my best.

And so I did. I went to the gym with Aliq and added to my workouts under his guidance. This resulted in new sore muscles, but after a couple weeks I got used to the routine and as Aliq predicted, I had more energy. I felt it in small ways, near the ends of matches where my forehand had a little more strength to it, my feet responded to my will better, and I wasn't breathing as hard. Over the first two tournaments, the extra conditioning maybe won me one match, a tough three-setter where I had the energy to fight off a break point in the third set so I could win it in a tiebreaker. It got me to a quarterfinal, where I lost to a kit fox who was ranked 67th in the world, but I felt better because I was being more and more competitive against better players.

So September slid into October and November, and the pain of Ma's death faded, though it never really went away. At the beginning of November I felt confident enough to take the high school equivalency test, and though I didn't do great, I passed. Danver and Aliq were the only ones I told, and both of them treated it as a curiosity, as though I'd gotten my fur styled a particular way: it was cool, but wouldn't really affect my tennis. I didn't text Marquize because if he hadn't taken the test himself, I worried I might be making him feel inadequate again. Our texts were still cordial and I didn't have the energy to put into changing that.

I also went out to gay bars more often, and twice I hooked up with a cute guy. The first time it was really weird and the second time it was easier; it helped that both times they wanted to exchange blow jobs, and that both of them were totally cool with using condoms for it. In neither case did I feel the need to keep in touch with them, nor they with me, though the skunk did ask for my phone number. I told him I was very private about that, and he shrugged and said he might run into me again sometime. I missed Marquize, but Braden had been right: having an outlet to have sex did a lot to relax me.

I saw Braden at the bars once or twice, but I stayed away from him. At tournaments we greeted each other and clasped paws, but I saw him more rarely; his ranking was climbing and he wasn't playing Challenger tournaments anymore. Aliq and I were doing well enough in doubles to be invited to a few Champions events, and that's where I'd run across him. He asked me once how I was doing after Ma's death and I told him things were getting better; I complimented him on his tournament wins and his top 20 ranking. But he stuck to his friends and I stuck to mine.

Aliq's parents invited me up for Thanksgiving dinner, and apart from his mother asking me once if I was doing all right, with concern in her eyes and the tilt of her ears, they didn't bring up Ma's death. It was a nice weekend overall, a good break going into the last tournament of the year, which Aliq and I were determined to win to bring our total to two for 2012.

I did pretty well in singles, getting to a quarterfinal which I had to play before our doubles semifinal. I was playing Keiran Lubovic, this tall, skinny fennec fox I'd seen around the locker room and knew mostly for his high, contagious laugh and the amused, collegial calls of "You asshole" that followed him around. This was probably his last Challenger event because he was now ranked #47 in the world and on his way up. I don't think he was ready for me, though I'd studied his game; I was still only #201. But I got an early break, and that flustered him, and I kept my serve steady all the way through, enough to win the set 6-4. He buckled down in the second set, and he was very good defensively, so twice he had a break point on my serve, but both times I saved it, and we went to a tiebreak.

In the tiebreak, with him serving to go up 5-4, he got a pretty good serve off and I got a good return back. I settled in to rally, but on my first groundstroke, my forehand clipped the net cord. It shot up like they do, and Kieran, back beyond the baseline, tore forward desperately. He lunged, but his racket came up a couple inches short as the ball landed softly just inside the sideline. Instead of 5-4 him it was 5-4 me. All I had to do was hold serve to win the set. I didn't waste the chance.

"You've gotten way better," the fennec said as we shook paws at the net and then walked toward the umpire's chair. "Hey, I should ask for your autograph. You're gonna be past me in no time."

"Ah," I said, "it's a good thing they don't put asterisks on wins."

He laughed and let me shake the paw of the weasel in the chair first. "No asterisk," he said. "One lucky bounce don't mean the rest of your play wasn't great. See you in Champions next year."

"Thanks," I said, and we parted ways then because it was a quarterfinal and there were two people from tennis blogs there who wanted to talk to me. I was starting to get to know them: a short, chubby wolf with a quick wit named Porter, and a tall glasses-wearing leopard named Cam. They asked about the net cord, of course, but also about the first set and about my progression.

"Welcome to the top 200," Cam said as we parted, and the significance started to sink in with me. I was going to be in the top 200. That was a milestone on the way to the top 100, the top 50, the top 10. It was another step, and even though I'd jumped farther in the rankings before, this time I was going to jump over that #200 barrier. I was going to have a 1 in front of my rank.

The euphoria from that lasted all of one day, because the next day I had to play Braden Longacre, who honestly shouldn't have been at this tournament at all, but he had a contractual obligation that predated his rise in the rankings, or something. And Braden was prepared for me, and I did not get a lucky net cord bounce. Honestly it would've taken about twenty lucky net cord bounces for me to win that match. The score was a respectable 6-3, 6-3, but I never had a chance. He broke my first service game and then kept up a high level of play, catching angles the same way I had against Kieran. I could make the excuse that I was flat, that I didn't have the drive I had against Kieran. Not because it was Braden, but because the win against Kieran had felt like such an achievement that I didn't know how I could top it.

I learned to overcome those kinds of feelings too, the insidious trap that lets you substitute a milestone for your eventual goal.

In the locker room after the match, I was almost changed when Braden came in from his interviews. A couple other players who happened to be around tried to greet him, but he brushed them off and walked right over to me. "Hey," he said.

"Hi." We'd already done our "good game" exchange on the court, so I wasn't sure what else to say.

"Want to grab a drink in say, an hour?"

I blinked. "Sure."

"Marquess Hotel bar." He half-turned toward his locker.

"You know I'm eighteen, right?" I asked.

He paused, a scowl on his long muzzle. "You know bars serve Coke, right?"

I grinned, and he went off to get changed.

* * *

The Marquess Hotel, to my eighteen-year-old eyes, wasn't as nice as the Calcott. Now I would look back and say it was nicer because it wasn't as ostentatious, but then I probably didn't even know that word, much less care about it. I appreciated when buildings showed their wealth, and the Marquess's soft white marble and fragrant flowers didn't really do it for me, nor did the bar with its gleaming dark wood and brass fittings. I hadn't learned to recognize fresh flowers as an expense (not only for the lovely arrangements but for someone to change them out every day), nor the attentive service at the bar as a luxury. I just thought that this hotel was a nice place to sit down for a Coke with an enigmatic fox.

He ordered a cranberry juice and soda water for himself to go with my Coke. "I turned 21 last year," he said, "but my trainer says no alcohol during tournaments. So." He made a face and sipped his drink.

"If you don't like it," I started.

"It's fine." He waved a paw over it. "I don't hate it or I wouldn't order it."

"You like alcohol?"

He eyed me, flattened his ears out a little. "I don't get drunk. But it helps me relax sometimes."

"Wouldn't relaxing be good for your game?" I sipped my Coke and raised my eyebrows. "I know Coke is the same everywhere, but this Coke tastes better."

"It's not the same," Braden said. "The stuff in bottles and cans is made at bottling plants, who are supposed to use a standard mix but might not. There's a plant that makes Dr. Pepper with real sugar and not corn syrup. But the bar gets the syrup and they mix it however they want. So it might be fresher, if that's a thing. Or they might be going heavier on the syrup so it's sweeter, if you like that."

I sipped again. "I never knew that."

He gestured to my drink. "They know they're going to be serving it with ice, which is going to water down the drink, so a little more syrup up front and it stays close to what you're familiar with longer."

"Wow." I shook my head. "So I could just dump the ice out and have the sweeter mix longer."

He cocked his head. "I guess. I never thought of that."

This was weird, maybe the first time we had an inconsequential conversation. I was smiling but Braden looked genuinely thoughtful, like I'd asked a riddle or something. So I said, "There's times when I'm done with a match when I really want a good cold Coke. I know it's not good for me, I need to hydrate and replace electrolytes and whatever, but I want it."

"I haven't had a Coke in years," he said.

"Really?"

He nodded. "I used to like it when I was a kid, but when I

started getting serious about tennis, I gave up sugar drinks."

"I thought you said Coke was corn syrup."

He narrowed his eyes, and I thought for a moment I might get a smile. But he just said, "Corn syrup is sugar, basically. I used to wonder why they had soda machines at Palm Gables."

"I miss those. Cheapest Cokes ever."

He nodded. "Hey, you still in touch with Coach Young? Frio?"

I tensed, and he must have seen it in my ears or eyes because he put up a paw. "Hey, sorry. Let me explain. I only just found out he was let go from Palm Gables."

"Right," I said. "Over a year ago?"

The cross fox grimaced. "I don't keep up on alumni news. And the one person I talk to from school didn't care to mention it to me."

"I only found out because I had lunch with a couple of my friends from there," I said to make him feel better. "Do you know why?"

He shook his head. "I was hoping you did. Not," he held up a paw again, "that I think you're close with him or anything. But your boyfriend was."

This, then, was the reason he'd asked me out to a drink. "Ex-boyfriend," I said, and Braden gave a short nod without changing his expression. "I heard…" I lowered my voice. "That it was a sex thing."

"So they caught him with a student and didn't want to make a big scandal about it." He tipped back the cranberry and soda and grimaced.

"That's my interpretation."

"Well…good. I mean, at least they're keeping him away from students now."

I nodded. And then I felt brave, so I went on. "I told you he tried to get me in bed, right?" He nodded, slowly. "You said he came on to you. Did you…?"

Braden stared at his glass, then picked up the straw and stirred it aimlessly. At least he hadn't told me to mind my own business. "Yeah," he said.

"I'm sorry." I meant it too. "Just him coming on to me messed me up for months. I think part of me is still messed up over it. Like if Marquize'd cheated with anyone else—anyone else—it would've been not as bad. But that guy."

"No, I'm with you." His ears were all the way flat now, his voice lower still. "I haven't talked to anyone about it."

"Ever?" It must have been five, six years ago for him.

He shook his head. "I was sixteen, he was twenty, so you know, it was almost even legal."

"I thought eighteen…"

He waved a paw. "If you're between sixteen and eighteen then someone within three years of your age is legal. In Pensa."

"But he was still your coach. That's not legal."

"No." He sighed and drank his drink. "And even if it was legal, it wasn't okay. Trust me, I know. I've read all the literature. I've seen the Lifetime movies. I've read the blogs. But none of those is *me*. I'm fine. I'm dealing with it."

In my imagination, I saw Braden in the hotel room at Pelotas

Rojas, Frio coming out of the bathroom naked. The cross fox younger, uncertain, but saying no the same way I had. Even though he'd made it pretty clear that he hadn't said no, that's how the image of the two of them stayed in my mind for a long time.

And that image served to do two things. It made me feel closer to him, but also it minimized, downplayed what had happened to him, and it helped me downplay what had happened to me. I was dealing with it too. I was fine. Compared to Ma dying, it was nothing.

(This was me at eighteen. Just want to remind you of that.)

So I said, "Yeah, me too. I mean, I told my Ma about it."

And there was a silent moment as Braden started to say something and then remembered that Ma was dead. "She help?"

"Yeah, she did. She, uh." I tried to remember. "She said it wasn't okay and that I had the option to do something about it." And if I'd followed that up, would Marquize not have had the chance to cheat? Could his betrayal come back to me? No, because I would've probably been gone from Palm Gables as well. Things would've been different in a lot of ways.

"But you didn't."

"No. We're here, you know, I mean, we were here, I'm here from a different country. I was here because of Palm Gables. If I made a stink about something, they could've sent me back home."

He searched his memory. "To Lunda."

"Yeah. I told you…"

"About your sister. It was a weird story." He set the drink down and scraped his claws along the table. "She still there?"

I nodded. "My manager's trying to get her back over here. There's a process, and a visa thing, and it takes a while. But she's safe now. With friends." As safe as she could be. But there'd always be that little worry in the back of my head until she was here in the States.

"I thought that money you needed…wasn't that to bring her over here?"

"It was to get her away from her husband," I said. "That's how Ma…"

"Right." His ears flattened again, and he lifted his glass. "Good luck getting her here."

"Thanks." I lifted mine and clinked it against his.

We drank, and when we put the glasses down again, he perked his ears. "You're getting better," he said. "The game today, you were good."

"Not good enough."

"I'm better. You could've taken a set but you weren't mentally all in it. Makes sense, I mean, Lubovic's good and you just beat him. That had to feel good. Probably too good; today felt like a letdown."

"A little," I admitted.

"You'll get over it. You'd think it would be easy to learn to take the games as they come, to forget the victories and defeats and play the game in front of you right now. Hell, they were teaching me that ten years ago when I was a skinny kid hitting with seniors at my middle school. But you can't really be told how to do it. You just have to go through enough that you understand it, that you feel it right here." He put a paw over his heart.

"Thanks." And I thought back to what he'd told me months ago, that tennis would be my only relationship. Marquize had left me, Ma had left me, but tennis was still here. And what I had to learn, what Braden was telling me to do, was give all of myself to it. To believe that the high moments needed to be earned again every single time, that the bad moments could be put behind me because the relationship itself wasn't going to go away, not if I kept putting work into it. And I knew, too, that I couldn't have been told this years ago. I had to experience it, to feel the letdown of defeat after the high of victory, to lose a tournament one week and win one the next, to understand that I had to keep putting the effort in every single week, every single day.

"Don't mention it." He grinned. "Someday you'll beat me in a match. A long way down the road."

Hope bloomed in my chest. "Maybe sooner than you think," I said.

His grin widened. "Come and get me."

Epilogue

N'Guwe holds serve here in the eighth game of the fourth set, but he's still down a break, and at 5-3 he's got only one more chance to stay in this match."

"Alastair, the crowd is on its feet here as Braden walks slowly to the baseline to serve. N'Guwe is ready on his end, and what must this young jackal be thinking?"

"Well, Daren, he's got nothing to be ashamed of. He's taken one set from a fox who's about to win the calendar year Grand Slam, and that's more than most people who've faced Braden Longacre this year have done. He's absolutely going to be top ten after this and I think this is just the beginning of a very promising run for him."

"But is that what's going through his mind right now? The future? Is he already looking ahead?"

"Oh, no. Right now he's thinking, if I can get a break here, we're back on serve."

* * *

I stare across the court as Braden walks to the baseline. The noise is crazy, loudest I've ever heard. This is the biggest crowd I've ever played for and every one of them is screaming, most of them standing. My ears are perked up so maybe the people think I'm listening to them, but they're aimed forward at the court and down. The hard surface reflects sound pretty well, so it's not like I can't hear them at all, but it makes every bounce of Braden's tennis ball stand out, like a rhythm confining the screams and cheers.

And that's all I need, to put those screams into a box so I can push them away even before the chair umpire calls for quiet. The bouncing of the ball grounds me to the game and confines me to the white lines on the court. There's no previous games, no previous sets, no previous points. There's only me, the ball, and Braden. There's only tennis.

His first serve is a smash right into the net. Automatically I register it: what was he trying to do? How will he adjust next time? Usually I'd move up a little for a second serve because we all take a little off our serve when we're facing a double fault, and while I'm not exactly tired, every little bit of energy counts. But I stay back because I've moved up the entire rest of the match, and I'm seeing angles in my head, and if I can put a little bit of a question in Braden's mind, that's worth a few extra steps.

Whatever the reason, he puts a little extra zip on his second serve. That's the kind of thing that sometimes, often, can result in a double fault. Not for Braden, not this year. He gets it right on the line, and fortunately I'm in the right position to return it. The angles for the return spin around in my mind and I process them with the sound of Braden's footsteps and the sight of where he is on the court and where he's heading and I act without making a conscious choice. I strike a forehand, aim it for the corner Braden isn't defending, and he sees it and lunges but it's already landing two inches inside the lines.

He gives a short nod and walks back to the baseline, and promptly responds with an ace down the middle when I'd thought he would shade it wide. He's still thinking, still outguessing me. So I do the same thing: I walk back to the deuce side and wait.

I get a racket on his next serve and put it over the net. He crushes it back and I'm on my heels but I get to it. Not only do I get to it, I get a pretty good backhand on it, enough to send Braden several steps to his left, which gives me time to set up. We exchange shots, his forehand to my backhand, which puts me at a disadvantage, and I know he's setting me up for a shot down the line, so I keep an eye on that side of the court with every shot, but he's being patient. And then an amazing thing happens. Whether it's the pressure of the Grand Slam or the pressure of that first serve return, I out-wait Braden. He gets impatient and he goes for the winner before he should.

I see it coming in a split-second, enough time to jump into it and get my forehand stroke on it. I shoot it back and Braden gets to my shot and tries to send it cross court. I watch it dip toward the line, too far away for me to get to it in time—and then it lands an inch outside.

But there's no call. I wait for the shouted, "Out!" but it never comes. So I raise my paw to challenge the call, and the umpire announces, "Rocky N'Guwe is challenging the call. The ball was called in."

I don't want to look up at the replay screen, but I can't help it. I watch the little cartoon ball dip toward the line just like Braden's did. The crowd is silent for a moment and then as the trajectory becomes clear, a slow roar builds and rises. It lands an inch outside the line, with clear blue space between the shadow of the ball and the white of the line.

"The ball is out. The score is 15-30."

The crowd is roaring again, but this time I feel like they're roaring for me. I won the point and they cheered. So it's my crowd, at least for now. My ears are up as I go back to the baseline, but not pointed at the court.

Again, Braden puts his first serve into the net. This time I move up for the second serve. It comes in strong again, and again I get a good hit on it. We rally, but this time I decide to surprise him, and on the third shot, I spin a drop shot over the net and away from him.

It's hard to get Braden with a drop shot because he's so fast. And it's a thing I do sometimes, so it's always in the back of his head. The thing is, he'll be able to get to it, but he'll probably try to flick it deep, past me. So I stay in the middle of the court, not letting him make a guess at where I'm defending, and then as his arm is coming up, I jump back a couple steps.

He sees it and tries to make an adjustment mid-stroke, to go cross-court along the net instead of deep. But even for the best tennis player in the world, making that adjustment running at near top speed with full extension is a hard ask. And Braden almost does it. Almost.

"Out!" comes the call, and then the umpire: "15-40."

There's no previous set, there's no previous game, there's no previous point. I'm dialed in now and I feel like anything Braden throws at me I can handle. He gets a good first serve in, I send it back, we rally, everything very standard. You remember how I told you that most tennis shots are very standard, not very exciting? This one's like that. I catch a ball a little bit off, it sails off my racket, lands long. 30-40.

And the crowd is still on their feet, still cheering, only I don't know what they're cheering for this time. But for some reason I think of Ma in that moment and how she'd advise me. Not any of my coaches from the past, nor the red fox sitting in the coach's box now not allowed to communicate with me in any way. But Ma, and how confident she was that I'd be a tennis star one day.

I haven't stayed up much with my faith. And Ori's not really observant anymore either, not after Raji and Sarya. But we both feel like Ma's watching us from Heaven, whatever version of that there is. And sometimes, in certain moments, I feel that strongly.

Braden serves at 30-40, and it's not a great serve. I jump on it and hit it right back toward his body. He scoots out of the way, but is off balance on his back foot when he hits it, and the ball doesn't have its usual crispness when it comes off his racket. I'm already running up to the net where his shot hangs like a practice volley waiting for me to put it away. And that's what I do.

* * *

"Simply incredible. Braden had the match on his racket and N'Guwe was too much for him. If the jackal can hold serve, he's at least on course to take this set to a tiebreak."

"Alastair, these two have delivered far more than we expected from this match. We're going to pause here, but don't you go anywhere. Will Rocky N'Guwe be overwhelmed by the moment? Will Braden Longacre return to form? We're on serve in the fourth set of the States Open. Stay tuned."

Patreon

Love Match was created with the help of Patreon, a web site that allows fans to support their favorite creators with monthly donations. Every week, another segment is posted on my Patreon site, with extra content available for those supporting at higher levels. If you'd like to continue to read about Rocky's adventures before the third volume appears, you can find them at http://www.patreon.com/kyellgold (URL for first part of book 2: https://www.patreon.com/posts/love-match-part-11741549). If you'd care to join the support for this book series, I'd greatly appreciate it! Patreon helps my income be more predictable and allows me to do things like commission more interior illustrations for this book than I've had in any of my others. And there are many other excellent creators on Patreon, so browse around and see who else you might find there.

My deepest thanks to all these contributors to the Love Match Patreon from April 2016 to June 2017 who have supported this book in whole or in part:

a stray cat	Buck Wolf	Cory
Adept Omega	buu38	Courtney
Aiden Fox	Canis Rufus	Strangewolf
AJF	Cassandra Mann	Crimson
Alex Bauer	Chandra	Curt Kihlmire
AnubiTitus	Charlie Payne	Cyle
Arrin Gerald	Chris Beningo	Dale Farmer
Ashley Jade	Chris Paw	daniel
"Blaze" Wiles	Chris	Dave B.
Athelstan	Christian Lopez	Diego P
Barium45	Christopher	Dmitry P
Baylei	Bryan	Donovan Elk
belladann	Clarke Macbeth	Dunkelpfote
BerryFox	Cole Stryker	Dynaphus
Bill Welsh	Colin Leighton	Early Wolf
BlackMoon	Colin Wolf	Edward Haynes Jr
blargh	Connor Laleff	EgoSaber

Emma Gibbs
erisil_lightarrow
Evey
Fabi
Felix seven
Felrnn
Flann Moriath
FlatFootFox
Foxon Silverfur
Furiia
Furtastic Voss
Geemo
Glassan
Grey
Grims
Gruffy
Guillaume Cauvet
Weidz
Ian Brandeberry
Injy
iqbunny
Ivy the Snivy
Jack Devries
Jake Hankwitz
Jakebe
Jared
Jase Anderson
Jasmine Smith
Jasperdesu!
Jeffrey Gardner
Jem
JLeet
Joe Brasen
Joey Watts
John Silver Fox
JR Puffer

JS
K Fox
K H
Kaily Spensor
Kairan Otter
Karmakat
Kato Okami
Keone
Kevin Frane
Kili
Kit Reynard
Kittopherson
Klarok
Kogawakenji
Korel Dagh
Kristofferson
L E
Laimika
Lazy Wolf
Lee Ford
Lennon Surcot
Lumble
M.C.A. Hogarth
Mad as A March
Hare
Malarwolfe
Malcolm F. Cross
mangowolf
Marc Gold
Marcwolf
Mark
Matt Wills
Michael Reyes
Michael
Mikasi
MrSolo

Mu Gamma
Nate Hopp
Nathan Martinez
NegaImage
Neil McIntosh
Nicholas
Nielas Sinclair
Nina
No name
Omegawolf
Wildpaw
Oryan_Winter
Oscar Landeros
oseyeris
Phenris
Pink Wolf
Pockets
Poi Wong
Pootie Fang
ProwlingPaws
Qball
Ragnar9
Raito
Ramuros
Rankine
Redx Wolfski
Rei Loire
Reilly Grant
Reyfar
Rhett
Riley Frits
Risus
Roger Gilson
Rooth
Ryan McKown
Ryan

sandcat
Scamp fox
Sean Hanson
Semilico Tiger
Setsune Wiefel
Shakal Draconis
Shane Elfield
shirou14
Silver
Silverfox 361
Silwer
Sirberus Khaos
Skandranon
Rashkae
Skeeter
Sketchy Wolf
Spirit

Stoatmeal
Streaks
sunkawakan
Tame Prince
Tau Switchblade
Taylor
Texas Lion
Thomas
Thorrn
Tiago
Tidal wolf
Tiger Stripes
Tiller Brown
Tiny Tallears
Tom Romsang
TomLeo
Trent Grasse

Trevor Bygland
Troy Ruggeberg
Tyfle
Vaska
Victor Dachs
Vulgus
Wanderer1708
Wesley Capelle
Wigwam
Will Cook
(Midnight
Hunter)
winterwolf3
Wolfi
Yifan Mai
Ysegrim
Zhathnor

Acknowledgments

Of course, this book has been supported with the help of Patreon and the patrons listed above. In addition, my writing group of Watts Martin, David Cowan, and Ryan Campbell continues to provide support and valuable feedback throughout the writing and editing process. For this volume, a fan named WildeCard reached out to offer advice in the details of the game of tennis, and his input has helped the tennis matches in this book be rendered a bit more realistically.

As always, Rukis has been more than just an illustrator. Her collaboration on many story points has helped the book along greatly.

And Kit and Jack continue to be the best family a fox could ask for. Without their love and encouragement, this book and most of my books would be greatly diminished.

About the Author

Kyell Gold has won twelve Ursa Major awards for his stories and novels, and his acclaimed novel "Out of Position" co-won the Rainbow Award for Best Gay Novel of 2009. His novel "Green Fairy" was nominated for inclusion in the ALA's "Over the Rainbow" list for 2012. He helped create RAWR, the first residential furry writing workshop, and has instructed at each of its sessions through 2017.

He lives in California, loves to travel and dine out with his partners, and can be seen at furry conventions around the world. More information about him and his books is available at

http://www.kyellgold.com

About the Artist

Rukis lives on a farm, where she spends most of her time working on art, caring for her animals, and hanging out doing tabletop gaming with her friends. She is a huge fan of old school D&D, White Wolf, and Warhammer, as well as studying and collecting exotic fish (Cichlids, mostly) and drinking a lot of Dr. Pepper. Her menagerie includes a rabbit, some fish, two wonderful dogs, and a whole mess of chickens.

She is the author of *Heretic,* the *Off the Beaten Path* trilogy, and *Legacy*, which take place in the world of *Red Lantern*.

About the Publisher

FurPlanet publishes original works of furry fiction. You can explore their selection at *https://www.furplanet.com* and find their e-books at *https://www.baddogbooks.com.*